# THE
# BANSHEES

# PARRIS

## AFTON BONDS
### NEW YORK TIMES
### BESTSELLING AUTHOR

*The Betrayers – The Texicans, Volume Four*

*The Bravados – The Texicans, Volume Three*

*The Barons – The Texicans, Volume Two*

*The Brigands – The Texicans, Volume One*

*Answering The Call*

*When the Heart is Right*

*Blue Bayou*

*Blue Moon*

*The Calling of the Clan*

*The Captive*

*Dancing with Crazy Woman*

*Dancing with Wild Woman*

*Deep Purple*

*Dream Keeper*

*Dream Time*

*Dust Devil*

*The Flash Of The Firefly*

*For All Time*

*Kingdom Come: Temptation*

*Kingdom Come: Trespass*

*Lavender Blue*

*Love Tide*

*Wind Song*

*Love and War on the Rio Grande*

*Reluctant Rebel*

*Made For Each Other*

*Midsummer Midnight*

*Mood Indigo*

*No Telling*

*Renegade Man*

*Run To Me*

*Savage Enchantment*

*The Savage*

*Snow And Ice*

*Spinster's Song*

*Stardust*

*Sweet Enchantress*

*Sweet Golden Sun*

*The Wildest Heart*

*Wanted Woman*

*Widow Woman*

*When the Heart is Right*

# THE BANSHEES

THE TEXICANS ★ VOLUME FIVE

NEW YORK TIMES BESTSELLING AUTHOR

## PARRIS
### AFTON BONDS

MOTINA BOOKS PUBLISHING

Text copyright © 2025 by Parris Afton Bonds
2nd Edition
All Rights Reserved. Printed in the United States of America
Published by Motina Books, LLC, Highlands Ranch, CO
www.MotinaBooks.com

Library of Congress Cataloguing-in-Publication Data:

Names: Afton Bonds, Parris
Title: The Banshees: Volume Five of The Texicans
Description: Second Edition. | Highlands Ranch: Motina Books, 2025

Identifiers:

LCCN: 2025943439
ISBN-13: 979-8-88784-067-3 (paperback)
ISBN-13: 979-8-88784-066-6 (e-book)
ISBN-13: 979-8-88784-068-0 (hardcover)

Subjects: BISAC:
FICTION/Romance/Historical/American
FICTION/Romance/Western

Cover and Interior Design: Diane Windsor

Dedicated to three of my life journey's mile markers -
Bonnie Winn, Diane Windsor, and Nicky Wilson-Kelly

# THE TEXICANS
## GENEALOGY

# THE BANSHEES

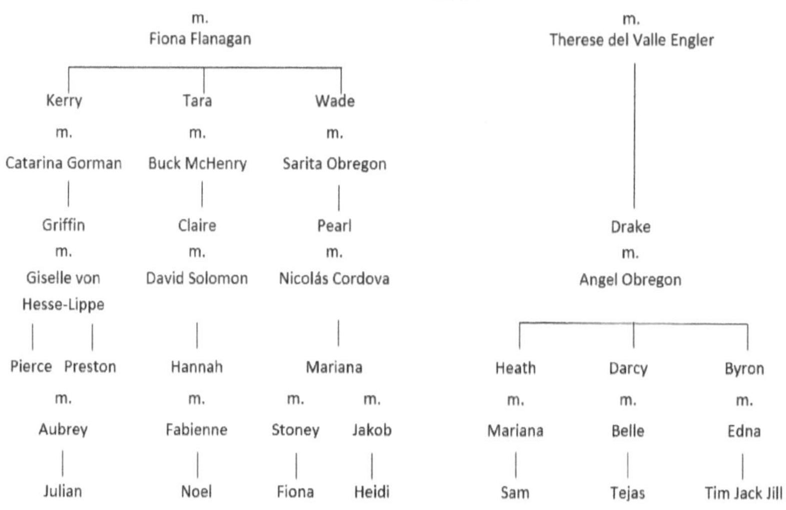

Amarillo
Red River
Brazos
Fort Worth
Dallas
Nacogdoches
El Paso
Rio Grande
Austin
Brazos
Trinity
Houston
San Antonio
Nueces
Galveston
The Barony
Corpus Christi
Gulf of Mexico
Rio Grande
Rio Grande City
Brownsville
N

TEXAS

# PART

# I

## BATAAN, PHILIPPINES
## APRIL 1942

Tim Paladín knew that he was fucked. He staggered forward in a never-ending line of Japanese prisoners-of-war. Like the others, he gripped the belt of the soldier in front of him in an effort to remain upright. To fall out of line, to stumble to the knees, meant a clubbing with a rifle stock or worse, bayonetting.

The thousands of Filipino and American prisoners trudged onward through the sweltering tropical heat. Toward late afternoon of the third day, they were starving and swaying. Tim saw the filthy water buffalo wallow alongside the dirt road. He veered off toward it, and other prisoners around him also broke ranks to drink from it.

Flies the size of thimbles skimmed its surface. What matter was dysentery when several hundred prisoners died daily—and that wasn't counting mass executions? Dropping to his knees, his hands cupped the dirty water to his mouth. He gagged down the slime.

Across the bank from him, a mounted Japanese soldier swept by the kneeling prisoners and decapitated one with his samurai sword—purely for the practice. The severed head bobbled for a moment in the pool of scum.

Immediately, the other prisoners scrambled back to join the plodding columns—as did Tim, prodded by a Jap sporting wristwatches on both arms, from wrist to elbow. Doubtlessly, the soldier had removed or hacked them off prisoners, both dead and alive.

The way the Japs had it, they were merely dealing with sub-humans and animals. Any warrior who surrendered had no honor and therefore was not to be treated like a human being. And by God if that son-of-a-bitch, Major General Edward Piss-off King, hadn't gone and surrendered to the Japs without General Wainwright's approval.

The next day was, if possible, grislier. Up ahead, a transport truck rolled over a prisoner who, unable to walk any farther, had staggered to the wayside and fallen. By the time Tim passed that spot, his combat boots squished what was left of the prisoner's body deeper into the mud.

That evening, word passed back along the line that those who were fortunate enough—or unfortunate enough, as the case might be—to survive the Death March were destined for slave-labor camps.

His gaze swept over the stick figures around him that passed for human beings. Some prayed for a swift death, right then and there. Others appeared content to plod on in this miserable existence that war had a habit of creating. But he was not content, not with his fate—or misfortune, or coincidence—or whatever it was that had landed him in this hell scape.

He recognized by now that he did not possess that dumb, animal endurance that was the sort of courage most soldiers needed. He was not ready to die—and neither was he ready to spend the remainder of his life in a work camp. He wanted to see Texas again—the brilliant sunsets coating The Barony in liquid gold, the soothing smell of mesquite fires when everyone gathered around for Christmas, and the mystical-like sagebrush that tumbled through in the bleak depths of winter.

He wanted to see his family.

At that moment, what he needed was a cigarette. Then, he needed to begin plotting an escape. After all, he was a Paladín.

Admittedly, as the adopted son of movie mogul Darcy Paladín, Tim had lived the easy life. At twenty-four, he possessed heart-throbbing good looks and more money than Fort Knox. He had a few B-movie roles under his belt, interspersed with lively periods of debauchery with Clark Gable, David Niven, and Errol Flynn. When patriotism called, Clark, David, Errol, and their club of fellow habitués had volunteered—and so had he.

Half a dozen years before, he had taken advantage of his Uncle Pierce's Paladín Air Southwest and had gotten his student private pilot's license. Like most of his efforts, he had lost interest and had not completed the course.

Upon volunteering, he had hoped for a plush duty station in a paradise like Hawaii or a plumb trainee position as ace fighter pilot, like his Uncle Preston in WWI. Such was not the case. Instead, because of his unusually sharp vision, he was assigned as aerial gunner based in the Philippines.

Obviously, to his great disappointment, he was never to " . . . slip the surly bonds of Earth and dance the skies on laughter-silvered wings," as the famed Pilot's Poem went.

Nope. Three months following the surprise strafing of Pearl Harbor, the Japs seized the resource-rich Dutch East Indies and its Clark Field—and thus, seized Tim Paladín.

The night before the surviving prisoners were to reach Camp O'Donnell, their captors bivouacked them beneath a jungle canopy of palms, acacias, and baletes.

"Do not touch that tree," warned a reedy voice in pidgin Spanish and English.

Tim glanced down at the little Filipino prisoner, as brown as nutmeg. At Tim's raised brow, the gnome added, "You must ask permission first of the balete tree."

Having spent his childhood in South Texas, Tim was proficient in Spanish, if nothing else—and to be sure, he was proficient at absolutely nothing else. He glanced around the prisoner-strewn encampment. Other prisoners already slumped against the forbidden trees. Nevertheless, he shrugged and humored the little Filipino, who identified himself as Marcos.

Managing an exhausted but elaborate bow before the gnarled tree, the actor within him beseeched, "I humbly ask permission to lean against you, Balete Tree."

According to Marcos, the tree was a species of strangler figs that fed upon other trees, later entrapping them entirely and killing them. "I tell you true, *Diwatas*—fairies—live in the baletes. White Ladies, the *Diwatas*, talk of death to come."

"Oh, that's just fuckin' swell." The White Ladies reminded Tim of the banshees from his Welsh-Irish origins. The banshees were female spirits in Irish mythology—omens of death and messengers from another world. If a banshee, a fairy woman, began to wail, someone was about to die.

Well, no banshee was about to get the best of Tim Paladín.

## FORT SAM HOUSTON, SAN ANTONIO
## OCTOBER 1943

AT FORTY-TWO, HANNAH PALADÍN Jackson still had exquisitely beautiful hands . . . if one discounted that both forefingers were nail-less. The tortuous extraction of the nails from their beds a decade earlier in Germany's Spandau Prison had seemed almost unbearable, but life was a great teacher. She had learned that she could endure almost anything.

Even this . . . this most painful neglect. But then, her second husband had never represented himself as anything but what he was—an easy-going cowboy veterinarian. He had shown up when she was at her weakest, a grieving widow.

True, Stoney was doing his duty, serving as a medic in the European theater. Yet somewhere even before that, somewhere in the history of their ten-year marriage, she felt she had been shuffled aside—as had his offer to move his practice to Dallas. And she knew she had been shuffled aside in yet another way, the most damaging to a woman's self-worth.

Having forsaken the position of buyer for her father's Dallas Emporium that required so much time away from home and global travel—derailed, what with the war—she had turned her empty hours in San Antonio to earning two back-to-back honors degrees from the University of Texas, where male enrollment outnumbered female four to one.

Yet that was not enough to stave off another emptiness.

Between her mutilated hands, she held two items—her ration book, every housewife's bible, and her Government Employee Pass. Both represented duty. The housewife and the harlot. Well . . . if thoughts were as good as deeds.

Under balmy sunlight, her '41 Woodie Station Wagon waited its turn at Fort Sam Houston's check point . . . while she gathered her courage.

The MP glanced at her Ford's windshield with its green "B" sticker, signifying her driving was deemed essential to the war effort. With the war raging, everything was rationed, including gasoline.

With a half-moon smile, she presented her pass to the young MP. He looked to be about the age of her nephew, Tim. The Filipino Red Cross reported he was in a prisoner-of-war camp. But then, she was about to drive into the entrance of one.

The guard waved her on by. The Station Wagon crept along the road, winding past a drill field, convalescent hospital, commissary, barracks, numerous native-stone buildings, and the airfield and its hangars. Everywhere, soldiers, trucks, tanks, trains, and planes were on the move.

Finally, she reached Fort Sam Houston's north side, with its tent-city of 170 six-man tents for both POWs and their American guards.

Newspapers dubbed the German prisoner-of-war camp "The Fritz Ritz." The prisoners had transformed their barbed wire enclosure by planting grass, adding flower beds, constructing beer gardens, staking out soccer fields, and making picnic tables. Beer and wine were available at the camp PX. These purchases were made with canteen coupons, provided to the POWs by the U.S. government as due payment for their military salaries and daily work.

As she left her car in the parking lot and walked past the front entrance, another guard escorted her to the mess hall-cum-library, where a bored soldier stood watch, his carbine lax in his arms.

Wedged in one corner was a library, consisting of donated books and magazines. It was large enough to do justice to an average high school. Paintings, family photographs, and chandeliers adorned the large mess hall. A phonograph was playing Bing Crosby, singing "Don't Fence Me In." Its scratchy sound indicated it must be a favorite with the prisoners.

Sitting at one of the bench tables, Colonel Jakob Nobel,

formerly with Rommel's Panzer Division of the elite Afrika Korps, was scribbling on a notepad . . . and waiting for her. When he heard approaching footsteps, his eyes moved quickly from his notepad to Hannah's face, and he rose to greet her, giving her a curt, formal bow.

She slid onto the bench opposite his. The combat-seasoned officer wore the common prisoner's attire, with the PW stenciled on both khaki shirt and shorts. His skin had been browned by Libya's fierce desert sun, though his squint lines were paler.

The Director of Internees had furnished her with the Colonel's dossier. Thirty-nine, the eldest son of Berlin university professors, Jakob Nobel had studied at Humboldt University. He had been a chemical industrialist and, in '39, began service in Hitler's army. The Nazis now made lethal use of his company's chemicals. He was married with one daughter.

He was also as harshly sculpted as she remembered from her first visit. Everything about him was square—from his jaw to his massive frame to his hands and even nail beds.

After her own bout in a prisoner-of-war camp, she always noticed hands. The hands of this enemy were the powerful kind that could choke the life from a man . . . or hold a woman desperately close. What was it about this German prisoner that could possibly attract her? And yet she uneasily was.

Resuming his seat, his slate-colored eyes studied her—her features, her posture, her clothing. She had carefully selected a conservative brown pencil skirt and jacket, bound her reddish-brown hair beneath a snood, in a schoolmarm's knot at her nape, and forsworn makeup completely.

She felt herself flushing. Of course, the prisoners were unused to seeing a female, but it was more than that. His heavy-lidded regard flustered her. "I did not think you would come, Mrs. Jackson."

She focused inordinate attention on removing her gloves. At the far end of the mess hall, two young men in khaki soccer shorts and shirts were playing ping pong. "Why not?"

"Last week, on your tour of our . . . our camp . . . you said you had spent time in Berlin. I have been informed it was not a pleasant time spent in my country."

The ping pong ball ricocheted off the wall, only to be collected and put back in play. *Puth . . . puth . . . puth.* The monotonous sound was disconcerting.

"On the contrary. Some of my time spent in Berlin was quite pleasant." She passed him the syllabus she had prepared.

"But not all of it?" He nodded at her mutilated fingers.

She folded them underneath her palm, placing them atop her purse in her lap. "Of course not. No one's life is . . . always pleasant." She tilted her chin at his stenciled clothing. Her gaze swept the large room. "I would not imagine your life has been one of supreme happiness, Colonel. At least, not at this moment."

Thick, spatulate fingertips stuck his pencil behind his ear and nudged aside the mimeographed German-language POW newspaper, *Spiegel,* on which he had been working. Catcher-mitt-size hands clasped the table, he leaned forward.

"Why did you volunteer to do this, *Frau* Jackson? To teach the Texas History class?"

The prisoner-of-war camp offered educational courses taught by qualified experts among the POWs. If there was a strong demand for a course about which few prisoners were knowledgeable, the course might be taught by an approved civilian in the area. Although San Antonio had been at one time mostly German, qualified linguists in the area were now serving in intelligence units overseas.

She forced her gaze to meet his. "I had spare time." She said it flippantly, as if surrounding herself with Germans was easy for her. What it would be—she hoped—was therapeutic. A way to confront her demons and dismiss them. A way to let loving memories of her late German husband take their rightful place again and banish the loathing gnawing in her stomach like acid.

She had loved Michael Kraft more than she ever thought possible to love another. She missed his German words of love whispered in the dark, the lovers' language spoken in that low, guttural growl that thrilled her.

But Michael had been brutally murdered, assassinated really, and she had been brutally tortured.

Yes . . . she might miss the German accent at times, reminding her of Michael's own, but it did not take long to be immediately flooded with disgust and anger, boiling right down to her fingertips, right where the Germans had mangled her nailbeds.

The dark paint brushes that were his brows furrowed. "Spare time? What is this 'spare?'"

Where and why had he learned English?

She stiffened. "Now why do I feel as if I'm the one who is being interrogated here?"

"Don't Fence Me In" had reached its end, and the phonograph needle's repetitious scratching was excruciatingly irritating.

He raised a dark black brow in contrast to his salt-and-pepper hair. *"Ja,* why do you?"

She clutched her purse. This was madness, volunteering when she had enough to do just keeping up with her and Stoney's nine-year-old daughter, Fiona.

Hannah went to rise, but his darkly tanned hand placed gently on hers gave her pause. She glanced down at their hands and thought absurdly of the bronze cast of the clasped hands of the poets Elizabeth and Robert Browning at Baylor University.

The guard flicked an inquisitive glance at her, and, after a tentative beat, her smile reassured him.

Someone changed the phonograph record, and the way too cheerful "Mairzy Doats" was blaring.

The German officer released her hand. "Come. Walk with me."

"Where?"

"In my garden."

"Your garden?"

"A vegetable garden. Working in it keeps my sanity."

"Of course." She knew that, per the Geneva Convention, captured enlisted men could be forced to do physical work, but not the officers. Officers were provided with their individual space and allowed the services of their enlisted valets. "I suppose you even have an orderly to make your bed."

A wry half-smile curled the ends of his lips. "That is of interest to you—my bed?"

She mentally cursed her deviation from the topic of gardening. "Why should I walk to your vegetable garden?"

He stood. "To discuss the Texas History course you will be teaching— without the"—he nodded at the ping pong players—"you call it commotion, I believe."

Outside, the perfect autumn day eased her reluctance, and she fell into step alongside the officer. She was tall, nearing five-foot-eight, but he was much taller—and massive. A Panzer tank. That was the descriptive word that kept coming back to her.

They passed POWs ambling about, as if merely on social outings— which she supposed they were, just behind the confines of the metal gates, observed by the multitude of guard towers. When she and the colonel passed the bakery, the yeasty smell made her stomach growl with hunger. She rolled her eyes. Just swell.

He grinned down at her. "You should stay for dinner. My men are having wurst, tomatoes from my garden, and even ice cream."

Just one more reason to hate him, his men . . . Germans in general. Her cousin Mariana, a D.C. senator, had told her that the War Department reasoned that food conservation would be improved—with prisoners-of-war trashing less food—if they were served healthy, appetizing fare.

Yet, she was so tempted. Not merely by the offer of food to alleviate her stomach's growling hunger, but also by the offer of a companionship to alleviate her loneliness. A companionship so very familiar to her in years long past. The companionship she and Michael had shared had been unique, special. He had been the unseen, unknown protector who had her back. They had long been friends before becoming lovers.

How she detested her shambolic emotions these days. "No, thank you."

Minutes later, mouth open, she stared at his garden. It had to be the size of half a football field. She was disgusted, appeased, and delighted.

She could not help but be disgusted that the prisoners were receiving far better food than that of American troops at the front who lived on C-rations but was appeased that the colonel was making an effort to feed himself and his men. And she simply could not stop the delight to be in the midst of something she loved so much—nature's cornucopia.

Earth's fresh soil was like a balm to her wounded hands. Her own garden was her retreat, its food her communion.

The colonel's garden was a feast for her senses. Brightly colored vegetables—gold zucchini squash, crimson strawberries, and purple podded beans—studded their green foliage. Every plant had its own scent. Oregano, sage, and mint tantalized her nostrils. As she followed him past a row of lamb's ears, she bent to trail her fingertips along its woolly leaves.

When she straightened, she caught him watching her. "You do garden work, *Frau* Jackson?"

She nodded and caught the wisp of his verdant outdoor scent. "Probably the closest I shall get to heaven here on Earth." She felt some of her body's tension slackening.

"Heaven? *Ja,* I have a part of heaven here." His chin jutted toward a dense grove of ornamental bamboo that screened off the camp's barbed wire and paved road, with its bustling traffic on its far side.

He strode on toward the wall of green, and she followed the stone path he took. The gentle rustling of the bamboo drowned out the noisy vehicles, and within its small enclosure came the musical sound of a rock fountain.

"One of my men is an engineer. He built the fountain. Sit." A sweep of his hand indicated the bamboo bench that anchored one curve of the timeless, secluded shelter.

Her stiffening posture must have given her away. *"Bitte—* please," he added. "We shall talk about the course you will teach."

She could feel resistance curdling like nausea in her stomach. Everything about him——his clipped speech, his Nazi training, his Aryan ideology with its supremacist concept, even his arrogantly virile demeanor—was anathema to her. Nevertheless, she had to walk through this if she was to reclaim the bold and enthusiastic-about-life young woman she had once been. She perched on the edge of the bench, like a grackle on a telephone wire prepared at any moment to take flight.

"You have my outline for the Texas History course,

Colonel." She could not bring herself to humanize him by using his name. "The days I am available. The materials your men will need. The topics I will be covering. What you will *not* have is Texas geography. Especially in reference to roads, water ways, railroads—and, more specifically—the Mexican border. I trust I make myself clear?"

He nodded. "However, I do not think you are clear at all about yourself, *Frau* Jackson."

Her brows collided. "What exactly are—do you want to be more clear, Colonel?"

"I have overseen both employees and soldiers. I feel I read people well. Your expressions, they betray emotions you try to hide. Your emotions are like one of those electric fans——you know, the kind that swing from side to side."

She shot to her feet. "One more thing I need to make clear. Your personal opinions will not be tolerated in my classroom."

And, with that, she did take flight.

## THE BARONY
## THANKSGIVING 1943

That morning, Paladín women bustled around the ranch's large, native-stone kitchen. Gold-and-silver-haired matriarch, Angel Paladín, had assigned each of them a dish to prepare. Wan sunlight spilled through the expanse of windows to fall on Spode and Wedgewood China, along with the silver service already brought out for the next day's Thanksgiving feast.

Perched on the wrought-iron kitchen stool, Aubrey flipped through the wooden box's index cards in search of the Crème Brûlée recipe. The recipe box had been Heath's grandmother's, Thérèse Paladín—a Frenchwoman, like herself and her sister-in-law Fabienne, who was at that moment shelling pecans.

One would think Paladín men had a penchant for French women.

Family recounting had it that Thérèse had been both French *and* feisty. The same could be said of Fabienne, Preston's elegant wife.

However, Heath's wife, Mariana, was most definitely Hispanic—and hot, according to radio gossip columnist Walter Winchell's staccato reports about "the Hill" senator. The horned rimmed glasses the black-haired beauty wore appeared to only add to her flair.

As for herself, Aubrey considered herself unquestionably low-key, flying under the radar, as was the phrase these days.

While both Fabienne and Mariana had the late Thérèse's talent for cooking and her zest for life and love, Aubrey's culinary skills certainly did fly under the radar as well.

But not her zest for love—her love for Pierce still made her knees go weak when he walked into the room—or rather limped, but she rarely noticed his prosthetic foot, as much a part of him as the sunshine of his smile.

And neither was her zest for life something low-key.

Since a young teenager in France during World War I, her gusto had taken her from Paris soloist ballerina to a French Intelligence spy to Pierce's lover, spaced over only a couple of years.

And now, she was his wife and a mother . . . and floundering.

With Pierce so caught up in the war effort, spending fifteen to sixteen hours a day converting his hangers near El Paso's Fort Bliss into one giant complex for the production of high-performance reconnaissance planes, she was finding her life utterly flat and fading fast.

At another time, she had also been fading fast, caught in the throes of opium addiction. The golden-haired Pierce had rescued her then. His unconditional love had brought her back to life. But now it was up to her to find her own life.

Mariana was untying her apron sash. "It's too damned hot in the kitchen. Aubrey, you up for a walk?"

Aubrey whipped off her own apron quicker than her ten-year-old Julian could hawk Sister Margaret's sterling silver rosary beads, which his father would claim was damned fast.

"Bring back a pumpkin from the patch," Angel called over her shoulder.

Frost still silvered the switchgrass and tufty grama grass, already withered white by a colder-than-usual fall. But that autumn morning was mild, with a crayon-blue sky and a dazzling display of brilliant red and orange leaves along the Nueces River. From the stock pens came a rooster's rowdy crow, doubtlessly delighted it was not his neck being wrung for the Thanksgiving dinner.

Mariana, hands thrust in her khaki pants pockets, briskly strode a path leading up to the ancient live oaks crowning the ridge. On the far side, slide paths made by river otters furrowed the bank leading down toward the Nueces. On the near side, the scent of burning mesquite logs drifted up from the rambling *hacienda's* multiple smokestacks and limed the crisp air.

The sound of Mariana's cowboy boots and Aubrey's brown-and-white saddle oxfords crunching the dried leaves filled their companionable silence. But as they neared the summit, Mariana broke it.

"So, do you miss the excitement of sneaking messages through enemy lines and bombs bursting around you?"

She sighed. "Julian provides more bombshells than have

been exploded in both world wars. Several times he has shut down classes in the Catholic private school we put him in. It looks as if I may have to find another place for him." She flicked Mariana a dry smile. "But I think even Huntsville State Prison would refuse him admittance."

At the ridge's crown, the two paused by tacit agreement beneath the giant live oak. Over a hundred feet high with a 125-foot canopy of nearly nude branches, the centuries-year-old tree stood watch over the well-tended plot with its marbled headstones of past Paladíns.

She felt almost as dead as they.

"Well . . ." Mariana drew out, "I need a social secretary, though only for the remainder of my legislative term. The city is full of prestigious prep schools. You think you and Julian would be up for it?"

Aubrey looked askance at her. "The city. You mean D.C. As in *Washington* D.C.?"

"Actually, Aubrey, I mean much more." She scuffed a few dead leaves with the toe of her boot, then looked her full in the eye. "Someone in high places—from the Cabinet to the Justice Department to Congress—is leaking information to the Axis Powers. Besides working for me, more of a powder puff position, you would secretly be working in liaison with the OSS."

Aubrey's heart stuttered into life. The OSS was a newly formed wartime intelligence agency. Pierce would be none too pleased about the time she and Julian spent apart from him. And Pierce would be even less pleased if he knew she would be working in intelligence again. There was no way he would countenance such a move. Not to mention, she was once more putting herself in jeopardy. The idea was absolutely out of the question.

*"Oui!* Count me in!"

"GOD BLESS OUR FAMILY, GOD bless The Barony, and God Bless America," Heath Paladín finished the Thanksgiving dinner's grace—delivered in the invariable Paladín style of importance first.

Family and land, these two essentials had been passed down through the ages—from The Barony's founding father, Don Alejandro de la Torre y Stuart, Baron of Paladín, to Griffin Paladín, to Drake Paladín, and now himself. From a Spanish land grant of 1767, the Paladíns had wrangled The Barony into the second largest ranch in the world.

And it fell on forty-two-year-old Heath's wide shoulders to sustain The Barony when all the world was falling apart. True, his seventy-year-old father observed from the wings and cued with advice whenever solicited, but at the moment, Heath felt he was spreading himself thin between his CEO demands.

Right now, he was striving to provide the military with beef while his man supply was being decimated by the draft. Luckily, the *Bracero* Program, a bi-national labor agreement with Mexico, was helping a mite to fill his Paladíneños' dwindling ranks.

Worrying him even more was the rocky relationship with

his wife. He glanced at the other end of the lengthy, hand-carved table where she presided. Regal, with the dusky beauty of her Spanish heritage, Mariana chatted amiably with the homely Gaila Barrett Bradford.

As U.S. Senator, Mariana was required to spend most of her time on the Hill. With all kinds of rationing, travel was severely limited these days. She had finessed this Thanksgiving trip back home to The Barony by including the Texas congressman, Garner Bryce Bradford, his wife Gaila, and their daughter, eight-year-old Gabby.

Likewise, Heath's cousins, the twins Preston and Pierce, along with their families, had managed to justify their Thanksgiving holiday travel through both their time and financial contributions to the war efforts.

"That's it," ten-year-old Julian proclaimed, whipping out his linen napkin. "No more praying—or I'm not staying."

Heath shook his head in amusement. Pierce and Aubrey had their hands full with the kid. Julian should have been Preston's son, instead of Noel.

Red-headed Preston, ever the Paladín's fiery rebel, had been tamed by the French minx, Fabienne, and had committed himself not only to marriage and their son, but also to the command of the USAAF's rigorous Navigator School at Houston's Ellington Field. Who would have thought he would have submitted to such a structured life?

Only Darcy and Byron, and their families out of state, were missing. And, of course, Hannah's husband, Stoney, who was serving in the European theater as a medic.

Heath rose to carve the turkey he had bagged and

smoked over pecan chunks for endless hours. At once, his ten-year-old son, Sam, clamored, "I got dibs on the—the leg, Dad!"

Heath plopped the drumstick on Sam's proffered plate, while at the same time eavesdropping on lanky, lantern-jawed Garner Bryce Bradford—a Hill Country brash and crass plowboy who had married into wealth.

With a decidedly Texas twang and an amiable manner, thirty-seven- year-old Garner was persuasively importuning Heath's cousin, Hannah. "As both a Paladín and a Jewess, Mrs. Jackson, you would be perfect for heading up our Operation Eyes of Texas, working right out of San Antonio where you live."

"I really don't see how that would be possible, Congress-man Bradford," auburn-haired, Hannah demurred.

"Sure, it would. Hell, The Barony Enterprises, with its Gorman Transportation, railroads, oil wells, aviation, and other business ventures, would provide lucrative oppor-tunity for the European refugee Jews' employment."

"The Barony might be perfect for your Operation Eyes of Texas but not me." She accepted a cane basket of buttery homemade rolls from Preston. "Between riding herd on both Fiona and my prisoner-of-war students, I have my hands full."

"Well, don't say no just yet," Bradford cajoled. "Kick my proposal around in the back of your head for a while. I can be a persistent cuss, ma'am. Isn't that right, Mariana?"

She smiled dryly. "That persistence is your strong point on the Senate floor—outside your good ol' boy appeal."

That persistence had won him the congressional election by a very narrow margin of votes registered in a heavily Hispanic county, many of its inhabitants deceased, lending him the sobriquet Graveyard Garner.

Heath's attention lingered on his wife. From behind those deceptive eyeglasses, Mariana's dark brown eyes regarded him for a long, promising moment. She had been his strength when she had represented him in a worldwide sensational murder trial, and she was his strength still, though a paradox—a woman with an avant-garde mentality and an Old World sense of dignity and charm.

After all these years, their love life still burned hotly. Yet, outside their bedroom, connecting with each other was daily becoming more difficult. They both had changed . . . taking their lives in different directions.

His, from Hollywood Hunk to heading up an international business that his forbearers had synthesized from southern plantation and Mexican ranchero operations. Hers, from impoverished law student to a confident and formidable U.S. senator—and somewhere in between, from his cousin once removed to his wife at a time when such a marriage was considered in Texas incestuously criminal, with prison-sentence penalties.

Like most married couples, the war had separated them, but he had to wonder, should life return to normal once the war ended, if Mariana would want to desert Capitol Hill to come back to The Barony. He wasn't sure if the changes they both had undergone were surmountable.

Or, if he even possessed the urgency to surmount them.

He feared the malaise that often claimed other couples would well claim them—that ease of drifting into a comforting pattern that did not demand challenge or growth.

GARNER B. BRADFORD AND HEATH Paladín, along with his son, were watching the trainer put Desert Thief through his paces on the racing course. The thoroughbred's stride was easy, effortless . . . and then he just exploded in a cloud of dust around the track.

Fall's leached-out light could not diminish the sorrel's majestic conformation. Paladín had combined a first-rate Kentucky thoroughbred with the crème de la crème of The Barony's own equines. The Barony's owner had built the grandstand just before the war's outbreak—with sights set on mint juleps and the Triple Crown.

Garner braced a highly polished boot on the lower rung of the grandstand's iron railing and propped his folded arms on the top one. "Yup, it's a nice spread you've got yourself here, Paladín. And a fine piece of horseflesh too. Is he for sale?"

"Desert Thief is mine," Sam Houston Paladín announced, the ten-year-old a spitting image of his father, discounting the pale scar bisecting the kid's upper lip.

He had been born with a minor cleft lip that, after surgical repair, had left one corner of his mouth with a slightly cynical curl for one so young and also had left him with an occasional speech impediment.

"When Desert Thief was a colt he got tangled up in a roll of barbed wire," Heath said. "His foot got infected. Thought we'd have to saw away the hoof, but Sam nursed Desert Thief back to health. So, Sam owns him—lock, stock, and barrel."

"Well, will you sell him to me, son?" He ruffled the kid's coal-black hair. Sam's matchstick-straight brows met into a single line, as if he were glaring against the setting sun. "Nope."

He rubbed the back of his sun-cooked neck. "Well, if Desert Thief is not for sale, is The Barony?"

Once seeing the magnificence that was its vast lands and the myriad scope of its holdings, everything that stood for Texas Big, he knew it was fitting for a man who thought on the grand scale.

The older Paladín's ebony eyes gave no quarter. "That's not even up for discussion, Garner."

He grinned. "Like I told your cousin, Hannah, I am a downright persistent old cuss."

AT FORTY-TWO, LT. COL. Preston Paladín, former WWI ace, chafed mightily at not being part of the action. The military felt he was more valued where he was, as USAAF's commander, giving him plenty of latitude in scheduling his time.

True, he had sworn never to leave Texas soil after waging dogfights over French countryside, then digging latrines in a

German prisoner-of-war camp in Karlsruhe. But he had always been a reckless soul, a risk taker—whether it be gambling, investments, or flying. And now was not the time to play it safe, damnit!

Not that living with a French wife, a charming vixen like Fabienne, was ever safe. How had she come to rule his world, when prior to working with her in the French Resistance the names of the women he had run through could fill a small town's telephone book?

Arms behind his head, he lay relaxed on the bed in one of The Barony guest rooms and watched its small aquarium's goldfish and bloodfins dart about.

He was reminded of Berlin's sparkling Wannsee Lake and Fabienne rowing their skiff—and the way sunlight and water had glinted off the golden skin of her honed forearms and the scimitar sweep of her cheekbones. She had been crisply discussing the hazardous plan to break Hannah free of Spandau Prison, and all the while he had been drowning in the bottomless blue of her beautiful eyes.

The bedroom door peeped open, and Fabienne slid through, closing it softly behind her. Eyes glued to his, she unbelted her blue belted blazer to reveal her crisp white shirt with its v-decolletage. Her sassy look caught his hungry gaze.

Six years younger than he, she still had an appealing child-like quality about her. Even after a decade, her wide smile, with its sparkly white, uneven teeth, continued to undermine him. "Hey, Cowboy," she said with her sultry French accent, "you're off duty, and Noel is tucked into bed. It's play time."

Her blazer slithered to the tiled floor, along with her blouse. Only her brassiere and her skirt with all its chaste underpinnings stood in the way of his ravaging her.

With a seductively teasing smile, she stepped out of her skirt, then slowly slipped her hands behind her back to unhook her brassiere. She gave it a provocative twirl, then sent it sailing—and, mouth open, watched as it spun across the bedroom and plopped into the aquarium.

Her dismayed gaze switched to his. He burst out laughing and held up his arms. "Come here."

Giggling, she crossed the intervening space and flung herself atop him. She began to rain butterfly kisses over his jaw, cheekbones, and forehead. Her sun-streaked tawny hair canopied their faces.

"You're gorgeous," he muttered. His groin came to life, and his hand began its tour of her thigh, bare of nylons due to wartime parachute demand.

"I bet you call all those WASPS gorgeous, too."

"Nah, not anymore, the fly girls shipped out of the municipal airport." He nibbled at her earlobe. "That's why I've moved you up to the top of my 'to do' list."

"Asshole," she moued. Then, "My brassiere."

"Let it drown," he rumbled against the valley of her collarbones. His tongue delved into the hollow. "You taste better than licorice. Delicious."

She laughed. "How romantic you are."

"God, I love you, girl."

Her clever hands worked at unknotting his officer's drab brown tie. "And I love how you love me, soldier boy."

His need of her and that supreme gratification was abruptly terminated by the hard, hurried raps at the bedroom door. He groaned, hoping whoever it was would go away.

"Ignore it," she whispered.

Not surprising, his hopes were dashed as the unrelenting knock sounded again.

"Fuck!" he rasped. "Let me get it."

With lingering regret, he covered her Venus-lovely torso with the bedspread and padded on stockinged feet to the door to slot it open.

His Aunt Angel stood in the corridor. The lines around her eyes were uneasy. "Preston . . . it's the INS. They're waiting in the parlor."

"The Immigration and Naturalization Service?" He plowed his fingers through his disheveled hair. "Why?"

"They're here to take Fabienne into custody. It seems the Department of Justice is suspicious. With her being German-born—"

Shock shot to his gut and galvanized him. "But her parents were French, and she worked with the French Resistance."

"Mariana is reasoning just that with the goons right now. But Fabienne has access to governmental information through both you and Mariana. Their orders are to take her to the German Internment Camp near Crystal City."

# LOS ALAMOS, NEW MEXICO
# APRIL 1944

Los Alamos was so secret that it was not on any map.

Like other newcomers, Byron Paladín, a very pregnant Edna, and fourteen-year-old Jack had ridden the train the year before into tiny Lamy, New Mexico, the nearest station to Santa Fe.

Then they had checked in at 109 East Palace Avenue in Santa Fe, where arrangements were made for everything from their luggage and household goods to their passes that would get them into the Secret City—and to Byron's newest employment.

Next was the thirty-five-mile trip to the northwest, taking almost four hours because of the steep, winding mountain road leading up Sangre de Cristo Mountains to Los Alamos Project's Main Gate.

Hastily built, large laboratory buildings sprawled atop Parajito Mesa. The table-top topography meant all entrances to its Site Y could be secured. On the mesa's west side, streets of four-family apartments dotted Bathtub Row, so called because they were the only housing in Site Y with bathtubs. Board sidewalks bridge mud from winter's melting snow and summer's afternoon monsoons.

Site Y had been chosen by the highly secretive Manhattan Project because of its isolation, access to water, ample space, and pre-existing buildings—part of the elite Los Alamos Boys Ranch School, which by right of eminent domain was now used for housing. The School's Fuller Lodge and Big House had been converted as social gathering places for project personnel.

No one who went to live and work at Los Alamos was allowed to tell friends or family members where they were going. Physicists, chemists, metallurgists, explosive experts, and military personnel descended like a flock of grackles on the isolated plateau for a single purpose—to design and build an atomic bomb.

An estimated thirty scientists were to work on the project. However, in a short time, the inhabitants grew to more than 6,000, causing severe shortages of housing and water, among other constant hardships. Little by little, a school, library, cafeteria, and soda fountain were added, making Site Y seem more like a town.

The central scientific laboratory operated feverishly and secretly in an isolated area. But at the Big House, weekly colloquiums were held where some degree of sharing in information occurred among the scientists and engineers from across the otherwise very carefully separated out units occurred.

These colloquiums ensured accuracy and forward

progress but also served to reduce the tension resulting from secrecy. Clearly, information could not be allowed to travel beyond the mesa. Fear was rampant that the Germans would develop a nuclear weapon first.

After all the theorizing and rhetoric settled, it still came down to the same concern—would a nuclear explosion burn up the atmosphere? Or the concern that the Gadget, as it was called, would even work.

That night, Byron trudged home from one of the colloquiums. He labored ten to twelve hours, six days a week. At work, he scribbled mathematical calculations on chalkboards, at home on the bathroom mirror, and at Sunday social gatherings on cocktail napkins.

On those Sundays, for relaxation, he and Edna sipped famously potent martinis at the director Oppenheimer's home, listened to musical concerts in Fuller Lodge, played canasta with other couples, or sat at home, comfortably working crossword puzzles. Or, at least, Edna did while he jotted calculations even in the newspaper margins.

They were flat broke. They had left behind everything in Roswell to risk undertaking this covert mission. For years, his beanpole of a wife and he had worked side by side in Roswell with the famed rocket scientist, Goddard.

Edna's dedication to Byron had always been his own particular rocket fuel. These days, it seemed she was his very breath.

When he entered the little apartment, she looked up. She was nursing the noisily slurping baby, Jill. He had to smile. When Sears & Roebuck delivery men became suspicious after orders for a dozen or more baby bassinets came from the same address atop Parajito Mesa, word was given out that the Los Alamos Boys Ranch had been turned into a home for unwed mothers.

Edna's usual wide, gap-toothed grin was subdued. "How did the colloquium go tonight, honey?"

He shrugged out of his sheepskin jacket and hung it on one of the wall pegs. "A real boxing match, sweetcakes. The guys were like schoolboys sparring over their theories."

His very own version of Olive Oyl offered up her lips for his kiss, then sighed. "I miss all that stimulation that we had in Roswell."

"What you wouldn't miss is a butt-load of egos. They're very, very bright and very, very ambitious." He grimaced. "But no doubt about it, there is steep competition to stand out. Jack already asleep?"

"No. In the kitchen, keeping track of the war, as usual—shifting those pins on the wall map."

Tissuing off the excess milk, she readjusted her wrap-around housedress and rose to put their sleeping infant into the makeshift crib, a dresser drawer, wedged in one corner of their tiny living quarters. Her back to him, she tossed the crumpled tissue in the wicker trash basket. "We had visitors, Byron."

He heard the concern in her voice, then saw it on her narrow face when she turned to him. Anything that could upset easy-going Edna, which was very little, had to be important. Very important. He crossed the oak plank floor that still smelled of sawdust and pulled her into the crook of his arm. "Okay, tell me about it."

She buried her face in the hollow created by his neck and shoulder. "Two FBI agents—they were here to question me about Andy."

"Andy?" Her brother had been killed ages ago, fighting for the Lincoln Battalion in the Spanish Civil War.

"Andy had communist sentiments and ties, honey. The agents were threatening to add us to the FBI's Custodial Detention Index—for arrest in case of some kind of national emergency."

"They were bluffing." He absently stroked the soft, fly-away hair at her crown. "That's their modus operandi for their investigations."

Why would the FBI be nitpicking over something as farfetched as a deceased brother with communist senti-ments?

"No, I think it goes further," she mumbled against his shirt collar. "It could get worse."

His hand stilled. "How worse?"

She raised her head. For the first time that he could remember, the oh-so-independent woman's eyes reflected apprehension. "They mentioned that the Manhattan Project Security officials could revoke your security clearance here."

Maybe it was the Paladín in him. His grandfather had maintained an arsenal of rifles and cannons pointed south in the direction of marauding Mexicans and west at the butchering Indians. Like the old Baron, Byron felt that a powerful offense was a good defense—and he felt the work he was doing in attempting to construct an all-powerful deterrent against the Axis was important. But apparently, someone somewhere did not.

"Well, well . . . another fine day." He unclipped his white security badge from his shirt pocket and lobbed it across the room into the trash basket.

## CRYSTAL CITY, TEXAS
## AUGUST 1944

IN THE VAST EMPTINESS OF SOUTHWEST Texas, duplexes, triplexes and quadruple barracks studded the Enemy Alien Control Unit like cloves in a Black Forest Ham.

The largest internment camp in the United States, its remote location—fifty miles from the Mexican border— made it ideal for the task of housing more than 2,800 internees of all three Axis nationalities. The constantly expanding camp contained mostly Germans or those with German ancestry, with a few Italians and Japanese also interned.

It was the nation's only internment camp established specifically for families, who for the most part considered it a place with not too many real hardships. Of course, the barracks were unbearably hot under that harsh, desert sunlight. Nothing, Fabienne Paladín privately lamented, like the cool tile corridors of The Barony's *hacienda,* from where she and Noel had been snatched.

Run much like a small community, the Family

Internment Camp had an infirmary, post office, bakery—even a German *biergarten* and a Japanese Sumo wrestling ring. Nursery schools and kindergartens were run by the internees.

Originally, female prisoners shared a few sewing machines, making curtains and children's clothing, but the sewing soon expanded into a parachute industry that occupied a majority of the female prisoners.

Sewing did not engage one whit of Fabienne's boomerang mind. In that internment camp, teachers fluent in English, Spanish, German, or Japanese were appointed to work with the children as foreign language teachers. Fabienne was fluent in French and German and passable in English, but so were many others in the camp. Approval of her desperately awaited appointment as a foreign language teacher looked bleak.

She also desperately awaited escape. Preston had said he would get her and Noel out, and she believed her husband. She knew he would walk through the fires of hell to do so. But, after six months at Crystal City, she had to face the stark reality' that he was still stuck somewhere in hell. As was she without him. As was Noel, if her son's battered face was an indication.

All around them the desert wind whipped dust devils that spun across the schoolyard and whirled effortlessly through the barbed wire enclosure. If only she and Noel could do so. "Behave yourself at school." Fabienne framed Noel's face with her hands and kissed him goodbye on the forehead.

"Mom!" the twelve-year-old groaned. "Not in front of

everybody."

She brushed the dark locks back from his forehead, and he winced when her fingers grazed a swollen bruise at his temple. "And no more fighting all those boys at once." Although, from the look of one of the bullies, her son had given as good as he got.

"But the krauts were pushing around Paola and calling her a wop."

"First, my son, you, too, are partly a kraut, if you insist on using that vulgar term."

"No. I'm a Paladín. A Texican."

"Second, you will take on only one at a time. And I want you to break his nose."

Noel's dark brown eyes mirrored his shock, then his face, scored in angles and planes by adolescence, screwed up. "They hang together, Mom."

"I shall take care of that."

That meant first addressing the problem of Paola Aliberti. The eight-year-old might still wear baby fat around her midsection, but she was a scrapper.

The family numbered among the few Italian ones interned at Crystal City. Her uncle had been Rome's mayor when her parents emigrated to Fort Worth, Texas. Her mother occupied a sewing table two over from Fabienne's. Her father, purportedly a member of the Black Hand, now served as an electrician and was also part of the camp's maintenance crew.

Fabienne envied the Alibertis being all together as a family, while she must cope without Preston at her side.

Although his arrest had not been ordered, he had been given the option to voluntarily join her.

A convening of the Paladín clan had made the collective decision that given his diversified connections with the power-shakers of the oil and banking industry, plus his contacts through the military, he could best spring her and Noel from the outside.

On the other hand, she had given Noel no option. Her motherly instincts shouted that her son still needed her foremost and had elected to keep him with her. Now, belatedly, she realized she had made a selfish choice. True, he was being given an eclectic education here at this isolated camp that many prestigious private institutions could not even approach.

But Noel sorely needed his father to provide a healthy balance between timidity and aggression. Fathers loved more dangerously. Noel needed that—needed Preston to guide him in the ways of a man, to learn how to channel his masculinity and strength in positive ways.

Paola had inherited her mother's intelligent Etruscan eyes and earthy electricity. As Fabienne suspected upon meeting with Paola's mother, the girl had not divulged her run-ins with the taunting German boys.

The mother Annamaria clapped her hands together as if in prayer and brought them to her lips. "Madonna, blessed saints. I will tell Paola's father."

"No, you won't. After school today, Annamaria, you and I will swim."

While the compound offered a variety of entertainment,

such as movies shown outdoors against a building wall and supervised picnics near the Nueces River, the swimming pool was by far the most popular form of entertainment.

Originally an irrigation pond, the prisoners had converted it to a giant sunken, circular pool of concrete. Two-hundred-fifty-feet wide, it might have been a resort beach if Fabienne overlooked the six guard towers with their brilliant searchlights, ten-foot-high barbed wire, the ferocious guard dogs, and her censored mail.

The pool was down a path bordering the school property. Walking to the pool's edge was a daunting trip of vigilance in order to avoid mesquite thorns, big red ants, stinging scorpions, and deadly rattlesnakes.

But they were nothing compared to Fabienne's Valkyrie expression.

With Annamaria trailing in her wake, Fabienne paused only long enough between the German and Japanese bathhouses to kick off her peep-toe shoes. Then, with perfect posture, she strode—fully clothed—into the water and waded thigh deep.

Atop the highest diving board at the pool's deep end, her son's mouth dropped open. Noel's astonishment shifted quickly to mortification.

Fabienne did not need to have the culprits pointed out. Three strapping German youths closer to the shallow end were dunking hapless kids. The nearest German boy glanced up to see her approach like a German U-boat. His sunburnt, contentious features registered shock. She seized his hair while Annamaria lunged to grab the ear of the second teenager.

At that point, Noel, surfacing close by, caught his mother's telegraphed "go ahead" nod. He charged into their midst, swinging furiously.

Behind, Paola was sloshing fast toward the circle of puerile pugilists. She swung her first punch, the boy wincing at the blow to his kidney.

Fabienne's eyes widened at the girl's pluck.

Automatically, the boy's fist drew back with his rebuttal.

That was when Noel delivered his walloping punch. A crunch, a yelp, and spraying pool water dappled Paola's grinning face and swimsuit a bloody pink.

## HOLLYWOOD, CALIFORNIA
## SEPTEMBER 1944

AFTER MARLENE DIETRICH'S scratchy, breathless voice finished warbling "Falling in Love Again" on the Hollywood Canteen's stage, Glen Miller's swing band launched into "In the Mood."

Belle Blevins Paladín scraped the bottom of her energy bucket to make it through another fierce jitterbug. At forty-four, she was too old for this—there was nothing like an aging screen star. Still, all too often on the Tuesday afternoons she volunteered, she would find herself surrounded by lonely soldiers while being spun, dipped, and flipped, then passed on to another, non-stop, until she thought she would flop like some ragdoll.

Volunteers—movie stars, directors, and film crews—waited twenty-four-seven on tables, cooking and cleaning up for the American servicemen, as well as the Canadian, French, Russian, and British soldiers—with even a few Chinese airmen coming in.

To cope with the two-story's limited size, servicemen entered in shifts. The rotation made it possible for more than 2,000 uniformed personnel to enter the club daily.

Food, dance, and entertainment were free for them. For the girls who showed up to dance, the canteen charged an admission of canned goods and items like sugar and flour. Strict rules of conduct applied. The dancers were to provide friendly companionship to the often-nervous men who were soon to be sent into combat—but no romantic liaisons were allowed between civilians and servicemen.

For the war effort, no matter how exhausted Belle was, she would show up smiling every Tuesday afternoon. After all, somewhere over in the Philippines, maybe Japan even, Tim was either a prisoner-of-war or . . . well, she could not allow her mind to tiptoe across that minefield—the loss that could bludgeon her heart.

Mariana was doing all she could through government channels to glean any information about Tim, but her efforts were repeatedly and inexplicably derailed. No one knew if Tim was among the 15,000 American soldiers taken prisoner or among those fallen. The entire Paladín clan was chafing at the bit to do something, *anything* . . . but their efforts were just as ineffectual.

Belle had been so young, just sixteen, when she had given birth to Tim. Her parents had disowned her. Struggling as a single mother to make a career on the radio, she had bombed. But Darcy had seen her potential and used the Paladíns' Double Take Studio to transform her into an international movie star, the Singing Cowgirl.

She had just returned early that morning from stumping across the country, selling war bonds. This particular Tuesday afternoon, she wanted nothing more than to crawl into bed and cuddle against Darcy's broad chest. Nevertheless, patriotic duty awaited her.

So, when a heavyset sailor had the audacity, as he escorted her from the dance floor, to grab her breast and try to French kiss her, she lost all patience and smacked him.

"Why, you . . . you *cunt!*" His paw flew to his red-imprinted jaw. Soldiers nearest them yanked him back from her. Arms swung, and the free-for-all was on.

Immediately, the band, as instructed in case of such a fracas, launched into "The Star Spangled Banner," and everyone snapped to attention.

Later, when Belle collected her purse, the chain-smoking Bette Davis who ran the canteen snapped, "He could have been a kraut for all I care. You don't slap him."

"Then you let him stick his tongue down your throat," she told the movie star, "not that he or any man with balls would want to."

Bette gasped, practically inhaling her lit Camel.

Aghast at what she had done, Belle cried all the way back to the studio. What the hell was wrong with her these days?

Her hormones were as out of control as the sailor had been. At forty-four, she was too old to be pregnant.

Taking a few calming breaths, she mentally ticked off the days since her last menstrual period. It had arrived three weeks before, scant and late though it was. Maybe she needed to make an appointment with her doctor.

Like she had time. Even now, she was running late. She should have been at the studio half an hour ago.

Given over to the U.S. Signal Corps, Double Take Studio was now known as the Army Pictorial Center. Despite the fact that both she and Darcy were proclaimed pacifists, it did not mean that they would not do everything they could for America and its sons—and her son, as well.

Darcy directed the filming and development of Army training and indoctrination films, and she had established a Red Cross blood drive center in the studio basement.

At the back soundstage, Elmer Davis, the director for the Office of Wartime Information, was on hand to monitor the filming of *Uncle Sam Wants You*. He and Darcy were deep in conversation with the film's star, Tyrone Power, shorter and not nearly as handsome as Darcy—at least, in Belle's biased opinion.

" . . . propaganda . . . depict the Allied armed forces as valiant freedom fighters" Elmer broke off as she joined them.

"Well, here is just the woman I wanted. Belle!" He gave her a peck on both cheeks. "Uncle Sam doesn't want you as much as Voice of America does. With your unique Texas twang, you'd be perfect, Belle. Have you given any more thought to my proposal?"

She sought out the shelter and support of Darcy's arm and managed a smile for Elmer. "I say I just want to get through the blood donation right now, then to Louella Parsons's party tonight, and then on home again, jiggety jig."

Darcy squeezed her shoulder and gave her a tight, reassuring smile that did not reassure her at all. "Well, you don't have to worry about making the gossip columnist's party, sweetheart."

She tilted her head to look up at him, her brows knitting. "Why?"

"Louella's secretary called us." He did not bother to hide his scathing tone. "She 'extended her sincere regrets that our invitation was sent to us inadvertently.'"

Belle knew there were some in the Hollywood community who had prowar attitudes bordering on hysteria and had chosen to ostracize Darcy and her for their pacifist stand. Others thought they had sold out by producing the patriotic films. They could not win for losing. Either way, it didn't help the bottom line of Double Take Studio.

She wanted to say, "Well, screw the vicious harpy," but she projected a cheerful grin. "I couldn't be more delighted in being uninvited." She stood on tiptoe to kiss his beard-shadowed jaw. "I'm too exhausted to go, anyway."

She then turned to Elmer Davis. "Count me in for your VOA program. Maybe 'The Battle Hymn of the Republic?'"

"That'd be swell, Belle!"

Taking her leave, she made her way to the stairwell of the basement sound stage where a Red Cross nurse was drawing blood in the huge, converted prop room. The goal of the blood drives was to process the donated blood into dried plasma on a large scale. Then hundreds of thousands of units of plasma were shipped overseas to come back home in the veins of wounded Marines.

At that late afternoon hour, only a few donors filled the brightly-lit, white-curtain-sectioned room. It smelled nauseatingly sterile. A cameraman Belle occasionally worked with sat straddle-legged on one chair, a tourniquet banding his arm.

She manufactured a peppy grin. "Hey, Charlie, how's it going?"

"Okey-dokey, Belle." His circled thumb and forefinger, flashing her the A-Okay gesture, but he looked ashen. She stifled a sigh at the male weakness when it came to needles.

Yet, after the old biddy of a nurse jammed the needle in the vein at the soft bend of her elbow, Belle immediately began to feel woozy herself. She, who fearlessly and effortlessly donated blood every other month. What the hell?

As the floor rose up to meet her, she knew something was terribly wrong.

# FORT SAM HOUSTON, SAN ANTONIO
# DECEMBER 1944

Daily life for the German prisoners was rather laxly structured. Reveille was at five forty-five a.m., and lights were turned off at ten p.m. Between those times, the prisoners worked, took care of their own needs, and entertained themselves with a large variety of handicraft—and, naturally, took advantage of the class Hannah taught through St. Mary's University.

The War Department had arranged for the extension courses. It was understood that the POWs' academic credits were to be accepted by the Germans whenever the war ended. Security had been very heavy those first few months, and she had been uneasy with the armed guard posted at the classroom door. But, as the German soldiers proved to be model prisoners, security became relaxed. Not one untoward incident occurred the entire term.

That last evening of the course, she stood before the class, limited to forty- eight students, and summarized in her slightly less than flawless German her four months of Texas history lessons. She doubted if all forty-eight young men were seriously interested in Texas history. Most of them, she sensed, merely came weekly to watch her, one of the few females they got to see, outside the old nurse, kitchen volunteers, and a few clerical personnel.

And then there was invariably the presence of the prisoner's commanding officer who watched from the back of the room—arms crossed, boots planted wide—like some Colossus bestriding two worlds . . . the Old and New, the Axis and the Allied, his and hers.

She had fervently hoped working with the prisoners would heal her battery- acid hatred that was hurting her far more than it affected the prisoners. Instead, working with them had opened her up to the forbidden—to a desire that had been dormant the past three years since Stoney had shipped off to war.

Or perhaps even longer . . . before she had discovered his affair with the young girl working his veterinarian office's front desk. Hannah did her best not to dwell on that heartbreaking discovery. What good did it do? Forgive and forget—was not that the noble act expected of a housewife whose husband had strayed?

Stoney had begged her not to leave, had sent the front desk girl packing, had pointed out the terrible consequences a divorce would have on their daughter Fiona, had sworn it was only Hannah he loved, had promised fidelity forever . . . and on . . . and on.

Shattered, wanting to hurt and humiliate him as he had her, she had struck back with insinuations and belittlements, like poisoned darts, until eventually she was even sick of herself, of the mean-spirited woman she had become. Their marriage had evolved into merely a matter of moving through each day, abiding one another's presence as tolerably as possible.

The letters they now exchanged while he was away at war said it all—because they said nothing. Nothing of depth, nothing that came from the soul, and everything superficial that disguised their inability to deal with the debris of each other's very human flaws.

The love and trust that had existed between them had been altered, and they both knew it was irreparable. Yet she continued to write faithfully, and he responded as often as his duty at the battle front permitted.

"Legend has it that the twenty-six-year-old commander of the Alamo Mission, right here in San Antonio," she explained crisply, "was faced with the probability of additional help fading fast. The story goes that Colonel Travis drew a line in the sand with his saber. He asked any man willing to stay and fight the Mexicans to step over the line."

She paused, her gaze slowly sweeping the desks' occupants but avoiding the brick-wall of a man standing watch at the back.

"Whether Colonel Travis actually drew the line or not, it's hard to say. But the fact remains that courageous men from all pursuits of life believed in freedom. The defenders of the Alamo stayed and made the ultimate sacrifice for freedom—their lives. The defenders were English, Hispanic,

Polish, French, Scottish . . . and German."

With that, she smiled. "I have enjoyed having each of you this semester." She paused again to reach inside the desk drawer and began withdrawing the forty-nine small boxes gaily wrapped in paper. She had filled them with fudge she had made from preciously hoarded sugar procured with ration coupons.

"Class is dismissed—if each of you will stop by my desk on your way out, I have a small Christmas present for you."

Immediately, a student in the first row, Pvt. Lars Steinweg, was at her desk. Shyly, he held out a brown paper sack. *"Frohe Weihnachten,* Professor Jackson."

She glanced inside. Pecans. Some prisoners were trucked out of the military installation to farms where they gathered pecans, picked peaches, cut wood, and baled hay.

Other prisoners were assigned jobs such as machinists, garbage collectors, bakers, truck drivers, and horseshoers.

A peck on Lars Steinweg's blushingly florid cheek would be *verboten.* She gave him a huge smile and said warmly, "And Merry Christmas to you, as well. *Vielen dank."*

Little by little, small gifts mounded on her desks. A Christmas tree ornament cut from an empty tin can, a loaf of dark German bread, a metal beer stein—doubtlessly forged in the blacksmith's shop. One by one, her students took their gifts of fudge and departed . . . until only the colonel was left.

She looked up at Jakob Nobel and, as always, felt intimidated by his size and authoritative manner. Her smile fixed, she passed him the remaining box of fudge. *"Frohe*

*Weihnachten,* Colonel."

*"Danke.* I like chocolate very much." He tucked the box into the pocket of his khaki jacket. "We walk."

Each night after class, he would walk her along the brightly lit street to the guard station parking lot, a good half mile distance. They would talk, mostly about inconsequential things. He, with his confident use of consonants and harsh-sounding staccato words. She, hesitatingly, sparingly, with the softer, gliding vowels of the Texicans.

She learned that he had no pro-Nazi sentiments. Of course, most prisoners would proclaim that. Only recently, had he revealed that his wife had cheated on him.

"I spent very much time building my chemical company. Not time enough with her. I wanted her and Heidi, our twelve-year-old, to have good lives. Instead . . . ." He had shrugged his yard-wide shoulders, his grimace slipping into a dry smile. " . . . she left me and Heidi for a dog trainer. He was visiting from Belgium." His English had been improving rapidly with the enforced use.

"Who is Heidi with now?"

"Back with my wife. She and I are trying to make it work. At least, that is what her letters inform me. That she wants this."

Sometimes they walked in silence. An easy silence, with no superfluous words forced to fill it. At other times, Hannah, too, would talk. "I have been married twice. My first husband . . . he reminds me much of you. Michael was German, Vice President of General Electric Corporation there in Berlin. Until he was assassinated."

"I remember reading the newspaper about that. I was . . . I think the English word is appalled. And your second husband—Stonewall Jackson?"

"Stoney is a veterinarian. Serving God knows where in Europe as a medic." She did not betray her husband's infidelity to the colonel.

This last walk with him would be different. Yes, she had familial duties to perform. There was still Christmas shopping to finish for Fiona. Her daughter had been well named for her tempestuous ancestor, Fiona Flanagan Paladín. The twelve-year-old was a mixture of fashion diva and burgeoning activist and both the bane and blessing of Hannah's existence.

Yet she knew that she had to make time for Jakob Nobel after class tonight. A closure of sorts, she supposed. She had moved past her revulsion of his people.

She hoped.

She collected her gloves and her hat. He took her wool jacket from her and helped her into it, his fingers grazing her nape. Her breath caught in an inaudible gasp. She tried to focus on anchoring her cloche hat.

Grasping her elbow, he steered her outside—not toward the guard station parking lot but along the flagstone path toward his garden retreat. She looked askance at him, puzzled by this change of direction, but said nothing. Instead, she gave unwarranted attention to donning her black leather gloves.

The entire POW camp was brightly lit at night, so she was not concerned at being alone with him . . . then again, she would not have been concerned were the place cave-dark. Ironically, she felt safe with this enemy of hers, intimidating though he was.

The evening was crisp and serene. As they approached the leafy bamboo enclosure, the fountain's splash tinkled through the quiet. "I have a gift for you. A Christmas gift for my American friend. There . . . on the bench."

Reluctantly—and she knew not why—she approached the stone bench in the shadows of the greenery. On the bench slab set a small package, much like the boxes she had given away. Pandora's Box, a voice within her whispered.

Fingers trembling, she picked up the gift box, peeled away the homemade Christmas wrapping paper, and opened the lid. Within nested two rings of carved wood. Peering closely, she could make out that each bore the emblem of the Star of David.

"Although Germany is famous for its master woodcrafters," Jakob said behind her, "I fall far short of them."

Two rings? What could this unshakable man be thinking? They both were married. She turned to find him standing close. "Thank you, but . . . ." She shook her head, bewildered as how to address this and slightly nervous.

"The two rings—for your two injured fingers. You hide them beneath your gloves. I feel you should draw attention to those fingers. To celebrate your great courage."

Moisture clouded her vision. Her lips worked to make some sort of response. No sound came out.

"Courage sometimes means being vulnerable," he

continued in that gruff voice of his.

She had screamed during the Germans' torture, but never had she wept. Not then. Nor since. Neither solicitous platitudes nor hugs meant to comfort had broken through her defense of stoicism. And it was not only the physical torture she had endured. It was the endless hours and days of mental torture, of fearing what awful thing next awaited her.

She collapsed against his solidity and sobbed.

His arms wrapped around her, supporting her. Gently, her enemy kissed each cheek, blotting her tears. Like a baby bird, her mouth turned up to find sustenance. And when his lips encountered hers, she knew she had found what she had been seeking but perhaps lost her soul in doing so.

## HARBIN, MANCHUKUO, MANCHURIA
## JANUARY 1945

WHEN IT CAME TO TORTURE, THE fifteenth century Spanish Grand Inquisitor Torquemada had nothing on the Japs at the Mukden slave labor camp to which Tim had been transferred. American prisoners were especially singled out for experiments by Japan's infamous biological warfare specialists.

In 1931, when the Japanese Army invaded Manchuria for its coal to supply Nippon Steel, the occupying army immediately began expropriating private property.

Foreigners, as well as Chinese, were kidnapped, tortured, and often murdered by the Japanese.

Now Japan was seeking something more than coal. It was searching for uranium ore in Korea and Manchuria, as far as Tim could figure out. But why? Unless . . .unless it had to do with something Tim vaguely remembered Uncle Byron trying to explain—the production of enormous energy from nuclear fission.

The Mukden camp deep in Manchuria, with its electric fencing and sentry boxes, assured that all contact with the outside world was cut off. It was part of a Japanese military base with the nearest city being Harbin, an exotic and international hellhole boxed in by Russian Siberia, Outer Mongolia, and Korea.

In his seven weeks at Mukden, Tim, along with thirty-four other Cabanatuan prisoners, had traded tropical ulcers that ate down to the bone and clothes that fell apart with mildew for frozen fingers and toes that broke off like icicles in Manchuria's sub-zero climate.

He had gone from killing and eating monkeys at Cabanatuan to killing and eating dogs that strayed into the Mukden camp—when he and the gnome, Marcos, and the other prisoners were so lucky.

Since the Japanese had never signed the Geneva Conventions treaty, they were not bound to treat their prisoners humanely.

Quite obviously, it was only a matter of time before he became a guinea pig with a glass tube shoved up his rectum, some kind of germ injection in his body, or chemicals sprayed in his face.

And he knew after that it would be even shorter a time before he traded his miserable life at Mukden's barracks for its ghoulish wooden warehouse, where the bodies of dead prisoners-of-war were stacked because the ground was too hard for burial.

Marcos, unaccustomed to the harsh clime, was already suffering, his little emaciated brown body a fluorescent blue with the frigid wind. "I tell you true," he said, his taxed lungs wheezing, "I hear the *Diwatas* wailing."

"Fuck 'em, Marcos. Banshees and *Diwatas* are bullshit." They were returning with other prisoners from a day of cutting logs. Their days varied—one day mining coal, another day moving rocks to build roads, and still another laying railroad ties.

Marcos's flat nose flared. "I tell you true—"

The whack in the Filipino's ribs from the barrel of a Jap handler's submachine gun sent Marcos reeling. Quickly, Tim hauled the gasping little guy to his feet. Beneath his breath, Marcos mumbled a raspy curse in his native Tagalog language.

Even on that late afternoon, Tim was to have no rest. Because of his strength and stamina, he was sent out once again on another detail, this time to clean a pit latrine. Who knew what kind of infectious diarrhea or intestinal worm infection he might contract or might bring back to the others in his barracks?

Not that it mattered. That evening, when he did make it back to Barracks Eleven, Marcos did not sit up, let alone open his eyes to greet Tim's malodorous self. One sniff of him, and even the dead would gag in their graves—which, Tim realized, was where Marcos would shortly be.

Now was the time to make a run for it.

Few ever attempted escape. All were caught. The Japanese method of execution was to round up the prisoners and force them to watch as gasoline was poured over the recaptured prisoner, who was then set ablaze.

Since the odds were the prisoner would die in the slave labor camp anyway, escape still would arguably be the best option.

Except guards had now put up signs declaring that if other escape attempts were made, nine prisoners would be executed for every escapee. Prisoners' barracks had then been divided into groups of ten. Naturally, the POWs kept a close eye on their bunkmates to prevent them from making escape attempts.

Well, fuck that. Marcos was dying, anyway. It was only a matter of hours or days at the most. There was no point in any further loyalty. He had to keep telling himself that or he would die with the rest of the lousy lot.

But that night, his exhilaration at the thought of escape was dismally dampened by Marcos's wheezing death rattle on the bunk to Tim's right. And on the bunk to his left groaned a nearly unconscious Chinese nationalist who had been taken prisoner five days earlier and beaten repeatedly.

Tim tried to blot out the awful, haunting sounds of both men by solely focusing on formulating an escape plan.

The details centered around escaping by way of the

latrine he had helped clean. It channeled through the compound to a canal twenty-five or so yards outside. The latrine's sturdy, thick-wired mesh directly beneath the concrete compound wall was the only thing standing between him and freedom. All he needed was a pair of wire-cutters.

He might as well be asking for a pair of blonde bomb-shells.

With time, he might secure something on the order of wire-cutters. But he did not have time.

All too quickly the five a.m. roll call sounded in the yard at the north end of the camp. Tim was trying to rouse Marcos, who didn't move. Laying an ear next to the Filipino's mouth, Tim tried to detect breathing.

"Hey, Paladín, get a move on it," Alabama yelled from the doorway.

"Give me a minute," Tim snapped at the nineteen-year-old and turned back to Marcos.

"It's not just your ass that's on the line," Alabama muttered and banged the door behind him.

Reporting late for roll call, after the bugle was sounded, meant two days without food for the tardy prisoner's entire barracks. Failure to show at all meant being roasted alive for the prisoner.

But thinking he may have heard a faint breath usher across Marcos's cracked lips, Tim could not yet bring himself to abandon the little man. Jesus! "Come on, bud!"

Suddenly, the door was reopened, letting in another blast of frigid air. This time, the barrack's warrant officer entered and directed a spate of Japanese words at Tim.

Shit!

From the little Japanese Tim had learned, the warrant officer was there to retrieve the Chinese guerilla fighter.

From the little Japanese that Tim had learned, the warrant officer was to retrieve the guerilla fighter and was ordering Tim to help drag out the nearly comatose man, apparently the nephew of the Chinese warlord, Jion. His bandits at the Manchuria borderland had kidnapped a Jap national and had arranged a hostage swap for Jion's nephew.

The warrant officer began to struggle to hoist the guerilla from his bunk. Tim did not even pause to give further compassionate thought to the harrowing fate of Marcos or the eight other barrack inmates resulting from his next course of action.

His locked hands chopped on the neck of the warrant officer, struggling to hoist the Chinese guerilla from his bunk. A mighty smash with the stock of the officer's sub-machine gun finished off the Jap's cranium.

Within seconds, Tim donned the warrant officer's hooded wool overcoat, now spottily flecked with brain matter. The overcoat was so tight on Tim's shoulders, he could not even come near closing the gap to fasten it. Next, he winched the much smaller and nigh-comatose Chinese guerilla up across his back.

While the prisoners hastened to line up for roll call, he shuffled his cargo across the frozen ground to the guard gate. Stooped by his human load, his disproportionate height was somewhat masked. Despite the frigid temperature and his light load, sweat broke out on his temples. At any second, he expected the alarm of a prisoner missing in the lineup to be sounded.

The Jap on duty at the guard station grabbed the blood-matted hair of the warlord's nephew and yanked to better present a view of the face in the predawn dark to others beyond the scope from Tim's furred hood.

"That is him," a voice acknowledged.

Tim raised his head, just barely, and caught a glimpse of a convoy of covered trucks, their tires affixed with snow chains and half buried in slush. Bandits, muffled head to foot in armor like knights of old, shoved forth an equally battered Japanese soldier in trade.

In the melee of the exchange, Tim deposited his cargo, as directed, into the darkened rear of the lead truck. Perceiving no one within, he scrambled inside to collapse face down beside the inert body on his left.

From outside, one Chinese guerilla quipped, *"Ch'ang chang, Tsai-chien*— Goodbye, goodbye, boss."

With relief, Tim heard the truck's accelerator being pumped, the choke notched out, and the engine humming with life. "Thank you, Jee-sus!" he breathed against the ice-and-mud-crusted truck bed.

Then he heard the distinctly feminine voice to his right say, "You are American?"

*Fuck!* He sprang into a crouch.

"No! No, you safe!"

The truck lurched forward, and his bony frame fell against the pliant body sitting at the truck's rear with him and the inert Chinese guerilla.

A soft giggle.

Quickly, he levered away and rolled to plop beside her. It was still pre-dawn dark and difficult to make out the other's features. "Who are you?"

"Ping Pong." Another soft giggle. "I learn English at Catholic Mission at Qingdao."

"Then you are Chinese?"

"No. Korean."

He grunted. Utter fatigue was claiming his spent body. "You don't by any chance have food on you—you know, a potato, a boiled egg, tofu, whatever?"

He could hear her digging around in her clothing. She passed him a small, flat package. Without even biting into it, he recognized it. In the ashen morning light seeping across the truck bed toward them, he made out a Hershey D-ration candy bar.

"Thank you, Jee-sus!" he muttered again. Ripping off the wrapping, his teeth tore into the candy bar. He closed his eyes and sighed with pure ecstasy. Too quickly, the chocolate was gobbled up.

All this time, the feminine figure at his side remained inordinately quiet, but he could feel her eyes upon him. Feeling some return of his depleted energy, he said, "How did you end up with these bandits?"

"I kidnapped in Qingdao . . . serve as a sex slave for Japanese military. Three months ago, Jion's militia, they rescue me in fight with Japanese troop I service."

"Holy shit."

The truck was lumbering down a mountainside, slinging him, her, and the unconscious Chinese soldier back and forth, and he would swear the brakes must have gone out by the way the truck flew around hairpin curves.

He shifted so that he was partially facing her. Already, the rising sun's cold light had steadily stolen across the truck bed to fall upon her hobnailed boots. "Look, can you get me to Qingdao? From there I could hop a steamer—"

"Chinese coast, it is blockaded by Japanese." He heard the alteration in her tone, from softly submissive to sly. "But I could get you to Korea . . . if you could get me to America."

"To America? Hell, I can't even get to America."

"Yes," she persisted. "When you go, big guy . . . I go as your bride."

The sunlight was at last far enough inside the truck to reveal her child-like face. It was breathtakingly beautiful . . . if he discounted the God-awful lines, tiny interlocked tattoos with a crude mixture of soot and hot peppers, that framed either side of her sparkling grin.

## CRYSTAL CITY, TEXAS
## FEBRUARY 1945

THE BATTERED DODGE EMERGENCY REPAIR truck creaked to a halt at the Crystal City Guard Tower. With just about every service vehicle in America commandeered by the military, the Del Rio and Wintergarden Telephone

Company had barely saved the dilapidated panel truck from being put out to pasture.

The repair truck might have been an embarrassment to the telephone company, which attempted to provide service to the incomprehensible vastness of the virtually empty, wind-swept Staked Plains, the Llano Estacado . . . unless one overlooked the panel truck's recently added dual rear tires and an engine hopped up days before by a couple of El Paso's old Prohibition bootleggers hired out by Pierce.

"Emergency ordnance repair," the serviceman told the young armed guard.

Border Patrol, a part of Internal Security and Surveillance which had authority over the camp operations, never had reason to question arrivals at the visitors check-in. That isolated camp had nothing worth sabotaging—or, at least, this was what Preston was counting on.

And, as for escapees, no escape attempt, successful or otherwise, had ever been reported. The Axis families taken into custody actually volunteered for internment at the camp, considered the showplace of the INS's internment program.

"Administration is second street to the left," the guard said, "third building on the right."

The repair truck rattled past the check-in point and skirted several tumbleweeds bouncing across the asphalt road. "Piece of cake," Pierce said from the passenger seat and doffed his appropriated Del Rio Telephone Company billed hat.

"Getting into hell is always easy," Preston told his twin.

"It's getting out that's the challenge."

Tension clamped an excruciatingly painful vise across the muscle-bound ridge of his shoulders. Accrued tension. All these months, he had battled The Hill with everything in his admittedly powerful arsenal, including his cousin Mariana's influence with her high-status congressional colleagues.

Even Garner Bradford's efforts seemed to have stalled. He kept counseling patience. Yet somewhere, someone, somehow, appeared to have more leverage. All requests and appeals for the reversal of the internee orders, for the release of Preston's wife and son, were inexplicably either denied or ignored and shuffled off to Never-Never Land.

From what he could extrapolate from bits and pieces in Fabienne's letters, she had a thirty-minute lunch break, coming up in seven minutes. Most likely, Noel would be horsing around after his lunch period on one of the athletic fields out by the water well.

Retrieving him was a walk in the park. Hands jammed in his pants pockets,
Preston's twin merely strolled toward the bleachers—well, almost. After all these years, Pierce's limp was damn near unnoticeable.

Preston watched his son glance up from the sidelines bench. His dark eyes lit up. "Uncle Pierce!"

Once Noel climbed into the back, Preston swerved in his seat to grab him, holding him tightly, so that his startled son could not see his face, see the glistening moisture that threatened to well over.

"Oh, jeepers, Dad!" his son said, pulling away. "I knew

it! I knew you'd rescue us."

Preston wished he could feel so confident about his abilities.

From there, with Noel directing, it was a short three block drive to the Mess Hall. This time, Pierce waited, along with Noel.

Preston strolled in, unchallenged. It took thirty or so anxious seconds for him to scan the room's two-hundred or so internees, taking their lunch break. He spotted Fabienne in the rear, at the next to last table.

At his approach, she glanced up from her sauerkraut and hot dogs, gasping.

He blinked rapidly again and swallowed hard. Damn, his wife was extraordinarily beautiful. If God did indeed exist, surely He had intended all along for this singular woman to be united in time and space with him, regardless of how lost his soul might be. And if God intended no such thing, Preston did.

He crossed to her, took her fork—stalled in mid-air— and, setting it on her plate, said, "Your Beretta's outside in my truck."

Her Beretta revolver had been a running gag between them since thirteen years before, when they had first met and she had helped him bust his cousin Hannah out of Germany's infamous Spandau Prison. That word alone— Beretta—signaled Fabienne to follow his lead.

Those eating around her paused to stare. She ignored them. Setting her napkin beside her plate, she rose and flashed him one of her wide-mouth gamine grins that just about knocked his legs out from under him.

What a woman. And now was definitely not the time for lust to spring to life at his crotch. But, damnit, it had been so long.

Gripping her hand, his own sweaty—and feeling the energy sparking between them—he led her outside, toward the curb and the repair truck, its motor running. He did not want to let go of her hand, but time was wasting.

Pierce leaned his golden head out the window to buss her on the cheek. "Hope you learned some Spanish while here."

Fabienne did not look surprised to see her brother-in-law. Nevertheless, puzzled by the remark, she glanced over her shoulder at Preston.

He hustled her around to the panel truck's rear doors. Neither did his wife look surprised to see their son in the cargo area amidst the various red and forest green mechanics tool chests.

"My fair-haired twin has managed to rent a *hacienda* outside Ciudad Acuña for a year or so," Preston explained, boosting his grinning wife inside. "However long it takes."

But Ciudad Acuña, across the border from its sister city Del Rio, was a good fifty miles away. And in another twenty minutes, Fabienne's absence at her sewing machine would be noted, as would their son's.

Once his son and wife were wedged among the toolboxes and covered with tarps, he steered the Dodge truck toward the gate entrance. At the guard house, one of the other MP's stepped out and glanced inside the driver's window.

"Kilroy's not here," Pierce quipped from the passenger

side.

Preston wanted to roll his eyes. This was not the time to get chatty. But the guard chuckled at the play on the war's famous graffiti phrase and waved them on past.

"*Kaput!*" Pierce pronounced.

Out of sight of Crystal City itself, Preston gunned the truck down a dirt road that shot like a compass needle straight south toward the Mexican border. In the rear, Fabienne and Noel wriggled out from beneath their tarps.

Behind Preston, Fabienne wrapped her arms around his neck and began smothering his nape with kisses. "*Mon amour, mon homme!*"

"Keep it up!" God, how he had missed her.

Noel's dimpled smile grinned back at him in the rearview mirror. "You did it, Dad. You sprang us!"

But Pierce, studying the side mirror said, "If that's not the lynching mob behind us, guys, then I'd say it's the Border Patrol."

From the White House's northwest gate, the regular White House correspondents filed through the Presidential offices' waiting room, checked in with the guards, and streamed down the hall into the Oval Office, where Roosevelt was opening up his news conference.

The President sat low in his wheelchair, and Senator Garner Bryce Bradford, standing at the back of the room, was once again impressed by the man's small size—relative to Garner's six-foot-four lanky frame—and impressed by Roosevelt's small head and narrow shoulders. Garner always expected to see a bull moose of a man.

Garner had run on Roosevelt's New Deal platform, and the President had found him to be an effective ally. A sharecropper's son, he identified with poor folk who had neither material possessions nor social status. There was a glory in helping the poor folk, yessiree. Black, Catholic, Jew—it made no difference.

Guarding the doorway stood a White House policeman

wearing a uniform, and stationed around the room hovered Secret Service men not wearing uniforms. Garner made it a point to acknowledge the Secret Service with his good ol' boy grin. He never knew when their policy manual might come in handy.

Of course, cordiality with the Press was a plus. Routinely, he visited the press gallery to pass out cigars to the newsmen, as well as visiting the House Guards and Senate Police to gift them, too, with cigars. A benign form of graft.

His close friendship with D.C.'s Chief of Metropolitan Police insured no tickets for Garner's speeding violations or occasional fender-benders—or more serious violations, when needed.

After Roosevelt wrapped up the news conference, Garner made it just in time to the Military Affairs Committee Room for the open meeting. Despite it being election year, the worst possible atmosphere, a lot of amiable chitchat was going on.

"What's up, Bradford?" one senator called out.

"Nothing much." He looked down his long nose at the man. "Just a lot of pressure being brought to bear to make me run again."

Another senator chuckled. "Of course, you're the one who's putting on the most pressure."

Garner grinned easily and shrugged broad, prominently bony shoulders. "Aww, shucks, boys. Guess the only thing I can do is bow to the pressure and run."

His hand, with its flashy diamond, clapped each committee member on the back. He smiled kindly, inquiring about a particular family member or health problem.

He was the master at gathering information, pinpointing exactly where a senator stood on an issue, ferreting out his strengths and weaknesses—whether it meant cornering a senator in the Senate cloakroom, on the floor of the senate itself, or hunting on leased land.

One day, he would entertain his sources from The Barony's own hunting section or its Olympic-size swimming pool. Rightfully fit for a president of the United States of America.

Easygoing, a twinkle in his eye, always available with a solution. That was him. Only Gaila and those closest to him knew his petulance, how rapidly he could become affronted when someone displeased him, his hypersexuality, and his overpowering fear of failure.

Vermin and pinworms feeding upon his already malnourished seven-year-old body, he had vowed to never be without again.

No more ass wipes with sheets torn from a Montgomery ward catalogue left in the outhouse. No more riding on a discarded bicycle's tireless rims. No more soup made from chicken feet or horrifically greasy, stove-cooked opossum.

Since those humiliating childhood days, he now always got what he wanted. Only the best, sooner or later. And he was a very patient man. Persistence combined with patience—an undefeatable team.

After guffaws and glad-handing all around, he took a seat at the committee room's long table just as the chairman was calling the meeting to order. Two seats over from Garner,

Mariana Paladín slid into her chair. Her glasses perched atop her head, she wore her dark hair gathered efficiently in an elegant knot at her nape. In a two-piece navy suit, she looked quite the professional.

He glanced through the documents the page boy had distributed to each member of the Military Affairs committee, along with a copy of the Austin- Wadsworth bill. Garner made a mental note. Nominate the Paladín kid— Sam, that was his name—for page boy when the kid came of age.

Mariana Paladín would most likely be against the nomination. Capitol grapevine said that after all these years, she was becoming wearied by the political infighting and the cold eye judgement of the Hill, but Garner figured it was his gesture that would count.

She gave him a smile one would give a colleague, tempered by warmth reserved for an old family friend.

Senator Austin was on hand to defend his bill—the National War Service bill that would solve the manpower shortage. The bill stated that every person had an obligation to serve the war effort "as he or she may be deemed best fit to perform."

Talking with his hands in quick erratic gestures, Austin finished by declaring, "All men between eighteen and sixty-five, and women between eighteen and fifty, would register under selective service. When manpower is needed for an essential activity, workers would be drafted at the same pay as plant employees."

A piss poor presentation, Garner judged. But he knew

better than to say so. His modus operandi was to soft pedal the criticism and lay on the shit with a trowel.

Mariana Paladín shot to her feet and yanked off her glasses. "Chairman, if I may?"

"Senator Paladín?" the chairman acknowledged.

"Premier Stalin of Soviet Russia declared that the United Nations would never have been able to turn the tide of battle without the vast output of munitions made by American labor. We did this without any kind of enforced act."

Garner shifted in his chair, suddenly alert. How deep went her knowledge of all things Russian?

She glanced around at the room's seven ponderous faces. "Why," she asked in an impassioned voice, "send our young men abroad to fight and die in a war against totalitarianism when it would be inflicted upon us here at home through a National Service Act?"

Over the years, she had become a formidable speaker. Before the meeting was over, she offered an alternative, which the Committee passed and approved as the Paladín Compromise.

Back at his office, he lit up a Lucky Strike, one of the forty or fifty he smoked a day, and leafed through his phone call messages. With a grin, he noted the one from Hannah. Hannah Kraft Jackson nee Paladín.

All along, he had known she would come around to his way of thinking. Her message conceded that she was ready to assume overseeing the undercover Operation Eyes of Texas that was enabling hundreds of European Jews to flee Nazi persecution to the safety of Texas.

Of course, she might also have been motivated to accept the position because she wanted to separate herself from the German POW camp, where she had been teaching until she had precipitously given her notice. That, she probably hoped, would effectively squelch her foolish infatuation with Colonel Jakob Nobel.

If Nobel were to be transferred to a prison with harsher measures, she would once again have need of Garner, when her cousin Marianas efforts proved fruitless. Yes, it paid to have eyes everywhere. The Eyes of Texas.

Besides, knowledge like this enabled him to help others, did it not?

He did worry about Aubrey Paladín. She was too intelligent, too curious, too inquiring especially now, working for her sister-in-law Mariana. Better he keep her under his thumb.

He had no delusions about his neediness and insecurities, leftover scraps from his impoverished childhood. Portions of that neediness and insecurity sought the enormous power generated from helping others on a large scale.

His thoughts turned to another woman, the young secretary with the poodle hair who worked in the State Department. He was to meet her and her boss, Jenkins, at the crowded Office Building Cafeteria for lunch. She was brazenly open to Garner's equally brazen advances wherever and whenever—even fondling under the lunch table.

His wife coped with his rages and his random sex encounters by hiding behind her public duties and her mother's role to their ten-year-old daughter. And the more

Gaila primly turned a blind eye to his misbehavior, the more he openly flaunted it.

If Gaila ignored his indiscretions, then everyone else followed suit. There was something to be said in having a wealthy wife . . . and even better in having power over one's wealthy wife.

He knew he needed to remain married to Gaila. He could continue to collect women as he desired, but he would never leave her for any of them, and he would never quit politics—not until after he had achieved that office of supreme power.

## WASHINGTON, D.C.
## APRIL 1945

PIERCE AND AUBREY WERE SOAKING UP the extraordinary beauty of the cherry trees' pink and white blossoms. From their rented paddle boats—he and Aubrey on one, twelve-year-old Julian on another—they drifted leisurely that afternoon along the Tidal Basin's Foggy Bottom, across from the sentinel Washington Monument.

The Cherry Blossom Festival was an annual event that heralded spring in the nation's capital. The nearly three-thousand ancient cherry trees had been a gift of friendship from Japan in 1912. But due to the ongoing war with Japan and its Axis allies, the Sakura Matsuri street festival, with its performers, martial artists, and vendors, was suspended.

Already four trees had been chopped down in protest to

Japan's treachery. Nevertheless, hordes of visitors seeking a respite of both peace and pleasure flocked to the Capitol that day to view the splendor of the cherry blossoms.

And it was a perfect afternoon. The buds of the cherry trees had unfurled, and their petals were magically carpeting the banks and dappling the water, their cycle an eternal sign of spring and romance.

Pierce found it astounding that after three decades, he could still feel just as strongly romantic as the callow downed airman he had been at eighteen in the first world war, when Aubrey and her father Julian rescued him.

She was willowy, with a ballerina's build, classy and intelligent—a Renaissance woman who just happened to hold in the palm of her hand his black heart.

And his heart was certainly black today. He was seriously considering kidnapping Aubrey and Julian, forcibly removing them from Washington D.C., and flying them back to Texas in the Paladíncraft Grasshopper he had designed and built. With or without his wife's consent—or Mariana's, for that matter. And he knew how much his cousin depended on Aubrey.

"I'll be home for Christmas, for good," she murmured. "You can count on it."

"I damn well am," he said with a mock growl.

They both were pedaling the paddle boat lazily. Her hands were curled around his bicep, her head at rest against his shoulder. That was the way he liked it. Hell, he was a love-struck kid all over again.

"I think I am on to something, Pierce." She looked up at

him then, and her pixyish nose wrinkled. "You know, I am cleared to run errands—mimeographing, transcribing minutes, printing testimonies—for both the Cabinet and the National Security Council's clandestine meetings. Things like that."

"Yes?" This was not like Aubrey at all. She was a bank vault when it came to government secrets. Of course, mail was censored, and telephone calls were monitored.

Aubrey and he exchanged so little over the past several years that he feared he was losing her, although he knew with a certainty she would never cheat on him. That just was not in her character makeup.

Sweet baby Jesus, he was just bowled over by this contradictory faunlike woman.

When he had agreed to her working in D.C. for Mariana, he had thought it would be for just the final year of his cousin's senatorial term. He had felt it was high time Aubrey's nimble mind be given that stimulating arena of The Hill in which to play.

But she had stayed with Mariana through her re-election. This separation from Aubrey, going on three years now with only occasional conjugal visits on the holidays, did not sit well with him at all. How his cousin Heath managed to make his marriage with Mariana work for all these years was beyond Pierce's fathoming.

Something had to change. For the past few months, he had felt strongly compelled to make this particular visit to the Capitol by Spring Break. Something in his gut shouted that he and Julian needed to be here, in D.C., with Aubrey.

And he knew better than to ignore his gut instincts.

He was supposed to be in El Paso now—at Fort Bliss—discussing among generals bristling with chest hardware the annexation of his aviation company with the Air Defense Center. His cousin Byron had gone to the trouble to initiate the contact through his connections with Goddard and the government's Guided Missile System project.

"One of the OSS operatives, the Russian diplomat, Arkady Borsov, alerted me earlier this week," she was saying.

"Is that unusual?"

The glinting sunlight betrayed the frustration in her eyes. "Normally, I just get an intelligence report in my inbox. But I received a ledger from the O.S.S. Reading Room, as well as a note from Borsov. He suspects a traitor in our midst. Right here on Capitol Hill. One of our policymakers, no less. He didn't indicate whom just yet, but this morning, I had paused by the Senate Cloakroom to jot in my shorthand notebook, when I over—"

"Hey, Mom! Dad!" Julian called out, waving. "Look, this duck's trying to climb aboard my paddle boat."

The duck's raucous squawking and wild splashing had Aubrey giggling and diverted Pierce's attention. So, when he felt Aubrey's head drop against his shoulder once more, he thought nothing of it . . . until he turned back to her again and saw the small, neat powder-rimmed bullet hole through her forehead.

PIERCE NUDGED ASIDE HIS HALF empty glass of whisky, almost tipping it on the desk's ink blotter. His third glass in as many hours made reading the small amount of intel and other briefings Mariana had been able to gather that week since Aubrey's murder rather difficult.

It was close to midnight. He buried his face in his hands for a long moment, then rubbed his eyes—red-rimmed from lack of sleep—and his stubbled jaw. How long since he had shaved? Three days? More? He knew he had to take better care of himself if he was to take care of his son.

And with that, he shoved away from his desk and made his way upstairs to Julian's bedroom. Light seeped beneath the closed door, as it had every night for the last week. Ironic how his son needed the reassurance of the light . . . and yet, with Aubrey's death, the light seemed to go out of Pierce. How could he go on without her? But he knew he must, for Julian's sake.

He knocked. "Julian?"

Silence, as always, during the past seven days.

His son, tight-lipped, had come out only to attend Aubrey's funeral and the prepared meals provided by well-meaning friends and only then because Pierce had insisted. Neither of them had the stomach to swallow more than a few bites. And, when after only a few minutes Julian shoved back his chair to return to his bedroom, Pierce didn't have the heart to stop him. They both were hurting.

Pierce knocked again, and, when no answer came, he opened the door. Julian lay on his back, his hands behind his head, and stared up at the light fixture. His face was almost as white as the pillowcase.

Like Pierce, he had shed not a tear since his mom's death, although the moment Pierce had gotten them back to shore and Julian realized his mother, cradled by Pierce, was dead, Julian had screamed and had not stopped until people rapidly began to gather. But then he had gone silent and cold as stone.

"It's late, son. You should be asleep." He went to toggle off the light switch.

"Don't," Julian said, his voice a raw whisper.

Pierce did not know what to say. He knew no words of comfort. What could he offer in the way of consolation or wisdom to a boy who has seen his mother murdered before him?

He shuffled to the narrow bed and, stretching out on his side next to Julian, slipped his arm under his son's thin shoulders. Julian stiffened but said nothing. Neither did he. He just lay there, with his cheek pressed atop the mop of smelly red hair. Apparently, Julian was becoming as lax as he with grooming.

"Why?" came his son's tear-rasped voice after a long while.

His throat clenched tight. Julian expected him to know everything, even about death. At last, he swallowed, knowing that all he could offer was truth. "I don't know, son. I don't know why your mom was shot. I don't even know why people or things have to die or suffer."

He wished he could have one more conversation with Aubrey, the kind of bedside conversation he imagined a couple had when one beloved lay dying. He would tell her how he loved her contagious smile, the happiness and joy she bestowed on those people fortunate to be in her presence.

She had been his rock through good times and bad—through births and deaths, weddings and divorces . . . through life. He wanted to apologize for letting his own life get in the way, so that he had not given her the full and focused attention she so richly deserved.

And now it was too late. He would never be given that opportunity for one last conversation. She had loved with all her heart, and now he would suffer eternal heartache without her. No one could fill the void she left: in his life.

He rubbed his chin into the cushion that was Julian's matted hair. "But I do know that bottling up our pain only makes it hurt worse." His chest was squeezing like a vice. He soon found that his own tears were trickling off his scruffy cheeks onto Julian's forehead. "That's not what your mom would want. She would want us both to move on with our lives."

A strangle outcry erupted from the back of Julian's throat, and he shifted suddenly to wrap his arm around Pierce's midsection and bury his face against his rumpled shirt. He held his son tightly as his small body heaved out the week of repressed sobs, and those thin arms clung to him like he was an anchor in a storm.

Relief flooded Pierce, but bile flooded his mouth. There was something else he knew. He would find and destroy the person who had murdered his wife, even if it took the rest of his life.

## LOS ALAMOS, NEW MEXICO
## MAY 1945

*THE NEW YORK TIMES* SHOUTED THE Associated Press's story under the headline "The War in Europe is Ended!"

Folding the week-old newspaper the mail had brought, Byron Paladín realized May 7 had been a day for Americas jubilation. And that kind of feeling was something the Paladíns seriously needed, what with the weight of Aubrey's ghastly murder the month before.

With the same mail came seventeen-year-old Jack's appointment to West Point by the Paladín family's good friend, Senator Garner Bradford.

It was Sunday, Byron's one free day, and as good a time as any to celebrate the doubling up of good news—the end of the war in Europe and his son Jack's appointment.

He grunted, thinking he should be feeling more elation. Yet something still muddled his mind. It was more than just Aubrey's murder—although assassination was a far better term, despite the investigation turning up nothing substantial.

With a time restraint exerted by the government on the Manhattan Project at Las Alamos, Edna alone had attended Aubrey's funeral—and had come back with outlandish tales regarding the Farm, O.S.S.'s training facility, and German and Soviet spies, as well as a mole within the Capitol staff.

He was well aware that despite the Manhattan Project's tight security, Soviet atomic spies had nevertheless managed to penetrate the program. At the moment, Russia was an ally, but who knew when she could turn on America?

Recently, U.S. intelligence had acquired information that Japanese scientists planned to conduct a test of a nuclear weapon near Korea's port city of Hungnam. Only recently did Byron and the family learn that his nephew Tim was indeed alive, a prisoner of war somewhere in the vicinity.

Because of the time pressure, Byron was forced to deal with dangers daily—spy infiltration at the top-secret laboratory's Y site, or worse, a momentary lapse in thinking that could set off an uncontrolled nuclear fission chain reaction. For him, a part of the job. But he also feared for Edna, who now worked on the Manhattan Project, and for their two children.

He rubbed his raspy shadow of a beard, noting that he still needed to shave. To celebrate the day's good news, the family was undertaking an outing to Edith Warner's famous Tea House, down the mesa on the Rio Grande, later that Sunday afternoon—a rare trip, what with the gas shortage. But well worth it if only for Edith's chocolate cake alone, if not also for the relaxed social gathering.

After the government, via Eminent Domain, had bought out the ranches around Pajarito Mesa, Mrs. Warner had been asked by the staff of the secret military facility to keep her Tea House running as a getaway for its employees.

Circling the ironing board Edna had set up in the small living room, Byron headed to the bathroom. He began lathering up and noted how the gray was seeping into his thick black hair. So far, his ruler-straight brows had escaped the wrath of time, as had the rest of his body—if he discounted the deeper brackets that edged his wide mouth and the ghostly shadows beneath his eyes these days.

He was tired, and it was showing. Six days a week of intensity and high-stress tension at work was bound to take its toll. Hell, make that seven days a week.

Edna's fabulous funny-face with her brown hair scrolled around her head like a Brillo Pad appeared in the mirror behind him. "You need to put your glasses on, old man. You missed a spot."

She gave him her picket-fence smile, then reached around him to dip a finger in his shaving mug and dab foam on his nose. He grabbed her wrist. Twisting around to yank her against his rangy body, he nudged his foamy nose against hers.

They both began giggling like two kids. It was always that way between them. Over the years, many a good-looking woman had made passes at him— or rather, at his Paladín good looks. But only rail-thin Edna fascinated him—her humor, her warmth, her refreshing remarks, her insightful intelligence.

Byron planted a foamy kiss on Edna's mouth, and their giggles turned to something more serious. Her arms curled around his neck. "Hmmm, Big Boy, maybe we ought to scrap the idea of the Tea House with the kids and—"

"Mom . . . Dad!" Jack stood in the doorway. A cowlick of jet-black hair flagged from the kid's crown. "There's someone here to see you."

Byron sighed. Edna chuckled.

They trooped back toward the small living room, where one of Byron's colleagues waited, hat in hand.

"Sorry to disturb you on a Sunday, Byron," Dr. Gruenwald said. "Morning, Mrs. Paladín. But, Byron, I'm on to something exciting. Would you mind stopping by the lab with me for a few minutes?"

Byron repressed a second sigh. A few minutes could turn into an hour. Hell, even several hours. But portly Gruenwald was not given to theatrics. "Sure, let me get my hat and coat."

He leaned over and pecked Edna on her lips. "Be back soon, sweetcakes. Jack, help your mom with the breakfast dishes."

"Aww, Dad."

He closed the front door on his son and his one-year-old daughter Jill's caterwauling. He hustled old Gruenwald down Central, past the Quonset huts, in as fast a walk as the physicist's overweight body could manage.

Byron was worn out and wanted only to get this revelation, whatever it was, over as rapidly as possible and just as rapidly get on with his family's Sunday outing.

Located in a rustic setting surrounded by tall pines, three modest wooden and asbestos-shingled buildings served as the principal research and design site for the Manhattan Project. One of the buildings had actually been an old icehouse.

Flashing their badges at the lab guard, who duly noted their arrival time, they went straight down a corridor of the icehouse, which had been enlarged since 1942.

Once inside the main lab, Gruenwald shed his coat and hurried across to the stainless-steel mixing tank. "What is this?" he exclaimed. "When I left, this was not how I anchored—"

Byron followed the physicist over to the tank.
The physicist quickly reached for a common screwdriver to hold apart the two hemispherical cups of the neutron-reflecting beryllium, which kept the assembly subcritical. Byron's breathing sped up at what he saw.

*"Scheisse!"* Gruenwald cursed when the screwdriver accidentally slipped, and the cups closed completely around the enriched uranium blocks.

As the rotund scientist worked frantically over the tank, Byron noticed that the red lamps that normally would flicker when neutrons were being emitted were glowing continuously. The hair on Byron's nape prickled, and his hands and feet turned icy. If Gruenwald's body reflected some neutrons back to the device, it could go supercritical.

"Gruenwald!" Byron warned. Quickly, while leaning back and away from the device, he simultaneously stretched an arm and yanked out a couple of the uranium blocks to lessen Gruenwald's dose of radiation and then hopped clear.

But not quickly enough. He saw a flash of light and heard Gruenwald roar, "I'm burning up inside! I'm burning up!"

In the next moment, the question exploded in Byron's brain—had he received a delayed body-cooking dose?

HER HEARTBEAT POUNDING IN HER ears, Edna sat on the hospital bay's hard, wood-backed chair next to a grim-lipped Byron on the bed and clutched his icy hand. How ironic that his flesh should feel so cold when his organs might at that very moment be broiling.

In another room down the hospital corridor, Gruenwald lay sedated . . . and dying.

"The best scientific minds in the world are right here." Was her voice a note too high? "You couldn't find better care anywhere."

Blood had been drawn. Urine samples taken. His body scanned by a Geiger counter. Doctors and nurses had come and gone. And now the agonizing wait for the reports.

She felt nauseated herself with fear. She couldn't imagine a life without Byron. At first sight of him, when she had answered his ad for a secretary at his isolated, small research lab, she had fallen hard. Not that she ever gave him the slightest hint she was fazed by his bespectacled good looks. Not when females everywhere were already throwing themselves in his path. And not that he noticed them.

His attention had always been caught up by rocket science, not by fawning, beautiful women. That was why she accepted the position, because she knew, given her smarts, she had a step up over the other females.

The door squeaked open, and her head snapped in its direction. Another white-coated doctor entered, this one the head of the staff. She and Byron had played dominos with

Dr. Gleason and his wife. He held a sheath of papers. At last, something. Both relief and fear fluttered in her heart. Byron's hand in hers went suddenly damp and tense.

Dr. Gleason adjusted his beer-bottle thick eyeglasses to better view the reports. "Well, you appear to be a very lucky man, Paladín. Our Geiger counter detected only a minute array of radiation particles, and your blood and urine samples have come up clear. Of course, it is still early, but we'll keep monitoring your fluids. The fact that you're not vomiting is a good sign. To be on the safe side, though, we will administer potassium iodide tablets to help block any radioactive iodine from being absorbed by your thyroid gland."

The tension in both her hand and Byron ebbed perceptibly. "Thanks, Doc. Am I free to go then?"

Gleason cleared his throat. "Well, not quite yet. A couple of government agents are waiting outside to question you, evidently about procedure lapse."

"Goddamnit, they need to question Gruenwald about those precautions, Doc."

Gleason shrugged apologetically. "Regrettably, that is impossible."

Minutes later, two bland looking men in nondescript navy blue suits entered, and she snapped, "Is this really necessary now? My husband has been through a lot today."

The shorter agent removed his hat to reveal a head wreathed by graying hair. "We won't take up too much time, Mrs. Paladín. We have only a few questions—about security lapse."

"Security?" Byron jackknifed up to a sitting position. "You mean Gruenwald's procedure violations, don't you?"

"No," the other agent said, his voice mild despite his grim expression. "No. We're talking sabotage."

Frowning in frustration, Byron plowed fingers through his rumpled hair. "Gruenwald was as loyal an employee as they come. Besides, why would he endanger himself if sabotage was his goal?"

"Exactly," said the first agent, staring at his hat as if its crease might hold the answers. "We suspect this was outside work."

The questions continued for a few minutes more, but after the agents departed, Edna was not reassured. It was not just safety at Los Alamos that was at stake, it would seem. Was she being paranoid . . . or was the safety of the Paladíns themselves threatened?

## THE BARONY, TEXAS
## NOVEMBER 1945

Heath lay in bed, hands behind his head, and listened as Mariana slithered out of her housedress. "You can turn on the lamp."

Her whisper was more a tired sigh. "I didn't want to disturb you."

That was what was bothering him.

In a haze, she had busied herself with last minute dinner preparations for Thanksgiving tomorrow. She had been back from Washington for a mere twenty-four hours. And, goddamnit, he was resentful. And jealous. He could compete with a mortal man for her love and attention. But how to compete with something as intangible as her life's passion, her work?

She slid between the sheets. He rolled to his side, turning his back to her. She glided her tapered fingers up along his thigh to dip across his pelvic bone and nestle against his groin. And, godawlmighty, it was treacherously leaping to life. With obvious deliberation, he removed her hand.

Her breathy words warmed the knot of tense flesh between his shoulder blades. "Heath, darling . . . what's wrong?"

His mutter was almost lost in his bunched pillow. "I'm just not in the mood for sex tonight."

Then silence. Screaming silence. Their sex life was strong, vibrant—especially with her gone half the time. His desire for her was a raging hunger when she was home. Maybe it was because he was afraid of losing her, as he had lost so many other family members lately . . . as if he heard some doomsday clock ticking away precious time.

Her reply was a pensive whisper. "All right." For a moment, all was still. Then she rolled to the other side of the bed.

EACH YEAR, THE PALADÍN THANKSGIVING reunion week served to remind family members of arrivals and departures from the clan . . . as Heath himself had been reminded all too clearly since last night. His wife Mariana had arrived and departed all in twenty-four hours if he counted her silent treatment today as a departure—which it might as well have been.

Looking around the crowded, oblong table, he took stock of the newly arrived family members. For better or worse, family was everything. A smile, wan though it was, tipped the ends of his mouth, bordered by deeper lines and a mustache that, like his brows, were still jet black, despite his forty-four years of ranch life.

From his seat at the head of the noisy table, he could see Belle with the youngest addition to the Paladíns. Against one diaper-padded shoulder, she cradled an infant son, even as she attempted to eat the turkey Darcy had diced into small pieces for her. Leave it to the Hollywood Ham in Darcy to name their son Tejas Alexander Paladín.

Nearer to the table's far end, another new Paladín sat—a Korean war bride, Ping Pong Paladín. Now if *that* wasn't a hell of a sobriquet.

Between Byron and Edna, Jill, barely one, wriggled in a highchair. Jack and Jill. One would think the Paladíns were destined for memorable names.

And, obviously, so too were the Garners. All three family members bore the initials GBB. Sitting as royally erect as the Queen Mother, Gaila was saying something about disc jockeys to thirteen-year-old Fiona on her right.

Everyone knew that Garner had used his influence in Congress to obtain broadcast licenses from the FCC for the small San Antonio radio station Gaila had invested in with her own funds.

An obviously besotted Preston had restored Fabienne and Noel back in the Paladín fold a couple of months before. After just barely eluding the Border Patrol by rocketing the telephone truck across the Mexican border, he had established his wife and son in Ciudad Acuña for a five-month hiatus. With the war's end, the INS had finally released them from its detainees list.

But there were also too many absent from the table.

Earlier that year, Heaths mom and dad had died within three months of one another, his dad of a stroke, his mom of a cardiac arrest—as if neither Drake nor Angel wanted to be without the other in this lifetime. He could understand that, to his everlasting torment.

And Stoney, one of the most decorated American soldiers—receiving every military award for heroism existing from the U.S. Army—had died in action.

Gone, too, was Aubrey. And, as yet, still not a clue had been turned up as to who was behind her murder, although a riled Mariana thought it had to be Russian-connected and vowed to bring the culprit to justice.

Glancing at her, Heath felt his smile, pasted that evening for Thanksgiving, slipping. Another member leaving. Well, maybe not leaving, but Mariana would be returning to Washington. And after what happened between them last night, it was obvious she was more committed to her job than their marriage. Could he blame her?

Before he got all maudlin, he stood and raised his glass of vibrant red wine. "A toast. To Jack's West Point appointment—and to the end of the war and Japan's surrender."

Glasses were raised in jubilation, but oddly, Jack did not look that jubilant.

Garner hoisted his aloft and drawled, "And a speedy end it was, thanks to Little Boy—and our boy, Byron, here!"

Relief that the Las Alamos docs had finally cleared his youngest brother Byron from any and all possible ill effects following the radiation accident a half year earlier eased Heath's mind.

Not so easy on his mind, as would be expected, was his cousin. Pierce should have enough to keep him busy, what with Paladín Aviation's production of high-performance reconnaissance planes well under way. It would seem he was filling the gaps left in his life and in his heart with Aubrey's death by his recent decision to become a lobbyist/consultant for the aviation industry.

Yes, Pierce's presence in Washington might be a beneficial change for him and Julian—and might just be Heath's one link to an also grieving Mariana. In addition to the loss of her sister-in-law, Mariana, Heath knew, carried the albatross of guilt hanging around her lovely neck. If she had not offered the sleuthing job to Aubrey, her death would never have happened.

And that day, he, too, carried guilt. In rejecting Mariana's gesture of desire for him, he felt as if he had violated that unique intimacy that had always existed between them. More than mere chemistry, their shared intimacy was tantamount to something sacred.

He watched his wife slip silently away from the table to prepare the final course of Mexican coffee and dessert. She had let the servants off for the holiday, and the Paladín wives had been helping all morning. Quietly, Heath excused himself from the table to follow his wife into the kitchen.

Cold rain was pelting the windows above the tiled counter that banked one whitewashed limestone wall, but the kitchen was warm and redolent with the lingering, mouthwatering smells of tart cranberries, toasted sweet potatoes with marshmallows, and turkey roasted on a spit in the kitchen's original fireplace.

He paused, watching her slice the pecan pie. The boys—Jack, Sam, Julian, and Noel—had harvested the pecans from the trees along the Nueces. Her hands, dolloping whipped cream on the warm pumpkin pie, moved as gracefully as a fandango dancer's. Along with her still slender waist and the way her hips gently flared out . . . .

"Yes?" she asked stiffly, not looking over her shoulder at him but obviously all too aware of his presence.

His fingers winnowed his hair. How to make reparation for his foolish, juvenile behavior last night? He slipped an arm around her waist, tugging her hips against him. He buried his face in her loose, brown-black tresses. They smelled of lavender and something else, something sweet, like honeysuckle. All he could manage to mutter was, "Forgive me."

Her hands overlapped his. She turned her head, so that his lips were now nuzzling her ear. "What was that all about, Heath? Last night?"

He could hear the deep hurt in her voice. He sighed. "I'm sorry. Really. You're gone for such long stretches, it's as if were strangers sometimes. And I had thought you were finished with politics. Then you announce you're—"

"But to . . . to pick up my hand and . . . and actually withdraw it . . . ."

His gut cringed. He had been tired and out of sorts. "As soon as I did . . . I knew I was a damn fool, Mariana."

She turned in his arms now. Her fingers, still sticky with the pecan pie's bourbon filling, held his face. "You—and

Sam—are what give my life meaning. I was just so close, working all those years with Aubrey, that with her death, I couldn't see the forest for the trees. I lost sight of priorities. I'll resign. I'll—"

"No." He turned his face to kiss the hollow of her palm. "We've weathered storms all these years. We'll make safe harbor through this one, as well."

"LAND WHERE I LIVED," PING Pong explained to the Paladín children, "Blind Man's Bluff, it is called ling dai. It means to bid—to take place of."

Fascinated by her fertile imagination, they listened to her cotton-candy voice explain the game. Tim strongly suspected that her awe-inspiring countenance with the tribal tattooed pleats at either side of her mouth also captured their attention.

She was no taller than the Paladín bunch, most of them twelve-and thirteen-years-old, who had gathered to begin the game in the hacienda's parlor—and she was not much older than they either.

But he could tell her devotion to children everywhere was most focused this weekend on his brother Darcy's baby, Tejas. When Belle had let her hold the blanket-wrapped infant, Ping Pong's eyes had glistened with unspeakable happiness—and longing. A longing that would never be fulfilled.

That first glimpse he had of her by the early light

creeping into the transport truck's interior had revealed what he thought was a beautiful woman with sloe-shaped, sensuous eyes and a dazzlingly laughing smile.

But those days following their hasty marriage, he realized his initial evaluation of her good looks was prompted by his lengthy time without a woman. And these days . . . well, he thought Ping Pong was astoundingly beautiful. She was fiercely protective of him, and he sensed she might even love him, although he was not sure. With this beguiling Asian nymph, he could not be sure of anything.

"Sam," she told the tallest, "you tie handkerchief over my eyes, please?"

"Oh, all ri—right," Sam agreed, though the hunch of his shoulders indicated it was with reluctance. At times, fewer as he grew older, his slight speech impediment surfaced.

"Let me, let me," Hannah's eleven-year-old daughter Fiona pleaded, waving her hand and jumping up and down.

"Next time you," Ping Pong promised her. "Then, next, you," she said, grinning at Noel. "Noel Nature Boy."

Noel grinned back, delighted with her nickname for him.

Hands jammed in his jeans back pockets, Tim watched from the hallway stairs as Ping Pong submitted to Sam masking her.

As Ping Pong groped with outstretched arms, the kids scrambled out of her way. If only they knew what they were in for, Tim thought.

She could easily contend with the Southwest coyote, the Irish leprechaun, or the hugely popular Bugs Bunny for an Oscar-winning performance of the Trickster. Her free and easy attitude combined with her mischievousness certainly kept him on his toes.

Only that morning, she had hidden his Bull Durham smoking tobacco bag in one of his boots. Three days before, she had concealed the pouch at the bottom of his shaving kit. Before that, it had been beneath his pillow. And before that, rolled into his underwear drawer. Always a place he would find sooner than later.

It was the same way with all the parts of his life that she had commandeered—whether it be helping him to gear up the Air Force veteran's group, along with filmdom friends, or calming his nightmares in his parent's Hollywood home, when he awoke in the middle of the night with a start, his heart thudding in his throat and his fists raised to defend himself.

She was as elusive as a firefly—and Tim was as off course as a plane without its compass.

The fallout from the Mukden slave-labor camp had left him unsatisfied with Hollywood's make believe. Fuck, he was so accustomed to skirting life's edges, he had no idea what to do with the rest of his life. How to earn a living.

He could act, but Ping Pong was shunned by the Hollywood community, wrongly associating her, a Korean, with the recent enemy, the formidable Japanese. That cancelled his acting career.

And he could fly. Pierce had offered him a job with Paladín Air Southwest. A steady, guaranteed income with routine flights.

Routine. An onerous word.

Tim would say life had lost its luster were it not for the fairy woman groping blindly in the parlor. Sharp and wily, funny, she was chockfull of an unsettling power that she had wedged into his life.

They had married in name only, a result of the deal they had struck to help one another. Initially, he had not a clue how to initiate sex with a sixteen-year- old, who had been used for nothing but sex. But he had forced himself to be patient . . . and tender.

He knew she did not love him, and he for sure did not love her. But they were in this together. She had gotten him safely to the Korean port city of Hungnam, and he had gotten her safely to America. Their debts had cancelled out one another. Yet, for some reason—and God only knew what that was—in staying together they found an ease to their lives.

He peeled himself off the hallway newel post and, entering the parlor's open double doors, threaded his way through the cluster of kids dodging Ping Pong's scrabbling hands. He placed himself directly in her path.

She would have recognized him by his height—should have. Yet her fingers continued their tantalizing climb up his slate blue chambray shirt. Standing on tiptoe, she slipped her little palms up to cup his face. Beneath the blindfold, a bright grin tipped her tiny teeth. "You. Big Guy."

Before she could strip the handkerchief from her eyes, he bent and gave her a quick kiss. Lately, those kisses had become drawn out, lengthening into further intimacy so that no longer was theirs a marriage in name only.

"You're it!" eleven-year-old Jill squealed. "You're it!"

"Naw, I think Julian should be it." He grabbed the shoulder of Pierce's taciturn son, standing off to one side, and pressed him forward. With his mother's death, the boy needed diversion.

The boy gave a heavy sigh and a shoulder shrug.

While Ping Pong knotted the handkerchief around Julian's head, Tim took the opportunity to escape the rumpus. Back in the hallway, Garner had taken up Tim's abandoned post at the stairwell. Watching his daughter Gabby and the other kids scramble around the room, he was puffing on one of his ubiquitous cigarettes.

"Want one?" He fished a white Lucky Strike package from his coat pocket.

Tim preferred to roll his own, but since he had not a clue where Ping Pong had last hidden his Bull Durham pouch, he drew out one of the Luckies. "Thanks."

"Don't mention it," Garner drawled. "I hear you're looking for a job."

"Yeah, me and half a million other G.I.'s." He was drifting badly, and he feared where his soul would wash up.

"You know, I'm on the Senate Armed Services Committee." Garner proffered his lighter for Tim. "The President's appointed me to NACA."

"Yeah?" Tim exhaled a helix of smoke. NACA was the National Advisory Committee for Aeronautics. "So, what's going on at NACA?"

"It's researching high speed flight."

Tim nodded. Earlier, Pierce had mentioned something

about a rocket- powered plane.

Garner flicked his cigarette ashes in a nearby potted fern and flashed his amiable twinkle. "NACA's looking for a test pilot to break the sound barrier. You interested? I'll warn you, its damned dangerous."

Why not opt in? He was fleeing Hells hounds of guilt. He was responsible for the certain execution of the nine prisoners he had left behind at Mukden's Barracks #Eleven. He couldn't flee that any faster than in a rocket-powered plane.

HANDS JAMMED IN THE POCKETS of his red plaid Mackinaw, Jack kicked a scuffed boot toe at the rock, skittering it off the path into the chaparral. At his side, his dad yanked his jacket hood over his head to ward off the mist that was thickening into a drizzle.

His old man had drawn him away from a killer of a dart game with Noel and Sam. "I want you to take a look at a mare I'm thinking about getting for your sister's birthday. A surprise for Jill, mind you."

Jack knew better. "What else did you want to talk about, Dad?"

His father slid him a sidewise glance, then ambled on a few paces. "Back there. At the dinner table. You wore the look of a condemned man at his last meal."

He picked up another rock and chunked it. His heavy sigh bore the mutter, "No shit."

"What?"

He could sense the fur on his father's neck bristling at his impertinence. "Look, Dad, I'm grateful for all you and Mom have done for me—and for Senator Bradford's landing me the plum appointment to West Point. But I'm not a foot soldier type. Nor a cavalryman. Aviation must be in the gene pool somewhere, 'cause I'm not the only Paladín bitten by the bug. And that includes yourself and all your rocket theories."

He glanced at his father, worried how he was taking what must be a gigantic disappointment—worried even more by how haggard his father looked. It was not just this disturbing bit of news. No, now that he thought about it, his father's complexion had been looking pale, lackluster, for some time now. And when had that furrow been carved between his black brows?

Staring straight ahead, his father cleared his throat. "Growing up, I was one of those pegs that never fit in a round hole. Glad now that I didn't, though at the time the snubbing by classmates made me feel like I didn't belong on Planet Earth. Like I didn't belong anywhere. Thank God your Grandmother Angel went to bat for me." He flicked Jack a glance. "So, what is it you want?"

Jack breathed a little easier. "An aeronautical degree— and where else but Texas A&M?"

In fact, he had been breathing a hell of a lot easier since his science lab partner informed him she was not pregnant. They had been sneaking a smoke behind the high school gymnasium when she had exhaled a perfect helix of smoke.

"Besides, we're both too young to be saddled right now with a baby."

Though the temperature had been a chilly fifty-three degrees, sweating beads of relief had dribbled down his sternum.

"Still," she had added, eyeing him askance, "we could get married. If you'd like."

He coughed. "Uh, I wouldn't." Fortunately, the bell rang, sparing him an apologetic explanation. After that, he kept a friendly but virtuous distance.

He was too young to be saddled. When you had a passion, you gave it all or nothing. You could not let duties or other obligations get in the way. And certainly not mere pheromones, testosterone, or lust. Nope, he had learned his lesson. Besides, his mother had always been right about him—his heart yearned to soar the skies, as his uncles had done before him.

★★★

RAIN SLUICED THE WOODIE STATION Wagon's windshield as Hannah, with a yawning Fiona in the passenger's seat, drove away from The Barony's expansive wrought iron gates that Thanksgiving and headed back to San Antonio.

Twice widowed. Never would she have expected her life to take that turn.

Absently, she rubbed the rings on each forefinger with her thumbs. She regretted skipping out on her family a day early. Well, Gaila and Garner were not family, but they might as well be.

It seemed to Hannah there was an almost desperation in Garner's craving to help others. Although Gaila never uttered a less than praiseworthy word about her husband, Hannah suspected his generous gestures somehow compensated for what psychologists attributed to something lacking in one's childhood . . . physical comforts such as food and shelter. Emotional ones such as attention and affection.

From what she could glean, and that was damn little, his childhood must have been one of hardscrabble. According to Mariana, his Capitol colleagues either adored him or despised him—viewing him as either kind and generous or as cruel and controlling.

Despite his reputation for being fast with the females, he had been nothing but kind and generous to the Paladíns and deferential to the females. Still, as she drove toward San Antonio, she had an uneasy feeling when she should be grateful.

Garner might have rough edges, but he was shrewd and forceful. Using his influence as Senate Majority Whip, he had arranged a Green Card for Jakob Nobel that established him as an alien registered resident.

This was a big deal. But, invariably, it seemed to her that life attached strings. She felt sorry for Garner because no amount of string pulling would get him what he wanted.

Every Thanksgiving, he offered to buy The Barony from its Paladín Enterprises, and every Thanksgiving Heath kindly but firmly rejected the offer, regardless of its amount. After a while, it had become a running joke between the two.

What she did not want was strings attached to that Green Card. Regardless, she had accepted it.

Time was running out. She had to get it to Fort Sam Houston's Prisoner-of-War authorities before Jakob was due to be repatriated to Germany—which was scheduled for the first of December—and she had to do it without Jakob's knowledge.

If he was sent back to Germany, he would be treated as a Nazi sympathizer and imprisoned by the occupying American forces. Back in Germany, a wife and daughter awaited him. Once established as a resident alien here in the United States, he could, in time, bring his family over. The decision would be his, but at least he would have a choice.

She had none. She had to simply carry on in what seemed like a gray, fog-bound world.

Almost a year has passed since Christmas when she had last seen him. Almost a year since that life-changing kiss. Almost a year of knowing her heart was betraying her wedding vows even if her body was not.

And then, she had received that cut-you-off-at-the-knees news that Stoney was not coming home—ever. That a bomb had left no remains to ship back.

That set her free. But not Jakob. He was still married. And never, ever, would she be a homewrecker.

She could claim that she knew how it felt to be the fallout from a homewrecker, but in all honesty, hers and Stoney's home had been crumbling at the foundation long before news of his front desk affair had flashed on the home front.

She flicked a sidewise glance at Fiona, slumped asleep against the car door. Her daughter missed her father terribly. She was beautiful, and, at nearly thirteen, Fiona was verging on the threshold of womanhood one day and acting infantile the next. Mostly, she was irritable and rebellious and resentful of her mother's excessive attention and monitoring. Her daughter needed her more than ever, of course.

Now, with the war's end, the Operation Eyes of Texas was over, and Hannah had worrisome empty time on her hands for which her overzealous preoccupation with Fiona did not compensate.

Her parents were badgering her to take over the reins of Dallas Emporium. Bittersweet memories were caught up with her years spent with Dallas Emporium as a buyer in New York, where she had met her first husband, Michael. She supposed she needed to put an end to the debilitating nostalgia by moving to Dallas and taking up the mantle as the Emporium's C.E.O.

Just as she needed to put an end to her last ties with Jakob Nobel. Do her martyr's good deed and be gone. Yes, moving back home to Dallas was a good choice.

Dear God in heaven, she hated the role of martyr or saint when all she wanted was to be held in the protective warmth of Jakob's cable-strong arms before she was too old to hope. Hope for what, she did not know anymore. Her personal yearnings felt so goddamn irrelevant.

At Fort Sam's guard station, she gave her name, showed her Government Employee Pass, and was cleared by the young M.P. The rain had let up somewhat, but a sleepy Fiona mumbled a yawning protest at getting out of the car. Which was just as well. Inside the Operations of Internees Management building, its Processing Office was a madhouse that evening.

With the war ending only three months earlier, staff personnel and prisoners jostled to fill out and record paperwork. The forms initiated the steps for release, parole, or repatriation to the prisoners' country of citizenship or ancestry. Names and instructions were being shouted out in both German and English.

Standing just inside the doorway, Hannah thrust her gloves in her coat pocket and searched her purse for the Green Card.

*"Entschuldigen Sie,"* one slope-shouldered prisoner grunted, excusing himself after being shoved against her.

In turn, she was jostled into someone else and in the crush, clutched at the arm—only to look up into Jakob's cast iron features. "You," she rasped. Nerves fluttered in her stomach like live wires.

Pointedly, his gray-eyed gaze jabbed down at her hand. "You still wear my rings."

She swallowed. Nodded. Tried to appear cool, calm, contained, when it was all she could do to keep from cringing with mortification. She had not anticipated this—actually running into him, here at the Processing Office. Well, maybe it was just as well. Deliver the green card straight into his safekeeping.

He took her hand and pulled her from the crowd out into the hallway. Then, clamping her elbow, he hustled her down the corridor, past other offices. "Why are you here?"

She managed to fish out the Green Card. "This. It's for you."

Sparing it only a cursory glance, he tugged her on past the mess hall and outside toward the barracks. "What is it?"

The cold, damp air slapped some sense in her. Her steps slowed. "Where are we going?" But, of course, she knew. To his garden.

She stopped altogether. "I don't have long. My daughter is asleep in the car." She waved the card aloft. "Here."

He halted his long, rapid strides and whirled on her. It was as if he were angry. "All right. What is that?" he asked again, taking time to look now at what she held.

"A Green Card," she said, a little breathless. Being around him did that to her, short-circuited her nervous system. "It will provide you residence here. You can bring your wife and daughter over here to the safety of the U.S.— if you want."

"I want to know what you want."

Her chest tightened. She clutched the Green Card to it, as if it were a flak jacket. "I want . . . I want peace of mind."

"Hannah, if you risk nothing, you have nothing. Then you become nothing."

"I don't want to hurt anymore." Was that her own pathetic voice?

"You can avoid pain, sorrow, but then you cannot love. I am willing to risk it." He nodded at the Green Card. "Give me that, but only if you want to risk it, as well."

## GALVESTON
## AUGUST 1946

The morning was already hot and humid. Hannah, along with her tight-lipped daughter, waited outside the Port of Galveston's holding room for Jakob and his daughter Heidi to clear the medical examiner's office.

Others were exiting, making their way through a maze of roped aisles to be greeted by family or friends waiting in the larger room that was more like a stifling warehouse.

Where was Jakob? Her mind darted from one alternative to the next. What if he—or even Heidi, for that matter—had not passed the medical exam, had been found unfit, and were already being turned away to be sent back to Germany?

Or, worse, what if at the last moment, he had changed his mind? Earlier that summer, he had written that he was officially divorced, at last. He had added that his wife was willing to agree to the divorce in exchange for the small amount of reparation money allotted him by the Pottsdam Agreement for his chemical factory the Nazis had confiscated.

But what if his wife had changed her mind about giving up Jakob? What if she had convinced him to reunite? Convinced him that their marriage was worth saving?

Half dizzy with relief, Hannah spotted him, striding briskly along the roped corridor with a cardboard suitcase in one hand and his other clasping a girl's shoulder, propelling her along with him. He looked different in his civilian's gray suit and hat, slanted low over his forehead. A little less barbarous, maybe.

Tall for a fourteen-year-old and painfully thin, his daughter carried her own worn cardboard suitcase. His dark head bent toward her, he seemed to be saying something. Her pale, strained features, framed by strawberry blonde hair plaited in a single braid, were a study in recalcitrance.

Then he glanced up, his metallic gaze homing in hungrily on Hannah. She had to hold back the choked sob rumbling up from her too tight chest. Three years of wanting and wishing and waiting. She didn't realize she was crying until his square-set face blurred directly in front of her. And then he was sweeping her against his broad chest.

Her spectator pumps dropped from her dangling feet. She wrapped her arms around him, burying her face against his neck, inhaling his masculine scent that was all his own. Her breathless words were a mixture of mumbling and weeping. "I thought you may have changed your mind."

"*Mein Gott,* how I've missed you," he growled. The way his eyes ran over her features—her nose, her eyes, her lips— she knew he wanted to kiss her but was refraining in front of both their daughters. One arm still wrapped around her belted waist, he let her slide to her feet, bare but for their sheer hosiery.

Her thick brows arched like Mexican colonnades, Fiona was holding the spectator pumps up in one hand. "You might need these. Mom." Her daughter wore an adult's chastising expression.

Wobbling on one leg, Hannah slipped one pump on, but when she went to put on the other, Jakob snared it and knelt to slide it on. Her hand placed on his broad shoulder for balance, her stomach fluttered at what seemed such an intimate touch of his blunt fingers on her heel. Then she caught Heidi's disapproving frown.

Hannah stifled a sigh. In their flurry of letters back and forth across the Atlantic, she and Jakob had discussed the issue of blending their families and had prepared for possible opposition from each side. At least, she thought they were prepared. What they had not discussed was what to do about the open antagonism.

"It's a long drive to my family's ancestral home," she said brightly. "A good seven hours or more, so we'd best get started. Your trunks?"

He hoisted his flimsy suitcase and grinned ruefully. "This is it. All my worldly belongings."

Germany had suffered heavy losses during the war, and she realized she had little idea what he and his family were enduring in the Reconstruction process. *We know so little about each other.*

Once everyone was settled in the old Woodie station wagon, she accelerated along the highway still referred to as the Old Spanish Trail. In stony silence, the two teenagers sat on opposite sides in the back and stared out their respective windows. Next to her, Jakob removed his hat and stretched his long legs, settling his honed torso as best he could. His commanding presence dwarfed the Woodie's interior.

There was so much she needed to discuss with him and could not. Not in front of their daughters. Subjects that written letters lacked the tone and nuance to articulate. Information she had uneasily withheld. Rationalizing that it was no use overwhelming him. And besides, he undoubtedly had his own private matters, accumulated over a lifetime, that he had yet to share and may never.

Jakob had no concept about the immensity of The Barony Corporation. Purposefully, she had refrained from explicitly referring to The Barony by name—or the Paladín name for that matter—when talking about the familial ranch, with its epic history and legendary wealth, though occasionally exaggerated. She preferred to maintain her independent and understated lifestyle. And even that, along with her modest home in San Antonio, bespoke of far more luxury than the one Jakob had left behind.

The touchy subject of wealth had led to another touchy topic she had refused to address in their letters, despite his repeated attempts. How would they afford to live? His bold, scrawling penmanship stressed often enough his need to find a way to use his chemical engineering degree. Yet, with so many American soldiers returning from war and seeking jobs, that would be problematic. He would most likely be passed over.

Breathe, she told herself and tried to relax her white-knuckle grip on the steering wheel. She felt both anxious as the future stepmother to an obviously hostile Heidi and nervous as a bride to a very virile Jakob with whom she had exchanged far too few kisses. "Fiona, if we arrive early enough, why don't you show Heidi the horse stables. Have you ever ridden, Heidi?"

A lengthy pause. Then, *"Ja."* Nothing more.

Hannah glanced in the rearview mirror. Both girls' faces were petroglyphs of antipathy. She tried again. "Tomorrow, Heidi, my cousin Heath is putting on a *barbacoa*—roasting a pig underground—to welcome you and your father to your new country. And afterward, you and Fiona may want to go swimming. You brought your swimsuit, right?"

*"Nein."*

So much for her effort at affable communication, Hannah thought dismally. Jakob lapped his catcher's mitt of a hand over her upper thigh. God help her. At his mere touch her breath congealed in her lungs . . . while the feminine fold between her thighs went damp. "Hannah, my daughter, she has changed her mind about moving here to America."

Her head swiveled toward him. She saw the deep sadness hollowing out those silver eyes.

"However," he went on, his tone emphatic, as if to impress upon his daughter his determination, "Heidi will be coming to visit on school holidays and summer vacations."

Hannah merely nodded. Yet another pothole in her and Jakob's road to a new life together. The interior of the car was heating up with the advancing hour, so they rolled the windows down. The wind whipped inside, slashing at the snood of her white pillbox hat and making further conversation difficult.

She grew more nervous as she, at last, turned off onto the gravel road that stretched seemingly endless through chaparral. Twenty minutes later, the wide gates came into view, emblazoned by the setting sun's golden rays. The sky had gone from clear blue to brilliant gold with streaks of cobalt.

The wrought iron banner rising from twin limestone columns and arcing high overhead boldly proclaimed *THE BARONY.*

Jakob's gaze swerved toward her. "Your family estates," he rumbled low, "they are this—" He made a jabbing gesture toward the arch. "You are one of *them? A Paladín?"*

Why had she thought he wouldn't have heard of her family? Her lips compressed.

She nodded.

His silver stare was the steam rising off hot ice. "We will discuss this later."

Was he going to back out of marrying her? Change his mind with this discovery of her deception?

At her suggestion, Mariana had arranged for a civil marriage ceremony for them that night. "I think simple and private is best," she had told Mariana, "given the tremendous amount of changes and adjustments Jakob will be facing as it is. And meeting our enormous family all at once could be daunting to anyone."

When a smiling Mariana and cordial Heath met them at the huge double-wide, metal-studded doors, Jakob clicked his heels, bestowing a slight nod of his head with his Old World charm. "Sir, Madam. Thank you for welcoming me and my daughter."

"Heath will do just fine," her cousin said, proffering a hand. "Welcome back to Texas—and I trust this time around, it's much better for you."

A faint smile tipping the corners of his broad mouth, Jakob returned the sturdy handshake. "Infinitely."

Ushering them into the cool, Saltillo-tiled *sala*, Mariana said with an easy smile, "I thought a light repast would be in order while we wait for the Justice of the Peace. I know you all must be famished and exhausted."
She glanced at the two girls, standing stiffly as soldiers and apart from one another. "I have Rice Krispy Treats—or still warm chocolate chip cookies, if you prefer." She nodded toward a silver service on the buffet. "And pomegranate punch. Help yourselves."

Heidi shook her head.

"No, thank you, Aunt Mariana," Fiona said.

Hannah knew both her and Jakob's daughters were angry and frightened. The Second World War, reaping away family members, and now the Cold War's tension, left little room for a child's trust. So this impending marriage between their parents, changing the very fabric of their lives . . . well, she couldn't blame either of them for their stone-wall attitude.

Mariana continued smoothly, "Then, why don't you show Heidi to her guest room—upstairs, the third one on the right. Afterwards, take her round to the Paladíñeros' *ranchito.* Old *Mamacita* should be casting her *bruja* spells with those awful petrified chicken feet—you know, for True Love and curses and all that fakery."

Both teenagers, their eyes lit up like solar flares, glanced at one another and grinned. Hannah could well imagine the colluding girls jamming pins through cornstalk effigies of her and Jakob.

"Be back by sundown," Mariana called after the girls as they clattered up the staircase.

"I don't have any of your fine German Riesling, Jakob," Heath was saying, as he headed toward the bar, "but would a local wine suffice? The winery has gone bust and closed its doors, so I bought up several cases."

"Actually, it is your beer I miss." Jakob hitched his trouser crease to sit beside Hannah on the tufted leather sofa, while she tugged over her knees her wrinkled, white-flowered wraparound dress. "Lone Star, if you have it."

Heath nodded. "Coming up."

"Hannah?" Marianna asked. "For you?"

"Any Pinot Noir left?" She felt this crazy desire to lean into Jakob, to absorb his heat and feel his solidity and strength.

"On its way," Marian said.

Jakob took the longneck bottle Heath handed him. "An uncle of mine owned a winery. I spent my summers working there, so the change to beer—it is good."

Mariana passed Hannah a glass and, her own goblet in hand, kicked off her shoes and dropped into an overstuffed chair, her legs tucked beneath her. "Mentioning changes, you both are facing monumental ones. But Heath and I want you to know we are here for you. To smooth the way however we can."

Jakob took Hannah's free hand in his. *"Danke.* But this is something we must do on our own." This was said amicably, but she knew now the heat emanating from him was a residue of his earlier anger at her deception. A sin of omission, she preferred to think of it.

Heath took a swig from his bottle. "My grandfather felt the same way. The old Baron expected us to work as hard as any of his Paladíneños."

From there, the talk skipped back to beverages and brews, with Heath joking about the head-slamming effects of the Paladineños' potent *pulque.* Then the room's laughter fizzled abruptly at the sight of Heidi and Fiona in the *sala* doorway, their expressions grim.

"He's here," Fiona said.

Hannah didn't have to ask who. The mustached man in the derby, hovering just behind the girls, had to be the JP.

She downed the remainder of her wine for liquid courage and stood. Maybe a little too fast because the room briefly spun. The drink, lack of sleep, long day of driving, tension, and most of all, wedding jitters, were taking their toll.

At once, Jakob rose, his hand at her elbow, supporting her. Introductions were made, and, smiling politely, the JP removed his derby. "Well, shall we proceed? I still have an inquest to perform."

Her knees felt as if they would collapse beneath her.

Breathe, she reminded herself yet again. Mariana looked at her, waiting, as if giving her the opportunity to back out. "How about in front of the hearth? Fiona and Heidi can stand to either side of us."

All too soon, with Heath and Mariana as witnesses, she and Jakob were making their vows, her voice a little too high, his a little too gruff.

"You are now joined to each other by love and respect," the JP pronounced in an officious tone, "two qualities you must always remember, even when times are difficult. I wish you the best of luck in your marriage, and it is my honor to introduce Mister and Missus Jakob Nobel."

IN HANNAH'S HEART-SHAPED FACE, her heavily-lashed eyes were wide with wariness. She should be wary. Jakob had been trained to snap a neck as quickly and easily as a matchstick. She had to know that.

She was backed to the guest bedroom's door, one hand still gripping the doorknob behind her. He could hear her breathing, rapid but shallow. In turn, he snatched a deep breath to stave off his fury—and inhaled her delicate, flowery scent, fueling instead his ravenous hunger for her.

She was all he had thought about for the past three years. Far more impactful than the trauma of the horrific war, she mucked with his dreams and occupied far too much of his waking moments.

He crossed to her, speaking quietly with each step. "Why

did you not tell me?" There was no need to clarify his question. She knew.

Her face was chalk white. The tip of her tongue swiped at her moist lips. A nervous gesture. Nevertheless, he admired her charade of composure. "Your damn German pride, Jakob."

Pride? After the news coming out of Auschwitz, any sane German had forfeited pride. But then, he doubted he was sane or rational these days. He braced his hands on the door, at either side of her head and stared down at her upturned face. His throat constricted at her incandescent beauty. "Why?" His voice was a low, rumbling snarl. "Explain yourself."

Her small chin shot up. "There existed the distinct possibility you would refuse to marry me."

His anger ignited. He was smart enough to know that the anger masked his understandable fear, but he could not shove down the need to strike back, to hurt her. With deliberation, he slowly lowered his face. Her long-lashed lids slipped closed in defensive reaction. Leisurely, his tongue traced the rim of those trembling lips.

When he drew away, her eyes snapped opened, searching his face for some clue to his intentions.

"Or could it be," he grated, wedging his knee between her legs, "that you simply had no trust in me?" He ground his thigh against her. "After all, for all you know, I could be a fortune hunter."

That she might so misjudge him, that she had no trust in him, ripped at still fresh but unseen scars. Suppurating wounds from being the defeated in battle. Festering pustules of shame and horror at atrocities committed by his Nazi comrades in the Fatherland. By association, he was just as guilty. His self-disgust was a weighty boulder in his heart.

Defiance blazed into flame, glowing hot in the hearts of her eyes. "Now you listen to me. It wouldn't matter if you were a fortune hunter. It wouldn't matter if you were a bigamist. If you were a murderer. I don't care. I want you, Jakob Nobel."

She released the doorknob to latch onto one of his splayed hands, tugging it down and shoving it between her thighs. "Touch me there, damnit, Jakob. I'm slick with wanting you. Needing you to fill me—and make me feel."

His heartbeat was roaring in his ears. Something hard and dark in him took over. He yanked her from the door and shoved her stumbling toward the wide four-poster bed. Before she could twist to face him, he mounted her pliant body, pressing her face down. He yanked the snood cloistering her hair, freeing it to fall over one shoulder.

She looked over it, her eyes wantonly wide and welcoming above the swath of hair, veiling her lower face.

It didn't matter whether she wanted him or not. He wanted her. He shoved up her skirts and ripped down her panties. Unzipping his trousers, he freed himself and found her as wet as she had proclaimed. "Is this what you want?"

Hands braced on the mattress, she nodded quickly in succession. "Yes!" and she raised her hips to accept him.

Disregarding a lover's preliminaries, his teeth nipped at her bared nape as he filled her with himself in a frenzied passion. Sweat poured from him. His heart hammered. At last, he groaned out his pent-up seed and held her prisoner beneath him.

Sometime later, when his breathing slowed, he rolled from atop her, pulling her into his arms with an intensity of need that scared him. Had his rapacious possession of her destroyed whatever tender feeling she might have felt for him?

Instead, her small, slender body was more than compliant. Her breath quickening, she raised her mouth to brush his. "Pleasure *me* now, damnit."

Shame smote him. With a gentleness he had forgotten he possessed, he cupped her face, planting soft kisses on her lids, her lips, and her ivory throat, arched to receive his gratifying touch.

He moved up over her again and, aided by her wetness, easily slipped inside. He tried to go slow, to prolong his stimulation of her with lengthy strokes, but a driving, primeval pace took over again. And something else, something strange to him, and he found himself incoherently blurting, *"Ich liebe dich."*

A vibrant shudder rippled through her, and she cried out, "I love you, too!" Then spasm after spasm left her trembling in his arms.

Some moments later, as he lay panting and staring at the spinning ceiling, she moved to lay half over him, her slender thigh lapping his heavier one, her wealth of hair falling around their faces. She gazed down at him, her expression serious. "I've been thinking."

He managed a depleted grin. "That is dangerous in this mood, *nein?*"

"You said you had worked in your uncle's vineyard."

"What do you think about our buying the vineyard that Heath said had gone out of business?"

He flicked away the strands of her hair caught on her moist lips. "That would require money I do not have. And I will not use yours, *liebe.*"

"Why not? Consider it a loan on which you make monthly payments." Her smile turned saucy. "As far as the accrued interest, that could be extracted in servicing my needs."

His hands framed her sex-luminous face. "That's a no to that loan part. But have I told you yet that I love you more now that you are *Frau* Nobel?"

Her laughter was low and husky. "No, but what about that servicing part, Herr Noble, beloved husband of mine?"

## SAN ANTONIO
## APRIL 1947

"I tell you true," Ping Pong said to Fabienne, Belle, and Edna, "Jakob, he plant more than grapevines."

Fabienne, her French background apparently not totally following Ping Pong's Asian humor, asked, "What do you mean?"

Ping Pong's small teeth gleamed with her grin. "He plant

pleasure in the Missus."

The four were taking a lemonade break on the shaded flagstone porch of the dilapidated and sprawling limestone house Jakob and Hannah had bought. Edna followed the young Korean woman's humorous glint to the line of old cottonwoods banking one side of the recently purchased acreage just outside San Antonio.

Sure enough, Edna could just make out the silhouette of the couple. If she was not mistaken, Hannah's German husband had her pressed against one tree, and her hands were clutching his ass. The couple was clearly canoodling.

Edna grinned. She may have years of marriage behind her, but she still could take pleasure in a rapacious romp with her man.

Still, it had been a while for her and Byron. A long while.

Farther along, where the creek cut through the estate, a passel of Paladín kids had switched from helping to set up the vine trellises to cooling off and futzing around in the shallow water. Their shouts and taunts and war whoops filtered up to the house.

"Those two girls," Ping Pong grinned, bowing the line of tattoos at either side of her mouth, "soon they make even Buddha's balls ping-pong."

Edna almost spewed her lemonade at the word play. Ping Pong was talking about Fiona and her stepsister, Heidi, who was visiting again from Germany for the summer.

And, indeed, Fiona and the German girl, wading up out of the water with their wet rolled-up jeans and shirts revealing every prepubescent curve, were turning the heads of the testosterone-driven teenage boys.

Sam, Julian, Noel—all their heads swiveled as the girls sashayed past. Even Jack left off with his post-hole digging to eagle-eye the two girls, who had become bosom buddies over the past two years.

Edna was not worried about her nineteen-year-old son. Ogle he might, but settle down, not likely. Jack's spirit yearned to soar, to take to the skies as his uncles had done.

No, she was worried about her forty-four-year-old husband. Byron was not himself lately. Of course, that complexly-wired brain of his was always at full throttle. Still, he seemed distracted.

She had thought his taking a break from work, a leisurely drive down from Los Alamos to join the rest of the clan in Hannah and Jakob's weekend housewarming—and helping with the vineyard restoration—would put Byron back into the groove once more. Back to nature and all that.

Back to her, back in their bed.

She found her lanky husband in the kitchen, popping a Shiner, laughing, and trading off quips with Darcy and Jakob and Tim. "I'm stealing your court jester," she told them, coupling her arm with his free one.

Winking, he hoisted his beer to the three grinning males, "My Queen of Heart summons."

They hooted good naturedly as she dragged him from the kitchen, out through the front of the house to the mountain laurel-lined dirt road.

Passing the Paladín's parked pickups and approaching their old Studebaker, he asked, "You aren't thinking about us leaving, are you, sweetcakes? 'Cause I told Jakob and Preston I'd help them get a start on re-roofing the barn later."

"No." Her arm linked in his, she continued walking. Smells of lavender dueled with a pickup's diesel. So much for back to nature. But there was still back to her arms and back to their bed.

She wasn't one of those simpering females who expected their mate to read their minds. She always spoke hers. Plainly. Clearly.

Staring straight ahead toward where the dirt road dwindled from sight among its bordering trees, she took a deep breath. "Byron, you've lost interest in either me or sex. Which is it?"

In life, there were sometimes long pauses that took you to your knees. She kept walking, waiting.

At last, he mumbled, "Neither."

"What?" She turned to look at him.

His bladed profile was grim. A tendon throbbed in his neck. "The radiation accident. It's made me sterile."

Her knobby knees did indeed almost buckle. She moved to stand in front of him. "Byron Paladín, as far as sterile, Jill and Jack—and you—are enough for me. Now I want to know about impotent. Did it make you impotent?"

He reared back and hurled his beer bottle off into the tree line. "Damnit, Edna, I haven't felt like a man since I got the potentially sterile-shit news three months back at my last checkup."

Why had he not told her then? When she had inquired

how his checkup had gone, he had merely muttered, "Oh, you know, the same old, same old." She grabbed his shoulders. "Have you tried jerking off, just to see?"

He hung his head. "No. I just haven't had the git up and go. "

"Well, let's get this settled here and now." She took his hand and tugged him to the scraggly scrim of brush and cottonwoods. Anyone motoring by could see them, but she didn't care. While he stood apathetically, she divested her sockless husband of his clothing and then hers.

"Now," she told him, lightly grasping his limp penis, "I want to see this cat eye weep and wink back at me. You hear me, Byron Paladín?"

Then, she knelt among the vines and bramble and began to give her man a blow job that, as far as she was concerned, would beat a vacuum cleaner all to hell.

With no response, Goddamnit!

She was giving it all she had. Her mouth continued to lick and suck that tallywacker and her fingers to caress his flaccid balls. But it was not all about him, either. She was mildly surprised that she could feel the excitement building in herself.

Her fingertips soon detected the faint throbbing beneath the sheath of velvety flesh, and then his large hands latched onto her shoulders, his fingers clenching and unclenching. Now was not the time to let up. "Come on, rocket man," she coaxed, "blast off!"

"Oh, God. Ohhh, God, sweetcakes!"

His weight toppled her, and he flung himself atop her

and began to pump rhythmically and rapidly like he was hoping to strike oil. The bramble was scratching her bare butt, and he was sweating on her and gasping and groaning, but she had never been so happy, so relieved.

When, hand in hand, they returned to the house to face Fabienne's artist brush brow, raised questioningly, Edna merely grinned and said, "You think Hannah keeps any calamine lotion on hand for poison ivy?"

# PART
# 2

## THE BARONY
## MARCH 1953

For a spring day, the temperature was well on its way to the branding iron-hot mark.

Shaded up under a mesquite, twenty-two-year-old Noel Paladín was fanning himself with his straw Stetson, as were his three cousins their own sun-heated bodies. Noel, along with his cousins, would have stripped off their sweat-pasted shirts were it not for the females who had come to watch the branding.

But it was not just branding time for Noel, the other Paladín males, and the Paladineños. It was swagger time. A chance for him and the others to prove their macho. Chaps, spurs, and six-shooters still reigned.

Even nine-year-old Tejas, visiting from Hollywood for two weeks, was out to prove he was as rough and tough as any of the Paladín guys. He was chasing a bleating calf, trying to grab its tail.

These days, the branding was more a celebration of spring rites than a requirement. By seven a.m., Noel had trailered his horse to the roundup spot.

One of the parked pickups was loaded with the irons, wood, and medicine and another with aluminum coolers of drinks and food. Other pickups carted those who were not on horseback. Nearly fifty or sixty folks—family, neighbors, townspeople—had shown up for the branding, merely to enjoy themselves.

As a teenager, Noel had worked weekends and school holidays alongside Julian, Jack, and Sam at the various Paladín cow camps for fifty cents a day. Now, on spring break and summers between college semesters, he and his cousins still took advantage of the outdoor freedom that The Barony jobs afforded.

That afternoon, he and Sam were trying to keep the calves to be branded down to a workable number, a couple hundred. A hundred or so had already been branded, and the vaqueros were taking a break for lunch and fire water.

In the background, the cattle bellowed along with a radio blaring "Rock Around the Clock." Fiona, back from Baylor, and Aunt Hannah's stepdaughter, Heidi, on summer school-break from Berlin, were swinging to it with a couple of the neighboring cowpokes.

Fiona was crazy about the song's spit-curl singer. Heidi, too. She was crazy about American music but hated its hot dogs and hamburgers. Hated meat, period. A vegetarian, she had told Noel she was—in that aloof, brisk way she had.

While Julian and Jack were showing off by arm wrestling on a pickup tailgate, Noel was watching another pickup spew a rooster-tail of dust as it headed toward them.

"Ever seen a green roper stop and turn his horse short, leaving the calf thirty feet from the fire?" the mustached Sam asked, tossing his empty Lone Star in the back of the nearest pickup. Noel's twenty-year-old cousin had just grown his lip rug and was proud of it.

"Next thing you know," Noel drawled, his attention more on the careening pickup, "Uncle Heath will have us using those new electric branding irons." He could identify the rusty green Chevy as a Barony one—and knew only his mother drove that recklessly.

The pickup rattled to a stop, so he deserted the guys and ambled toward the dust-coated vehicle.

From the driver seat, his mother got out and, with a wide smile, hailed him. "You are just the one we wanted to see," she told him in her French-accented English that years in the States had done little to tarnish.

However, it was not the sight of his mom that snagged his attention but the young female emerging from the passenger side of the pickup. A cloud of reddish-black hair mantled her shoulders. She wore a men's size sloppy white shirt, hanging out over jeans rolled to just below her knees, and sneakers.

Something about her was familiar. His mother linked arms with her, and the two sauntered toward him. Watching the young woman walk toward him was like time tunneling backwards through the recesses of his memory . . . a ten-year-old girl, her pigtails dripping pool water, her fist connecting with his tormentor's ribs, then blood from the boy's nose Noel had smashed polka-dotting her face and bathing suit.

In the next moment, Paola Aliberti recognized him as well. Relinquishing his mother's arm, Paola's steps quickened, then slowed as she drew nearer. Her eyes took on a disbelieving look. Her words tumbled out breathy. *"Dio mio,* Noel! You . . . you've grown."

His arms went as useless as a Slinky's coiled springs. His mouth opened and closed. He dragged his gaze from the twin mounds stretching her shirt taut. "So have you."

A slow, saucy grin curved her lips, a sort of grin that made him feel slow for his age. "Your fetching freckles haven't faded."

She leaned close and pecked him on his cheek. "And beard stubble!"

"It's you, Paola! Really you!" All of the unhappy memories of the Crystal City internment camp receded temporarily.

While his mom hobnobbed with The Barony's neighbors and friends, he introduced Paola around and could not fail to notice how the guys were gawking. Snatching up a couple of long necks, he latched onto her hand and tugged her toward his Ford pickup. "Come on. I'll show you around."

Since she would have already seen the ranch head-quarters, he drove her past the grandstands, the horse track, the vaccinating chutes, and on past the dirt landing strip to pastures afire with wildflowers. He knew every single location of the ranch's 318 windmills, and as he drove her out to the most scenic one, they reminisced over the past and caught up on the present.

"Yes, I am engaged," she told him, flashing him her left hand with its sparkly ring.

"Who to?"

"Luca Buonocore. His father is the president of Italy's telephone system." He could hear a slight boasting note in her reply of which she was probably not even conscious. Coming from a relocation camp, a kid could only hope to climb the ladder out of the shame. "I met Luca when visiting relatives in Rome—and I stayed. I flew back to the States so *Mamacita* and I could trousseau shop at The Dallas Emporium."

"Of course." He had forgotten her parents had lived in Fort Worth before their internment at Crystal City. He grinned. "The Dallas Emporium is the place to shop for those with a fortune to spend. Where is your mom?"

"*Mamacita,* she does not feel so well these days. So, I flew on to San Antonio alone to meet up with your mother and revisit old times."

"What? No chaperone?" This was more than just catch up they were doing. He sensed they were—or, at least, he was—struggling to reestablish their old rhythm. What had they been? Eight or nine during that unsettling time?

They had moved from puberty to maturity, and he was not certain how to bridge the chasm. He felt sort of like a tight-rope walker.

She shrugged. "It's not so much like the old days. Still, my parents, it was they who introduced me to Luca. They felt we would make a good match."

He pulled up before the windmill and shut off the engine.

Something in the tone of her voice told him this was not a match made in heaven.

"Luca is a good man." She slid him an oblique glance. "He is rich and will make a good husband, Noel."

He shrugged. "Well, too often, it seems to me, we fall in love in a hurry. Maybe your parents got it right." He swung open the pickup door. "Come on, let's shuck our shoes and cool our feet. The tank's not as big or deep as the Crystal City pool was, but it'll do."

She met him around the front of the pickup. "Brings back a lot of memories."

They picked their way around the cow patties to the tank. She paused to unlace one sneaker, then the other. "Like the time you dumped that pail of garter snakes in the pool." She laughed and, holding his bicep to balance, tugged off her white socks. "Never saw the pool clear out so quickly."

The V of her shirt had fallen open to give him a glimpse of the narrow valley between her heavy breasts. She caught him gaping. "I didn't have these back then, did I?"

His gaze raised to meet hers. It was a clear invitation that he would have had to be blind to miss. "I think it's high time we cool off in the tank."

Hell, he was not opposed to a roll in the hay, having recently screwed his brains out with the more-than-obliging sister of an A&M buddy, but with Paola? He could not imagine having sex with someone who'd been such a good friend in his youth. One of the guys. Jeez, it'd be like having sex with a dude.

Boots and socks peeled away, he slung both legs over the

side of the tank and waded in. Paola watched him, then followed suit. The tank water lapped above his knees and clung to the hem of her shirt and to her jeans at the apex of her thighs.

He turned away, thankful that the water would take the edge off both the oppressive heat and his scorching ardor.

At least, it did until she reached her arms around his hips and, with both hands, palmed his expanding crotch. Caught off guard, he jerked away, almost falling face first into the tank. Recovering his balance, he turned to face her. "Look, this isn't such a good idea at this moment. We need to give us a little time. You know, to get to—"

She grinned, even as her fingers flicked down his zipper.

## THE BARONY
## NOVEMBER 1953

THE BARONY WAS A HAVEN for trophy wildlife.

The four horses picked their way through thorny chaparral stretching beyond The Barony ranch proper. The conversation of the Four Horsemen of the Apocalypse, as the four Paladín men good-naturedly dubbed themselves, naturally centered on aviation—not sex, which was where Tim's mind was tending to wander that Thanksgiving morning, after Ping Pong had awoken him with her skillful little hands.

Jack shot Tim a joshing grin and wisecracked, "As the

Fastest Man Alive, I hope you have your insurance paid up."

Younger than Tim's own thirty-five years by a decade and more, Jack was chafing at the bit to be appointed to the Aerospace Research Pilot School, the new human space flight program created by the government's National Aeronautics Council.

"Tim was the fastest man." As a kid, Julian had been the most irascible of the Paladín lot. Still was, but after his mother's murder, he had become more introspective, more withdrawn. Yet, he still maintained a record he had set in one of his dad's single engine jet aircrafts.

"And Tim will be again a few days from now," Noel defended, nudging his mount up alongside the other three, "If our uncle Pierce has anything to do with it."

As a Washington consultant and lobbyist for the aviation industry, the fair-haired widower knew what went on behind the scenes.

Only Garner, perhaps, knew more. But then, Garner kept tabs on everything and everyone. The Barony was lucky to have him on their Board of Directors. Now that Aunt Mariana had retired from politics, Garner's access to the Capitol grapevine continued to keep the Paladíns abreast of current affairs that could impact them.

Tim had flown the B-58 Hustler, the first US supersonic bomber, capable of Mach two, at a time when Soviet fighters were scrambling to attain that speed. He was also one of the first American pilots to fly a Communist MiG 15 during the Korean War.

But, damn it all, two years before, the Navy had bested

him with its D-5558-11 Skyrocket. The Skyrocket had reached twice the speed of sound.

In all reality, he should be concentrating on two days from now, when he was scheduled in the Air Force's X-1A to attempt to beat the Navy's Mach two record. Bur his train of thought kept drifting back to Ping Pong.

Ping Pong, his Korean banshee bride, even after ten years. Ten years later and she still hid his Bull Durham. That morning, he had found the tobacco pouch hidden behind his Old Spice Lather Shaving Cream in The Barony guest room's medicine cabinet.

She had taken every inch of his life and every inch of his heart. From early on in their marriage, he had fallen victim to the combination of her childlike innocence and siren's seduction. Their love was both the blessing and curse of the human's need for another.

As their married life progressed, she and he together had battled so many of her venereal diseases. The sulfa drugs and penicillin and other medications had defeated the crabs, syphilis, chlamydia, gonorrhea, and a host of others.

However, her two years as a sex slave for the Chinese army had left her infertile. There were surely enough Paladín kids to supplant the void in her womb and both of their hearts, but he worried if the hepatitis jaundice was taking both its revenge and ravages on her liver—and he was scared as shit.

So was she, although none of the family or friends would guess, given her goofy little grin. No matter what happened, nothing seemed to faze her. Except by this time, he knew her too well.

Despite her jaunty and imperturbable nature, she had her moments—like their fifth anniversary, when she had ripped off the string of expensive Mikimoto pearls he fastened about her neck after she learned they were from Japan.

As they scattered around the floor like a child's marbles, she had spat repeatedly on them. "What you think?" she had shouted. And that was it, he had not been thinking, had forgotten the bitterness tightly tucked away.

Like him, nightmares plagued her over the years after their escape from the Japanese prison deep in Manchuria. Gasping, she would bolt upright, eyes wide, a keening howl pulling from lips bard in a rictus of terror. He would gather her against his chest, shushing her as one did a child afraid of storms, smoothing her sweat-damp strands of black hair from her tear-damp cheeks. "I'm here, my love. I'm here."

If someone took a scalpel and opened him up, they would find that being in love with the little banshee never went away . . . find that helpless feeling of being in love was always there pestering him.

Perhaps it was his preoccupation with the fear for her festering in his gut like a cancer that he was not attentive to his roan's sudden shift in gait as a jackrabbit bounded from nearby scrub brush. His mount reared, and Tim found himself embarrassingly unseated. He, who had spent so much of his youth at The Barony and could ride like a Cossack.

He struggled to sit up, and it was as if a giant sledge hammer slammed into his chest. His lungs collapsed like bellows. He was in such pain that he fell back, gasping. "My ribs," he wheezed to the others.

"Jack, get Doc Warren!" Julian said, immediately dismounting.

"It's Thanksgiving," Noel reminded him, grabbing the loose reins of both Tim's side-stepping, nervous roan and Julian's bay.

"No, Jack . . . no doctors—no hospitals," Tim told Julian who was struggling to lift him to his feet. Any report of his injury could damn well end up having him removed from the flight mission. "Fuck! Just get me back to the ranch . . . without rattling loose anything else inside me."

The efforts to move him detonated an explosion of pain in his ribcage. He damned near passed out. "And if you dudes can't do that," he wheezed, "just shoot me, please."

Somehow, by Indian drumming or word of mouth, his accident must have been telegraphed back to the hacienda, because Ping Pong was running from its wide veranda to meet him and the guys.

Her black pupils in her pixie face were expanded with fear. "Here. You lean on me." She nudged the towering young men away, as if they were mere boys.

Her arm barely lapped the back of his waist, but, impossibly, her head supported his battered side in such a way that the rest of the walk was not too jarring. Her long-lashed eyes peered up at him with searching concern. "I fix you."

His sigh was exhausted exhalation. "Yeah, hon, you do that." Others would most likely find it odd that their relationship had most likely developed from mutual assistance between two fundamentally different personalities to an unbreakable bond of respect, devotion, affection.

And, yes, he supposed, that mysterious and bewildering yet rewarding emotion might well be termed love . . . a love understood, though verbal acknowledgement of it had never been considered by either of them as being necessary.

Excruciating minutes later, he was flat on his back on the bed in their guest bedroom and stripped of his shirt. If he was careful not to move, he felt somewhat better.

That was until Ping Pong returned minutes later from the kitchen with a wadded towel, a bowl, and a glass filled with a dark liquid. He was not sure if it was the contents of the bowl or the glass's contents—or both—but the odor was reminiscent of roadkill in July.

She plopped Buddha-like beside him on the mattress and a groan bellowed out of him. "Easy, girl."

"No, no easy. You need to do deep breathing. Like hard cough. Here, you swallow this."

Dutifully, he swallowed. And whatever it was tasted worse than roadkill in July. More like an outhouse in July. "What the hell is this?"

She grinned wide. "Magic medicine. I tell you I fix you. Pain will be better." She dipped her small hands into the bowl and came up with a brownish unguent and began to gently massage it onto his bruised, inflamed ribs.

"Shit!"

"Good for you, my Tim. Need to move here," her small fingers piano-keyed along his ribs, "or lung get infection."

It wasn't the thought of lung infection that concerned him. "Look, Ping Pong, our livelihood is depending on my flying the X-1A in mere days." Perhaps it was her potion he had swallowed, but he was already feeling somewhat drowsy and unguarded. "Ain't no way I can seal its latch, banged up like I am."

"You no worry, I tell you truly." She placed the towel, with its freezing ice cubes, atop his ribs. "I fix that, too."

But he *was* worried. He drifted off to sleep with black clouds swirling around him. When he awoke, moonbeams, not sunlight, shafted through the window's slatted shutters, and his uncle Pierce, not Ping Pong, sat in the easy chair, watching him.

Tim grunted. "I'm trusting this is not a wake."

The older man smiled. Rarely did he grin or laugh, not since Aubrey's death. The guy really needed a woman to make him laugh again. As Ping Pong had evoked Tim's own laughter.

"Brought you a little get-well gift," Uncle Pierce said, holding up what looked to be the end of a broom stick and some kind of device attached to its tip. "Fashioned this for your mission the day after tomorrow. Ping Pong's idea, really."

Tim started to get up, groaning with the pain-shooting effort, but pushed through the pain to sit erect anyway. The sheet fell aside to reveal his now greenish purple ribs. "You gonna tell me I can ride a broomstick, Uncle Pierce, instead of an X-1A?"

"No, I'm going to tell you that you can use this as an extra lever to seal the X-1A's hatch."

"Fuck!" he groaned and collapsed back onto the mattress. "Just swell."

But days later, the broomstick-lever did, indeed, seal the hatch, after he folded his body into the airplane's claustrophobic cockpit, with a great deal of labored effort and resulting stabs of pain through his chest.

A B-29 ferried Bell's X-1 aloft and then dropped it. The Bell tracker's voice commanded his attention. "What cylinders are on, Tim?"

"Number Three coming on now."

"We have your time."

"Okay. All throttles go." As the plane hurtled upward toward 80,000 feet, Tim's splintered ribcage slammed repeatedly against his rattling lungs, and he was scared he was going to blackout with the pain. But the "Hot damn!" and "You got it!" cheers from the earth-bound Bell tracker kept him focused.

And then he did it, achieved that goal in the treasured Pilot's Poem that he had thought beyond his reach as a young man.

Upon beating the speed record at Mach 2.44, approximately 1,650 mph, Tim experienced an exultation like no other, as though his spirit was momentarily AWOL from his body. It was an exhilaration like the ecstasy of having Ping Pong wrapped in his arms.

Then the X-1A began to shudder. His eyes scanned the panel's gauges. Nothing . . . no explanation as to the reason for the loss of aerodynamic control. Rapidly, his fingers flipped through the array of switches. Still nothing. Rolling and pitching and yawing, his plane fell 12,000 feet in twelve seconds.

He watched the control panel's indicators spinning wildly and knew that his own life had sped out of his control . . . and he had never told Ping Pong he loved her.

## SAN ANTONIO
## APRIL 1955

Twenty-three-year-old captain Julian Paladín had been kicked out of more private schools than Brackenridge Park had alligators, and, by San Antonio's last count, that numbered in the dozens.

He had been a lone wolf hell-raiser growing up. He had sneaked into Juarez's opium dens and trolled Washington's Hooker Street . . . and he had seen his mother shot between the eyes. Not much fazed his twenty-three-years of fast living.

Flying Lockheed's U2—nicknamed the Dragon Lady —for the CIA pretty damned near beat everything combined.

During the Korean War, he had been recruited by the CIA and had not flown combat missions. Instead, at Randolph Air Base's Air War College's in San Antonio, he had graduated from a workhorse trainer to the U2.

A reconnaissance aircraft, the single-jet engine provided all-weather intelligence-gathering, day and night, at ultra-high-altitude of 70,000 feet—twice the altitude of commercial aircraft.

Once in rarefied air, the U2 would glide like an eagle on a thermal, but when closer to the ground, the powerful single-seat plane was difficult to keep stable and landing was hell-on-wheels—precisely because the U2 had no conventional landing wheels.

In addition, its aluminum wings were nigh butterfly thin. At times like this, he could only admire how Tim had been able to pull his X-1A out of that spiraling death-dive the year before. After the aviation boards review and his medical release, the family had gathered around him at The Barony for a blowout celebration.

Tim might have been hobbling around like an old man at the time—and for a few months afterwards—but the lightning looks exchanged between him and Ping Pong was a blistering testament of young love.

Julian's tall frame was compressed into a bulky orange spacesuit with its fishbowl helmet, and in turn he was compressed into the miniscule space allotted beneath the canopy. Normally, pilots of his rather tall frame were not accepted into the program. But his aerial skills had earned him the spot.

Cleared for takeoff, the spy plane's engine roared to readiness. Taxiing down the runway, he slammed the throttle with his left hand, unleashing more than eight tons of thrust. In less than ten heartbeats, the U2 rocketed into a brilliant cerulean sky and zoomed toward the edge of space.

Due to so little room to move even his head, his view was limited but still mind-warping. He could see the curvature of the blue earth and the firmament as it gradually blackened at its outer limits. Off to his left, he could see the sun and to his right, the white hot full moon.

The feeling was at once exhilarating and depressing. So far from family, from earth—experiencing the kind of utter loneliness enforced by isolation and the kind of dark, dank space surrounding him. All this—and not to mention he was so close to being extinguished should he suffer rapid decompression sickness, vertigo, or just sheer lack of focus for a second.

Few humans experienced this, and he hoped to soon be the first man projected farther into space itself. As to whom the space agency would select, well, damn, the race was on between him and Jack, who had the benefit of seniority and, admittedly, the prestige of officer ranking in the U. S. Air Force.

Either way, it seemed appropriate for a Paladín to be among the first to pioneer the frontiers of space as they had the frontiers of Texas.

In the nose cone, cameras collected intelligence, radar information, and high-resolution photographs of places like Korea and Russia and other trouble spots for analysts who would be able to distinguish artillery installations and even armored trucks.

Besides an aerial sweep of the communist Republic of China and the Soviet Union's Gulag—a collection of forced labor camps—he was ordered to do a flyby near Moscow.

Khrushchev, the prime minister of the Soviet Union, in response to NATO actions, namely the rearming of West Germany, had just concluded a military defensive alliance known as the Warsaw Pact. It allied Russia with Albania, Bulgaria, Czechoslovakia, East Germany, Hungary, Poland, and Romania. The Cold War was, indeed, escalating.

After Julian's nine-hour mission was completed, with a quick layover at an Iranian airstrip at Zahedan, he aimed the spy plane back toward San Antonio.

Running through the checklists, he prepared to descend—the most challenging part of the mission. He had his hands full. With its bicycle landing gear and long wingspan, the U2 had to be stalled mere feet above ground, and he struggled to keep the wings level while the cockpit shook as violently as his heart.

The ground crew rushed to disconnect his numerous belts, straps, hoses, cables, and communication lines. "Great landing," Skunk, a retired Pan Am pilot, called out.

Julian acknowledged him with a casual two-finger salute and climbed down the step ladder, where a van waited to take him to his follow-up physical exam and then the intelligence debriefing.

But on the van's lower step, he paused as the two Special Agents went to work, removing the reconnaissance pods of highly classified information from the stealth plane's nosecone housing. This was standard operating procedure, except the agents were not the usual pair.

The motor pool driver was waiting for him in the van, so Julian climbed aboard. He figured when he got to Administration in Building 100, known as the Taj Mahal with its blue-and-gold dome, he would inquire the Brass about it, but Dr. Bridget Malone torpedoed all cognitive thinking.

Neither did she do anything to help his blood pressure.

Blonde tousled hair caught in a careless swath atop her head, she was tom- boyish-slim with a toned, strong body, an impudent smile, and an intelligent gaze that studied him through cat-eye glasses. "So you're Paladín, Prince of the Pilots. I'm Doctor Malone, your new Assistant Chief Health and Medical Officer. Come along."

Like a puppy dog, tail wagging, he trotted behind her to the lab station, where she began the usual post-flight scrutiny tests—pulse rate, blood pressure, urine sampling, body temperature, and various other measurements.

He had been sweating in a pressurized space suit for nine hours, and his fire-red hair, out from under the flight helmet, looked like rat fur. When she placed the stethoscope against his bare chest, surely his heartbeat accelerated to Mach 3.

Finishing her notes, she smiled up at him. Appearing

to be in her late twenties, she had pouting pink lips that looked way too versatile. "Make sure you eat plenty of protein and take the next twenty-four hours off, Airman. Allow your body time to recuperate from the mission. Doc's orders."

He stood up from the examination table and began shrugging into his long-sleeve blue shirt. "Twenty-four hours would give me just enough time to take you to Brackenridge's Chinese Tea Garden."

She tucked her pen into her white smock's pocket. "I make it a practice not to date military personnel, younger men, or bad boys." She turned and walked away, her hips swaying provocatively, as if to taunt him.

"It wasn't a date," he called after her. "I was going to feed you to the Garden's gators, Doc."

Without bothering to look back, she held up a hand and flashed him the finger.

He was in love.

## WASHINGTON, D.C.
## SEPTEMBER 1956

NORMALLY, K STREET WAS THE ABODE of the lobbying industry, but Uncle Pierce's firm was ten blocks closer to the Capitol.

The August G Street Northwest now embraced the special-interest groups, but in earlier years, it had harbored warehouses, liquor stores, and the spillover of Hooker Street's red light district.

Working as she did for her Uncle Pierce as a lobbyist for the aviation industry, twenty-three-year-old Fiona Paladín realized there were those who considered her, and lobbyists in general, in some respects like a hooker.

Oh, sure, lobbyists could be nobly described as intermediaries between client organizations and lawmakers. Their job description could be said to explain to legislators what the organizations, which Paladín Practical Solutions represented, wanted and, in turn, could be said to explain to PPS clients what hurdles legislators faced.

But her job was also to charm, challenge, and convince her mark of the sensibleness of her firm's position. Of course, she did much, much more. With her Uncle Pierce so caught up with Paladín Aviation and Air Southwest, these days she practically single-handedly ran PPS, which catered to the light aircraft industry.

Of course, she was willing to hustle, but only to a point, and that point did not include spreading her legs, as was expected from the far too few female lobbyists. To reinforce a no-nonsense image, her business attire consisted of boxy suits with padded, square-shouldered jackets and pencil-straight skirts.

That evening, she had a black-tie gala to attend, and her attire would be more feminine, with a tight smoky gray bodice and its billowy, long silk skirt redolent of the Victorian era. Her gown was conservative but with pearls encrusted along the bodice and a lustrous pearl choker to add a softer, classy image. A wise, safe choice. Surely, few would recognize her as the tomboy of The Barony.

Since J. Edgar Hoover, Director of the FBI, and Garner lived in the same neighborhood, Fiona had maneuvered to talk alone with Hoover for a few minutes at one of Garner and Gaila's informal socials. She merely mentioned she had a crush on Steven Douglas and was looking forward to meeting him at the upcoming National Business Aviation Association gala.

The soiree was being held at the Library of Congress's Great Hall in the Library's Thomas Jefferson Building, an 1890's beautiful two-story room decorated in the Italian Renaissance style with murals, mosaics, and vaulted marble ceilings.

The Library of Congress was the largest library in the world, founded in 1800 to serve the needs of Congress. Tonight, she was hoping the Library of Congress would serve her needs.

While her job for PSS was to entertain, on behalf of the National Business Aviation Association, certain congressman and Hill staffers, who dined on the $2500/ticket provided by PSS, her need that night was to seduce Steven Douglas, Librarian of the Library of Congress.

Well, not seduce but induce. Specifically, she needed to induce him into permitting her to view highly classified files in the Library of Congress.

Steven Douglas, famed Southern poet and writer, and

regarded as a gentleman and a scholar, was not hard on the eyes—a Gregory Peck in glasses and navy seersucker suit that hadn't spent much time with an iron. Douglas' quiet dignity was intimidating and kept would-be opportunists at a distance. The faint graying at his temples hinted he had to be in his late thirties or early forties.

As Librarian, he had enhanced the Library's reputation as a major cultural institution. He also drafted speeches for the President and represented the government at various high-level meetings. All this, besides being an adjunct professor at George Washington University.

But what was most important to her was that Hoover deferred to Mr. Steven Douglas.

The Cold War had given the Bureau new power and the merciless power- mongrel Hoover new glory. His dossiers on his enemies were immense, as well as his command of Congress and his manipulation and intimidation of the press.

When he reformed the Bureau's files, he took something old—the Department of Justice system—and something borrowed—the Library of Congress's strategy of extensive cross-references. Used by most US research, the cross-references provided access to the content of the FBI files.

The Library of Congress's National Archives and Records administration, an independent agency, maintained and protected these extensive records of the

Federal Government. Some of those were the very files that had been transferred from the Registry Office of the former OSS, now the FBI.

Obviously, presidents were made aware of the records' secrets during their term of office, mostly relating to military matters and national security. Access was available only to Library staff, congressional offices, and archivists with security clearance.

However, Uncle Pierce's wife, Aubrey, had had access to the OSS's Registry Office files before she was assassinated. A notation in the small black book she had left behind indicated she suspected a mole in the upper echelon of the U.S. legal system.

Fiona wanted access to those files, now buried in the highly classified section of the National Library of Congress and not open to the public. Searching through the hundreds of thousands of records could easily take a lifetime or more.

Regardless, she felt compelled by something beyond her ken to dedicate herself to that formidable and possible life-long task. While she had not enjoyed the luxury of spending much quality time with her Aunt Aubrey, the woman's grace and courage were legendary . . . and you do not murder a Paladín and get away scot-free.

At least, that was what both her uncle Pierce and her Aunt Mariana had given her the go-ahead to do, to step-in and step-up the investigation into Aunt Aubrey's death before the trail went entirely dead.

Aunt Aubrey's son Julian had no interest in pursuing the investigation, letting Fiona know he only wanted to get on with life. This, she could certainly understand. Sometimes pain was so great it could only be dealt with at a distance.

Still, there was something relentlessly integral within Fiona that, when she committed herself, nothing short of death would let her give up. She didn't understand exactly why she was like this. Some might ascribe it to the Paladín gene pool. All she knew was that, for her at least, a life without passion as its motivating force was not a life.

The gala sponsors did the inviting and dictated who sat where, but thanks to the mincing and natty-suit-dressed Hoover, she found Steven sitting to her right when that particular gala appeared on her calendar.

Of course, females of all ages flocked to the eligible and handsome widower—and throughout the dinner, she either studiously ignored him or replied to his efforts at courteous conversation with a brevity that had to disconcert him.

She would hope.

She attempted to focus her attention on others at her round table for ten—particularly the very powerful and very boring Senator Joe McCarthy.

His Red Scare, hyper crusades, and accusations against suspiciously disloyal public servants and left wingers, in order to prove the government was packed with traitors and spies, were so intimidating that few people dared to speak out against him.

But the slightly paunchy McCarthy just might have something there—that traitors and spies abounded on Capitol Hill.

The senator was also slightly drunk, as usual. He was a notorious alcoholic. His Glenlivet sloshed in his glass with the expansive gestures accompanying his grandiose comments. Nevertheless, she smiled attentively, and her red snapper ceviche and filet mignon went practically untouched.

Later, when she declined his offer to dance, he slurred, "Do you realize who I am?"

"Well, if you aren't John Wayne or James Dean, I don't care."

She had grown up with five rowdy male cousins. She had fought to attend the all-male Texas A&M but had stood about as much chance gaining admission as Rosa Parks had sitting at the front of a bus, so Fiona knew more than a little about wrangling with the male sex.

Females she had not resonated with at that young age, either. She remembered in middle school the agony of eating alone during lunch because the girls apparently had considered her unworthy. She had put in a lot of time and effort to change that image.

Of course, that same Paladín gene pool had helped evolve her into the "Willowy Westerner," as her Baylor annual had dubbed her.

"Listen here, sweetheart," McCarthy snarled, "you corporate folks want us at your table, and I'll be—"

A distinctive low-pitched drawl intervened. "Miss Jackson has already promised this dance to me."

Reflexively, she laid aside her damask napkin and rose to accept the long, elegant hand held out to assist her. Only then did she look up into the face of Steven Douglas, a face that was all angles—squared jaw, sharp triangular cheekbones, a broad rectangular forehead, even his overly-longish dark hair grazed one rim of his eyeglasses.

She permitted him to draw her out onto the dance floor, where couples glided past to "Love Is a Many Splendored Thing." He splayed his right hand firmly at the small of her back.

"You are a fool to risk losing your job purely out of gallantry."

He looked down at her, and his smile rattled her composure. "You are a fool to take on McCarthy purely to cultivate me."

Her heart free fell. Had Hoover betrayed her? She had no choice but to bluff her way through. "Are you always so arrogant?"

"Are you always so disarming?"

"Only when I want to get my way."

"And what way is that?"

Always stick as close to the truth as you can. "I want my way into the National Archives' Secret Intelligence Room."

A dark brow raised above the black rim of his glasses. "Well, I suppose that could be arranged—if you are willing to let me have my way."

Here it comes, she thought dismally. Huge disappointment weighted down on her. This kind of crude sexual pass, coming from a man respected by many for his basic decency. Nevertheless, she stayed in the game. "And what way is that?"

"I want to go hog hunting at The Barony."

## THE BARONY
## NOVEMBER 1956

Everything was said to be bigger in Texas, including the feral hogs.

In the brush country of Southwest Texas, the population of feral hogs—quite prolific breeders—had exploded to enormous proportion. Weighing up to four-hundred pounds, in herds they presented a dangerous threat with their four long tusks.

Heath made sure the ranch lived up to its reputation as a paradise for trophy wildlife, ranging from white-tailed deer to Nilgai antelope. Corporations such as Dallas's Dresser Energies and Texas Instruments were willing to spend eight dollars an acre for a lease, sharing the scrubland with the cattle.

"Bait and wait," he whispered to Douglas. In the scrubby clearing, Heath had set out a feeder, one of the better methods to lure a hog out into the open, since hogs could smell some odors anywhere from five to seven miles away.

"Yeah." Steven shifted his bow grip so that his index finger brushed his thumb. "Back in Georgia, as a kid, I loaded our feeders with oak mast, but your son tells me you use corn."

Steven Douglas was one surprise after another. Cultured and cosmopolitan on one hand and down-home Hemingway on the other. Heath had expected to provide the distinguished college professor with a rifle, but the man showed up with his own bow and quiver.

Heath had expected him to make a pass at Fiona while here for the Thanksgiving holiday, but he had arrived two days before and was leaving tomorrow morning, Thanksgiving Day, without much more than a "howdy" and *"adios"* for her.

Steven and he hunkered down, concealed behind a thicket. They had arisen way before dawn to hunt because the hogs were usually nocturnal. The weather that morning was frosty, and Heath wiped the sleeve of his denim jacket across his runny nose.

At the rustling in the scrub beyond, Steven slowly raised his bow. It had an impressive sixty-five-pound pull.

A two-fisted poet, the man was.

When the rustling ceased and no hogs made an appearance, Steven lowered his bow. "You've got a fine son in Sam."

He had to smile. "Sam reminds me a lot of myself at his age. Tomorrow morning, he and the younger guys will be headed out hunting. You know, that piece of business about us men facing down our fears and testing ourselves against nature."

Steven peered through his glasses at him. "I suppose you might say that's why I made this jaunt. I wanted to find out what 'this piece of business,' as you worded it, has to do with your niece. Exactly what is Fiona doing, testing herself against the U.S. government?"

He eased in a chilly breath. How far could he trust Steven Douglas? Fiona had said she only shared with the man that she was researching her Aunt Aubrey's backstairs work in D.C. and her mysterious death a decade earlier—and had mentioned nothing about a suspected government mole.

After all, what did he really know about Douglas? The news media capitalized on the romantic backstory of Steven's marriage with his late wife, a Greek opera prima donna. Evidently, he still pined for her because a dozen or so years had passed since their infant's and her death from childbirth complications in Athens.

But just how deeply was the man entrenched with government service? "That 'piece of business' you're talking about," Heath said, "is purely business. Fiona's business. You'll have to trust her."

At another rustling, Douglas moved with a blur, coming into focus at full draw and letting his arrow fly. The hog squealed once and toppled dead.

Heath didn't know whether to be relieved the man was on Fiona's side or fearful he was on the other. And that was the problem—no one knew what, or who, that other side was.

WITH PROVISIONING FOR Thanksgiving dinner the next day in mind, twenty-three-year-old Sam Houston Paladín and his three cousins set out in the dark of morning from the twenty-nine-room rambling *hacienda*.

The guy Fiona had invited down from D.C. to hog hunt had already taken one, the meat of which, tastier and leaner than pen-raised hogs, he had donated to the Paladineños at *La Baroncita*.

Nevertheless, the muscular wild boars provided for The Barony males a great opportunity to hone their hunting skills.

Rifle ready, Sam crept through the dense vegetation of the Nueces river bottom. Noel, Jack, and Julian, as good of tracker as he but not quite as good a shot, followed close behind. Jack was a skillful roper and Julian a centaur of a horseman, and Noel was probably one of the best all-around cowboys on the ranch.

All four were taking advantage of the opportunity The Barony offered to spend time in the field. The weather had turned wet and cold, as was the marshy water into which Sam's left boot sank. "Shit!" he muttered, his breath frosting his mustache.

"Look," Noel said, kneeling off to the right to point in the mud at the sunken hoof print.

Jack, at twenty-seven and older than the others by three or four years, joined Noel and whistled low.

"Well, I'll be damned if that hog don't weigh a good

five-hundred pounds if it weighs an ounce." Julian grinned, gesturing in the track's direction.

Farther along, Sam bent over to examine scat between his fingers. "Still mighty warm, guys."

Up ahead, Troubles, Sam's old Catahoula cur, began baying. The four glanced at each other and exchanged grins.

"Hunt's on!" Like his other three cousins, Noel shared the Paladíns' extraordinary height and remarkably wide shoulders and had in common with Julian the Irish side of the family's red hair.

The closer Sam got, the louder the hogs were grunting. He stayed downwind, as the hogs had a heightened sense of smell and hearing to compensate for their bad vision. He paused to load a .30/06, about the only thing that would penetrate that tough hide with its stiff, bristly hair.

Besides, with the feral hogs' lightning speed, loading time would be out of the question when once actually on the jousting field. "The boars sound pi . . . pissed off."

His speech impediment only revealed itself in times of urgency, whether it be stress or exhilaration. That morning, it was both. Some even compared his stutter to Jimmy Stewart's screen one. It was almost as embarrassing as the congenital hitch to the outer corner of his mouth that, ridiculously, the opposite sex seemed to find attractive.

For the most part, an Old West gunfighter's mustache that drooped over the ends of his mouth hid the imperfection. Nonetheless, Sam felt driven to prove himself among his peers, for which excelling in school and sports only marginally compensated. It was as if a yawning hole just waited for him to slip up, to reveal his charade, and tumble in.

With his cousins quietly trailing behind, he approached a clearing maybe fifty yards off where Troubles had bayed at one huge hog. The warning clack-clack of its teeth echoed eerily among winter's skeletal trees. The Catahoula was snapping furiously and darting back and forth, just beyond the thrusts and swipes of the temperamental hog's razor-sharp tusks.

Silently, Sam signaled his cousins with an upraised hand for a halt. But not quickly enough. Suddenly, the enraged black swine swerved and charged toward Sam. Troubles was in quick pursuit.

Sam jerked his rifle to his shoulder and fired. Sweat beaded his upper lip in as quick of time as it took him to fire again. But the rifle kept hanging up. A feral hog was more like a wounded lion than a farm pig.

His hands trembled. Once more, he fired. The swine hurtled in for the fatal goring—and at the same time, Troubles sprang at its rear hind quarter. The two wrangled in a swirl of mud and a splatter of blood drops.

Behind Sam, Noel's Remington Model 7600 exploded, laying down lead. "Damn!" Noel muttered, lowering his pump rifle.

Once the cordite cleared Sam's nostrils and the dust settled, his field of vision took in first the dropped wild male hog, shot clean through from mouth to ass, then Troubles, his inert body tossed several yards off.

"No!" Sam was not sure if the word had been a yelled denial or whispered as a beseeching prayer.

He sprinted the intervening distance and, dropping his rifle, knelt to examine Troubles. The dog blinked, whimpered. He had been disemboweled. "Oh, Je . . . Jesus Christ!"

He stripped off his camo jacket and, carefully gathering Troubles' entrails, tucked them back in and bound the dog as best he could with the jacket. He scooped up his limp Troubles, supporting him against his chest.

"Got your rifle," Noel told him.

Panicky, with only an anguished afterthought for resorting to horseback, he set off loping along the long path back to the hacienda. Noel was close in step with him. He reckoned Julian and Jack stayed behind to field dress the wild boar. A couple of times he stumbled, not so much from his load but from his vision, blurred by tears.

Troubles had been a gift from his father on Sam's thirteenth birthday. The five-week-old frisky puppy had slept with him every night until he had gone off to SMU to study law.

At the moment, Trouble's soft whining just about gutted him. Despite being able to bench press over two-hundred pounds, Sam's arms were growing numb on the nearly three-mile return trip.

Noel glanced at him anxiously. "Want me to spell you?"

He shook his head. The fast pace had him breathing heavily. He barely reached the *hacienda's* high, wrought-iron arch, proclaiming The Barony, when his blood-soaked jacket with its beloved burden began to give away. He grappled to hold on to Troubles and shuddered when his dog yelped. Noel, shouldering both rifles, could not lend a hand.

In the driveway, a white Corvette convertible was pulling up beside the tiered fountain. Arriving for the Thanksgiving holiday, eighteen-year-old Gabrielle Bernadette Bradford emerged from the driver's seat, took one look at Sam, and hurried across the lawn toward him.

She was wearing an expensive winter-white wool coat that could only have come from the Dallas Emporium, and he watched, stunned as, uncaring of the blood and gore, she cradled Troubles between them. "Quick," she ordered, "the stables."

Then to Noel, "In my car, grab the black bag."

This . . . from quiet, stand-offish, distant Gabby? As a child, Garner's daughter had been as rowdy as the Paladín kids, but somewhere along the teenage years, she had acquired an unnerving aloofness at The Barony gatherings, often withdrawing to the music room to tinker on the piano.

In tandem, Sam and she headed off toward the stables. In the first vacant stall Sam and she came across, they gingerly laid Troubles on the bed of straw. Doc Warren, the resident veterinarian, would be away for the holiday—and, like family announcements, emergencies always seemed to happen at that time.

Peeling away his blood soaked jacket, Sam cringed at Troubles' whimper of pained protest. "You're going to be okay, fella." But he really wasn't so sure of that.

On her knees, on the other side of his dog, Gabby shook her head. "I've seen recovery from worse injuries. A Peruvian girl disemboweled by a single swipe from a jaguar's paw."

The past two summers she had spent in Spain and then Peru with the Experiment in International Living. Her knowledge of Tex-Mex Spanish had qualified her for the volunteer EIL program, a result of a bill her father had introduced to recruit an "army" of young Americans to foster peace and democracy in third-world countries. Perhaps that explained the soft, old world patina glimmering off her.

Noel returned with the bag and Sam said, "Fi . . . find my father—tell him to get a vet bo . . . booked on a flight to The Barony ASAP!"

"Gotcha covered." Noel wheeled to sprint back to the *hacienda.*

Already, Gabby was rummaging through the bag, a medical kit from the looks of it. Iodine tablets, calamine lotion, tweezers, insect repellent, rehydration salts—all spilled from the bag, as her fingers searched expediently through its contents—selecting a few, discarding others.

"EIL's answer to on-the-job emergencies," she explained briskly, setting to one side her collection—adhesive tape, scissors, an antibiotic ointment, sterile gauze pads, and surgical tape. Pushing back her chin-length, bluntly cut brown hair, she looked up at him and gave a twisted, wry smile. "Comes equipped with even cough drops and condoms."

At nineteen, other girls would have said that last word with a feigned coy giggle, but she was obviously indifferent to flirtatious byplay.

"Do you want to go get cleaned up for Thanksgiving dinner, Gabby? I can take over from here until a vet arrives."

She bestowed him with a fleeting half-smile, but that prim and proper mouth said, "Fuck Thanksgiving dinner."

FOR FIVE GENERATIONS, THE BARONY Ranch had been ruled by a Paladín family member, with Heath Paladín currently at the helm of The Barony Enterprises.

Noel's uncle clearly held the staunch opinion that family members, Paladineños, and other employees were to emulate his dedicated work ethics—rising at four in the morning and on the job from five until ten that night, six days a week.

So it was no surprise that even that Thanksgiving weekend, a number of family members were summoned for a board meeting. Though usually an informal one, this meeting seemed to carry more weight—though for the life of Noel, he could not fathom how this one impressed him as being any different from others.

Admittedly, he had yet to drop in on The Barony Ranch's new corporate offices, located on the fifteenth floor of a San Antonio skyscraper some ninety miles away. This one would be a first.

He settled his Stetson on one starched, jean-encased thigh and prepared to suffer through the tediousness. The board meetings tended to be about as exciting as his last term class in Statistical Regression and Classification had been. He'd much rather be riding fences or chasing strays than saddled to the uncomfortable hardback chair he straddled backwards right now.

Uncle Heath stood behind his desk, arms akimbo, and waited for the room to quiet. Aunt Mariana, as ranch attorney, sat on her husband's right, and to his left, long-time trusted family friend and knowledgeable board member, Senator Garner Bradford.

In Noel's mind, Uncle Heath, at fifty-four, was the last of the legendary Paladín patrons. After the inflation following the Korean War, the Federal Reserve had made monetary policy more restrictive. Almost overnight, The Barony had become land rich and money poor.

Uncle Heath had rescued the ranch from the ensuing tax foreclosure by negotiating a lease through Noel's father with Humble Oil for oil and gas exploration on The Barony.

As a result, the Barony's share of its oil royalties enabled The Barony not only to pay its back-due taxes but also to acquire vast expanses of pastures in Australia, Cuba, Europe, South America, and even Florida, creating a worldwide cattle kingdom.

The Ranch had developed into the largest beef-producing operation in the United States. Uncle Heath also sat on the board of Texas A&M and Corpus Christi's newest hospital. Obviously, he was elated when he realized the Paladíns could maintain the glory of the land they held quite dear.

"Because the Barony Enterprise requires my spending more and more time away from Texas and the ranch," Uncle Heath was saying, "I have called this meeting to announce that I want to appoint the task of running the home ranch's three divisions to the most capable man I can think of. I want to hand over the reins of the ranch to my nephew, Noel."

Noel started. He was not sure he heard right. Across from him, Sam, worn out from his all-night vigil over a recovering Troubles, nodded and gave him a thumbs up. By all rights, the most logical successor to the throne should have been Sam, but Noel knew, as Uncle Heath must have, that Sam's career sights were already on public service.

Noel's dad, standing with arms folded next to his twin Pierce, nodded his approval.

Uncle Heath now looked at Noel. "I know I sprang this on you. The fact that I haven't even had a chance to closet myself with you, regarding this, supports my objective today—you at the helm of The Barony Ranch."

His steely gaze scanned the room. "As you know, Noel has also been trained at Harvard Business School, focusing on agribusiness. But that is far less impressive than the fact that he knows what to some may seem insignificant details—like exactly how much gas is guzzled by the pickup of each line camp caporal."

He looked back at Noel. "Well? Are you game?"

Noel rubbed the back of his neck. "This does put me in a deuce of a spot, Uncle Heath. You all know I'm not much of a flannel mouth."

In truth, he had been flirting with the idea of making the military his career, as Jack and Julian were doing, but had realized he would never be happy with a structured life . . . and hobbled to a desk seemed pretty damned confining, even if it was The Barony's.

Back in '43, at ten-years-old, he had watched FBI agents arrest his mother and then ransack his family's home. Then, his family had decided it was best he be reunited with his mom in the internment camp.

There, he experienced that horrible feeling of confinement—as if he had done something wrong. America did not just lock up people for no reason. He still carried that stigma that he wasn't quite worthy enough to take his place in society.

And now he also carried that leftover vestige of Crystal City—of Paola and him, coupling wildly in the windmill tank like two river otters. By now, she would be a married woman, and he both wished her well and hoped Luca Buonocore had the stamina of a stallion.

"I don't know if I can be of that much use to The Barony," he said. "What all you're talking about, Uncle Heath—supervising the entire agricultural side of the business, I can do. But watching over the hardware store and the saddle shop in San Patricio as well as the cotton warehouse in Galveston and our thoroughbred farm . . . well, I plain don't know."

"Give Noel time to think it over," Garner said, stabbing out his cigarette in the yucca's terra cotta pot behind him. He ambled toward the center of the room in his cowboy boots, hands clasped behind his back, and stared down for a moment at the braided area carpet, as if trying to gather his own thoughts.

Noel wasn't fooled. The whole family knew how proficient Garner was at collecting information and then confronting his target with it. Wheedling, accusing, or joking, he wooed the opponent into his camp. His bushy brows raised and lowered as he overcame every objection before it could be voiced and with a smoothness that was not to be denied.

Noel couldn't deny that through these various ploys, Garner was accomplishing much on behalf of America's downtrodden.

At last, his sights cut to Noel. "To keep the profits rolling in, The Barony Enterprises needs to become a highly competitive agribusiness, which makes you perfect for the position, son. You understand its nuts and bolts."

He paused and glanced at the others seated in chairs loosely scattered around the room. "Still, when success is based on the bottom line of The Barony's financial statement, the Paladín bonds of family can only link so far. With older family members retiring or dying, The Barony Enterprises must think about moving into the next century as a global organization."

Uncle Heath paused in rolling the sleeves of his light blue chambray shirt up his forearms. "Exactly what is it you have in mind, Garner?"

"Heck, Heath, I'm just suggesting The Barony will need to become more progressive. That at some future point, I feel we board members should form a search committee of sorts—to take a vote to look around for chief executives outside the family. You know, specialists in the economics of long-run commodities, enhancement production, the supply chain of microeconomics. Things like that."

Noel rose and clapped his hat on his head. "Alex and Fiona Paladín created The Barony. Our family has fought droughts, depressions, and government interference to keep it with the same determination as our forbearers. I reckon we'll find someone to fit the bill you describe to run the show. In the meantime, I'll do my best to run the shop."

TWENTY-THREE-YEAR-OLD HEIDI Nobel dragged the scooter's rear brake to a stop next to the Polo White Corvette, parked by the tiered fountain. Her turquoise Vespa was no Harley, and she was no Marlon Brando, although her father and stepmother might indeed be inclined to think of her as "The Wild One."

She had missed the Paladíns' Thanksgiving dinner altogether. It was not unusual for her to miss out on command performances of any kind, wherever they may be. She rebelled at prescribed expectations from anyone, including and most of all, family. Besides, there was still the tail end of the weekend to navigate with the Paladín family.

And what a family her father had married into. The colorful, challenging, and most oddly loving people she had met. Perhaps that explained why she occasionally bothered to show up for these get-togethers—and explained her father's contentment over the last eight years with Heidi's stepmother, Hannah.

Of the family members, Heidi missed Fiona most. They both had been rebellious hellions, as Hannah had often commented with a roll of her eyes. But then, Heidi was sure the terms unconventional or quirky were never applied to Fiona, as they were in a more derogatory sense to herself.

Just behind missing Fiona came missing Noel, a full two-years younger. He only ran a close second because Heidi's pleasure in their youthful companionship had been tarnished over the years—at least, in her eyes—by her growing awareness of him that went beyond friendly bounds.

The way his voice had deepened, and his upper arms had muscled up. The way beard now stubbled his jaw when returning from a dawn's hunt and the line of wiry, coarse hair that ran up from his low-slung jeans to his navel. She was quite aware of the changes in Noel.

One day, when she should have been taking biology notes, she found herself doodling Noel's name inside a heart. She knew then she had better cut her losses, cut back on her visits to America. Because he had never, and would never, evidence any interest in her beyond friendship. His kind would be the All American Girl.

But that didn't stop her from inscribing his name elsewhere. Sort of like the G.I.s and their "Kilroy was here."

After rocking the scooter onto the kickstand, she dusted off her cuffed jeans and scuffed motorcycle boots. No conventional Mary Janes or saddle oxfords for her. She struggled out of one sleeve of her father's old black Luftwaffe flying jacket, minus its insignias. No use inflaming the Americans any more than necessary.

"Need help?"

She looked over her shoulder to find Noel immediately behind her. Her lids closed in suppressed exasperation. Why could it not have been her father or Noel's Aunt Belle or Fiona?

He took the dangling other sleeve of her jacket and slid it off her shoulder.

"Thank you." She tossed the jacket across the saddle seat. "Why are you not with the rest of the family? You know, horsing around . . . drinking Lone Star . . . playing poker . . . contending for bragging rights. Those sorts of things."

His muscled shoulders shrugging, he grinned. He tucked his thumbs into his pockets. "I'm heading out, you might say. Fixing to make a pilgrimage of sorts."

"A pilgrimage? Out here? In the middle of nowhere. And exactly to where would this holy expedition be headed?"

His jaw jutted up toward the live oak-crowned bluff. "The Paladín family burial plot. Figured I should get some advice from the Wise Ones regarding an offer I just received from The Barony Board of Directors."

"A *seance?*" *An* unlikely interest for one who majored in the staid and starchy subject of agribusiness. Would wonders never cease? Mimicking him, she likewise wedged her hands in her jean pockets and smiled drily. "But, of course."

"Yeah, in a way. Pretty creepy idea, isn't it?" He nodded at her Vespa. "Hey, can I try out your scooter?"

"Only if I ride with you."

He hiked a brow. "You don't trust me? The best bronc-breaking cowboy in the Southwest?"

"I don't trust anyone."

He looked down at her oddly. And only then did she notice his height had shot above hers since her last visit, and she was tall for a woman.

She shrugged. "Growing up with the splintering of bombs, bank accounts, and your parents' marriage sort of makes you wary."

Avoiding the searching look in his long, lazy eyes, she shrugged back into her leather jacket. Her very bones and teeth vibrated from the jarring ninety-mile trip she had just made from San Antonio, but could she truly pass up riding with Noel? Just this once, a voice urged. Play it cool. "Are you going to climb in the saddle or not, cowboy?"

He slung one lanky leg over the Vespa, and she swung on behind, wrapping her arms beneath his denim jacket and encountering his washboard stomach.

He launched the scooter down the long drive, out through the arched gates, and then off the blacktop road into the scrubland to pick up the trail grooved by a countless number of Paladíns across a span of more than a century.

He actually accelerated on its hairpin curves up the bluff, spraying dirt. The headwind lashed her reddish-blonde braid as she leaned her head close to his and laughed. "So, you can be reckless?"

"Reckless, no." No laughter colored his own words. "But I may take calculated risks."

At the crest, he parked her Vespa beneath the lone, soaring live oak. Beneath its broad evergreen canopy, off to one side, was a collection of tombstones encompassed by a wrought-iron picket fence. Below the bluff sprawled the hacienda, with pungent mesquite smoke curling from several of its chimneys.

They dismounted, and she followed him to the live oak where he abruptly slumped against its rough bark base, hands clasped over one upraised knee.

She slid down beside him. As a teenager, early on I used to resent coming here. To the Barony. It represented everything I did not have. Home. Family. Security. Wealth. Prestige. I would watch you and your cousins play. As if there were no hunger or hurt or need for hiding."

He looked sidewise at her, again with that strange look in his eyes, almost a feasting.

"I do not know when everything changed, but gradually I began to look forward to my visits here. It became a constant in my life. A stability. A refuge, when schoolchildren were still kneeling on all fours in hallways, hands covering their necks, during bomb drills."

"I knew you went off to Paris to . . . to some—"

"To *École des Beaux-Arts.*"

"And over the summers you still work with my Aunt Hannah and your father's vineyards."

"*Ja* . . . yes." Her fingers toyed a spit curl back into place before one pierced ear, where a golden hoop dangled. Her father had gone bananas when he sighted the piercing. No good girl would ever pierce her ears.

"But what do you want to do with the rest of your life?"

"Actually, I have been giving it some thought. I want to open an art gallery . . . in San Antonio." She tensed, waiting for sound of the ball-peen hammer to bang with her admission.

"An art gallery?" A thoughtful pause. "Yeah, it would suit you."

"My father thinks it's bad judgement. That San Antonio is so isolated there's not enough clientele to support the business. That it is too frontier to be interested in the arts—and I am too funky to make a respectable go of it."

"Funky?" He palmed her kneecap, a casual gesture expressive of that easy friendship established by years of familiarity. "That's part of your charm."

"What? My weirdo ways charm the no-nonsense Noel?"

He flashed an appealing grin. "Hey, you got major mojo, Heidi."

She pointed with her chin at the small cemetery. "So, what do the Wise Ones have to say about your dilemma?"

His gaze followed hers, and his mouth thinned. "I think they would agree with you. Only the truly reckless rock and roll."

Her instincts told her that despite the evidence that Noel was a hardliner, a by-the-book kind of guy, he would not expect her to conform to society's expectations. Besides, some of The Barony's illustrious members had been notorious for not conforming to set rules.

"Well," she grinned, "Einstein said, 'You have to color outside the lines once in a while if you want to make your life a masterpiece.' And that was one German who always seemed to know what he was talking about."

He chuckled and threw a companionable arm around her. "I like that. See, I found my solution up here after all. I'm glad you came."

If only she felt that companionable easiness. But what she felt unsettled her—this attraction, this awareness of him that was only growing stronger. Unfortunately for her, Noel was bound to The Barony and its people. And she was not one of them.

The shortest and most exclusive railway in the world was the U.S. Capitol Subway System, only accessible by Legislators and approved guests. Fiona Paladín was one of those few privileged guests, as long as she was accompanied by Steven Douglas.

For the past eight months, since last Thanksgiving, Steven dutifully met with her at the John Adams Building and descended to the River Styx, as she styled the little-known-spur of the U.S. Capitol Subway System. As promised, he was paying off his debt, the opportunity to hog hunt at The Barony.

The underground train sped them through a labyrinth of murky tunnels to the massive National Archives and Records Building. From there, his governmental pass sped them through the many archivists' security checks into the nation's most inaccessible and little-known reading room, as well as its Special Intelligence Section.

Despite a score or more of these meetings, hers and

Steven's exchanges during those short excursions to the National Archives remained cordial but formal—the kind of cursory conversations between acquaintances regarding upcoming functions, the weather, people they knew.

She was beginning to wonder if there was any substance to the good looking man, notwithstanding the profundity of his published poems and stories. But it was common knowledge his deceased wife had loved him wildly, as he had her. So there had to be something of substance to him that Fiona was overlooking.

She often wondered if Douglas suspected her of finagling to steal the Rotunda's Declaration of Independence or some plot even more dastardly, regardless of her assertion that she was merely researching the unusual O.S.S. career and death of her aunt for a biography.

She was discouraged, exhausted, and stretched thin by both her lobbying job and her research efforts—involving hundreds of thousands of files and ledgers. Only a scattering of Request Slips revealed Aunt Aubrey's signature as having checked out the files.

Those 1940s files held nothing suspicious in regard to a mole. They were mostly descriptions of the lowering of the German military draft age or Japan labor and manpower or Italian weaponry. All Axis powers at that time. Innocuous subjects, it would seem, when in search of a mole.

"Good morning, Fiona." Steven greeted her with his

polite, perfunctory smile in the bowels of the nearly empty Capitol Subway. It was Good Friday, and not many legislators had bothered to show up for work—a perfect opportunity for her to get in some research time. "How was your week?"

She swung into the rattling car's nearest vacant seat, and he slid in beside her, jamming the knees of his lengthy legs against the empty seat in front. Only an Air Force colonel and a Reading Room female staffer in khaki trousers were aboard.

What the hell, let's throw him for a loop.

Foregoing her customary glib reply of "Wonderful, thank you . . . and yours?" she said with a blazing smile, "It was crappy. I had to wage a hand war with a congressman fondling my thigh last night, I spilt blazing hot coffee on my skirt this morning, and the only pair of hose I could quickly find had a runner. Then, to compound the injustices of my life, I have to endure yet another politely boring ride to the National Archives."

One brow peaked above the rim of his glasses. "Well, I should be able to take care of that." His hand splayed across the back of her head, turning it toward him, and his mouth captured hers.

Aware of the two other commuters—and their perfectly good pair of eyes—she stiffened instantly. But as his lips continued to move softly back and forth over hers, she forgot the other two passengers, forgot where she was, and slipped her hands up and around his shoulders.

From a distance, she heard his rumbling, "Mmmmm."

Only when her purse and pad clattered to the floor did she come to herself. He released her as she blinked and cleared her throat. "Err . . . uhhh, I was beginning to wonder if since your wife's death you had become a monk." She half expected a blistering setdown that she was venturing into his revered privacy.

Instead, he drawled, "You know, Fiona, I was also thinking just how utterly boring these trips are and how much I dread them. And believed them to justify my opinion of you as insipid, banal, and priggish."

Anger smoked her eyes. "You supercilious, stuffy, puffed-up—"

His self-satisfied smile creased parentheses around his wide mouth. "I think I may have changed my opinion of you—and I hope I have changed yours of me, as well."

## WASHINGTON, D.C.
## AUGUST 1957

AT TWO A.M. SAM WAS MAKING phone calls. As tired as he was, if he was not careful, his stutter would stumble through his message.

For Majority Leader Garner Bryce Bradford, days and nights were nothing. Especially now. His entire career—indeed, his entire life's dream—hinged on this seemingly hopeless bill passage. Garner needed its passage to make him acceptable to both liberals and northerners. If it passed, his lifelong drive to be President of the United States was more securely nailed. If it failed, then Garner was just one among many aspirants for the nation's highest office.

As the steamy month of August commenced, both the bill and Garner's aspiration looked doomed to fail.

At that time of night, Washingtons high-end residential enclaves were asleep—until Sam's call. The senator would answer in sleep-drugged tones, and Sam, in his repeated messages, would say, "This is Sam Houston Paladín, Senator Bradford's legislative secretary, calling about the Civil Rights bill with its amendment to be brought before the floor tomorrow."

Garner was adamant about passing the first civil rights legislation since Reconstruction. He sincerely wanted to help the Negroes, and that was why Sam was committed to this legislative genius of a man. As Garner had told him, "If we're going to have any civil rights bill at all, we've got to add this negra jury trial amendment to it."

The ultra-liberal Senator Edmund McKay's response to Sam's late-night call was, "Everyone knows the bill is deader than a doornail."

Weary beyond words, Sam slumped back into his chair. Words were all he had left. Together, he and Garner were working the cloakroom, the corridors, and behind closed doors with every ounce of persuasion they could muster.

"Everyone seems to know that the bill is dead, Senator McKay—except Senator Bradford." His hand scouring his mustache, Sam sighed heavily. "Look, all the compromises and deals that have been chiseled out in the past months have put the two sides at a standoff. Unless there can be some way of finding a middle ground, the haters will take over. The Negroes will lose it all. We need your help."

From Garner, he had learned the importance of the words "we" and "us." He needed to imply they were on the same side—and make both sides believe that.

He was trying to make the biggest deal of his career for the biggest dream of the Negroes—a civil rights bill that would include not only an existing civil right, the right to vote, but would also ensure southern Negroes a new civil right, the right to sit on juries. The bill lacked so much, but at least it was a start.

"All right, you've got my vote tomorrow," McKay conceded, probably only because he wanted fervently to go back to bed.

During the months of refining the civil rights bill, Garner had kept under the radar, rarely appearing on the Senate floor and using his masterful persuasion skills huddled with senators either in the Capitol or in his offices in the Senate Office Building. "If ya can't finesse 'em, stress 'em," he'd remind Sam.

But that next morning, Garner was on the floor ready to do battle. And Sam was not the only warrior he had summoned to be present for that historic showdown. In the gallery sat Gaila and Gabby.

Glad-handing and smiles were few that morning. The Minority Leader, Senator Wayne Wynn, was telling reporters—and the White House and Vice President Ellwood—that everything was going fine, reiterating his confidence that "at least thirty-nine to forty" Republican senators would join at least a dozen Democratic liberals in voting against the jury trial amendment.

And that morning, Sam was still making his calls. After several of them, he erased the number that he had placed next to senators' names in one column on his tally sheet. Votes were volleying back and forth, and White House pressure might well force some votes to change yet again.

By evening, the debate was well underway, and the debate came down to the wire. Sam watched as a freshman senator, cued by Garner, sprang upright from one of the back row desks to speak.

Sam reviewed his smudged tally sheet. As the hands on the clock approached the bewitching hour of midnight, Vice President Ellwood came in to take the presiding officer's chair. A page set a lectern on the Majority Leader's desk, and Garner himself stood to deliver the last and most crucial speech.

While Sam had been working tirelessly to change the minds of the Senate, Garner was now eloquently swaying the room to his way of thinking.

Sam glanced over at the Press Gallery, where rows of reporters were jumping up like Jack-in-the-boxes and sprinting up the stairs to the telephones in the Press Room.

At three a.m. that same morning, Sam flew with the Garner entourage to Texas. Garner and Gaila were ebullient. The Civil Rights Bill had passed, assuring Garner's Presidential nomination. But Gabby sat quietly at a small table toward the jet's rear section and stared out the small window. Weary, Sam slid into the padded seat next to her.

"Worn out?"

She smiled faintly. "Completely exhausted by the dog and pony show." Amid all the posturing and dissemination of Capitol Hill, Gabby Garner was refreshing. She had no agenda. He admired her. Her watchwords could well be, "I live to serve."

He draped an arm over the back of her seat. "You know your presence makes a difference in your father's career. Solidarity. Stability. Family loyalty and love. All of that—it appeals to American ethics."

She arched a brow. "And what about my life? Am I allowed to have one?"

He understood more than she realized. Sometimes the individual had to cede his interest for the greater good of the group. In both their cases, the family often took predominance.

"You know, I've frequently thought, being in the spotlight with the Paladíns as I am, how wonderful it would be to have someone who liked me, not because of my triumphs, but despite my failures and vices."

The sudden moisture glistening in her eyes took him fully by surprise. But she gave a soft laugh. "Then that person would have to be blind."

At that, he chuckled. "So, my flaws are that obvious?"

Her generous mouth, wide like her father's, crimped. "Are you kidding me? Pride. Ambition. Relentlessness. They're carved on your face like Hamilton's is on Mount Rushmore."

"Maybe," he joked, "I should be depicted there as well?"

She sobered. "My father will beat you to it."

"Do I detect a smidge of resentment?"

"Of course. The family of civil servants also have to endure the blinding spotlight of fame and censure. I detest it all more than words can say. But . . . when I see my father beam . . . beam at me . . . I know it's worth anything."

"A daddy's girl, huh?"

"Yes," she replied unequivocally.

That evening, with but little time to rest and freshen up, the celebration of the Civil Rights bill passage took place at Austin's legendary Driskill Hotel. Garner and Gaila's wedding had occurred there, and it had been his campaign headquarters throughout his career thus far—and, Sam knew, would also serve those purposes in Garner's upcoming bid for the Presidential nomination.

In the ballroom, red, white, and blue bunting looped its walls, and at either side of the dais the Stars and Stripes and the Lone Star stood sentry. A magnificent chandelier sparkled dancing lights over the multitude of guests and reporters. A band played "The Eyes of Texas." On the dais, a tired but grinning Garner, his long armed lapped around the shoulders of a smiling Gaila, waved for the press.

When the band immediately followed with "Deep in the Heart of Texas," Garner spontaneously led Gaila around on the dance floor with a quick two-step and the crowd went wild.

As Garner and Gaila retired back to the dais and others began to dance, Sam felt obligated to ask Gabby to dance. Her eyebrows shot up in surprise. "Go ahead," Garner urged, "enjoy yourselves!"

Once in Sam's arms, the pliant-in-public Gabby moved stiffly. Sam inclined his head near hers. "You've told me how flawed I am, but am I truly that bad of a dancer?"

From beneath thickets of eyelashes, she glanced up at him with poignant eyes. "You know our families are orchestrating our pairing." She nodded toward the dais. "Nothing would make my father happier than to see us married. Combining two dynasties. It would ensure his presidential bid."

Knowing Garner, Sam was not shocked by this, but he had never really considered marriage, much less marriage to Gabby. She was more than a friend, true— between them breathed something elemental and fierce —but what was the adage? "Never mix business with pleasure."

Yet he found himself doing just that. "To he . . . hell with politics and parents. Look, I have a banjo upstairs. Let's go slumming at Congress and Sixth Street. Some gr . . . great country music acts are playing in the dump." Damnit, if he could only put his Chevy governor on the speed of his spoken thoughts.

She tilted her head back and chuckled mirthlessly. "My mom owns the radio station down the street from the dump. But like you said, to hell with them."

The beer hall he had in mind was much like the dives on either side of it, a framed-out bar sporting a floor matted with sawdust—but the duo, a harmonica and a banjo player, was rather good.

Swigging beer, Sam and Gabby sat at a small table wedged in a corner and listened until the guys wound up their gig. By that time, Sam was feeling relaxed, and, apparently, so was she because conversation came easily. They discussed everything from Picasso to the Washington Redskins to peanuts—and avoided politics like the plague.

Idly, she peeled the label from her beer bottle. "So, did you ever skinny-dip at the old Nueces swimming hole out back of The Barony?"

His relaxed gaze ricocheted from the scruffy dude playing his banjo badly to her. From beneath dense lashes, she was studying him. "Yeah, off and on over the ye . . . years." He realized that over those years, she had never commented on his occasional stutter, just accepted it. "And you?"

A rueful smile transformed her strong features, softening them. She wasn't quite beautiful, but her father's long nose and determined chin were held in check by her soulful yet sensuous eyes. "No." She returned to peeling off the label. "Jokes were leaked at The Barony's holidays about the Paladín kids, boys and girls, caught sneaking off to skinny dip. I longed to do just that—throw caution to the wind."

He allowed himself free rein with his next words. "Gabby, I think it's time you raised a little hell."

She merely nodded, but later her spirit caught fire. At two o'clock that morning, another act, a guitarist, launched into a sultry fandango. She surprised Sam by rising from her chair and clapping her hands with sinuous movements. Slowly, she circled their table, never taking her smoky gaze off his face.

As she completely surrendered herself to the pleasure of the unguarded moments, he could only stare and hope he wasn't drooling. He was mesmerized by her previously unperceived passionate nature. It was time to set his intentions toward getting to know Gabby Bradford better.

That afternoon, Garner greeted Sam with a slap on the back and a "Shave that outlaw mustache, Sam. It's time for you to begin to make your name out in the front runners for a congressional seat."

Sam should have been elated, backed by the support of such a powerful politician as Garner Bryce Bradford, but something in Sam, perhaps alerted by Gabby's earlier statement that she would do anything for her father's approval, made him dig in his feet.

Sam was not sure whether or not he wanted to run for a congressional seat, but he was sure as hell not shaving his mustache.

## WASHINGTON, D.C.
## SEPTEMBER 1957

SITTING IN THE PASSENGER seat, Steven cleared his throat. The Cadillac Coupe de Ville gliding along a shady, forested drive of Rock Creek Park was headed in the direction of the public horse stables. Was this why she had instructed him to dress casually?

"What?" Fiona asked, sliding him one of her maddening smiles. "You don't like my driving?"

She handled the luxury car's steering wheel undoubtedly with the same ease at which any Paladín worth their salt did the reins of a horse. "Uh, this surprise outing of yours—does it involve horseback riding? Because equestrian, I am not." A decidedly unpleasant memory loomed of a Shetland he had been riding as a kid tossing him and then tap dancing across his chest.

"Oh, ye of little faith."

That was just it. Despite three dates, the community affairs kind, he felt he understood so little of her on which to base a deep and trusting faith. Oh, he was very familiar with her passionate responses—the small sighs of ecstasy escaping from her beard-chapped lips, the trembling of her small body, imprisoned by his against her front door, those same hands that now held the steering wheel slipping beneath his jacket to claim his belt and draw him even closer.

And then there were his own responses. His scrotum tightening, his simmering blood rising to a molten point that he strove to keep in check.

Without a doubt, they both wanted more from one another, wanted the consummation of the electrical change that sparked non-stop between them. Perhaps he wanted even more than that. He feared he was falling in love with her, and that could be even more difficult to keep in check.

The move would be his to make. And, damnit it all, he sensed this would be no passing fling—not the way he was drawn toward her as inexorably as the compass needle was drawn toward north.

But he was not sure if he was ready to risk loving fully again. He knew love could be nothing but heartache. No . . . better to keep a little of oneself in reserve.

Avoiding a pair of riders trotting their mounts, she parked in the dusty lot off to one side of the stables. He shot her an accusing look. She dimpled. "Patience. Follow me."

Careful to skirt the clumps of manure, he trailed her into the large barn and, hands tucked into his jeans, watched as she strode across the mucked straw. Her hips, set off very nicely by jeans rolled up to her calves, swayed gently in time with hair that she had pulled up into a ponytail.

She spoke briefly with a billed-cap older man raking the littered straw. Nodding, he set aside the rake and crossed to an empty stall. Well, not entirely empty, because he rolled out first one, then another . . . bicycle.

"All yours," he told Fiona. "Return 'em by six or another day's rental."

She beamed at Steven. "Ready?"

His responding smile was most likely a little dicey. "Umm, it's been a long time since I've ridden one. A couple of decades, give or take. But, hell. As it's not a horse, I'm game."

After a rather wobbly start on his part, they were off and riding down an obviously well-traveled, wide dirt path that soon led into a forested oasis within the nation's capital. Once he got the kinks out of his leg muscles, he began to enjoy himself.

Songbirds warbled, a deer waved its white tail as it thrashed in retreat through underbrush, and up ahead, a coyote padded calmly across the trail and vanished.

The knotted muscles and ligaments in his shoulders relaxed. The fresh breeze, scented with evergreen, ruffled through his hair and revitalized his stale lungs. Renewed energy pumped refreshed blood throughout him. He turned to her and grinned. "You did good!"

She grinned back widely, and he glimpsed in her eyes

the same lightning struck look he was feeling. Her attention diverted, her bicycle threatened to sideswipe his. Quickly, she swerved back on the track and giggled. "Oops! Maybe I should stick to horseback."

After they cycled past a water-powered grist mill, she called out, "There's a scenic spot up ahead. At the base of one of Rock Creek's falls. What's say we take a break?"

"Sounds good."

The place they parked their bicycles' kickstands was delightful. It was bracketed with aromatic wildflowers and drowned with nature's chattering squirrels. He followed her down the slope and noticed water tumbling over a short ledge of rocks. She found a grassy bed beside the creek, dropping down, and he joined her.

Reclining on her forearms, she glanced over at him as sunlight filtering through the leaves glinted off her gold earrings. "Makes you forget for a while the strife of politics."

"A respite in the midst of greed and graft and double dealing." He plucked a blade of grass and tucked it between his lips. "Thank you, Fiona. I mean it sincerely. My beleaguered spirit needed this."

She shrugged dainty shoulders. "Part of my job. Not you," she quickly amended. "But my uncle Pierce's clients. Providing some stress relief to the demands of their everyday life."

"Speaking of demands, the President has requested that I attend an upcoming swearing-in ceremony. Why, I cannot imagine."

"Why not? You are an urbane, versatile, and resource-ful man. Not to mention attractive."

This was an offhanded remark, but the calm deserted their conversation, replaced by a sudden silence . . . and an unbidden awareness of the ineluctable draw between them.

Not knowing how to reply, he watched with affected interest a bald eagle winging overhead.

Bracing on one forearm, she shifted toward him. In a beautiful face usually graced with absolute confidence, he thought he glimpsed vulnerability and wariness, and he was caught off guard. "Steven, I won't chase after you. But neither am I the kind of woman to play hard to get. If I am off base, tell me now."

So, this was it. The gauntlet thrown down.

His lips tightened. He swallowed.

"You are not finished living, Steven," her whisper reached him. "Nor loving if you give it a chance."

Too many years of stiff-lipped mourning had left him desolate, his authentic feelings locked up. His teeth clamped hard on his lower lip. "In everyday life, I might be a disappointment. I mean in returning expectations. You know, the kind that can wither—"

"Why don't you let me decide that?"

He reached an arm to gather her lithe body against him and dropped his forehead against hers, sighing. "'Fools rush in, where angels fear—

She drew back to search his face. "Am I competing with an angel for your love because that's an impossibility for any mortal woman."

"My wife was no angel." He brushed his lips over her trembling ones. "No, you're rescuing a man who has been a fool for far too long." He realized he had been feeding off his emptiness. "A man who is hungry for your love."

## SAN ANTONIO
## JANUARY 1958

"Bridget Malone?"

"Yes?"

"It's Julian Paladín. And it's New Year's Eve. I'm in San Antonio on a layover. I want to see you."

Her voice came back just as crisp as he remembered—and scornfully cool. *Julian? Julian who?*

"Meet me in the Menger Hotel at six thirty." His own voice came back confident and in command, though he was anything but. Oh, his uniform sported the hardware of one in command, but his accelerated heartbeat right now proved that a lie.

In agony, he waited through the ensuing silence. His waking hours had been occupied solely by his career, his love of flying. But, when he did daydream, more often than not those flights of fancy were of Dr. Bridget Malone—with and without her white medical jacket.

His sleeping hours were all too often haunted by a single gut shot and his mother's empty eyes. His father was constantly reminding him to "get on with his life because that's what your mother would want for us." And, by God, that was exactly what Julian was doing.

He cleared his throat. "Bridget?"

*At last, a response. "We've crossed paths once—and that was, what? Almost a year-and-a-half ago?"*

"I'll be in the bar, the last stool to the right."

*"You've got to be kidding me. I've got a date."*

"Ditch him."

Click.

Well, should he have expected anything else? Slowly, he rubbed the back of his neck, telling himself what a besotted imbecile he was.

Nevertheless, at six twenty that evening, he staked out the designated bar seat. Maybe a dozen or so couples had arrived early to welcome in the New Year. Twists of glittering ribbons spiraled down from the bar's crystal chandeliers and bunting sparkling with "Happy New Year's" draped each wall.

He ordered a scotch on the rocks. "Dewars—and make it a double." He was probably going to need it if she did not show up—and most definitely if she did.

More couples arrived, commandeering the remaining seats at the bar. The walnut-paneled room was growing stuffy, insufferably confining, and annoyingly noisy. He glanced at his wristwatch. Six-forty-five. He'd give her another fifteen minutes.

He finished off the drink and ordered another. He was thoroughly out of sorts. He could see more couples, decked in monkey suits and ballgowns, streaming down the corridor toward the bank of elevators and the Grand Ballroom. Hell's bells. He glanced again at the time. Seven-oh-five.

He sighed heavily, downed the last of the whiskey, and, signaling the bartender, went for his wallet.

"Put your wallet back, flyboy," a crisp voice said behind him. "My time will cost you more than a couple of drinks."

He swiveled to find Bridget, arrayed in some kind of golden gauze, and smiling cautiously. "Even if we're going against military protocol, fraternizing and all?"

She settled onto his knee and plunked her small purse on the counter. "Fraternizing? Is that what it's called? Lusting the hell out of one another?"

He lapped his arm about her about her waist, drawing her against him. "And is that what you want?" He nodded up toward the hotel's floors of bedrooms above. His heart beating against his chest like a snare drum, he waited for her reply.

Her eyes, their golden-rimmed irises larger in the bar's dim light, searched his face. "Truth is, I've thought about you off and on. Okay, a lot. Like a schoolgirl, I've followed your career, researched your records. I know flying claims your soul. But it's your body I'll settle for from here on out, Julian Paladín. Whenever it's available. But just your body. After all, I've got my own career to concentrate on."

Bingo! What could better fit his lifestyle?

Of course, if he had a heart, he'd most kindly give that to her, too. He so badly wished he could love, but that was something of which he was not capable. He fearfully suspected his heart had begun to wither with the outrageous pain that came from seeing a corpse that once breathed life, that once loved you in return.

He fished keys from his pocket and, grinning, dangled them. "It just so happens I've pulled strings and reserved us a room tonight."

## WASHINGTON, D.C.
## JULY 1958

PHOTOGRAPHERS' FLASHES lit the Oval Office as reporters, pad and pencil in hand, stood ready to capture every word of the President signing into law the National Aeronautics and Space Administration. The United States had built a vast highway system across America, with the Interstates springing up everywhere. Now, it was building a highway to the sky.

Standing next to the President during the NASA signing ceremony, Texas Senator Garner Bryce Bradford's lantern-jaw face beamed, matching the twinkle in his eyes, for the multitude of cameras.

The President then placed the commemorative pen he had used to sign the bill into a royal blue box bearing the presidential seal and passed the box to Garner with a

"Thank you for all your help, Senator Bradford."

After the Russians surprise launching of their satellite Sputnik, America itself was launched into a crisis, part of the larger Cold War. Immediately, Garner began to acquire an expert's knowledge on aeronautics development. Persistently, he harangued for a full-blown drive to put a man in space.

Of course, the Sputnik's launching was not that big of a surprise to him. He had had hints. Over the last decade or so, his intelligence contact in Russia kept him informed on everything from the value of a ruble to Khrushchev's bowel habits.

Knowledge was indeed power. Garner used knowledge he dared glean, where others pussyfooted around, to help in matters that would most benefit the United States.

Of course, the Russian's expedient elimination of Aubrey Paladín had been one of those nasty little aspects of politics. Most unfortunate but necessary.

He might have been able to prevent her neutralization, but she had come too close to jeopardizing his life's work on behalf of the disadvantaged folks. She had stood in the way of all he could do in leading the United States to its greatness.

Yet, had he not made up for that unpleasant little oversight in divulging that intelligence report by time and again providing opportunities for the rest of the Paladín tribe?

Oh, he was well aware of his vices, foibles, frailties,

and shortcomings. But he felt his generosity and magnanimity compensated for these less sterling attributes.

The reporters were rushing back to the press room and its news wire. And he . . . he had a date to keep with young Senator Carnegie's luscious secretary, who was even younger than her boss, younger even than Gabby, but who talked most freely of her boss's behind-the-scenes tactics.

## MERRITT ISLAND, FLORIDA
## JULY 1959

Receptions, graduation parties, and other significant life celebrations were staged at the Officers' Club, the social heart of Patrick Air Force Base.

The base was the Joint Long Range Proving Ground installation at Cape Canaveral. You could come to the installation's base to dance, or you could come there for dinner, or you could come there for bingo and canasta.

Second Lieutenant Bill Herndon, Jack Paladín's best friend and drinking buddy, had come there to get married. His father, a hardscrabble Okie, had been employed at the base as a civilian locksmith in the early 50s. In his mess dress uniform—epaulets, bowtie, cummerbund, and the whole shebang— Bill stood waiting as his bride to be walked down the aisle. The piano plinked out Mendelssohn's wedding march.

First Lieutenant Jack Paladín stood just in front of the artificially flowered arch with Bill and watched, along with the rest of the guests, as Bill's plumpish betrothed,

Susan, walked in measured paces toward them, a bouquet of fragrant orange blossoms in hand.

Well, actually Jack was watching her maid of honor, Regina, off to one side. Like the rest of the bride's wedding party, she wore some kind of red knee-length formal, but the way she moved was royalty personified. All she needed was a jeweled crown topping that mass of upswept deep dark brown hair instead of the pillbox hat with its ridiculous fluff of veil. "She is firecracker-hot."

"I take it you're talking about Regina and not my bride-to-be," Bill fired back from the side of his mouth.

Jack winked at her.

Regina rolled her golden brown eyes.

She had studiously ignored him throughout both the rehearsal and the rehearsal dinner last week. Which made him all the more determined. A four alarm fire siren sounded in that primeval part of him. He would definitely be playing with fire if he tried to seduce Regina Prendergast of Florida's famed Rancho del Sol lineage.

However, playing it safe merely for peace of mind was not his style—or else he would not be part of NASA's dangerous space race with Russia for world leadership, especially now that the Soviet Union was outpacing the United States in the production of new, nuclear-capable inter-continental ballistic missiles.

His father and Uncle Pierce's partner, Robert Goddard, had been right all along about rockets being the future.

No, playing it safe for peace of mind resulted in a

mediocre state of mind.

He winked at Regina again, and her chin shot up. Of Seminole Indian blood, she had a dusky beauty that reminded him of tintypes of his great-aunt Pearl. And Regina was indeed a queen, if one took into account that her father was a cattle baron.

Of course, other cattle ranches—like one in Australia and the Prendergasts' own Rancho Del Sol near Saint Augustine, Florida—were large, but not nearly as diverse as The Barony.

The Barony businesses included not only cattle but also citrus, cotton, hogs, sugar cane, turf grass, and, of course, oil—as well as, thoroughbreds, one of which had won the Kentucky Derby and Preakness.

The Board's search committee Garner had put together had hired Melvin Knopf as The Barony's chief executive, and he appeared to be quite capable and respectful. He had attended the University of Texas and had worked his way up to corporate consultant for a large family-owned ranching company in the Texas Panhandle. He could scarcely stay in the saddle, but his executive skills were renowned.

He was not overbearing but definitely bulldog tenacious. Very likeable if you could overlook the irritating way he sucked air in over his bottom teeth each time he launched into speech.

Yet it bothered Jack that someone outside the family had such a major role in The Barony's operations. He wondered if, had he been Noel, he would have taken the usurpation so well. Of course, Uncle Heath still held the reins. And Sam did not want them. Never had.

Nevertheless, Jack would have liked it if The Barony were still solely family operated, as was Regina's huge family spread.

At nineteen, she was only a couple of years older than his sister Jill, but Regina was light years ahead when it came to Eve-like seductiveness.

Once his and Regina's toasts made to the bride and groom in the reception room and his perfunctory waltz with Susan were completed, he claimed Regina for the next dance, "The Sea of Love."

His hand at the small of her back could feel the ramrod-steel spine running through her slender waist. She looked over his shoulder, barely flicking him a glance, as if she were merely enduring their obligatory floor presentation.

"There's a dive located on the wrong side of the Banana River. I'm splitting the reception. Are you coming with me?"

Her sizzling gaze alighted on his. "Do I look like a 'dive' sort of diva?"

He laughed. "You look like you're bored. So either it's this Royal Command Performance boring the hell out of you, or it's me. And I know it can't be me. I charm women out of their clothes."

A grin sneaked up to grace her sculpted face and was then abruptly erased. "I don't think you could handle me, cowboy."

So, she knew his ranching lineage, as well. He released her waist but held onto her opera gloved hand and headed out the ballroom doors for the parking lot. But when he tugged her toward his battered pickup, she tugged back. "No, my car . . . besides, my purse is there."

He shrugged and let her tug him now. Her car turned out to be an old Army jeep. "Some coach, Cinderella." He would have expected a Jaguar or Cadillac.

With no door to open, she climbed in bereft of his would-be gallantry, stripped off her gloves and pillbox hat, and revved up the engine. Soon, the Jeep was speeding down 520 with the heat, salt air, and wind taking their toll on her elaborate coiffure. Her exultant expression hit his crotch like a blow job.

"Where to?" she shouted against the wind.

"The Tiki Hut. Merritt Island side of the Banana River."

Sadly, as a result of post-war land speculation, the great Florida Land Boom had transformed the bucolic countryside from mosquito country into upscale neighborhoods and shopping areas. And now NASA had transformed the landscape into a space age stepping off point to the Universe. But tonight, cruising along 520 with Regina was sheer magic.

She did not bother to talk during the drive, and neither did he, which was a pleasant change for him. Most women immediately attached themselves to him and chattered like tickertapes when they learned that he was one of the Paladíns or that he was the lead candidate from Project Mercury's seven-man flight team for the first manned space flight.

The Tiki Hut was a great waterfront bar. Actually, it was a WWII Quonset hut with a dock for boaters enjoying the beer and juke box. Wanda Jackson was belting out "Hard-headed Woman." The billiards tables were clustered by scruffy patrons who looked like a motorcycle gang but most likely had more money than a shrimping fleet had shrimp.

He grabbed two bottles of Lone Star from the cooler and led Regina to the outdoor tables, lit by white Christmas light strands running from the rafters and along the dock. Only a handful of patrons braved the sultry night air to sit outside, bereft of the Hut's humming air conditioning unit. He shrugged out of his white mess jacket with its heavy sleeve braids and loosened his tie.

She slid into the rattan chair he pulled out for her and nodded at the long necks. "What if I don't like Lone Star?"

He grinned. "Oh, these two are for me. Starters, while you try to make up your mind what kind of frilly cocktail you want."

She canted her head, eyeing him with a frown. "Your cowlick is sticking up, cowboy."

"The cowlick's part of my phenomenal charm."

A crusty old waiter, cigar dangling from his mouth and wearing a grease-stained apron, shuffled to their table. "What'll it be?"

"I'll have the same," she told him. "Lone Star. But three up front."

After the waiter ambled away, Jack turned back to her. "Think you can drink me under the table?"

She smiled sweetly. "I expect that anything you can do, I can do just as well if not better."

"Oh, yeah?" He took a swig of his Lone Star.

"Yeah."

So this was to be a game of bragging rights. "I sincerely doubt you could make it through the astronaut's survival training in the Nevada desert much less pass the psycho physiological criteria or undergo a flight simulation test of a Redstone Missile."

The waiter returned with Regina's beers, and she took a deep draught then slowly wiped her mouth with the back of her hand, all the while watching him. "Sure I could, cowboy. All I would need would be the same training you received—and, of course, someone of import putting forth my name. Someone like Senator Garner Bradford."

"Lady, you're nuts. I qualified because of years of training and studying as an air force test pilot, and I faced a shitload of danger. I earned my rightful position by the sweat of my brow."

And speaking of sweat, he watched sweat bead and run down her chiffon- ruffled cleavage as she tilted back her head and slugged down the remainder of the first longneck. He tried to keep his jaw from falling open.

She smiled at him like the Cheshire Cat. "Do you

know anything about working cattle, cowboy?" He drained the remainder of his first Lone Star and started on his second. Swallowing, he drawled, "Put in my time on The Barony."

Now he was blustering. Sure, he could brand cows and castrate bull testicles, but summers on a ranch could have taught any dude that. It was not bred into his blood like it was into Noel's or even Sam's.

"You probably used a lasso to muster strays." That was uttered with a blistering tone of contempt.

He removed his cufflinks and began rolling up the sleeves of his starched, white pleated shirt. "Well, now, I sure didn't do it with a motorcycle or helicopter."

"Here in Florida we muster cattle another way. You've heard the term Florida Crackers?"

He took another swill from his long neck. Perspiration was trickling down its sides, as well as beneath the armpits of his shirt. "Sure." Where was all this leading?

"Florida Crackers . . . the early Anglo pioneers who settled in Florida." She tilted her bottle to her juicy pink lips, quaffed the last of her second Lone Star. "There's that. But there's another meaning bantered around."

She reached for her last bottle. "Florida Cracker cattle were brought here even before the *Conquistadores* arrived. Ponce de Leon might have searched for the Fountain of Youth, but he left a lot of stray cattle. Those cattle go further back in history than your Texas mavericks. The Florida cowboys who work the cattle crack their whips instead of throwing limp lassos."

Limp lassos? He almost choked on his beer.

Over the rim of her bottle, her eyes gleamed like gold doubloons. "I was cracking whips by the age of seven. My Seminole grandfather taught me how."

He'd heard of the geezer. A cowboy, he had been among the last of the Seminoles hiding out in the Big Cypress Swamp, staunchly refusing to cave to U.S. military removal to the Brighton Indian Reservation. The Seminoles had a strong reputation for non-surrender. As obviously she did.

She lifted a dark-winged brow. "Care to see a demonstration?"

"Here? Now?"

"Give me five minutes. I'll grab my whip. In the meantime, you grab your beer and wait for me at the end of the dock."

Her high heels clicked across the wooden deck, and with lust, he watched her backside as she re-entered the Hut. What kind of female kept a whip in her car? What was she going to do, swat mosquitos?

He sighed, picked up his remaining long neck and strolled out to the end of the dock. The high tide of the Banana River sloshed nosily against the pilings, and the smell of dead fish permeated the muggy air. He slapped at a couple of whining mosquitoes.

He was finishing off the last of his beer when she returned. Bemused, he watched as, whip in hand and hips swaying deliberately, she sauntered across the deck like it was some Paris couture's runway. Shit, she was some-thing else.

She stopped on the dock, less than a dozen feet from him. "All right, cowboy. Put the bottle on your head."

"You're serious?"

"Where's your renowned Paladín courage? Or is it just sheer bravado?"

"Hell, no." But he shrugged uncomfortably.

"That charming cowlick you're so proud of should help balance the bottle."

Shit, the family's illustrious name was at stake. With a couple of adjusting tries, he stabilized the bottle atop his head.

The few patrons on the deck had turned to stare. He felt like a screwball. And if he should feel the slicing sting of her lash, well, then he would deserve to be shot at dawn. He could lose an ear, an eye. Goddamn, he could lose his career as an astronaut—and with it, the adventure of being the first man in space.

Slowly, she swiveled the eight-foot bullwhip above her head. Now sweat was sluicing down his ribs. Even his cummerbund was wet with sweat.

She popped the bullwhip a couple of times overhead. Sweat riveted his crotch. He held his breath. Balanced precariously on the top of his head, the bottle wobbled.

Then, flicking the whip up and behind her, she snapped it forward with a loud crack. He flinched. But the beer bottle went sailing, snatched by the bullwhip's curling tip. He fought to keep his knees from buckling.

She dropped the whip and, hand on one hip, sashayed toward him. "I will say, you got balls, cowboy."

And he was glad he still had them. He prayed his voice did not squeak. "The name's Jack."

"While we're on the subject of balls, you ready to beat me in a game of billiards inside?"

"You've read the Taming of the Shrew? If not, you need to read it before our date."

"Date? Why would I want to date you?"

"Because you want bragging rights at billiards, and besides, you can't resist my extraordinary charm." And, if he were honest, he would add that he wanted her in bed, sooner than later.

But, as it turned out, Regina planned on it being much later, if ever. When he would phone her, she airily turned down every date he proposed.

"Jack Paladín here, Regina. I'm off duty next Thursday and have two tickets to Orlando's Museum of Art—it features the world's largest collection of Louis Tiffany."

No young woman of Regina's class could pass up on Tiffany. "I can pick you up that morning and have you back in time for High Tea with your family." Or whatever a family of her royal pedigree did with their afternoons.

"Jack. Great to hear from you. Thank you for thinking of me, but I've already made other plans. Take care of yourself." *Click.*

"Regina, Jack here. Weather looks to be great this

weekend. Sunny, no wind. Perfect for a beach outing. If I supply the beach blanket and food, would you supply your delightful company?" Trite, but he was feeling a tad nervous and, damnit, he didn't like this unfamiliar feeling one bit.

"Oh, Jack, how sweet of you to call. The beach outing sounds divine, but regrettably I can't make it. Other obligations and all that. Still, I know you'll enjoy the sand and surf. Maybe another time." *Click.*

He was about ready to write off the ace-high kind of woman as either impossible to please or playing hard to get. Either way, not worth the effort.

Then, determined this was to be his last ditch effort and not even bothering to exert the full force of his Paladín charisma, he disgruntledly tossed out the idea of playing cards one evening at Bill and Susan's.

"Texas Hold 'em, Regina. Even though it's obvious that Texas just plumb ain't your style," he added, falling back on his southwest Texas lingo to irritate her further.

"You're rootin' tootin' shootin', cowboy—count me in. Meet you there." *Click.*

And she fit right in. Maybe because Susan was a close friend . . . or maybe because Bill and Susan Herndon liked seeing them together. Either way, when they greeted her with hugs at the door of their small apartment, she was affable and at ease, even bestowing him with a lighthearted kiss. Though a quick one, to be sure.

Her smile as sparkling as a West Texas sunrise, she pulled up and straddled a chair backward at the second-hand table. "What're the stakes?" She wore pink pedal pushers with some kind of sleeveless pink top knotted at her waist.

A jackass might as well have kicked him in the forehead.

Susan returned from the postage stamp size kitchen with a tray of nuts and beers. Bill took a bottle and grinned. "We're broke sons-of-bitches, Regina. It's penny-ante poker here."

Jack grabbed a handful of cashews. This was going to be good, watching her sink like lead.

"In that case, at the end of the evening, if I win, I brand the Jack of Hearts here," Regina told the couple and nodded at him. "An engagement ring from Tiffany's would do nicely."

Jack coughed and almost choked on the nuts. She had gone from zero interest to marriage quicker than the countdown to blast off. "Uh, I'm a go-it-alone kind of guy."

"I thought your kind was a risk taker."

He cleared his throat. "And if I win?"

She shrugged and flashed him another pretty smile. "You won't. But should my calculations go terribly awry and you win, then I'll give you a blow job."

Bill slapped his knee. "Hot damn, if that don't beat all."

Jack could only stare. He had yet to get anywhere near her pretty pouty lips, and she was staking an engagement ring on a blow job? Hell, he could always get out of an engagement.

"And if I should win," Susan smiled as she slid into her chair, "you three clean up the place at the end of the evening."

"I win," Bill said. "You three wash my Beetle."

"Done deal," Jack agreed.

The gambit took three hours to finalize. Bill and Sue had long since surrendered their chips. Susan sat with her gaze ricocheting between Jack and Regina. Bill, standing behind Susan, his hands on her shoulders, stifled a yawn. "You don't think you two could take up this battle in bed, do you?"

"Hell, no," Susan said, "I want them to help you clean up this joint."

"Read 'em and weep," Jack told Regina, fanning his cards on the table with a sweep of his hand. He had beat her two pair, aces and kings, with three deuces.

He reached across the table to collect her remaining chips and her palm slammed over his. "Not so fast, cowboy."

Hand still anchored by hers, he raked a brow. "You a sore loser, Regina?" Nothing could have pleased him better at that moment.

"High card draw. You win, I sign over the title to my 25,000 acres of Rancho del Sol. I win, I win your name in marriage—after a suitable engagement, of course."

Both Susan and Bill stared with open mouths.

"Why do you want me so badly?" he asked, suspicion needling his gut. While Regina sorely tempted him to ride the trail for a while with just one woman, he was not ready to settle down. Nope, in high school he had come perilously close to forfeiting his heart's dream.

Regina didn't flinch with her reply. "I could say it's because you're the one and only thing I want. However, that's not the full truth. Another part of that truth . . . ."

She paused, grimaced, looked down at the spread of cards, and then back to him. "I'm falling hard for you, Jack Paladín. But I'm a smart cookie. I know you'd never willingly commit long term. You love the wide-open skies too much. Still, I'm willing to risk that you will fall hard for me, too. Enough to commit." She tapped the table. "There, I've played all my cards. This is it. Take my offer or hit the road, Jack."

Recognizing her courage in the face of her enormous pride . . . it was the closest he had ever been to feeling an affinity for her or any woman, other than his mom and sister. "Sorry," he said, shaking loose her hand, "I am not up for grabs, and . . . well, I think I'll just blow off your blow job I won."

## SAN ANTONIO
## SEPTEMBER 1959

"All you need is a moonshine distillery," Noel said, swatting away a nettled yellow jacket, "and I'd quit my job at The Barony in an instant and hire on as Lavender Hill Vineyards' resident grape picker."

"And resident wino," Heidi teased. She was balanced on a step ladder in order to reach far behind the latticed vines to pick the berries. She held her garden clippers in one hand and a cluster of rich, blue-purple grapes in the other.

Her rebellious, red-gold hair was restrained in its customary single braid, yet damp ringlets managed to escape and plaster themselves to her temples and at her nape. Wearing rolled-to-the-calf jeans and a man's denim shirt, she reeked, nonetheless, of earthy sensuality. Twilight with its autumnal haze suffused her with an ethereal titian light.

He should have been tracking a gang of cattle rustlers using eighteen-wheelers. He should have been worrying about how to clear away sagebrush encroaching on The Barony's *hacienda*. Or he should have been puzzling how The Barony had gone from one ranch to four to a parcel of dozens under The Barony's new CEO. The old Baron would never have approved of divvying up the land grant.

It was troubling.

Noel was not a fan of Melvin Knopf, although under his stewardship, he had managed to increase The Barony's bottom line five-fold through his compartmentalizing concept.

Noel needed to get away from its operations, and Aunt Hannah and Jakob's Lavender Hill Vineyards needed all hands possible for its harvest time—and the mindless work of grape picking was both satisfying and distracting for him.

Surely this was a bit of Tuscany here in Texas hill country. Adjacent lavender fields were in unseasonable full bloom and flooded the senses with their sweet, exotic smell. The wine was the same, reflecting the terroir—fruity, with peach and apricot flavors and refreshing in a way that Texas wine should be on a Texas summer day.

However, the best time for grape harvest was late in September, in the cooler hours of the evening and night. Still, that evening it was hot enough that he had shed his shirt.

Among the rows of trellising, other volunteers also labored. Fiona and Steven, in addition to friends of the family, collected the grapes in blue bins that weighed fifty pounds when filled. Maybe that was what kept Heidi's body looking so sleek.

Once the grapes were sorted and tumbled into crushing tubs, the volunteers' work was finished. Beyond, on the hill's crest, the one-hundred-year-old renovated limestone house promised the workers rest and libation on its colonnaded porch.

Jakob and Aunt Hannah had intentionally designed Lavender Hill Vineyards as a small scale operation, with most of its harvest sold to other customers. Jakob and Aunt Hannah concentrated on the plump Spatburgunder grapes, keeping only enough to fill the oak barrels for local sale and consumption.

"Hey, Noel."

He looked around just in time to see Heidi, a dozen yards away, pelt him with a grape cluster. His gaze dropped to take in his sun-browned chest, its dark hair now clotted with purple must.

He scooped from his bin a handful of grapes. As his long legs ate up the space between him and Heidi, her eyes widened. His arm imprisoned her waist. His free hand squeezed the grapes, dribbling juice over her face.

"No, no, help! Help!" She tried to twist from his grip, but she was laughing. Her head turned up, her mouth open like a baby bird's to partake of the sugary sustenance dripping over her.

Watching her tongue steal out to swipe at the sticky juice bluing her lips, he began laughing, too. They used to laugh like this as kids, but somehow time and distance had seemed to dampen their friendship. For him, something further was imprinting on it. And in that moment, he realized what it was—he was looking at her not only as a friend, but as a highly desirable woman.

His gaze dropped from her juice-coated chin to her right shoulder, below which the overly large denim shirt had slipped. A blood-red tattoo was inscribed into the soft curve of her shoulder. He had never encountered a female with a tattoo and was a little shocked—but he was even more shocked as his gaze took in the single word inked into her flesh—*Noel.*

Suddenly, she stilled.

He looked from his name branded on her shoulder to her eyes, sparkling like blue diamonds.

"I never expected anyone to . . . ." Her whisper died away.

The primeval smell of damp, fertile earth filled his nostrils. Dusk with its accompanying silence abruptly surrendered to the celestial star-lit night. Around them, crickets clicked like castanets. Lanterns flickered on. Distant voices could be heard murmuring from here and there among the vineyard rows. And all he could think to say was, "It must have hurt . . . the tattoo."

She managed a shrug. "I did it on a whim." Her voice held a defiant tone.

He nodded but had yet to release his grip. He was trying to find his bearing here. "You're quite the bohemian, aren't you?" He nodded at her bare shoulder. "What's a bohemian called these days? A beatnik?"

At that, she smiled and tugged loose from his grip to pull her shirt up over her shoulder. "How about *avant-garde?* And before you get the big head, Noel means Christmas in French."

"And you have Christmas tattooed on your arm because . . . ?"

Her blue-burnished lips cinched. "Because I like the magic of Christmas, smarty pants."

He didn't believe her, at least about the name source for the tattoo, but he said nothing, only jammed his hands in his pockets so they would not be tempted by her earthy siren's call.

He had never noticed it before, how this, this *fascination* he had for her—how it was like the grape picking itself, both satisfying and distracting at the same time.

He shambled back to the berm and his grape picking, as did she, but something had shifted. Permanently. And he didn't know what the hell to do about it. Or if he even wanted to do anything about it.

He dated around here and there—had had a couple of long-term relationships, if you counted six months or so long-term. Most of them from the international horsey set. Deauville, London, Palm Beach, Riyadh. He also dated friends of the family—a young waitress working her way through UT. An Aspen ski instructor. A Ballet Folklorico dancer. An assistant editor at *The Cattleman* magazine.

And yes, there was that one scorching afternoon

sporting with Paola in the water tank.

But Heidi . . . well, hell, all those summers and holidays she spent in the states, they had played together from corrals to tennis courts. He could remember her first summer's barrel racing contest—and giving her the going-away gift of a box of fancy personalized stationery when she went off to that art college in Paris. So they could keep in touch.

They hadn't.

Maybe because they had not needed to. They knew each other better than they knew the lines in their palms. Or so he thought.

Uneasily, he finished grape picking an hour so before dawn and went to shower before joining the rest of the family and friends on the flagstone porch that overlooked the vineyards and neighboring lavender fields.

A half dozen loyal friends of the Nobels were also straggling out onto the stone-arched portico. Fiona and Steven had yet to make an appearance, and Noel could well imagine what delayed the two lovers.

As the sun began to peek over the hills, mimosas and coffee were served. He poured a tin cup and settled into one comfortable pigskin chair. The early morning vegetation smelled fresh, cleansed of the prior day's striving. Usually, at the end of a night of grape harvesting, he would feel relaxation seep into him, but the newfound tension between him and his supposed close friend plagued him.

To one side of him, Aunt Hannah and Uncle Jakob sat in a porch swing, and on his other, Heidi reclined on the chaise longue. At the far end of the serving table, a few other friends had joined the party but were not sitting close enough to eavesdrop on the conversation which concerned changes at The Barony.

"We hear Knopf is doing great things," Aunt Hannah said to him. Nearing sixty, she had let her shoulder-length hair go completely gray. It was striking in contrast to her dark brown eyes and brows and still youthful skin. Her palms cupped her ceramic cup, and, as always, he was thrown off balance at the sight of her nail-less forefingers.

"I don't know." He took a sip of the aromatic coffee while he stalled. He didn't like bad-mouthing anyone. "No one can criticize his efficiency. Our pre-tax profits have tripled. Our debt has disappeared. We have a whopping amount in cash and even more invested in securities."

Uncle Jakob leaned forward, his muscular forearms braced on his knees, his mimosa flute fragile between his cigar-size fingers. His silver hair was buzzed in a military haircut that emphasized the sharp lines of his Slavic cheekbones. "I hear a 'but,' Noel." After all these years, his voice still rasped with his heavy guttural German accent.

Noel shrugged. "Knopf spends most of his time at our San Antonio office." He shook his head and grunted. "I just don't like being kept in the dark like a mushroom and being fed bullshit. Pardon my language, Aunt Hannah . . . Heidi."

At that moment, Fiona, her dark hair tousled, showed up with Steven close behind. Flute in hand, she took up the chair next to Heidi. "Speaking of bull, y'all, I trust Knopf about as far as I can throw a bull. And you know, even at our rodeos, our Paladíñeros can't throw a bull more than a few feet."

Noel noticed that only Heidi had kept her gaze fastened on the rising sun, now painting the hills with glittering gold opulence. As if, after all these years, she was suddenly shy in his presence. Without looking at him, she asked, "What do you think he could possibly be hiding?"

And now he could not take his eyes off her. "I don't know, but I am thinking about doing some serious sleuthing."

And perhaps spending serious time with Heidi. But, then again, maybe not. She was the antithesis of what The Barony was about. She, a vegetarian, when it was about beef. She, an activist, when it was about military aviation. She, a German, when it was about Texas. No, best he turned his attention to the home-grown beauties.

## MERRITT ISLAND, FLORIDA
## MARCH 1960

"COME ON," SUSAN CAJOLED. "Give the guy another chance. It's just a clambake for God's sake." She turned her beat-to-shit Studebaker off onto the beach front road. "It's not like you're stuck on a deserted island with Jack. There'll be several other couples from the base there."

"Yeah," Regina muttered, "but they're partnered up already." What could she and Jack Paladín possibly have to say to one another? "Jack *does* know I'm coming, right?"

The windows were down, and Susan tugged loose from her neck a swatch of hair whipped from her topknot. "Of course."

The way Susan's mouth twitched told Regina that he was probably none too thrilled with this setup either. "This is your chance to show him you're over him."

"Yeah." Through salt-sprayed sunglasses, she watched out the cracked windshield as the sea breeze slithered sand across the pitted pavement. Dear Jesus, why was she submitting herself to another put down by Jack.

Six months of self-prescribed therapy—shopping, traveling, spas—had worked their magic, restoring her wounded ego. She thought she was an expert on the male sex. Then she found out she had been wrong the whole time. There were men out there like Paladín who could easily trample her heart.

Susan parked on the edge of the road, lined with other old cars, and pushed her sunglasses atop her head. "Look, you two have off-the-charts chemistry. And you have common values and interests. Anything worthwhile is worth—"

"Worth fighting for. I know." But fighting seemed to be what they both did best. Could someone as iron-willed as Jack love just as strongly?

She spotted him among a couple of men digging a hole in the sand. He was shirtless, and the muscles beneath his sun-browned shoulders shifted with each shovel-load he hefted. Beyond, some barefoot guys and gals were playing volleyball. Others were still wading in the bay's shallows with their buckets and digging for clams.

She sighed. "Let's get this over with."

She and Susan got out and hefted the two picnic baskets from the rear seat. Pasting a smile on her face, Regina set off toward the revelers, her sandals digging into the warm sand with each determined step she took.

Drawing closer, she could hear his deep voice, " . . . basic chores like washing my underwear and cleaning a commode, Bruce, but that's my limit when it comes to domestics."

"Nothing more than any self-respecting man should be capable of," she said, coming up behind to join them. She flashed him a cool smile while her pulse hammered in the hollow at her throat. "Good to see you again, Jack."

He tossed back a low-key smile. "Same here." His eyes raked over her casually, taking in her jean cutoffs and length of bare legs, returning to meet her defensive stare. "How have you been?"

"Busy, you?"

"The same."

Bill, his pants' cuffs rolled up to reveal heavy and hairy calves, rescued the stilted conversation. "Regina, this here is Bruce Atkins." He gestured toward a stubby young man who bobbed his head enthusiastically. "And the guy over there piling up stones is Wayne. Hey, Wayne, say hi to Regina."

Wayne, his nose and cheeks slathered with zinc paste, waved, and she returned his wave with a much friendlier smile than she had allotted Jack.

Susan nudged her arm. "Looks like Debs and Bunny

could use our help." With a flick of her hand, she indicated two young women in Bermuda shorts sitting on overturned buckets in the lee of a dune. They were chopping vegetables into paint cans. "You can wield a paring knife? Right?"

She grinned. "Does Jayne Mansfield sleep on her back?"

Chuckling, Sue drew her over and made the introductions. The young woman in a beat-up safari hat, Bunny, grinned and nodded toward a cluster of empty paint cans. "Have at it."

Debs paused to give a jaunty smile and salute with her knife, but Regina did not miss her speculative look.

Using their picnic baskets as seats, she and Susan fell into easy conversation with the other two while they filled their cleaned cans with potatoes, onions, tomatoes, and assorted herbs and spices. When Regina realized her paint can was meant to be shared with Jack, she was tempted to dribble sand in it and forego the vegetables.

Debs shredded some parsley into her can. "So how long have you and Jack been an item?"

The question, coming so casually, caught her off guard. Susan saved her. "Jack and Regina were members of our wedding party."

While the clams and cans cooked over the hot rocks and seaweed, people began drifting toward the game in play at the volleyball net. Feeling totally out of place, Regina trailed the base wives across the sand. Where was Jack? Her gaze darted among the players, then searched among the figures wading in the surf and was relieved to spot him and Bill sitting on ice chests placed strategically to catch the breeze rippling the water. They appeared to be laughing.

She plowed on through the grainy sand. What, three or four more hours of easy socializing? Or, at least, acting like it was easy. Then she'd be scot-free.

But, of course. Jack was not the kind to play it safe. From the corner of her eyes, she saw him snag two beers from the ice chest and stride toward her. The breeze riffled up his short, dense hair, and the setting sun's light gilded his bare chest.

Her palm found her own chest, as if to still her thundering heart. No use running like a rabbit. She muttered a quick, "I can do this. Be the bigger person," and paused to wait for him.

He passed her a bottle. "Not Lone Star, but it'll do in a pinch." He did not even bother with one of his engaging smiles.

Wordlessly, she accepted the bottle and a took a fortifying swig, grateful for something to fill the void and grateful for the chilled brew easing her suddenly dry throat.

He cupped her elbow, steering her away from the group. She fell into step with him. Circumventing a bend of the beach's tall, marshy reeds, they left the romping and shouting behind. The silence between them grew intolerably heavy. She was tempted to prattle like some giddy middle-school girl and bit hard into her lip. She felt just as awkward. Her salt-dusted skin turned clammy. This was a huge mistake.

As they approached a large piece of charred driftwood, he turned to her, taking her bottle to set it alongside his on the log. His dark gaze, very serious, was gauging her features, ranging from her eyes to her mouth and back. "Either we have everything to say to one another—or nothing."

Why deny it? It was a losing battle, controlling her push-and-pull attraction to him. Not when his very nearness wreaked havoc with logic, not to mention most likely sizzling her skin worse than any sunburn she could recall. She just wanted to be with him, whatever the means.

Her smile had to be as radiant as the sunset. She stood on tiptoe and, wrapping her arms around his muscled neck lifted her lips to his. "Later. We have a lot to say. We can talk later all you want."

## SAN ANTONIO
## MARCH 1960

THE SAN ANTONIO LIVESTOCK Auction's pungent scent of hay mingled with dust and manure assailed Heidi's nostrils, though after all the summers and holidays spent at The Barony, she should be familiar with those particular ranching odors.

And after all these years, she should be familiar with Noel. They had practically grown up together. But that familiarity had taken a turn at September's grape harvesting. She knew it, and he knew it.

Their altered relationship fared no better that Thanksgiving and Christmas at The Barony. Throughout those holidays, they moved amidst the family members, exchanged hugs, badinages, or reminiscences, pausing to snatch Mariana's homemade cookies or bottles of beer or flutes of champagne . . . and all the while, it felt as if they were joined by something unseen but as fragile and vital as an umbilical cord. Every so often, their gazes would intersect.

She suspected that, like herself, he was assessing, evaluating their feelings. Were they something as common and old as time? Did they merely have that inextinguishable desire to mate, the frenzied rutting that was careless about consequences?

Or could a future be created between them once lust was satisfied?

As pragmatic as Noel was, he had to be entertaining these questions. She might be the opposite of practical, but given her childhood, she figured caution should never be dismissed. So, she warily agreed to join that afternoon in his bid for a prize Brahma bull he wanted for The Barony.

Since it was a special sale, the auction barn was not crowded, and she sat on the lower bleachers next to him, shoulder to shoulder, absorbing the warmth his powerful frame emitted. When a handsome man in a tux and bowtie could turn her eye at the snap of a finger, how could Noel with his strong but not necessarily handsome features—and in jeans and boots— make her knees go weak?

One by one, livestock was paraded into the arena. The auctioneer talked in a rapid-fire way that could have been Mandarin for all she knew. Off and on, other ranchers shot up signs in bidding. Noel sat easily.

Every once in a while, he would lean close to tell her the qualities to watch for. "That calf there, with the patches missing from its hide—could be a sign of an underlying health issue."

But she was not watching the calf. She was watching Noel's mobile mouth and inhaling his masculine scent.

But then came a magnificent, snorting black bull. The way Noel's muscular frame went on full-scale alert, she knew this was the one he wanted. He knew his mind.

A helper shouted, "Yep!" A numbered sign flagged the air. The auctioneer rattled off another string of nonsensical words. Rather than use a sign, Noel only made a hand signal. Then another sign jutted up. A couple of times more, Noel signaled. And then, almost before it started, it was over.

He turned to her, his sexy mouth hitched in a one-sided grin. "We won."

They drove around in his pickup with its stock trailer to wait with other winners in the loading chute area. Sitting on the far side of the bench seat, next to the window, she glanced over at him. "How long will it take?"

His Stetson shaded his features. He shrugged. "Thirty, forty-five minutes, I reckon." He turned his direct gaze on her. The cab's confinement was electrical with his animal heat. "You got anywhere you need to be?"

"No." He was watching her mouth, and she found it disconcerting. She swallowed. "Nowhere else I'd rather be."

"Good, because there's no use beating around the bush and no better time than now. I've made up my mind, Heidi." He reached over and, lapping a broad hand around her nape, drew her across the worn vinyl upholstery to him. His mouth brushed her lids, tipped her nose, then moved to graze across her lips. His whisper was husky, raw. "How about you?"

For answer, she grinned and tugged off his hat, tossing it onto the vacated seat next to her.

He did not give her a chance to change her mind. His mouth slanted down over hers, one hand digging into her hair, holding her fast. "Oh God, Heidi . . . you've driven me plumb insane."

Her moan echoed his in intensity, and, within minutes, they flattened his Stetson.

## SAN ANTONIO
## APRIL 1960

Surely, it was a sacrilege, surely—shagging in a convent. Well, a two-hundred-and-fifty-year-old convent converted to a high-end hotel.

Consummation of that wild passion that Dr. Bridget Malone could arouse in Julian, even after almost four years of dating, would surely be more closely associated to lovemaking than shagging.

In fact, it was damned close to a spiritual experience, as he made love to her on practically every square inch of their River Walk lodging that weekend—discounting the ceiling.

They had just attended the world premiere of John Wayne's *The Alamo,* which had been filmed outside San Antonio, but they had barely made it to the hotel before they were stripping each other's clothes.

He toed off his shoes, slung off his black bowtie, slid out of his white mess jacket and shirt, and shucked his trousers. She tore down his briefs and then rucked her dress over her head as he wrangled her bra off her breasts and nearly ripped

233

her panties off. He broke out the condoms and she, in her haste, sent her cat-eyed glasses sailing. They skittered across their target of the bathroom counter and plunked into the commode.

They both erupted into laughter that immediately returned to lust. They now lay entangled in the bedclothing. She snuggled in the crook of his arm, one bare leg lapped over his thigh. Her fingers were tunneling through the sweat-dampened, dark red hair carpeting his chest.

He captured her hand. "I'm starving, kiddo. Let's get something to eat. Enchiladas at Mi Tierra?"

"No, please." Worry laced her usually crisp in-charge voice. "There is so little time left."

"There's plenty of time, Doc." He glanced at his Timex. "A good seventeen hours left to us."

Unless there was something else she wanted to include in this romantic rendezvous. Like talk of marriage? Like a wedding at the Alamo?

She had more than once accused him of being emotionally unable or unwilling to meet her on the deepest level of a relationship. But that meant surrender of the self, according to her, and, hell, he wouldn't run up the white flag until his dying breath.

Besides, on one of their leaves together, he and she had deadheaded on a military transport bound for D.C., and he had taken her to meet Sam and Gabby, who had started steadily dating, at a quaint little restaurant there. Did not that count for something, meeting family?

He and Bridget both possessed physically and mentally

challenging careers that demanded their total focus. Stressful lives that allowed not even marginal room for errors. Marriage had never been even alluded to, if for no other reason than under military law, such a marriage would make her ineligible to remain in uniform, and he knew how much she enjoyed and valued her job.

True, he loved all the little things about Bridget—the way she walked, her refreshing manner of speech, the way she surreptitiously winked at him over her cat-eyed glasses, her moxie. There was no other female he wanted to spend his free time with.

It was just he had so little free time. And, as she had told him, in an all too short seventeen hours, their idyllic interlude would end.

And his Top Secret mission would begin. Of course, it was general knowledge that America's U2s did flyovers of adversaries' territories. But this next mission was to be an extraordinary intelligence operation on his part. The CIA wanted a covert aerial reconnaissance over the USSR.

At all costs, Julian was to avoid being caught because that would not only jeopardize the Paris Summit, but it could also cause the Cold War to escalate to a substantially more dangerous level. To that end, he was to carry in the outer pocket of his full body pressure suit a suicide pill. Actually, it was a silver dollar coin with shellfish toxin embedded in its grooves, should he need it.

"It's just . . . " Bridget murmured, her voice raw with unshed tears. "What if . . . what if something should happen, something—"

Why was she so worried about this particular flight, after all the ones he had made? Did she know—sense—something he did not?

Her lips trembled, and she whispered in a shaky voice their recital to one another from the children's prayer, reinterpreted . . .the line about when she went to sleep and his love she prayed to keep.

He kissed first one damp eyelid, then the other, finishing his line, his own voice raspy, " . . . should die before I wake . . . I'll return to you, never mistake."

Her mouth found his, and his arm tightened around her, tugging her lithe body halfway beneath his. "I think the enchiladas can wait."

But, all too soon, Uncle Sam had Julian winging 35,000 feet altitude from home base in San Antonio to a U.S. base in northern Pakistan. Then, with eight hours sleep behind him and a high-protein breakfast of steak and eggs, he was once again airborne, this time 70,000 feet above central Russia.

As the Soviets had no idea of his covert mission, and MiGs and SAMs could not fly that high, he felt relatively safe, barring a slipup of his own making. But he was both competent and confident, so he settled back into his ejection seat as comfortably as he could get, considering he exceeded the maximum sitting height, and his legs were far too long.

All in all, though, the flight was running smoothly . . . until that first surface-to-air missile exploded some distance below him. Its blast wave bounced his spy plane around like a Mexican jumping bean, which caused his heart to do the same.

What the hell was going on?

The following missile exploded just off to his left. His plane had reached the coffin corner, the narrow margin between the Critical Mach Number and the Stall Speed. Shockwaves hit the plane, and the U2's instrument panel stopped responding.

God awlmighty! Instantly, an image assailed him—his mother, collapsed against his father, black powder rimming the hole in her forehead. He knew his own death was imminent.

His plane was out of control, nose pointed to the sky and spinning violently in a downward spiral. Next, his tail section was ripped off. Then the wings peeled away. He was breathless, and his ears buzzed.

He was slammed forward against the instrument panel. His helmet's face shield cracked. Automatically, he went into survival mode. Yelling out the legendary Texican battle cry, he groped for the yellow ejection handle between his legs and yanked.

Shit!

One of two oxygen hoses popped loose and was cracking like a whip. Its metal connector crashed into his helmet. Frigid air blasted his face. His heart leaped to his throat, choking off his involuntary cry.

Before he lost consciousness high above the Russian steppes, the thought flashed through his brain—someone had alerted the Russkies!

And then the next thought, quickly fading with his fading

consciousness . . . Bridget. Behind his lids, he saw, oddly, her honeyed hair fanned out on a pillow, her lips moist, her pelvis raised to meet his in that lifegiving way of hers.

He should have crossed that line in the sand and begged her to marry him, there at the Alamo.

## LOS ANGELES
## JULY 1960

"SECOND ON THE BALLOT to that fucker Carnegie?"

Calmly, Gabby watched her father slam a fist through the wall of their Biltmore hotel suite, where the Democratic National Convention was being held. She knew his anger could be volcanic but usually subsided quickly.

"Now, darling," her mother said from the tufted sofa where she sat knitting, an outlet for her in times of stress. "You'll find a way to turn this to your advantage." Her needles clicked in and out of the yarn again before she added, "You always do."

"Actually," Sam said, hands on his hips as he turned from the television screen newsfeed, "this could work out much better even than you anticipated."

Rubbing his scuffed knuckles, her father snapped. "How the hell do you figure that?"

Sam took a seat in the overstuffed beige chair and, hands clasped between his knees, leaned forward, his tone earnest. "If the Carnegie team is smart, and they are, they'll offer you the position as running mate so they can remove the threat you offer as Senate Majority Leader."

Gabby crossed the plush carpet to settle on Sam's chair arm. "Sam's right, Dad. By accepting an offer as running mate, you could better your political career and be in a better position to become president with the next election."

She draped an arm across his broad shoulders, feeling their tense muscles bunching. They were rock hard. Fitting, seeing as how he had been her rock since they had started dating.

It was Sam who had encouraged her to pursue her neglected interest in humanitarian organizations like EIL and UNICEF.

It was Sam who gave her room to vent when the dutiful daughter role became too much.

It was Sam who remembered her birthday when her parents had not and had surprised her with a romantic picnic on The Barony's bank of the Nueces.

He surprised her now. "Garner, I want to marry your daughter. I love her more than I thought I could ever love anyone or anything." His smile was a half jest. "Including The Barony." He glanced at her searchingly, and for once, he looked a little unsure of himself. He clasped her hand laying in her lap. "That is, Gabby, if you're up to taking on another politician in your life."

Her eyes went damp. Her hand squeezed his. All through their dating, though they had been intimate, though she had given herself to him without any expectations, and though he had told her he loved her and shown it over and over, she had feared the Paladín independent streak ran too strong in him to commit. Her joy spilled over tremulous lips. "You've got my vote."

Her father gave a clap of his large hands, his anger at once dissipated. "Great running mates—Bradford and Paladín."

"Soon to be Paladín and Paladín," Sam shot back.

## WASHINGTON, D.C.
## AUGUST 1960

THE PHONE'S SHRILL RING JERKED Sam from a deep sleep. Disoriented, it took him precious seconds to glance at the room's only source of light, his alarm clock— two thirty-six a.m.—and then to react and grapple for the phone.

"Paladín here," he rusked, half expecting to find Garner on the other end of the line, as always demanding prompt service twenty-four hours a day.

"Sam, it's Bridget."

He could hear the tears in her voice. Not surprising. Since Julian went missing in action last month, presumably dead, his entire family had been stunned. He himself had been desolate. His whole life was peppered with cherished memories of his cousin, who was more like a brother. Even the small release of heartbreak that could come with mourning was denied by the government's hush-hush policy.

When Khrushchev released to the world that an

American spy plane had been shot down in Soviet territory, the Air Force assumed their pilot had died. Few survived ejection from a U2, much less one being shot out of the sky.

Immediately, to avoid jeopardizing the all-important upcoming Summit meeting in Paris, the U.S. had concocted a cover story that the crashed plane was a weather research aircraft, not a spy plane, and that the pilot had radioed in that he was experiencing oxygen difficulties while flying over Turkey—that the plane could have continued off its path, despite auto-pilot.

Understandably, Bridget had refused to accept it—and so had the Paladíns. The family leapt into coordinated action—badgering government and military officials for further information, calling one another daily to report any gleaned data, checking in with Bridget, supporting her in her darker moments, when even they held little hope. She fiercely continued to persist in her own behind-the-scenes efforts.

She hiccoughed. "You told me to call you first if I heard anything."

He propped up to a slumped position on the side of his bed and shoved back the haystack of burnt-black hair from his forehead. "Yeah. Yes, yes?"

"I'm sorry it's so late. I'm here at the airport."

"You're here? In D.C.?"

"I co-opted a flight from Randolph Air Base." He heard her sniffling. "Look, earlier tonight, I was opening a pile of condolence notes that had been piling up. But this envelope I opened, well it's—"

His spine jerked upright. His brain fought free from sleep

paralysis to focus sharply.

"Listen, Bridget, you know the restaurant where you and Julian lunched with me and Gabby? That first time he brought you to introduce you to us? Meet me there at noon—and say nothing to anyone. About the envelope or our meeting."

It was not that he didn't trust certain people in the government. He did not trust anyone in the government. His few brief years in politics so far had crushed his idealism and, in its place, had installed cynical caution that bordered on caustic.

He questioned whether he should go through with this gut feeling and run for Congress. His gut feeling insisted there was some greater purpose for mankind than mere existence. But how could he hope to serve constituents when so many compromises were demanded? When there existed that fine shading between compromise and circumventing?

At half past eleven that morning, he drove aimlessly for half an hour, just in case, before he crossed the Potomac River into Washington, D.C., and entered Chadwick's, a popular Georgetown restaurant.

Dr. Bridget Malone hailed him from her corner booth. She was dressed in Air Force blues with a beret angled low. Her hands were knotted before her on the damask-covered table.

He leaned over and pecked her on her cheek. His gaze took in her nails, bitten to the quick. However, behind her cat-eye glasses, her haunted and hollow eyes glimmered with excitement.

"Sam, he's alive. Julian!"

His pulse leaped. "What? How do you know this?"

"I received a letter with a Havana postmark," she said in a hushed voice. He nodded. The Cuban capital was a hornet's nest of international spies and a foothold for Russian military.

"No return address. But—" She broke off at the approach of a waiter in black tie and apron.

"Two iced teas for now. We'll order later." Hands clasped, elbows on the table, he leaned forward and nodded for her to go ahead.

"But inside was just one sentence—and no mention of a name."

"Then what makes you think—"

"Because of what it said."

His brows knit. "What?"

The starchy young woman actually blushed. "Silly, I know. But it was a line from the children's prayer. You know, the one that goes 'Now I lay me down to sleep?'"

With a nod, he canted his head, puzzled. "Yeah?"

"Julian and I had our own version. That was my part." She reached into her purse and passed him a wrinkled envelope. "Read the sentence. That was his part."

He extracted the page. His eyes skimmed the line and reread the last words again, ' . . . die before I awake, I'll return for you, never mistake."

"That was my and Julian's love code. No one knew this but him!"

Both elation and spine-tingling dread jockeyed for first

place in his racing brain. Khrushchev could be laying a political trap for Eisenhower—by announcing that the U2 spy pilot was alive and well in one of their prisons. Maybe not so well but alive, at least.

Her eyes darkened to bleak, bottomless pools. She uttered his fear. "I've heard about their prisons."

He covered her cold palm with his. "I'll bring him back to you."

In what seemed a protective gesture, her palm dropped to her jacket's brass button at her waist. "To me—and our child I'm carrying."

## VLADIMIR, UNION OF SOVIET SOCIALIST REPUBLICS
## OCTOBER 1960

VLADIMIR PRISON, BUILT IN 1789, resembled a medieval bastion. Inside, medieval torture went on methodically. Repeatedly, by rote, Julian gave his name, rank, service number, and date of birth, all of which was readily available on his dogtags.

He knew the code of the United States Fighting Force— to evade answering further questions to the utmost of his ability, to make no oral or written statements disloyal to his country or harmful to its cause, and, most importantly, to never forget that he was an American, fighting for freedom, responsible for his actions, and dedicated to the principles which made his country free and to trust in his God and in the United States of America.

But those responses were not what his torturers wanted.

What his torturers wanted, other than classified information, was what amounted to a pathological desire to control the minds of U.S. prisoners. They were not hesitant to use gruesome torture as tools in their efforts to exploit U.S. prisoners into making public statements that appeared favorable to the communist Cold War effort.

Lack of food, sleep deprivation, absence of medical aid, and subhuman treatment became a daily way of life for him. His training had not prepared him for this new battlefield.

But just as his Texican forebears had fought at the Alamo and San Jacinto, regardless of the outcome, so did he—despite the fact that his naked body, with multiple breaks from the U2's ejection, was suspended by his wrists iron from a chain hooked to the high ceiling of one of the interrogation rooms and his ankles anchored to the cleats in its cement floor.

Ice water was dashed in his face. His tongue flicked thirstily at the water droplets. Between water-spiked lashes, he blinked at the bright spotlight. Behind it, cameras were rolling. From what he could piece together, it had to be around late evening.

Back in the States, it would be early morning. What would Bridget be doing? Groping for her eyeglasses she invariably misplaced? He was afraid and lonely and exhaust-ted beyond endurance, but fastening his thoughts on her kept them from straying into dangerous territory that could weaken his resolve.

"I will ask you again. Did you have crypto clearance?"

"I am a Paladín." Now where did that come from? He was losing it. He tried again. "My name is First Lieutenant Julian—"

His interrogator backhanded him violently, slapping his face so hard to one side, his neck popped and blood splattered from a displaced tooth. The Husky Russkie, as Julian mentally referred to him, was furious with Julian's terse replies after this first week of torture.

But this . . . this coming torture warranted from Julian a valor he feared he did not possess.

While three other comrades looked on, Husky Russkie circled him, knife in hand. "I have given you every opportunity to cooperate," the burly blond purred. He paused directly in front of Julian. "This is your last chance to confess that you have committed a grave crime."

Shit, was Husky Russkie going to castrate him?

"Did you have fucking crypto clearance?"

Julian managed to spit bloody saliva at the hulking man's boxy face.

The man's free hand wiped away the spittle, then shot out to knuckle Julian's buzz cut, yanking his head backward. "A pilot without eyesight . . . well, cannot fly, *nyet?*"

He pressed the knife point just below the lower lid of Julian's right eye. He felt the knife slit through the thin flesh at the socket's rim. Involuntarily, his head jerked, his body torqued, and a loud guttural noise rolled up from between his clenched teeth.

At that moment, the siren's wail warned of lights out and bedtime, but to Julian the wail was more like that of the fabled banshees. Unbearable pain ripped through him—along with the stark realization that his eye socket had been gutted. He knew what that indicated about forthcoming torture.

He let his head hang down, desperately attempting to hold on to the Paladín bravado.

# WASHINGTON, D.C.
# NOVEMBER 1960

That evening was the first ever televised election debate, and, like the rest of the nation, Fiona and Steven watched it from the comfort of the cozy chintz sofa in Steven's colonial revival estate along Georgetown's Rock Creek waterfront. The den was well appointed but as rumpled as the suits he wore.

"Carnegie's wily. With that full head of hair, his telegenic youthful good looks will win him the election."

"But Ellwood is much better qualified," she protested. "He's a seasoned lawmaker and the Vice President."

Steven's fingertips graze-stroked the curve of her shoulder. "But look how Carnegie plays to the television camera, not to the reporters."

Steven had that delicious habit of touching her, even just in passing, letting her know he forever found her desirable, even after a year of being lovers. Lovers but not man and wife. She suspected Steven saw himself as a one-husband-forever type of man. And even that role had ended with the death of both wife and baby.

Come Thanksgiving weekend, The Barony would be celebrating another wedding—and it would not be Fiona's.

"Well, Ellwood has been ill and lost a lot of weight," she countered. Indeed, his suit hung on him like cast-offs on a scarecrow. "But given the Vice President's vast experience . . . well, that should give him the edge. His responses are much more informed."

After all, following an illustrious career in the Senate, Ellwood had spent nearly eight years as the country's second in command.

And now it looked like a very pissed off Garner Bryce Bradford might be playing the role of second-in-command under Marcus Carnegie. The two detested each other. However, Carnegie, with his upper-crust Northeastern speech, knew fully well he could not be elected without the support of traditional Southern Democrats, most of whom supported Garner. So Garner was going to have to settle for second best.

"On the radio, yes," Steven conceded. "The pundits will give the win to the incumbent Ellwood. But not on television. I predict it's going to be damn close, my love."

She looked up into his patrician-handsome profile, his horn-rimmed glasses illuminated by the television's glare. As always, she felt that thrill. Yes, something about him, something indefinable, pulled her like the moon pulled the tide.

"If the Democrats do carry the election, Steven, will you be concerned? I mean about keeping your job at the Library of Congress?"

His expanse of chest let out an almost inaudible sigh. "Technically, yes. The presiding president does select the Librarian of Congress and no term of office is specified. But the Senate still has the power to veto a president's nomination."

She was not that worried. If Carnegie won, Garner, running as his Vice Presidential candidate, would use his influence to keep things status quo—which had been anything but for Americans since the U2 spy affair and the consequential Summit Meeting crash.

For the Paladíns, it was much, much worse. Vladimir Central Prison, one-hundred miles north of Moscow, now housed one of theirs. Ten years of hard labor . . . that was a hell of a long time for an espionage conviction.

With elections coming up and Julian supposedly confessing to being a spy, though no proof had been put forth, Garner could not risk being involved. But she knew Sam was working behind the scenes to get Julian released.

"The staid Eisenhower years have been stagnant and reactionary," Carnegie was saying on the small television screen. "The Republicans have both lost Cuba and allowed the dangerous missile gap to develop. Why, the Russians have overtaken the United States in the building of missiles capable of delivering nuclear warheads. Tell me, is this the future you want for your children?"

She and Steven finished watching the debate, but Steven was not finished with her. In his bedroom, which she shared four or five nights a week, he was anything but the consummate Atticus Finch gentleman. Gentle, maybe—in one moment, but the next, he was ravishing her until the sheets were wringing wet.

"Ewww, we are *stinky*," she murmured afterward, naked in his embrace. His whispered words, each breathing a note of passion, stirred the sweat-dampened tendrils curling near her ear. "You can't even begin to imagine how stimulating I find our smell."

Yes, she could, if his arousal prodding her backside was any indication. Nevertheless, drained to limpness, she fell asleep instantly . . . only to be awakened in the middle of the night by a vague dream with a vivid, repeated word—*Russians.*

Finding herself drenched in sweat again, she partially propped up on one elbow. She nudged Steven's shoulder. He shrugged, rolled toward her and, still asleep, lapped one long arm around her, corralling her back into his embrace. "Steven," she mumbled into the matted hair of his chest. "I need to get up. We need to get up."

"Hmmmm. What?"

She pried herself a little away from his chest to better breathe. "I need you to take me to the Library of Congress."

This time he stirred sleepily awake. His dark hair tumbled across his forehead. "What? You're serious?"

She tugged away to sit fully up, the sheet clutched above her breasts. "Russians. That word kept recurring in a dream I just had."

One hand tunneled through the swath of hair, shoving it from his eyes. "Of course, it did. Senator Carnegie made the

Russians' technological advantage a major point in his TV speech."

Steven was right, but . . . .

"Listen, Steven, the majority of files my Aunt Aubrey checked out usually covered the Axis—Germany, Italy, Japan. But files on Russia were invariably among the others. Why? Russia was an ally in World War II."

He sighed and reached for his glasses. "And I don't guess this could keep until morning?"

An hour later found them rattling on the ultra-private subway coursing beneath Capitol Hill. They crossed the Archives' vast marbled entrance lobby to sign in with the night guard. Other yawning guards passed them through various checkpoints.

Dawn's light, creeping through the single high-set window in the Special Files room of the Intelligence Section, found her and Steven huddled in front of a microfilm monitor.

The Special Files department was an immense vault-like room where extensive dossiers were stored. Cabinet after cabinet contained highly classified reports, newspaper articles, lab results, photos—all on microfilm reels.

After sitting in the chilly room for a couple of hours in front of the monitor, her joints were getting numb. The sudden clacking of teleprinters signaled that office hours were beginning.

When she rubbed her hands together for warmth, Steven stood. "The cafeteria should be opening. Let me get you some hot coffee."

By the time he returned, her eyes were blurred, and her shoulders ached from hunching over the microfilm reader. She wrapped chilled fingers around the hot Styrofoam cup and scrolled another microfilm reel into view.

Her enthusiasm was dimming swiftly.

So, why that nagging tic at the back of her beleaguered brain?

And why had she wasted all her spare time all these years to try to find Aubrey's killer? There was more to it than Fiona loving a challenge. If the killer were still out there, he could kill again . . . maybe another Paladín.

"Fiona," Steven said, slipping an arm around her waist, "Give it up. It's been fifteen years since your aunt was murdered. Whoever did it, whomever she suspected as the mole, might be long dead by now."

She was cold and tired and irritated with his logic—and even more irritated with herself, with her crazy stubbornness. Nevertheless, she snapped, "Or the mole might be even more deeply entrenched in our government by now."

He pulled away slightly and lifted a derisive brow. "Well, by all means, let's start at the top then. With President Eisenhower."

"Don't patronize me, Steven Douglas!"

"Then don't act irrational." His fist thumped the desk. "What about the time you've wasted, time you could have spent on yourself instead of the damned Paladín clan, time we could have spent together." He drew a calming breath, then leaned toward her, his tone contrite. "Listen, I do realize—"

She slapped at the pacifying palm he held out—and gasped as her cup tipped and scorching coffee sloshed over both their laps.

Simultaneously, she and Steven jumped to their feet. His fuming gaze raked over first his stained pants, then her skirt.

Her gaze clashed with his and she saw that he, too, was recalling that same moment on the subway, when she had complained to him about spilling her coffee—and their first heated kiss that had followed.

She tried to steer away from that most memorable passionate moment. "Well, if you would for once—"

He grabbed her shoulders and arched her back over the desk. "You are damned dangerous with your coffee cups."

His kiss this time was nothing like Gregory Peck's gentlemanly role in Atticus Finch but more like his rogue's role as Lewt McCanles in *Duel in the Sun*. She could not decide which she reveled in best.

"And you are damned dangerous with your kisses," she gasped, grinning.

## THE BARONY
## NOVEMBER 1960

"ALL RIGHT, READY?" THE MINISTER'S heavily hipped wife asked and, without waiting for a response, ordered, "One, two, and three—and begin."

Mariana watched, as for the third time that afternoon, the wedding party began its rehearsal march down a red carpet toward the gazebo. It was decorated with Chinese lanterns provided by Ping Pong. For tomorrow evening, she had also staged fireworks to light up the sky.

Over the years, that little puff of an ageless woman Tim married had come to be one of the most cherished members of the Paladín family. Children adored her, and adults gravitated towards her generous smile and mirthful nature.

Not to be outdone, Garner Bryce Bradford was providing a flyby at twilight of four F-100C Super Sabres—in honor of its missing man, First Lieutenant Julian Paladín. But then Garner, who was patiently awaiting his role in giving away the bride, was always a big onstage production.

The fall weather was cooperating, just cool and crisp enough. The trees along the Nueces were putting on a show of autumnal colors—pumpkin orange, red-hot cinnamon, and brown sugar—Gabby's colors chosen for the wedding.

She looked vibrant today, and one had to wonder how anyone could ever have overlooked her quiet beauty. Sam, of course, looked in love—and anxious to be finished with the wedding frivolities.

Somehow, the quiet family affair Mariana knew her son and Gabby had wanted was nevertheless escalating into a national event. The decisions of the parents of the bride had prevailed, namely those of Garner's.

He had wanted a big Texas-style wedding for his daughter. Only The Barony would do as a venue. He had even requested that a press room be set aside at The Barony.

The estate crawled with both reporters and secret servicemen.

Not that he was in any mood to celebrate. The week before he had been elected to office—but as second-in-command to President-elect Marcus Carnegie. What a come down for Garner's presidential aspirations. Nevertheless, as Vice President-elect he meant to make the most of this Thanksgiving weekend by generating positive publicity.

Mariana went over her checklist in her mind. Tomorrow morning Pierce was having fresh flowers flown in from Mexico. Hannah and Jakob were driving in this evening from San Antonio with cases of champagne and wine.

Fabienne, assisted by Edna, Belle, and Heidi, had taken over in the kitchen with the side dishes.

Tim, Noel, Preston, and Jack were cooking three hogs, buried in wet burlap feed sacks underground—and the four guys were already swapping tales over Lone Stars that Preston had arranged to be trucked in.

Mariana inclined her head to whisper to Gaila, "The cake?"

"In flight now from Washington," she whispered back. "If not, our chef's head is on the chopping block. And Bob Wills and his Texas Playboys have already left Amarillo, and with luck, their bus should arrive sometime tonight."

"We can put them up in one of the bunk houses."

Mariana sincerely liked the quiet, gracious woman and wondered how Gaila put up with Garner's affairs when everyone on the Hill knew about them. Fortunately, his randy lust was balanced by his deep-seated concern for the underdog. And Garner had to be top dog, so the cautious offer of office of Vice President was an affront to his monumental ambitions.

Nevertheless, he had always come through for the Paladíns. His devotion to them, his own family, and his country could not be questioned. And yet . . . .

"Look, Gaila," she said, "can you keep an eye on things while I check in with Heath and the others?"

Those "others" were Pierce, Fiona, and Steven, secluded in the office where Mariana was to meet with them and Heath. At her entrance, those three looked glum. Smoothing her skirt beneath her legs, she took a seat in the deep-cushioned, cowhide-covered armchair. Nothing went wasted at The Barony. "Something new?"

Pierce's presence suggested the hastily-called meeting had to be about Aubrey's murder. Since Steven had stepped in to help, the trail had grown warm again.

Fiona's gaze ricocheted from Steven to her uncle Pierce then to her. "Steven has found something that may prove fruitful."

She glanced now at him and, to Mariana, her niece's bemused look revealed a hopelessly love-struck female.

Steven stretched out his long legs and fished a small spiral from the pocket of his tan suede coat. "Well, Mrs. Paladín, while running a check on radiograms buried deep in piles of minutiae, I found a message coming from a short-wave radio in Moscow in 1945 from one of our sleepers that—"

He paused as Heath entered the room balancing a tray of

cups and with a booted foot kicked the door closed behind him. He handed one from the tray to her, and she grabbed the energy pick-up with a sigh of relief. The coffee was sweetened with two dollops of sugar, just as she liked it.

Her lanky, old cowboy, still Hollywood handsome, knew her so well. Knew both what she needed and craved—him, more than anything. She could not imagine her life without him in it. After all these years, she had grown not only to love him more every day but to admire him right along with it. He was far larger, far grander, in real life, than those fictional screen images made him out to be.

To the others, Heath passed out cups of Mexican hot chocolate. "Felt it best only the five of us needed to be present during this conversation. Steven tell you what he unearthed?"

"He was just getting ready to," she said, taking another restorative sip of the coffee, still so hot it came close to burning her taste buds. She nodded for Steven to continue.

"Back in 1945, our intelligence decoded a radiogram from one of our Moscow counter agents—Candy Bar. I found the radiogram, alerting us that he feared his cover had been blown by a mole inside U.S. intelligence, whose identity is still unknown today. What we do know is Candy Bar's encrypted radiogram revealed the Russian agent name G.B. Borsov. That was Aubrey's last notation—the same day she was . . . was shot at the Tidal Basin."

He directed a glance at Pierce. "I am sorry."

Pierce nodded, but she could not miss the flexing of his jaw muscles. How did he shoulder such horrendous and heart-wrenching catastrophes—losing a foot in WWI, then his wife's murder before his own eyes, and now their son, rotting away somewhere deep inside Russia?

With elbows on his chair armrests and hands clasped before his still taut stomach, he leaned forward. "An obvious intelligence leak. That's why our discussion goes no farther than this room. And as for our Russian agent? I seem to remember an Arkady Borsov in Aubrey's notes."

"That's right," Fiona corroborated.

Pierce expelled a soft grunt that hid a wealth of heartache, then shifted his prosthetic leg to a more comfortable position. "What happened to Borsov, Steven?"

"Two days later, before his Moscow CIA handler could debrief him, he fell from a platform at Moscow's Arbatskaya metro station." Steven shrugged. "Needless to say, our own family jewels have their respective blemishes, as well. You name it—the CIA's Cuba assassination attempts, infiltration of leftist groups, tests on unwitting U.S. civilians with pharmaceutical drugs, wiretaps and surveillance of journalists."

"So, who stood to gain the most by killing our Russian contact?" Heath asked, then added, "And Aubrey?"

"A better question to ask," Fiona said, "is who had the power to cover it up?"

Mariana sighed. "So many. The Mafia—if you remember, they sided with the Fascists in '45. Stalin, of course. Even the Ku Klux Klan. Hell, if you want to talk power, it could be anyone in our political system, playing both sides merely to cover all bases. A counterspy with a personal agenda, if you will."

"A politician with a big ego fits the bill, as well," Steven mused as he methodically cleaned his eyeglasses with his crumpled pocket handkerchief.

Mariana wondered why he had yet to propose to Fiona. Was he still that much in love with his late wife?

"Is there any other kind?" Fiona asked, grinning dryly, "begging your pardon, Aunt Mariana, but is there any other kind of politician than one with a big ego?"

SAM DREW GABBY ASIDE FROM the chaos of the preparations. "Meet me on the bluff, beneath the live oak in half an hour." He knew it to be a place secure from eavesdroppers or possible listening devices.

Looking up distractedly from a list in her hand, her smile faded at his serious expression. "I know you too well by now to think you're having second thoughts about marrying. So, it has to be pretty serious."

He nodded. "It is."

Thirty minutes later, he slipped away and climbed to the venerable live oak that stood guard on the bluff overlooking The Barony's *hacienda.* She sat erect, arms wrapped around her knees, staring sightlessly at something far beyond. She had not changed out of the yellow silk wrap dress she had worn for the rehearsal.

As she said, she knew him so well. His life had not started until she had become a part of it. She was his reality in a venue that had the trappings of excess, of unreality. The two of them were more alike than naysayers realized.

She glanced up at his approach, noiseless though it was. He slipped down between her and the tree trunk, his knees and arms encompassing her. He drew her taut body back against his chest. At that, she slumped into his embrace, her head lolling in the cradle of his shoulder and neck.

He nuzzled her temple, and she twitched at the tickling of his mustache.

"Let's run away," she said, without looking over her shoulder at him. "Now. Skip the wedding and hightail it to some third-world country, where reality is reassuring. The dripping of rain. The sifting of coffee beans through the fingers. The intoxication of orchids in an Amazonian forest. Peru—its people—is so out-of-this world beautiful."

He hated doing this. "Julian, he's alive. He's being held at Vladimir Pri . . . Prison." She would, of course, recognize his high voltage tension, betrayed by his rare stutter.

Her face whipped up to his. "What?"

"In Russia. It's infamous as a torture prison." He need not tell her that it was aimed at destroying people psychologically, that its conditions were so horrendous prisoners resorted to suicide. "I need your help, Gabby, to fr—free him."

Her eyes widened. "How can I possibly be of help?"

This was certainly not the time—not the night before their wedding, when romance should prevail—to discuss hard, cold tactics. But in this case, time was truly of the essence. Upon learning Julian had been taken prisoner, U.S.

wags would soon be demanding why he had not swallowed the coin's suicide toxin given him.

But he had been under no orders to take his own life. The toxin was available to use voluntarily should he choose to—perhaps in the face of unbearable torture. But they did not know Julian. He was a fighter. He was a Paladín. He was a Texican.

He had survived ejection, although communiqués indicated the wind had torn his helmet off, broken blood vessels in his face, and snapped one of his legs.

Yes, he would fight back until beat senseless by one of his captors' rubber truncheons—or beat to death.

And that was what Alexandr Shitov, a Soviet intelligence agent and currently a journalist for Tass, was trying to prevent.

Barely observing below the caterers setting out tables on the *hacienda* grounds, the Secret Service agents patrolling its perimeter, and the household help scurrying around the gazebo, Sam spoke quietly, his breath stirring tendrils at Gabby's temple.

"Come Monday, a Russian agent by the name of Alexandr Shitov is to be dispatched as cu . . . cultural advisor to Cuba, but in the three-day interval between now and then, he is attempting to arrange with Soviet intelligence to swap Julian for one of their agents, who's serving a twenty-five-year sentence at a Louisiana penitentiary."

He paused, drew a fortifying breath. Goddamnit, he loathed the inextricable position in which he was placing Gabby. Once again, being used. She had been used all her life as a political pawn, although she would assert it was by her own choice.

"The only hi . . . hitch is that Khrushchev's policies are erratic. He could change his decision at any moment. And, too, Shitov seems to have reason to feel that staffing surrounding our present administration has more holes than a sieve. For this reason, he has specified that he will deal only with family members. Specifically, you."

He felt Gabby go rigid—could actually feel her heart pounding through the back of her ribcage. "Me? Why? I'm not a family member."

"You will be, once we're married. And as to why . . . because you have traveled the world with the Experiment in International Living and UNICEF. Because you, among all of us, have managed to remain neutral."

"And how would this . . . this trade . . . be accomplished?"

"If your father can convince the President to go through with the exchange, our honeymoon itinerary would add a stop after Salzburg—in Berlin."

She shifted so her hands could frame his face, and he felt the chill of her fingers. "Of course, I'll negotiate this trade you're talking of. Isn't that what family is all about? Both our families?" Her lips tried kicking up a smile, but it was feeble. "All for one, and one for all and all that."

He could not smile. "God, I fucking hate all of this! But I'll be right there with you, Gabby, I swear to you."

Her mouth wobbled. "I know that."

His lips were buried in her hair—as if at that moment to lose bodily contact with her would mean losing all contact forever. "You've heard the fable of the haggle-toothed, sewage-smelling witch who was forced on Sir Lancelot as his bride?"

"Hmmm, no."

"As her bridal gift to Lancelot, she gave him the choice. Her, as a beautiful maiden by day—or by night? And he replied he would allow her to make the choice herself."

He heard Gabby's half-sigh, half chuckle. "You are saying your bride-to-be is a repugnant haggle-toothed, sewage-smelling witch?"

At this, he expelled that breath he had been holding. "No, I am saying the moral of the fable is that what a woman really wants is to be in charge of her life. I just want *you*—haggle-toothed, sewage-smelling and all."

Her forefinger reached over to trace his mustache. "And I shall do this—this exchange—because I want you, snot-mop and all." She grew more serious. "And I want you to remember this—that no matter what, whither thou goest, I go, and thy people shall be my people, Sam Houston Paladín."

COLD FEAR SHIMMIED A SPINE-freeze down Jack's back.

The third wedding in the year and a half since his and Regina's first date. After Bill and Susan had played match-maker—inviting both Regina and him first to a poker party, then to a beach picnic the following month—the chemistry between him and Regina had overridden both their strong wills.

Flicking a sidewise glance at her now, he could tell she was primed this time to either unite her famed name with his or separate his testicles from his groin with a flick of her famed whip.

A harp, classical guitarist, and flute trio were playing. With her younger eighteen-year-old brother Rex trailing, Regina and Jack walked the daisy lined red carpet leading to the gazebo.

Rex was as proud and arrogant as his sister—and, sharing the same gene pool— was most likely as thermodynamic in bed. Which accounted for Jack's bicep-tightening response to the way the darkly handsome lad had cast a predatory glance at Jack's sister.

One of Gabby's bridesmaids, Jill, was waiting on the patio for the processional march. Surely the testosterone-driven punk knew that Jill was a definite underage seventeen-year-old—and definitely off limits.

"Down, boy," Regina murmured to Jack. "Jill can handle my brother on her own."

They took seats on the groom's side of the aisle. Jack draped an arm around Regina. She laid a gloved palm on his thigh, and it twitched in response.

Of all the women who had come and gone in his memory, she alone had that power over him. This Seminole Indian maiden matched him—on the sparring floor and in the bedroom. She could handle the pressure of fame and power as easily as she handled dirt and deprivation. As at home in blue jeans as a ball gown.

But he wondered if she could so easily negotiate the treacherously ever-changing boundaries of love and marriage, commitment and apathy, trust and deceit that he observed in other married couples on the base.

After all, she was spoiled, privileged—and impulsive. But he'd say this for her. She was never boring.

Regrettably, the Senate Chaplain that Garner had arranged to officiate the wedding ceremony was monotonous. He droned on until Jack found himself yawning, and Regina elbowed him. Nevertheless, his lids started to droop. His faux pas was avoided by the woman who belatedly slipped into the seat beside his.

Bridget Malone, her tawny hair caught up in an elegant Grace Kelly knot, slid him a sidewise glance through those saucy cat-eye glasses and gave him a half-smile.

She was radiant with maternity—and about to deliver if the size of her ballooned silk blouse was any indication. Occasionally, she would visit The Barony with Julian a couple times a year, but Jack had not seen her since a couple of months before Julian's plane went down, and the family learned of her pregnancy. "I'm glad you could make it to the wedding."

"Oh, I'm attending more than the wedding," she whispered back. "I got a backchannel message—about the exchange, Jack. I intend to be there in Berlin for Julian's release."

"What?"

Heads swiveled at his raised voice.

Behind her glasses, her eyes grew wide. "You didn't know?" she mouthed. "About the exchange—on Sam and Gabby's honeymoon?"

His grin accompanied his murmur. "It's going to be one hell of a honeymoon with both the Paladín clan and the KGB performing chivaree for Sam and Gabby."

## BERLIN, GERMANY
## NOVEMBER 1960

The quaint potsdam lakefront on Wannsee had all the European charm conducive to providing a most romantic honeymoon if one could turn a blind eye to the two machine-gun bunkers built in the '40s.

Nearly three decades earlier, Sam's uncle Preston had spirited away his imprisoned cousin Hannah and a top German physicist from this same area. Sam knew his uncle Preston and Pierce meant to do the same for Julian, given that, if all went well, the CIA would get dibs on Julian for debriefing purposes.

The Cold War had frozen Berlin in time, divided by the four victors of World War II. West Berlin remained under western control, but it was located deep inside Soviet-controlled East German territory. The divided city spot-lit the sharp contrast between the communist and capitalist systems.

Sam stood, arm wrapped around Gabby's waist, at the tree-lined, western side of the steel bridge that spanned Lake

Wannsee. The bridge provided a photogenic vantage point with a view of Schlosspark Glienicke, its castle grounds, as well as Babelsberg Castle and its park.

His gaze skimmed the paltry, milling crowd at the nearby Old World plaza. With winter approaching, the tourists and civilians were few that breezy and chilly afternoon.

Out of sight, waiting by one of the bunkers, poised a CIA handler and his Soviet prisoner, a KGB colonel, recently released from his Louisiana prison cell. The two looked like idle tourists, perusing a street map. But they were ready to move at the given signal.

Garner had readily agreed to Gabby's service as liaison, provided he could persuade the President to give his nod to the trade, which, of course, Carnegie had. The trade would be a great publicity coup.

Also, nearby—hovering around the plaza's nigh-empty kiosk—were Bridget, Regina, Jack, Preston, and Pierce. All flown in by the latter on his turbojet. Sam, and the CIA, had fought against this family conclave. One misstep and the deal could be blown.

But Bridget had determined that she was coming, whether requested or not. And Jack was determined to safeguard her. Regina was determined to be at Jack's side. Uncle Pierce was determined to retrieve his son back home to the States. And, hell, Uncle Preston was best adept at negotiating Germany's governmental mazes.

Damn, the Paladíns should have staged their family reunion in Berlin this year.

Within minutes, the trade for Julian would go down at

the center of the Glienicke Bridge, which connected the American sector of Berlin with the East German town of Potsdam. The border between East Germany and Western Allied-occupied West Berlin bisected the middle of the bridge. A few pedestrians braved the cold to traverse the bridge from both sides. Despite the Cold War, civilian life continued blithely on.

From the bridge's far western side, Sam, with his height advantage, spotted the KGB's signal before Gabby did—the flurry of a hand-held white handkerchief.

He glanced at his wristwatch. Two o'clock precisely.

His arm tightened imperceptibly around her slender waist. He inclined his head and nuzzled her temple. "It's time."

She nodded, looked up, and brushed her lips quickly across his. "I love you and your outlaw mustache, Sam Houston Paladín."

She started walking across the bridge, her red wool coat the only color against the drab backdrop of a communist winter.

As each spy waited, along with their handlers, at their respective ends, she and a man in a gray overcoat and felt fedora negotiated in the center of the bridge, where a white stripe that represented the Iron Curtain divided East from West.

God, what if something went wrong? What if something happened to Gabby? He sensed movement from behind and turned to find the familiar faces of his family gathering around him. He blinked away moisture, undoubtedly due to the cold air from the lake.

Finally, the Soviet spy and Julian were waved forward from their corresponding holding positions, accompanied by their handlers. Although Sam had been warned against it, he followed the Soviet spy and handler at a discreet distance, with his family buttressing him.

At two-oh-six p.m. Berlin time, the two handlers and their prisoners—red-headed Julian limping—reached the white stripe, where waited the Soviet negotiator and the woman in the red coat.

Anxiously, Sam watched, straining to overhear what would be said. From his viewpoint, Julian did not appear too much the worse for wear, and Sam felt the breath ease from his lungs.

Then, came Gabby's howling scream of rage—and clips of her words spit like bullets from a magazine clip. "No! What . . . you . . . to him?" He saw her fling herself at the man in the fedora, " . . . not the agreement!"

All parties whirled toward the scuffling two. The CIA agent managed to pry her loose from the Soviet negotiator. But from beneath his overcoat, the Soviet agent whipped out a handgun. Julian reached out, latched onto the man's coat collar. But after a fleeting moment of tussle, the Soviet agent shrugged free. He leveled the handgun, this time at Julian.

## SAN ANTONIO
## MARCH 1961

LIKE BLUE-UNIFORMED SOLDIERS, the bluebonnets stood sentinel against a cloudless blue sky, along with the Indian Paintbrush and other wildflowers blanketing the hills.

It was not illegal to pick the bluebonnets, the state flower, but it was certainly bad Texan karma—and Julian knew something about bad karma.

From his limited view, an orange-and-black butterfly flitted from one bluebonnet to another that afternoon. Fortunately, because he was older, the inability for his one eye to triangulate did not hinder his depth perception, so he had little problem with self-sufficiency.

From a mesquite, a mockingbird twittered. Spring was unfurling new life in all of nature . . . all except the flitting glow within the husk that was his body. Bridget, however, was enrapt with motherhood. He felt like a curmudgeon. Gratefulness fell far short of what freedom felt like to him. And the prospect of fatherhood? It was both wondrous and daunting.

At the crown of the hill, she had positioned a pair of antiquated turquoise metal outdoor chairs she had rescued from an about-to-be demolished old motel. Her rented home, more a bungalow than a cabin, occupied barely two acres that were seven miles outside San Antonio.

"A perfect place to recuperate," she had told him with a too-bright smile.

The sun warmed his up-tilted face, easing the prickling

nerves in the shriveled pink flesh that welted the hollow left on the right side of his face.

Supposedly, he was fortunate to reside in San Antonio, with the availability of a world-class medical post close at hand. The Air Force Hospital at nearby Lackland Air Force Base was renowned for its advanced medical treatment in all specialties. He had even been fitted with a prosthetic eye. Nevertheless, the irritation and persistent tearing rendered its wearing not worth his effort.

He heard Bridget approaching through the tufted grass, a good twenty yards behind, but did not turn his head.

The rusted chair protested as she took a seat to his left. His peripheral vision captured her in a maternal portrait. She slipped loose the top buttons of her floral-pattern blouse and folded down her bra cup's left flap. She shifted their baby in her arms so Julia could more easily nurse. When proof of Bridget's pregnancy had been discovered, the Air Force had automatically discharged her from service.

He could hear his daughter's little mouth suckling with mewling noises and smell the sweet, musky milk odor. Once again, nature's will to survive was exerting itself. His daughter nursing should have been a beautiful sight, but his ability to perceive beauty seemed to have withered.

Yer there was that indefinable tug at his heart—Julia. That small mite of life that was part of him, valiantly struggling in her new environment. As he was his.

"Have you made up your mind?" Bridget asked.

He turned his head slightly in her direction. Sunlight glinted off her glasses, and a swatch of sunlit hair straggled from the knot at her nape to tumble over her shoulder. "About what?"

She bit her lower lip, emitted a soft sigh. "Flying is in your blood, Julian."

He tunneled fingers through his unwieldy crew cut that had grown out. "No, balancing on the narrow rope of danger was in my blood."

"You'll feel different, once you get into the cockpit again."

"The cockpit of a commercial plane is vastly different than that of an ultra-high-altitude plane."

"Your father said you'd be able to get a medical cert and could rely on your instruments to—"

"Damnit, Bridget, I told you flying isn't in my blood."

"I didn't ask that," she said, her voice maintaining its even tone. "I asked if you had made up your mind—about the commercial pilot's job with Paladín Air Southwest."

His gaze swiveled back to the patches of wildflowers. He felt lower than worm shit. Why she put up with him, he could not figure. Without his black eyepatch, he looked like some grotesque Halloween mask. And his mood was just about as grisly.

Most days, he wished there on the bridge the Soviet agent's bullet had taken him out, but the quick crack of Regina's fabled whip had prevented that. Its whipcord had snapped away the gun, its misfired bullet harmlessly rippling the gray river below.

"Stop it! I know what you're thinking. Julia and I need you. And your family needs you." Abruptly, she changed tactics. "You're being a horse's ass, refusing New York's tickertape parade."

"Don't you think it beyond-belief bizarre that America labeled me a traitor because I didn't use the suicide coin but wanted to proclaim me a hero for being maimed?" He hated being heralded as some kind of Superman, returning time and again from the brink.

Once more, she shifted the conversation. He had to give her that. She was unpredictable. And she was brave. "I have taken a job as a staff doctor with the San Antonio State Hospital. It's nearby, and, given my M.D. degree, they're willing to let me work part-time."

"Of course they are. The San Antonio State Hospital is desperate." An asylum, it was badly overcrowded, under-staffed, and faced with the problems of low budgets, antiquated buildings, and an unacceptable staff-to-patient ratio. With her experience and training, she was vastly overqualified.

Her mouth tightened. "Just because you've been an asshole doesn't mean you have to continue to act like one."

He stifled a repentant grunt and watched her secure her bra flap with one hand and re-button her blouse. He should offer marriage but could not bring himself to saddle her with a derelict of a man. She deserved better.

A man with a future.

And living with her pity would be more painful than the actual gouging of his eye from its socket had been. Despite loving her maddeningly, or maybe because of it, he considered off and on setting her free. Is not that what one did when loving deeply?

He shifted his gaze to the shimmering horizon. "When would be a day good for us to go to the courthouse and get married?"

The slight amplification in her voice told him her head had swiveled toward him. "Married? Why would I want to marry you?"

"Because my daughter is a Paladín, and she needs my name."

"She needs a father, not a self-absorbed asshole." Her rusted metal chair squeaked as she rose. "And I need a husband who's passionate about me." She Hung out an arm before his vision and flipped him the finger. "If you can't provide that for Julia and me, we'll get along on our own just fine, thank you!"

He shot to his feet. Lifting the tiny Julia from Bridget's arms, he cradled the treasured bundle in the crook of his arm. The first time he had done just this, he had been trembling so hard, he'd feared he would drop her. Now, it was second nature. "We're going to The Barony to get married, Doc. Then to see Pierce in El Paso—to get work for me."

Her mouth crimped ruefully. "Wow, what a romantic proposal. I hate you right now. But, to my self-disgust, I still love you, too. Let's go."

## SAN ANTONIO
## APRIL 1961

PALADÍN FAMILY MEMBERS AND household staff hustled to prepare yet another marriage ceremony—that of Julian and Bridget's.

Noel already knew it was going to be a hellhole of a day. Julian's spur-of-the-moment wedding was scheduled for six p.m. at The Barony. Aunt Mariana was making hasty arrangements for the various last minute details and serving as Bridget's matron of honor.

As best man, Noel had to be there by five o'clock, which meant he had to leave the noon grand opening of Heidi's Chaparral Art Gallery no later than three—then it would be pedal to the metal, unless he could commandeer one of the Paladín Airways two-prop planes.

Heidi's non-conformist spirit was sorely constrained by the enormity of the grand opening of her gallery, which could not be cancelled—not with all the brochures and word-of-mouth already circulated. But she, Aunt Hannah, and Jakob were planning on making the ninety-mile trip for the reception later that evening, after she wrapped up the grand opening.

Her entire heart was bound up in the success of this event. Hors d'oeuvres were already arranged as closely as possible to the staging area, interspersed with pedestals.

She was wearing a fresh, wildflower wreath in her hair, some kind of short, bohemian gauzy dress with laced-up, knee-high Indian moccasins that sent his blood pressure into overdrive. God, he wanted her so. All the time. Good times. Bad times. They had been lovers through the best and the worst.

He would bind her by marriage if he could, but he knew she would never be his—at least in that way. He knew she was in love with him. He would have to let her come to him on her own. Whenever, wherever her whimsical spirit called her to him. She was not one to be cajoled.

The opening was eight minutes away, and she took a nervous sip of champagne from her flute. "Dad and Hannah should be here by now." They were alone in the gallery's backroom, jammed to the latilla ceiling with stored artwork.

"They'll be here soon. It's probably taking your mother longer than planned to locate a florist that carries fresh daisies."

"What if the guests don't really like anything in the show?" she whispered. "What if they want to visit the artist at his studio to see whether he has anything there they might like better?"

He leaned down and brushed her lips with his, tasting the sweet bubbly on her lips. "Your radiant energy will hold them captive here."

She grinned. *"Mein Schatz,* did I ever tell you how much I love your freckles? They reassure me that fairy dust magic does exist in this humdrum world."

*Mein Schatz? My darling?* "Marry me," he fired back, "and I'll keep the magic coming."

His tone was joking, but he was weary with importuning the wild child and not a little hurt by her penchant for the new culture springing up that forewent the traditional ties-that-bind values. "Hell, Heidi, we could make it a double wedding ceremony tonight.

"I doubt Julian and Bridget would want to share their—" Her phone rang before she could finish her reply, and she grabbed for the receiver, listened, then, with raised brows, passed it to him.

Puzzled, he frowned but took the receiver. "Paladín here."

"Noel, this is Mel." The guy had an annoying habit of sucking his breath in between his teeth. "Tracked you down to The Chaparral. Congrats on Heidi's Grand Opening. Look, the board just met, and a matter has come up. How soon can you meet me at the corporate offices?"

Noel glanced at his watch. "Can this wait, Knopf?"

"No. It's urgent."

Corporate offices were twenty minutes away, in downtown San Antonio, but Noel would be damned if he would leave Heidi in the lurch. Today was important to her. "I'll be there in an hour and a half."

"That's the best you can do?"

"No, I can do better. It's the best I want to do. See you at one thirty."

He cradled the receiver and smiled. "Pleasure before business."

"Noel, if it's impor—"

"*You're* important. The only thing that's important." He bent to kiss her but at the tinkling of the gallery door's bell, admitting her stepmother and Jakob, only grazed her lips.

He grinned. "Show time."

Heidi rushed to help his Aunt Hannah with her armful of daisy bouquets that Heidi had wanted. After hugging his aunt, he relieved the German Goliath of several of the vases he toted. "One day, I hope to be as tall as you."

The stout man grinned and patted his stomach's slight pooch. "*Ja,* but you should hope not as round."

The tinkling bell signaled more arrivals. While Heidi greeted them and her mother placed the vases of daisies advantageously throughout the galley, he caught up with Jakob and the vineyard's operations.

By all accounts, the grand opening could be acknowledged as a success, being well attended, and Noel deemed it socially safe to take his leave an hour later.

However, the board meeting hours earlier was not likely to be acknowledged as a success. Not with Knopf summoning him precipitously.

Somehow, by hook or crook, the fourteen-member board now contained eight members outside the family. Only Uncle Heath, Noel, and his cousins—Sam, Jack, Julian, and Fiona—remained on the board as the six familial representatives.

Noel rode the elevator to the fifteenth floor, occupied entirely by The Barony Ranch Enterprises. A pert little secretary ushered him into Knopf's office, a softly-lit expanse of windows, shuttered by blinds. The mahogany desk was nearly large enough to seat the President's cabinet.

As chief executive officer of The Barony Ranch Enterprises, Mel Knopf could help make a higher profit, but not stage a coup—the Paladíns had made sure of it. Still, with unanimous support from the eight non-family members, which included Garner, Knopf could very well fire Noel today. Except that was highly improbable.

Garner could be damned uncomfortably persuasive, as any member of congress could testify, and could most likely persuade the board against taking such a step.

Then, too, Noel had introduced the cattle prod to move the cattle along faster when they were in their pens. To open up more pasture, he had devised a plow pulled by a massive, specially designed bulldozer that could clear four acres of brush an hour. And the cattle and farming portion of Barony Enterprises that Noel oversaw had garnered a five million after-tax profit each of the past three years. A record best.

Of course, five million seemed like a hell of a lot of money—unless it was divvied up among the more than forty heirs still alive on the family tree and holding stock.

Knopf's countenance was shadowy until a smile creased his doughy face. He rose to shake Noel's hand. "Sorry to inconvenience you, Noel, but this is serious business."

Noel slipped open the middle button of his denim blazer and, hitching his trousers at the knees, slid into one of the leather nailhead chairs. Forearms draped on its armrests, he asked, "What's up?"

Knopf settled back in his swivel executive chair, hands clasped over the small mound that was his stomach. His soft looks in no way diminished his stature as an astute business executive.

"It's the Board of Director's meeting held this morning.

Of course, you, Sam, Heath, and the rest of the family, what with the wedding, couldn't be present for it. But even so, the majority of the Board felt the ranch can no longer continue to provide for so many Paladineños. They've got to go."

"What?"

Knopf leaned forward, his folded hands now atop the polished desk. Not an inbox or paperwork or manila folder in sight. "Look, Noel, the Paladineños' villa on the ranch shelters nearly five-hundred workers and their families. With modern machinery and vehicles, the Paladineños are Stone Age relics. The company can't justify providing for that many."

Noel knew times had changed. Range bosses were nowadays called unit managers and cow camps and chuckwagons were a thing of the past, but to layoff the hundreds of Paladineños—*vaqueros,* whose ancestors had loyally served Alex Paladín, the patriarch himself—the idea was incomprehensible. The villa of La Baroncita contained their multitude of homes, two schools, a small library, and a well-staffed clinic, as well as a mom-and-pop grocery store.

"You're telling me, Knopf, the Board wants me to face these people who are like family to us and inform them they are history?"

Knopf nodded.

Anger bristled Noel's hackles. What had looked like a hellhole of a day now looked like a hellhole of a job. Not only that, but he was late for Julian's impromptu wedding—which spared no time to talk to the family about this stand-off with Knopf.

# SAINT AUGUSTINE, FLORIDA
# APRIL 1961

Jack was not in the best of moods.

A week earlier, the Soviet cosmonaut, Yuri Gagarin, became the first person in space to make an orbital flight. Americas orbital flight was not even on the drawing board until late this year, at best.

Meanwhile, Jack was scheduled for a mere suborbital flight in three weeks. Granted, he would be the first American to make a suborbital flight, but, damnit, it was not anything in comparison to what the Russkies were doing.

And then there was Regina Prendergast. She and her damned whip continued to garner more media attention than he did as Americas lionized astronaut.

A Belgian tourist just happened to capture the exact moment of the Berlin prisoner-trade with a photo of Regina, her whip popping forward to snap the KGB agent's gun. The photo had spread around the civilized world as quickly as the Black Plague.

But the worst was yet to come—their engagement party at the home of her parents.

Home? In reality, Rancho del Sol was an *Architectural Digest* of a grandee's Spanish castle. The Barony's rambling haphazard design, a blend of both Old World and Tejana adobe, while warm and inviting, looked like a border town *jacale* in comparison.

Although Jill was handling all the hoopla with aplomb, their parents appeared flummoxed. After all, they had lived the greater part of their lives in substandard housing in the isolated town of Los Alamos in northern New Mexico.

Even Byron Paladín's participation as part of the group of renowned scientists who had designed the atom bomb for the U.S. in '45 had been kept mostly under governmental wraps.

From the back seat of Jack's Rambler Rebel, his mom asked, "Do you think Mrs. Prendergast would have some private time to cement wedding plan details over cocktails one evening?"

"I'm sure she would, Edith," Byron said drily from the passenger seat, "as long as it's Dom Perignon and not mezcal."

"Especially with its worm, Mom," he said, mustering as much humor as he could, given the ordeal he was about to undergo.

From the backseat, Jill playfully whacked both him and their father upside the back of their heads with her beaded purse. "Mom's serious, bozos."

So were Regina's mother and father. Maybe speculative

was more like it. He introduced his parents to them, Regina, and her brother Rex. Both families were to greet guests at the bottom of a Saltillo-tiled staircase wide enough for a B-52 to taxi down.

Rex was the only one who seemed in a lighthearted mood. Of course, he could be feeling a little cheerful because he had just been released from quarantine, following the onset of an adult case of chicken pox, to pursue his sexually predatory habits. Too bad the pox hadn't ravaged the young man's macho features, a masculine version of his sister's blatant beauty.

To be generous, Jack recognized his sex-driven self at that age. But his own sister Jill was way too vulnerable to Rex's raffish charm.

"Well this engagement has to be a match made in heaven," the handsome lad said of him and Regina. "America's Hero and Heroine." For a mere nineteen years, he was astonishingly self-possessed.

Silver-haired Mrs. Prendergast displayed a smile that would look good in newspaper photographs the next morning, and old man Prendergast said heartily, "Like the rest of America, we couldn't be more delighted with this fairytale union—heirs to two of the world's largest ranches."

Of course, Jack had met Regina's parents several times, and they had been quite cordial, despite the suspicion that his playboy's reputation must have preceded him. They probably hoped that, given both Jack and their daughter's forceful personalities, their romantic relationship would eventually fizzle.

After the guest line dwindled to late arrivals, while their parents exchanged polite conversation, Regina led him from guest to guest, her hand tucked at his elbow. He felt paraded around like her pet poodle.

If he did not delight so much in her raunchy humor and daredevil antics and . . . damnit, everything about her. Almost. She could afford to be a tad bit more compliant to his whims and wishes, though he conceded they could be outrageous at times.

His glittering champagne-cognac-colored engagement ring, from the world's biggest mine in western Australia, sparkled on her finger as brilliantly as any on Princess Grace of Monaco's. His astronaut's salary might be meager, but his Barony Enterprises royalties were not.

At last, she tugged him away from the press of guests that included the governor of Florida, the president of the Florida Cattlemen's Association, and reporters from the Miami Herald, the Austin American Statesman, and the New York Times. A subscriber and crossword puzzle aficionado, Jack's mother would be thrilled to meet the last reporter.

He followed Regina's lead out to the terrace with its stone-bordered waterfall and Olympic-size swimming pool, fashionably enwreathed by palms and exotic plants.

Abruptly, she spun, her chiffon-and-satin champagne-gold gown swishing around her stiletto heels and, hands on hips, faced him. The lavish beauty of her features was molded into a frantic frieze. "I want to call off the wedding."

He blinked several times. "What? Now . . . tonight? Look, I love you. And I've never told another woman that. And I want you in my life. But you were the one who wanted this . . . this charade of a Command Performance. I'd be just as happy if we showed up at the courthouse and—"

"No, that's my point. I was the one who wanted to get married. Not you. I'm calling off the wedding. Period. No wedding. No marriage license. No Command Performance." The last words were fired at him like missiles.

"You and your high-handedness. Have you lost your marbles? You invited the whole goddamned world of blue bloods and jet sets tonight!"

Her unforgettable golden-brown eyes glared at him from above the sweep of sculpted cheekbones and small, hard-set jaw. "No, I've found my sanity, and its reasoning has overruled my fascination with a narcissistic Jackass. That's with a capital J. Jack the Jackass. You never wanted this marriage. You're always searching over the next hill. Another horse to ride. Another galaxy to explore."

"Narcissistic?" His fists jammed on his hips. "This coming from you, the most indulgent, raucous, egocentric female on the planet?"

She slapped him. That gal could pack a punch. His cheek burned. He grinned. "Does this mean I can have the engagement ring back?"

# CAPE CANAVERAL, FLORIDA
# MAY 1961

AS RIGOROUS AND GRUELING as the Project Mercury countdown review at Cape Canaveral was, packed into every waking moment over the next three weeks, Jack welcomed its diversion.

No one could completely understand or communicate the complexity of the operation's activities that went on before the launch. Activities which allowed no time to devote serious reflection as to how Regina's accusations might just have a grain of truth. A very small mustard seed size grain of truth. If any. Really, none.

Vaguely, he seemed to recall a quote of Aristotle's— something about man aspiring to know himself and his universe and that his deepest passion was to become godlike. Well, Jack readily admitted, for himself, that was a tough tight wire act, balancing between hubris and humility.

He wanted to attribute their volatile argument to pre-wedding jitters. He certainly knew he had them, and she had to know it, too. Several times, he went to pick up the phone and call her. But she was too strong-willed. Crawling back now might very well mean crawling all his life.

Would she call him? Time before the launch was dwindling down. The ticking of his internal clock irritated him.

As the days got down to the wire, he realized she was not going to contact him first but knew he had to forget Regina Prendergast and concentrate solely on the flight. The main medical problem he would face, other than the anticipated post-flight low blood pressure, would be simple personal hygiene.

And then a giant medical problem presented itself.

He had the goddamn chicken pox, thanks to Rex. He was scrubbed from the flight by the Mission Control Center.

The next day, an insistent knock at his bungalow's front door disturbed his already miserable lethargy. He was feverish, a jackhammer pounded in his skull, and he itched like crazy. He dragged his body, clad only in his stinky, ratty pajama bottoms, from the rumpled bedsheets.

Regina stood at the front stoop, on her arm the same picnic basket she had carried to the clambake. Memories of that sweet reunion flooded back. Under any other circumstances, he would feel the flicker of elation that came with renewed hope.

Remarkably for her, she looked a little uncertain. "I heard . . . about the scrubbed flight." Her compassionate gaze scanned his spotted, blistered face, and he spotted the brief flare of perverse amusement in her face. "And your chickenpox."

He plowed fingers through his matted hair. A half sigh, half groan shuddered through him. "Look, I'm not up to parrying with you. I feel like—"

"I know, I know." She sidestepped him, going inside. "I'm here to take care of you."

Closing the door, he turned to stare after her. She was wearing a man's shirt, it's untucked tail nearly reaching the knees of an old pair of jeans.

She sat the basket on the kitchen table, took something

from it, and headed to the tiny bathroom, he heard her drawing water, so he padded after her. She was kneeling by the tub, shaking a container of oatmeal into it.

He scrubbed his scruffy jaw. "What are you doing?"

She looked over her shoulder at him, her expression quite serious. "We're going to take an oatmeal bath, and then I'm—"

His brows popped up. *"We?"*

"—going to rub you down with calamine lotion." Her lips curved in what he interpreted as a repentant smile. "And then I'll read you to sleep with passages from the *Kama Sutra*—or I can just tell you over and over again I love you and have missed you."

He managed a feeble grin. "I'll take all of the above."

**THE BARONY**
**NOVEMBER 1961**

NOEL HAD ARRANGED FOR THE whitewashed, limestone homes of the oldest Paladineños—homes they had lived in since birth—to be freighted off The Barony, relocated to the place they desired, and given to them as a reward for their service. It was the least he could do.

And it laid him low to see them leave.

The mythical Paladíns had dominated Texas, not the other way around. They had carved something beyond their wildest dreams into a reality. But an era was coming to an end. He was not the visionary Alex Paladín was, nor any of the legendary Patron's successors.

Noel could keep the course, and that was the best he could do.

True, he had risked expanding ranching operations overseas with land purchases in Argentina, Australia, Colombia, Spain, and Morocco—and with the oil royalties flowing in, no one in the family was complaining.

Uncle Heath had gotten rid of the company's foundering cotton warehouse in Galveston, a lumberyard in Conroe, and a horse farm in Kentucky. So for the moment, all was stable at The Barony.

However, Noel's love life was not. Perhaps unstable was not the right word. Better would be in . . . limbo. But, at thirty, he was ready to settle down. He wanted children traipsing in his boot tracks. And he wanted Heidi, though Heidi was content with their life together as it was.

The traditional Thanksgiving family reunion at The Barony that frosty November afternoon should have been a joyous one, what with the pirate- looking Julian, black patch and all, back in the fold and the celebration of his marriage to Bridget. Interesting, how no matter where they were, what they were doing, every so often their heads would turn toward each other, like sunflowers toward the sun.

Jack and Regina seemed to be faring well, given their off-again/on-again wedding was less than four months off. In fact, Regina looked radiant and Jack rather pleased with their state of affairs, as if they had come to terms with one another's mercurial temperaments.

And Fiona and Steven appeared well matched. Unlike Noel, both seemed content in a relationship that did not require the bonds of marriage. Although lately, Noel wondered about Fiona. He thought he sometimes detected a melancholy in her eyes, so unlike her vibrant nature. Then, too, it could have nothing to do with her and Steven and everything to do with the stress of her covert investigations.

Further along the table, his parents exchanged brief glances and grins, communicating more than any loving words could. Preston and Fabienne acted like two teenagers—always had.

Sam and Gabby appeared genuinely happy with one another as well. Gabby's parents, Garner and Gaila, had been married for close to forty years.

Anyone could see they understood each other well, accepting one another's foibles and shortcomings and turning them into strengths.

At the table's far end, Noel's oldest cousin, Tim, was recounting his latest attempt to track down his missing Bull Durham pouch, " . . . then, right quick like, I figured out Ping Pong had hidden it in a rubber glove in the commode tank."

Laughter filtered along the table. Noel did not miss the squeeze Tim gave Ping Pong's small hand.

For Noel, that small, insignificant gesture was monumental for himself. The straw that broke the camel's back.

Following the prolonged dinner, he tracked Heidi down to the kitchen, where the women were hanging out following clean-up. Mariana could have kept on a staff for the holiday, but she both preferred they have the day off and the Paladíns have their special time alone.

With wine glasses nearby or in hand, the females either sat on stools around the blue azuelejo-tiled center counter or flitted about, restoring recently cleaned china and silver-ware to the vintage Mexican sideboard.

As the lone male in the decidedly female regime, he was out of place, but it did not matter. For this, he would brave the lionesses' den. His Aunt Belle waved. Aunt Edna raised a glass in salute. Aunt Hannah winked. And his mom nodded in the direction of the fireplace girded on either side by pots and pans.

He nodded back and strode on toward the hearth. Heidi and Fiona were hovering near its dying embers, laughing easily about something—just what, he could not hear. At his approach, both glanced up. Heidi's alert expression relayed that she perceived something was amiss with him.

The kitchen at once went silent. The others, too, felt the unsettling energy that had wafted in with his entry.

He took her hand. "Pardon me, cuz, but I need to palaver with Heidi."

"Back in France," his mother said, smiling gently, "we call it a rendezvous, a tryst."

He would call it a showdown.

He tugged an unresisting Heidi down the hall and outside toward the gazebo. The denuded trees cast withering setting-sun shadows on the winter-grass. Once they reached the shelter of the white-painted gazebo, he turned toward her and released her hand. Shivering in the frigid weather, they faced one another.

She stood as if frozen by the weather, all but her hands that twisted together. "What?" Her breath frosted the air.

"At last, Heidi, I know what I need to do. I need to set the caged bird free."

She bit her lip. Her arms wrapped around each other to stave off her shivering. "What if the caged bird isn't sure it still wants to be free?"

"Isn't sure?" Was that the even-tempered Noel's grated response? "Oh, the caged bird is very sure. I have been caged far too long with this unproductive longing, waiting for you to want to share a married life with me. No more. This bird is taking flight. I'm out of here."

ANY RELIEF NOEL MAY HAVE felt at finally flying the coop was cut short within half an hour after re-entering the *hacienda*. He had joined the men in Uncle Heath's office for the customary cheroot and cognac.

Over the century, the room had barely changed but for a few of its rustic furnishings. Its occupants were all relaxed, glad for the holiday reprieve. Nevertheless, business was bandied about.

Uncle Heath was one of those rugged men who could ride herd not only on cows but also on dollars. Noel did not envy the Paladín schmuck who would eventually take his uncle's place as leader of The Barony.

He strode over to the sideboard's decanter and poured himself a liberal dose of cognac. His lamebrain was still on Heidi. He might have lost her, but he had to make a stand, or he would wind up losing her anyway.

He was burnt out with their drifting relationship—and burnt out with desk work. What he desperately needed was to be back, riding the range again. As always, comfortably alone, at one with himself and nature.

*Nature Boy.* Wasn't that what Ping Pong had once dubbed him?

Behind him, Sam responded to Uncle Heath's report. "If our dividends are going to remain on the up side, Dad, we have no alternative but to position ourselves where we can diversify further, not rein in on our investing."

Noel turned back to face his kinsmen and, drink in one hand, braced the other on the sideboard. Next to him lounged sixteen-year-old Tejas, trying to look as macho as the rest of the males, despite the obvious—the bottle he drank from was a Grapette and not a Lone Star.

Uncle Darcy and Aunt Belle, Noel knew, worried Tejas might all too soon be drafted into an all-out war that appeared to be looming with Vietnam.

"We can always expand our Saddle Shop," Noel's father drawled from an old buckskin couch, where he and his twin sat, their denim clad legs sprawled. Uncle Pierce balanced his tumbler on his board-flat stomach. "You know, luggage, purses, boots—that sort of thing."

Now that each of the fraternal twins, one once a redhead, the other once a blond, had gone nearly gray, it was difficult for strangers to tell them apart.

Uncle Byron chuckled. "If that won't beat all. Purses! What next? A makeup bag?"

"Preston has something there, Byron," Uncle Darcy said. "With television Westerns so hot these days, Hollywood would go great guns over leather items. Put our brand on some tooled leather and I'd wager we'd have a sure—"

Suddenly, from behind his desk, Uncle Heath rose, snifter in hand. All eyes rebounded expectantly toward him—only to watch the snifter tumble from his clutch and his tall, lanky frame crumple across a fluttering of papers.

"Dad!" Sam's strangled shout reverberated against the office walls.

Noel was the first to reach the body, collapsed on shattered glass and cognac spreading like blood.

HOURS LATER, NOEL WAS BACK in the gazebo.

"The Corpus Christi coroner's office is with your. . . ." Heidi's voice faltered, ". . . the body now." She stood framed in the entrance to the darkened gazebo.

Noel, hunched forward on the wooden bench, did not reply. He had wanted a little time alone, away from the others, just to grapple with the impact of Uncle Heath's death. Working day in and out alongside Uncle Heath, Noel was closer to him even than he was to his cousins, who were more like brothers.

His gaze drifted back to his hands, clasped between his

knees. He heard her knee-high boots click across the puncheon floor.

She sat down on the bench beside him, sliding her arm around his shoulder. "Noel, I know words don't heal a hole left in the heart. I know how close you were to your uncle Heath. But I am here, if you need me—and I'm hoping like hell you need me, because . . . because I need *you.*"

He heard her voice choke and glanced over his shoulder. Saw the pain in her eyes. "He was good to me," she murmured, "a Paladín clan outsider, and I respected him and admired him."

He turned his gaze back to his interlaced hands, rhythmically knotting to the heavy thudding of his heart.

"I know I'm frivolous and flighty and self-centered." Her free hand reached to clutch his clasped ones. The brilliance in her eyes dueled with that of the rising moon. "And capricious and stimulating and . . . but I love you so much. Give us a chance, please."

He straightened. Her palm, damp despite the cold, still overlaid his hands. "What exactly do you want, Heidi? I'm tired. I love you, too. How could anyone not? But I want-"

"I want what you do, Noel—our pairing to be a union solidified by marriage . . . and celebrated by our families and friends. But I just need time. A little more time. Until I can get the gallery up and running. I'm tired too and frazzled. Please understand."

He grunted, then enfolded her hands between his. "Then, you've got it. But I want you to be damned sure about this because I won't—"

He broke off at the sight of his father, beckoning with a motion of his hand from the patio doorway. "Something's up," Noel told her, pulling her to her feet with him.

When they reached the flagstone patio and doorway, Noel could see the grief in his old man's face at the death of his cousin. Deep lines grooved either side of his mouth. He and Uncle Pierce had joined the Air Force together with Uncle Heath in the first World War. They had seen so much, been through so much, lost and won so much. But this had to be one hell of a loss.

"Your Aunt Mariana wants to see you," his father said. "Alone—in Heath's office."

"I'll wait in the den," Heidi said, squeezing his hand reassuringly.

Tentatively, he opened the office door and found his Aunt Mariana at the massive desk, her fingertips tracing the contours of the black telephone console off to one side. The gray in her hair glimmered faintly, and her eyes were sunk into their sockets like distant starlight.

She looked up at Noel. "I can almost feel his energy around this piece of shit. All the calls Heath made and received, all the time wasted on someone's bullshit."

He knew she was angry at being robbed of the love of her life. He closed the door behind him but did not take a seat. He just stood there, watching her closely, because he knew what was coming and did not want to hear it.

She switched her dark, damp-eyed gaze to his. Her throat worked, either choking back tears, he suspected, or getting out the necessary words.

"The bad news is a Paladín has died, Noel. The good news is that a younger, healthier Paladín has been appointed to sit astride The Barony saddle. You."

# CAPE CANAVERAL, FLORIDA
# FEBRUARY 1962

J ack groaned out a song as he scrubbed Regina's back in their shower after their lovemaking.

It was their last hours before he had to report for duty—one that would eventually hurtle him toward galaxies, black holes, and fame—if he but made it through this mission as the first American astronaut to orbit the Earth aboard the *Friendship 7.*

"You never played by the rules."

"I did, too, you insufferable Cracker—engagement ring and all, if you will recall."

She turned in his arms. Tears, mixed with shower water, spiked her lashes. "Now I want that wedding ring." Her attempt at smiling barely created commas in her cheeks. "I can't have you bailing out on our wedding like you did our engagement, cowboy."

He framed her face, plastered with wet strands of hair. "I'm not bailing. I want you more than I want fame and glory."

Her fingers played with his buzz haircut. "Come home to me, Jack Paladín."

"You should know by now, nothing can keep me from you."

She struggled with a smile. "Just return to Earth to claim me as your bride come April."

Their future was all up to Mission Control and the gods who threw the dice.

THE SEVENTY HATCH BOLTS HAD been secured and the liquid oxygen propellant valve positioned. The countdown had gone perfectly—and then blast-off.

Jack's mission was to circle the globe three times during a flight lasting five hours. It was all the exhilaration he had anticipated——with none of the fulfilment he had hoped.

Hours before, he had submitted to the last medical procedure, a mere cuff that took his blood pressure. How archaic, considering his pulse climbed to a hundred and ten beats per minute after he was catapulted from Launch Complex Fourteen.

He had Garner partly to thank for this. The Vice President testified before the House Committee on Science and Astronautics in executive session that Jack should be given premier position over the other seven astronauts due to his outstanding performance in Project Mercury.

And then, to crown this achievement, Garner scored a coup for Texas in arranging Mission Control Center to be moved from Cape Canaveral to the NASA complex to be built outside Houston within a couple of years.

"Zero G and I feel fine," he relayed back to Mission Control.

Below him, as he passed over Perth, Western Australia, its residents were turning on their house, car, and streetlights. It was a sight that almost rivaled the Milky Way but would never rival his fiancée's radiance those moments he brought her to the Big O or, simply, her smile when he had handed her a cup of coffee he had brewed in the early morning hours before he had left their bungalow.

Regina had a glamour that mere beauty did not approach. He was in awe of her social poise, wit, and outrageous antics. Since last year, when she had moved in to take care of him during his recovery from chicken pox—and stayed—they had somehow come to terms with their confrontational natures, had somehow managed to cherish rather than battle the gifts their strong wills brought to their relationship.

A light flickering on a gauge to his left snatched his attention back. It might only be a small problem, but small problems in space could rapidly expand to disastrous ones. Quickly, he went through correction procedures . . . and nothing.

Flight Control contacted him. "The Automatic Control System is failing. A major yaw adjustment is necessary. You will need to take control."

He glanced down and noticed that his altitude indicators disagreed with what he observed were the true spacecraft altitudes. "Roger. I'll allow the spacecraft to continue to yaw until it is facing its flight path."

As he struggled with his task, the muscles in his shoulders tightened like tension cables. The veins in his temples were pulsing. His heartbeat pounded in his chest, as if it were exceeding blast-off speed. He drew a slow, deep inhalation from the oxygen hose.

At the proper moment, he adjusted the yaw thruster. Even with the incorrect instrument readouts, he was pleased to be facing forward instead of backward on his orbital path. At the same time he was busy manually keeping the spacecraft altitude correct, he was also trying to accomplish as many of the flight plan tasks as he could.

But what really bothered him as he crossed over the Canary Islands, what no one at Mercury Control had anticipated, were the fireflies dancing outside the spacecraft. This was no hallucination on his part. They had no connection with gas from the reaction control jets. Something was seriously awry.

"This is Friendship 7. Reporting luminescent particles dancing around the spacecraft." His suit temperature felt too warm, but he couldn't take time to adjust it.

Worse were Mission Control's next words. "Uh, tracking operations at both the Nigeria and Zanzibar sites have noticed a twelve percent drop in your secondary oxygen supply."

Another warning light came on, indicating that the fuel supply for the automatic control system was dropping.

Mercury Control's delayed response, "We recommended that you let the spacecraft altitude drift to conserve fuel."

"Umm, it's hot in here." Could the heatshield on his spacecraft be falling apart?

Silence. Then, a jaunty voice. "Keep cool. And just keep in mind that three orbits should meet the minimum monthly requirement off our hours' flying time." And then banteringly, "You'll also be certified as eligible for your regular flight pay."

Fucker. "If I make it home."

## SAN ANTONIO
## MARCH 1962

RARELY WOULD HEIDI consider herself levelheaded, disciplined, or responsible. She was astounded that Noel, so solid and dependable, had found anything worthwhile in her that appealed to him, much less to love.

She had not seen him in months, and he seldom called. When he did it was a casual, "Just checking in to see how everything's going," type of telephone call.

Yes, she knew that taking over the reins of The Barony Enterprises was consuming all of his time these days—and she knew, too, that he was complying with her request for more time.

But their relationship had stalled, and she was not sure what to do about it. She knew she was being both childish and foolish to entertain hopes and yearnings for some grand romantic gesture from him.

Several times that morning she had picked up the gallery telephone to call him, then replaced the receiver in its cradle and returned her attention to checking the gallery's records of acquisitions.

But it was no use. Her enthusiasm for her work was lagging. Not to mention the niggling worry that he may have found someone else, someone with his values, someone more fitting, more desirable.

Her gallery's records—dates, provenances, sales figures—were blurred by images of him.

His boyish features and laughter at Blind Man's Bluff . . . holding fast to his muscled shoulders as he careened her Vesper up a rocky path . . . at the grape harvesting, his assessing gaze, noticing her from a new point of view . . . and his hunger for her branded on his chiseled features at the auction barn, as his name had been branded on her shoulder.

Once again, her hand went to the phone to dial his number . . . and once again thought better of it. Instead, she dialed the number of a Santa Fe gallery director about an exchange of artworks she really needed to finalize. "Emily, it's Heidi at the Chaparral Art Gallery. Regarding that—"

The gallery's front door bell tinkled, and she sighed at the interruption. "Emily, my apologies, let me call you right back."

She parted the back office's beaded curtain and strode toward the front, only to halt. Her stomach started a freefall.

A denim jacket hitched by a thumb over one shoulder, Noel appeared to be perusing a sculpture of a roadrunner. Hearing her approach, he turned to her. Beneath the

Stetson's brim, his face was shadowed, even more so by the stubble rimming the box set of his jawline.

When he removed his straw hat, tossing it on the roadrunner's tail, she bit back a gasp. His eyes were hollows, their whites veined with red. With quickened steps she crossed toward him. "Noel, what's happened?"

He ran fingers through hair flattened by his hat band, then sighed. "I guess I'm burnt out by The Barony work. I had to get away for a while." Wearily, those shadowed eyes shifted down to meet hers. "And here, to you, is the only place I could think to go right now."

Her lips trembled. Both she and Noel prized their individualism, though in different way. And both were willing to fight for it, but he was also willing to fight for her. She could not think of any grander romantic gesture than this one.

He glanced around the gallery, as if looking for any customers. "Look, if this isn't going to work for you . . . if now's not a good time—"

She cupped his scruffy face. "How do you feel about going to Mexico for the weekend, instead?"

"Mexico?"

She shrugged. "Well, you know—cheap booze and cheap tattoos."

One brow climbed. "Tattoos?"

"I've been thinking I could use a tattoo on the other shoulder." She knew she was babbling. "Maybe something like . . . *Frau* Paladín.'"

A slow grin lightened his haggard features. His arm

encircled her waist, and he drew her up against him. As exhausted as he looked, the hard mound pressing against her pelvis assured her he still found her desirable.

"So," he asked, nuzzling her hairline, "do you think our differences—little things like your being a vegetarian and me a co-owner of one of the world's largest cattle ranches, wee issues like that—could present a problem?"

They were no wee things, but they had not stopped her from wanting him, needing him. She knew a life without him would become tedious, boring.

"Mexico's booze will help us work out any small problems this weekend. And if not its booze," she flashed him a saucy smile and pressed her hips against his suggestively, "there's always this. We've got a lifetime to work on our differences."

## EL PASO
## MARCH 1962

JULIAN GLANCED AT HIS wristwatch. The Triple Crown event listed a post time at twelve forty-five p.m. The Paladín entry, Pistol Packer, was a major contender that afternoon. In the festivities that followed the thoroughbred racing, Marty Robbins would be performing his latest hit "El Paso" before a packed Sunland Park.

Most importantly, though, eager citizens from both sides of the U.S./Mexico border had been drawn to the Park to observe the momentous meeting of their respective presidents. A historical meeting, to be sure, as they both sought to iron out the Chamizal Dispute, raging since 1885.

Julian's father Pierce had invited Bridget and him to join Noel and Heidi for the festivities that afternoon. The couple had just returned the week before from an elopement to Mexico that took the entire family by surprise. The Acapulco's intense sunlight had burnished their skin—either that or their delirious lovemaking. They looked ecstatic.

The Paladíns had seats in the grandstand's prestigious upper private box. It was draped respectively with red, white, and blue bunting and red, green, and white bunting in honor of Presidents Carnegie and Mateos.

The two Presidents stood in the center of the private box and waved in acknowledgement to the cheering spectators while around the Presidents, Secret Service agents swarmed to avert an assassination attempt.

Noel and Heidi were down on the track with Pistol Packer's trainer. Julian's father, Pierce, who spoke fluent Spanish, sat next to President Mateos, with Bridget seated between President Carnegie and Julian.

She was explaining to the President about Pistol Packer's upcoming race. "—a maiden stake race. Our jockey, Arturo down there in the purple and red silks, is a three-time Kentucky Derby winner."

Easily, she had slid into El Paso's slower paced lifestyle. However, two days a week, she volunteered at a free clinic, treating the border's poor, and Julian's father had come to depend on her to take up some of the social slack left by

Aubrey's absence.

That afternoon, Bridget was wearing some kind of wide-brim, beflowered hat that Julian thought made her look mysterious and sexy. Despite being parents, the attraction between them still burned hot enough to scorch their sheets.

His disgruntled rush to wed may have soured their marriage at the outset. She had cashed in her chips, for all intents and purposes, writing off their relationship as terminally stagnant. It had not helped their relationship's stability that women everywhere turned to look at him with his pirate's patch. Of course, children stared too, in wondrous acclaim.

But Bridget loved him, maimed face and all. Dense dolt that he was, he just had not known it, known he needed to express it with his body, soul, and heart, until it was almost too late.

He finally convinced her he would be with her, regardless of his absorption with their daughter, Julia. "You've been my life's compass all these years, before Julia."

He had even taken the confining routine job of flying for Paladín Air Southwest, when his spirit yearned for daring and risk.

But, when you love someone, you will do anything.

As the gate crew led the horses into the narrow stalls, Noel and Heidi rejoined all of them in the private box.

Pistol Packer was reluctant to load in the gate, and Julian's father glanced at Noel. "Did Arturo say anything about Pistol Packer's last workout?"

"Only that he has been acting temperamental all day."

The doors sprung open, and the horses were off. Each thoroughbred had a running style solely its own. The pacesetters liked to take the lead right away, while others preferred to hover just behind the lead horse and then make a break for the lead in the homestretch.

But Pistol Packer was a closer, what Julian called a heart-stopper, because the thoroughbred liked to lag at the back of the pack and make one big run at the end.

And, damnit, if Pistol Packer did not do just that—waiting until the eighth pole, a furlong from the finish line, before making his break. It was a tight race. At this point, even both Presidents were on their feet, yelling with the rest of the spectators in the stands.

Bridget grabbed Julian's hand and screamed, "Go, Pistol Packer!"

He held fast to her, just grateful to hold her once again.

Those last twelve seconds were the longest seconds for The Barony Horse Farms and the shortest for Julian. He was reluctant to release Bridget.

Dust flurried, obscuring the galloping horses. Then he sighted Pistol Packer, crossing the wire first. He threw back his head and closed his eyes in relief. Around him, a mighty roar went up from the spectators.

As the horse made the trip to the Winner's Circle, Bridget released his hand to clap and jump up and down, like a child at Christmas.

Then President Carnegie was grabbing her hand and pumped it and shouted his congratulations. Suddenly, a man—a Mexican by his looks—somehow managed to jump the box railing. Whipping a gun from beneath his sports jacket, he aimed it toward the pair.

Amidst the cheering, the pop of gunfire went undetected.

WHEN JULIAN'S LIDS MANAGED TO slit open, the wavery image of Bridget appeared. At one point, he had heard her watery whisper, "Damnit, when are you going to quit playing hero?"

He had felt her damp kiss on his shriveled eye socket. "I need you, Julian Paladín, because my life without you lacks luster."

Later, he had heard her barking orders. "Goddamnit, I may be a doctor, but even a staff nurse knows you should first contain the bleeding. I want you to get an IV antibiotic started—now!"

Then, the crisper image of his father Pierce and Noel was coalescing before Julian's medicated vision.

He took a deep breath, stirred against his uncomfortable bed for support, and felt pain blast through his ribcage. Shit! "Are you two here for the last rites?"

"I'm here, hoping you can perform one of your Superman feats and save The Barony, son."

"What?" He blinked, trying to refocus not just his vision but his befuddled brain.

"While you were snoozing," Pierce said, "I learned Knopf has little by little been calling in his markers for a showdown. He is—has been for a while—steadily manipulating for possession of The Barony."

Julian struggled to make sense of his cousin's statement. "And you want me to . . . ?"

"As soon as we can get you out of this damned hospital and on the mend," his father said, "I want you to find a way to block Knopf before he can preside over a dissolution of the corporation."

"But Noel . . . *you* run The Barony."

"The ranch. But Barony Enterprises—hell, I'm swamped as it is just learning the corporate ropes. It's the ranch I love, cuz, not the corporation."

"What about Sam or Jack or Fiona?" The three, other than Noel and Julian, qualified as the eldest heirs.

"You're the only one here in Texas and readily available."

"You mean the only one bedridden and unable to avoid your wily manipulations. Dangling this carrot to get me up and out of here, are you?"

"I'd do it myself, son. But I've got a project of my own."

"Like what?" His voice sounded whiskey raspy in ears.

"Like finding that son of a bitch who fired that bullet—and finding just whom the bullet was meant for—the President or the Paladín."

"Can't you let the FBI or the CIA handle that?"

"Or maybe, better, the Texas Rangers?"

"Then you don't think the assassination attempt was aimed at Carnegie?"

His old man shrugged. "I don't know, but I trust the Fed's agencies only a little more than I trust Knopf. So, what do you say? Will you help?"

He took another painful breath. "Well, seeing as how I won't pass the commercial aviation flight medical right now, I suppose you could say I am, in fact, readily available."

"Forget commercial aviation forever, Julian. You save The Barony, by damn, I'll see you get the job as its CEO."

# WASHINGTON, D.C.
# OCTOBER 1962

The Soviet buildup in Cuba and the Bay of Pigs fiasco the year before had been a huge embarrassment to the Carnegie administration. Heads had rolled, beginning with the Director of the CIA.

That particular morning, Garner could feel the tension in the Cabinet Room in the West Wing of the White House. It was as thick as the fog off the Potomac.

The Cabinet Room adjoined the Oval Office. Thus, in an emergency summons, President Carnegie could convene the Executive Committee of the National Security Council—known as Ex-Comm.

Listening to the terse briefing, it was clear to Garner and Carnegie's aides and cabinet members that never before had the survival of human civilization been at stake as it was now. With the Russian missiles found in Cuba that week, nuclear war was imminent—a war that could destroy the entire damned Northern Hemisphere.

The secret doomsday plan to safeguard the government

had already been put into effect in Washington. But what about ensuring the survival of the people the government represented? Garner had to wonder at the callousness of Carnegie and his Ex-Comm.

As it was, Garner was devoting his valuable time that morning to the stagnating meeting of conformist jerks, when he could better serve the poor folks.

His efforts the month before to get the negra Meredith enrolled at the University of Mississippi campus had nearly been sabotaged when Carnegie had trucked in U.S. Marshals and 3,000 Federal soldiers, setting off a deadly racial riot.

"Damned groupthink inhibits you men from raising controversial issues," President Carnegie snarled at the Ex-comm. "Or alternative solutions, for that matter."

The fifteen men, reputedly the brightest minds on Capitol Hill, squirmed in their chairs around the long table. Some suddenly focused on doodling on their pads, while others stared out the windows at the fog-bound rose garden, as if hoping for an angel heralding insight.

"I need some renegade thinking here," Carnegie continued in an executioner's voice that chopped each word. "Independent mind mapping. I need you guys to challenge both my staff advisors' judgment and the plans the CIA is putting together."

"I have just the man for you, Mr. President," Garner drawled. "Sam Houston Paladín."

From the center, east side of the highly polished table, Carnegie's nasal, northeastern accent was sarcastic. "Family politics, again, Bradford?"

"No, sir. My son-in-law has a mind as sharp as a razor, and I'd wager he is better informed on Cuban-Russian matters than your staff advisors, the CIA, or anyone present at this table."

The President arched a derisive brow. "Assistant Secretary of State for Economic Affairs, isn't he?"

"No, sir. Paladín is the Assistant Secretary of State for *Legislative* Affairs."

Carnegie rose. "We'll call a break, you guys. Bradford, have Paladín in the Oval Office at 3:00 p.m. The damned world clock is ticking down."

"Get Paladín here in my office by one o'clock," Garner told his young, nubile brunette secretary he had once groped in his senate office in front of his staff aides.

Earlier, she had reported that Sam was hunkered over a stack of files with his lobbyist cousin Fiona and the Librarian of the Library of Congress, Steve Douglas. Garner was beginning to feel a little concerned. Fiona could stumble onto something, although he had been damned careful to cover this tracks.

She turned to comply, and he said, "And, also, I want the list of files Fiona and Douglas checked out of the Library."

At nine minutes past the appointed time, Sam strode into the office. Garner put a lid on his irritation. He wanted the young man in his pocket. "Have a seat, son."

Unbuttoning his suit jacket, his son-in-law settled into the cushioned arm chair. Granted, Sam Houston Paladín was good-looking, but he needed to shave the damn mustache if he wanted to make a run for congressional seat. Sure, he had his heart set on following in the footsteps of his namesake, Sam Houston— "By seeing for Texas the realization of all its potential glory."

Too damned idealistic.

"Another disaster, one of worldwide repercussions is imminent, Sam. We have a meeting with the President in two hours, and I need to brief you."

Quickly, he went over the salient points. "US spy planes have discovered Soviet nuclear missiles are being deployed in Cuba at nearly completed bases. The weapons are capable of striking major American cities, including Washington."

Sam grunted. "Russian sons-of-bitches."

"Tonight, Carnegie is going on TV to inform the public. What he must also tell the public is what we are going to do about it.  The hawks are pushing for another Cuban invasion. They are claiming the Russian missiles are a reckless and provocative threat to world peace. The Joint Chiefs of Staff are urging the President to order a 'surgical' strike to take out the missiles and put U.S. military forces around the world on DEFCON 2."

Sam looked askance and sighed heavily. "You do realize, Garner, such action could precipitate the very nuclear war we are wanting to avoid. Should we do this, it is disturbingly evocative of Japan's attack on Pearl Harbor in '41. It's tantamount to US government-sponsored terrorism."

"The President is not looking for any moral lecture," he snapped. "So what if it means bad press in some friendly countries? Carnegie wants a solution. Meet me at the Oval Office at three p.m. with one."

Between then and the appointed time, Garner paced his office, cigarette after cigarette dangling from his fingers. He could use a glass of Cutty Sark. Or a cunt.

If Sam bungled this, he would brand his bunghole. Sometimes, when pressured, Sam would stutter. But he would come through. He was that kind of young man—responsible and resourceful.

Hell, with Sam's idealism, charisma, and dynamic approach to politics, he had already captured the imagination of the younger generation. His patriotic enthusiasm was contagious. Newsweek and the popular TV news program, the Huntley-Brinkley Report, had interviewed him. He would be an asset on Garner's team.

Now if Sam would only come up with a palpable solution.

At 3:10 p.m., the buzzer at the West Wing secretary's desk rang, and she nodded primly at Garner and Sam to make the trip down the long hallway to the Oval Office.

The President greeted them, shaking Sam's hand heartily. "Howaya today, Mr. Paladín?"

"Fine, Mr. President, thank you."

The three seated themselves at the grouping of sofa and chairs before the immense *Resolute* desk, gifted by Queen Victoria. His hands clasped between his knees, Sam presented his plan.

"To begin with, Mr. President, I su . . . suggest a naval blockade around the island to prevent Khrushchev from sending in additional mis . . . missiles."

Garner inwardly cringed, hoping that the damned stuttering did not grow worse. But then Sam's Jimmy Stewart stuttering appealed to millions of film fans.

"This will both demonstrate how serious we are," Sam continued, more confidently, "and will also provide a cooling-off period when we can, with a hell of a lot of luck and prayer, nego . . . negotiate a settlement."

Carnegie perked up. "What kind of settlement?"

"A settlement that will diffuse this missile crisis and ensure peace. A tradeoff, if you will, Mr. President."

Now Carnegie leaned forward. Garner watched. Yup, his boy was solid. "What would you suggest as a trade-off?" Carnegie asked.

"That's easy. The Russians get out of Cuba, and we adhere to international law and remove any threat to invade the island."

Carnegie shook his head doubtfully. "Cuba and the U.S. might gain but not Russia. There's not much incentive for them to—"

"Begging your pardon, Mr. President, but there *is* an incentive. We also offer to withdraw our missiles in Turkey."

"What? Our whole armament strategy has been to encircle and contain Russia. This would be unthinkable."

"If I may, sir—I have been doing some research for the last hour or so. I have learned that our missiles in Turkey are obsolete. That already, a budget is being proposed by our House Armed Service Committee to upgrade the nuclear threat to a far greater one. We have nothing to lose and everything to gain."

Carnegie paused, staring down at the carpet's Presidential Seal. He nodded once. "You may have something there, Mr.

Paladín."

Garner smiled. Once he and Sam were clear of the Oval Office, he slapped Sam on the back. "You did well, son."

"We are damned lucky we don't blow up the world," Sam muttered. "And no thanks to the political or military leadership of this country."

"Maybe it needs some new leadership."

Matching strides down the corridor, the young man flicked him a skeptical look from the corner of his eyes. "The next presidential election is a long ways off for you, sir."

"I was thinking more along congressional lines. My old Texas mentor, Sam Rayburn, is dying. Pancreatic cancer chewing up his gut. I think it's time I put your name forward for the special Congressional election coming up."

"Well, I'm appreciative—"

"But there's a tradeoff. As always, with everything. A compromise. That is what politics is all about, right?" He needed young blood like Sam who would help him carry Texas.

"And that would be, what? The trade-off?"

"Your old man is gone now. As are the days of the Wild West frontier. And blood dynasties are dying out. One day soon, The Barony Board of Directors—who care nothing about sentimentality, only the bottom line, and rightly so—will be recommending the ranch become a wholly owned subsidiary. Before that day comes and the place is turned into a goddamned museum, I get first option."

"Our family would never agree to—"

He grinned and slapped Sam on the back. "Just saying.

You might want to give it some time and thought before answering."

And if Sam Paladín's answer was not what Garner wanted to hear, well, he reckoned he could always swap horses, from finesse to stress.

## EDWARDS AIR FORCE BASE, CALIFORNIA
## MARCH 1963

BELLE CLOSED THE DOOR behind her and crossed to the other side of the curtain. A single bed occupied that half of the sterile cubicle. On the wall behind the bed, an array of switches were banked between two globe lights, their glow falling softly on Ping Pong's pallid features. The base hospital was one of the best facilities in southern California, but even its staff was futilely battling the rampaging diseases of sex trafficking that had snared Ping Pong as a child.

Her lids opened, and her eyes shifted to take in Belle. A wan smile, bracketed by her tribal tattoos, displayed tiny teeth. "You came."

Belle slid into the chair next to the bed and reached over its railing to grasp the small hand. "Of course, my precious friend."

All the times flight duties called Tim away, she and Darcy had been taking turns visiting the ward. But at five that morning, Tim's exhausted voice awoke her. "Belle, Ping Pong's asking for you specifically. I know you were just there yesterday afternoon, but do you mind dropping by again?"

Over the years, she and her daughter-in-law had grown extremely close. To her, the little Korean woman was like a sister, a daughter, and even a wizened mentor.

"This I tell you, what your man Darcy does to you," she once advised when Belle complained their love life had lately turned routine, "he likes it, too. You touch him back in places he touches you." Then, with a mischievous grin, she'd added, "Feathers, handcuffs, they nice, too."

She squeezed Belle's hand now and fastened those dark brown eyes on her. "This I need to ask you. You do. No one else."

Belle blinked back tears. "Anything."

"You hide for me my Tim's Bull Durham. This last time."

## THE BARONY
## APRIL 1963

FROM FAR OFF CAME THE MOURNFUL HOWL of a coyote. The coyote mated for life and only sought out a new partner when its previous one had died. For years, Fiona's uncle Pierce had been the lone coyote of the Paladín tribe, never taking a mate after his beloved Aubrey's murder.

Now, at midmorning, another lone coyote joined him. Fiona's cousin Tim stood at the bluff overlooking the Paladín fortress.

Directly in front of him was the freshly turned earth that

mounded Ping Pong's grave, amidst those of all the other Paladíns' who had departed the earthly plane.

A fine mist was falling. April showers to bring May's flowers—wildflowers like Indian Paint Brush and Bluebonnets that were already carpeting the bluff.

After a plump and eunuch-looking Father McGuffey had finished intoning the Canticle of Luke and the Antiphon John, he said in his high, officious voice, "We now ask for Ping Pong Paladín's soul to rest and pray for mercy and forgiveness of her sins."

At that, Tim's head snapped up. Reddened eyes glared out of the Paladín visage, distraught by raw grief. His dark head swiveled toward the white-robed priest. "If there was a pure soul in our world, Father, it was Ping Pong's. She needs no forgiveness. You've done your good deed for the day. Be on your damn way. Now."

The priest stiffened, looked to Noel and Heidi, who had made all the funeral arrangements.

In unison, they nodded their support for Tim.

With a huff, the priest pivoted sharply. His cassock swirling around his puffy, white-stockinged ankles, he stomped out of the wrought-iron fenced graveyard.

None of the funeral's thirty-odd attendants moved one muscle more than the actions necessary for lungs to expand and contract.

Instead, all watched as Tim withdrew a packet from one of his black corduroy jacket's pockets. Head down, tears dripping one by one from his beard-shadowed jaw, he slowly circled Ping Pong's mounded plot, sprinkling tobacco flakes from his Bull Durham pouch.

Sniffles and gulps from the attendants whispered through the air. Ping Pong had been beloved by each of the Paladíns.

Fiona, her chin quivering, watched for as long as she could. Next to her, she caught Steven observing her with concern.

Afraid she would burst into tears, she back-stepped away from the mourners, then spun and, exiting the graveyard, stumbled down the pebbled path. Fog-shrouded, it led her on a treacherous journey back to the brightly-lit hacienda below.

She headed, not to it, because the asinine Father McGuffey most likely would already be there, waiting to collect his fee for his services. Instead, she took refuge in the gazebo, wreathed in wisps of mist.

Curled in a fetal position on one slatted bench, she bawled. Not just for the loss of the infectiously funny Ping Pong, but for Uncle Heath, Aunt Aubrey . . . and all of life's losses. Did life's gains balance out the outrageous accumulation of losses? Was this all there was to life, trying to walk the middle road between euphoria and despair?

Fiona knew she should be grateful for all she had. Yet thirty-plus years loomed on the horizon, and all she could think was how little she had to show for thirty-past years of striving.

And of yearning. Just to hear those three important words. Clinging to futile hopes and waiting that seemed to always outstrip her patience. What was the purpose of seeking, vainly, what seemed always just out of one's reach?

Ridiculous, her self-pity. But then, she could attribute her maudlin feelings to what she could no longer put off acknowledging—her hormones were geysering, gushing, and short-circuiting her natural body processes, along with her missed period.

How could that have happened? Was the new birth control pill not as effective as claimed, or had she missed taking one?

Even now, her body was betraying her. She felt as if she were going to throw up, so she struggled to sit erect, her fingers barely muffling her sniffling gasps. Her panic battled with her practicality.

What-next questions assailed her. She was logical, strategic, an A-to-Z planner. Assets that had put her at the top of the lobbyist game. But she had no clear idea of what plan B should be, much less A.

Fear as biting as acid choked her hiccoughing sobs. And then, Steven was there, gathering her into the stronghold of his arms and pulling her drained body to slant across his lap.

She pressed her face against his chest, and a snotty snivel escaped her trembling lips. "Oh, God!"

His fingers smoothed back the strands of hair sticking to one tear-damp cheek. "My love," he crooned, "Tim, all of us, can't hold the rose without feeling its thorn. But the pain . . . this, too, shall pass."

She tilted her head back so that she could better watch his expression. "No, the reason for what I'm feeling won't pass, Steven." She wanted to burst out into maniacal laughter. "I'm pregnant."

He blinked and behind those brown-flecked irises, she could see he was trying to absorb the enormity of it all. "You . . . you're certain? Sure about this? I mean . . . the doctor? Your cycle? Have you missed—"

She felt every muscle in her stiffen so that her words came out sounding more sarcastic than she intended. "I was hoping to hear joy . . . pleasure . . . excitement. Or something similar."

Still cradling her in one arm, he tunneled fingers of his free hand through the thick swath of hair that had tumbled diagonally across his forehead. "You'll have to forgive me, but you did have a head start in knowledge of this."

"Not much." She edged away as far as his grasp permitted. "And, no, I haven't seen a doctor. But, at nearly thirty, I know my body. NASA could time the moon's orbit by my cycle."

With both hands, he tugged her back into his embrace, his jaw nested atop her forehead. "Now listen to me, Fiona." Her hair softened his words but not the tension behind them. "My surprise has nothing to do with whether I want the baby—"

"*Our* baby."

"Yes, our baby. I need time to adjust to that and all that it implies—a baby, a marriage. To acclimate to a different standard of life with different routines."

She heard the wild panic undertowing his low, muted voice. She squirmed, trying to extricate herself, but he held her fast. "Well, I don't want any dutiful, run-of-the-mill marriage, Steven. I want a commitment that comes out of our love and passion for one another."

He raised his head and tilted her chin up, so that her eyes were forced to meet his gaze, intense and deadly serious behind his glasses. "Our child came out of our passion for one another."

"But you would never have mentioned marriage were it not for the fact that I'm carrying our child."

His mouth tightened. "No. I love you too much."

"What kind of cop out is that?"

His shoulders slumped. "All these years, I don't know . . . I think I've tried to ignore the loss—the deaths—of family. Told myself you don't let your head hang down. You suck it up and move on. Just don't love so much the next time. I didn't want to love you. And when I did . . . ."

"That's not my point. You've told me often enough—and demonstrated-—your love. Given my preoccupation all along with the investigation and everything, I'm surprised you didn't get fed up and leave. My point is you loved me enough to stay . . . but not enough to commit."

"I'm not sure why I haven't. Maybe I thought if I kept you at a safe distance . . . I could keep pain—the pain of loss—at a distance." He had the grace to look embarrassed. "As time went on, and our lives together went on, I never gave it much thought."

She framed his long face with her hands. "What did you just tell me about the rose and the thorn?"

He rolled his eyes, and his mouth crimped in a sheepish smile. "You should know better than to listen to any smooth-talking Southern gentleman. Honey, I don't want

Father McGuffey marrying us."

She smiled through tears that glossed her eyes. "I never said I'd marry you, Steven Douglas."

"If you don't, I'm blackmailing you. Want to see what I found that may identify the mole we've been searching for?"

She jackknifed upright. "What?"

"Say yes, first. Say you'll marry me—because you don't know when you may catch me again at a weak moment."

She made a moue. "All right, all right, if you must force me to marry you."

He grinned. "How romantic you are, my love."

"Steven Douglas, what did you find?"

"Remember that radiogram, with the encrypted message and your Aunt Aubrey's last notations?"

She nodded. "Yeah?"

"But do you also remember we had talked about who could possess enough power to cover up such an infiltration in our government hierarchy? A politician with a big ego, right?"

He fished in his jacket pocket and produced a florist card. "This was attached to that big floral spray at the church funeral service this morning."

She took the card and squinted at the writing.

*Our deepest sympathy,*

*Gaila and GB Bradford*

She scowled and looked back at him. "Are you putting me on? You're trying to connect that radiogram with this florist card?"

"Look at the signature again. Look at Garner's name."

She shrugged. "What about it? Because the initials are run on with his surname?"

"But on the radiogram, so were the initials of the suspected mole's name— GBBorso. Borsov's first name was Arkady. Think about it, Fiona. Garner's ego is so gargantuan, even his wife and daughter's names share his initials. And I think your aunt Aubrey's hasty jottings ran the two names together."

She inhaled softly at the impact of his theory. Then practicality took over. "That's pretty far-fetched, Steven. We'll need proof. And trying to prove something like that— a connection between the signatures—could be difficult."

He eyed her grimly. "And could be deadly."

## IDAHO FALLS, IDAHO
## OCTOBER 1963

Suit jacket slung over one shoulder with his tie loosened, Julian approached the Victorian house on Riverside Drive, just across from the Snake River. This was the thirteenth home he would be calling upon.

Nevertheless, he reminded himself of the first rule of corporate power. Quite simply, the person who controlled the votes of the stockholders ultimately controlled the corporation.

Eighty-six-year-old irascible Emma Wilder might be the unlucky thirteenth, but she was also—because of the luck of inheritance—The Barony's largest individual stockholder, with somewhere between seven and nine percent of the stock, if his arithmetic was correct.

The basic fact was that the stockholder who controlled fifty-one percent of the stock was able to run the company pretty much as wished. Julian meant to see that the Paladín heirs influenced fifty-one percent of the voters.

With more than forty heirs still alive on the family tree

and holding stock, it was a race between his attempt to corral the shares in the Paladín favor and Knopf's recent attempt to call a stockholder meeting. The only hedge Julian had was a stockholder meeting would require a couple weeks' advance notice.

This gave a still febrile Julian time to call upon the stockholders wielding the most power—and wheelchair-bound Emma Wilder held the crucial vote.

She was a formidable harpy that Idaho Falls denizens went out of their way to avoid. Her aunt had been Sarita Obregon, the wife of one of the original four Paladín offspring and daughter of their nemesis, Guillermo Obregon—also known as Liam O'Brien.

As a child, Emma had occasionally visited the ranch. Later, she danced in the Ziegfeld Follies, married an air force officer, and gave birth to Oliver, her only child. At twenty-one, he had received the stock in a trust. However, when he died, single and with no heirs at twenty-eight from pneumonia complications, all of her Barony Ranch stock reverted back to her.

"With the eyepatch, young man," Emma wheezed in a throaty, bitter tinged voice, "you look like a pirate." She blew a smoke ring from the cheroot she puffed. "So are you here to plunder like all the rest of your Paladín ancestors did?"

"I beg your pardon?"

"I imagine Alex Paladín would turn over in his grave if he knew that an Obregon would be controlling the fate of his dynasty and the lands he stole." She was a heavily painted, crusty old woman with enough blubber to out-live an

Eskimo. "How ironic. An Obregon, at last, decides the fate of a Paladín."

Well, he might as well get this onerous duty over. The week had been fraught with stockholders reluctant to commit one way or the other just yet. He eased into the doily protected cushioned chair. Decades had yellowed the doilies. Knick-knacks cluttered the stuffy living room, blind-shuttered and dimly lit by one frilly-shaded lamp. The room's window A/C unit wheezed as loudly as she.

"I would imagine my great-great grandfather would have wanted the Paladín legacy and tradition to continue," he said, more in a reflective tone than an idle comment to his hostess. "I think he and Fiona believed there was more to The Barony than the wealth it provided."

The land defined the Paladíns, and they defined the land they had tamed—but he was not sure how to convey such a concept to the old hag across from him.

"Legacy? Hogwash. Alex Paladín most likely did whatever it took to keep expanding his tumbleweed king-dom." She took another puff from her cheroot. She reminded Julian of the Hookah-smoking Caterpillar from *Alice in Wonderland.*

Her seamed mouth pinched into an upside down horseshoe. "Just maybe he believed ordinary people, the minions of his world—chiefly the Obregons—should be sacrificed to a larger cause, that being his empire. Stories passed down through the years has it that he swindled, stole, or sold his soul to possess ever more land."

He smiled grimly. "Not stories, Mrs. Wilder. Legends.

Myths. Alex Paladín was larger than life. So were his deeds and his misdeeds."

"Through my decrepit veins runs not only Paladín blood, young man, but also Obregon blood. And from all reports, Guillermo Obregon suffered greatly from the Paladín greed."

He leaned forward, hands clasped between his knees. "Look, all I can give you is my opinion and advice. Whether you're in the Paladín or the Obregon camp, Knopf isn't the kind of leader I would want to follow into battle. And my advice is for you to seek legal counsel. Because this upcoming stockholder meeting on November twenty-first is going to be a morass of legalities."

"Do you have a family? Children?"

"A daughter, Julia. She's eighteen months."

"I had a son." She shot him a rancorous look. "Oliver was about your age when he died."

"And I am still alive and he's not."

Jumping Jesus, he wanted to dance the dangerous edge but facing off with this old biddy was self-obliteration.

"A parent should never have to bury their child, Mr. Paladín."

He fell back on his charm and silver tongue. He delivered a megawatt smile. "Mrs. Wilder, keeping the family and the ranch together is more important than any ancient feud between the Paladíns and the Obregons."

"Hogwash. I suggest you and your ass both take your leave—go home to your precious family."

Well, his instincts had always been shot full of holes. He

nodded and stood. If only he could cinch his clicking tongue that was about to destroy all the plans and hopes and dreams, not only for his and his family's future but, also, for the very existence of The Barony. But if he had no values, no principles, what in the hell was he about?

"The Barony was created by a family which fought for their land with determination and passion, Mrs. Wilder. The Paladíns have loved and lost and rebuilt an empire like nothing the world has ever seen. And we will do it again—on our own—and to hell with you and the Obregons."

And if the old harpy from hell did not bring his day to a new low, then his father's phone call did.

"I ran upon a dead end, so to speak, son. One of my contacts at El Paso's Border Patrol said they located the Mexican who shot you—floating down the Rio, dead as driftwood."

## THE BARONY
## NOVEMBER 1963

AT THE SAME CENTURY-OLD, hand-carved desk at which had labored a line of his forebears—Alex, Kerry, Tara, Drake, and Heath—Noel himself now scratched out a plan for The Barony's survival.

Shambolic financial statistics and bloodlines mired him. Never had he felt more inadequate. The thought of losing what his predecessors had worked so hard to build made him want to vomit, again, and he was gulping Tums like they were M&Ms.

How he hated for the ship to go down on his watch. He had never wanted to be at its helm. He had just loved standing at its bow, gazing out on The Barony's sea of grass and blood-red sunsets. It was the only place he felt he belonged. On the land, not in an office.

The stockholders' meeting was in less than a week, and right now, at one o'clock in the morning, he figured he could squeeze in five hours more to work on it before he had to ride herd on his daily job.

Once more, he tallied the stockholder's proxy votes and those attending on whose votes he felt he could count. All the immediate family, of course.

No surprise that Knopf had scheduled the stockholders meeting on the same day as the special election to fill the vacant senatorial seat, for which Sam was running. He, along with Aunt Mariana, had perforce tendered their proxies.

Julian's solicitation trip had most definitely garnered additional support, but, really—from all Noel could figure—it came down to The Barony, Inc.'s largest stockholder.

Emma Wilder.

According to Aunt Mariana, who, since retirement from Congress, once again acted as The Barony's legal counsel, Mrs. Wilder's proxy vote had yet to come in. And according to Julian, the wheelchair-bound woman was too incapacitated to travel.

Once the votes were in, Noel figured that he and Heidi might just well be out on the streets, as destitute as some of the Paladineños, thanks to Knopf.

The rap on the office door jerked him back to the present. The door slit open enough for Heidi to poke her head in, her braid swinging like a pendulum. *"Mein Schatz,* we've a visitor."

He blinked, scrubbing his jawline. "At three in the morning?"

She nodded and slipped further inside. From the hem of her plush, pink terry cloth robe peaked her pink-polished toenails. "I left him in the den with sugar cookies and a cup of Mexican chocolate."

"Him. Him who?"

"He says his name is Val. Noel, he can't be older than eight or nine years old. How he got past the gates and guards is a mystery, but he won't talk to anyone but you."

His brows peaked, but he stood and, arm and arm with Heidi, made the trip down the long hallway to the front of the house and its mysterious guest waiting in the den.

The boy had a mop of curly black hair, and his black eyes stared him down. His blue jeans and hooded jacket were rumpled and filthy. He jumped to his feet and thrust out his sugar-sticky hand. "Pleased to meet you, sir."

"Pleased to meet you, as well." The kid had a foreign accent. "Have a seat." He and Heidi dropped onto the sofa opposite him.

Heidi cleared her throat and, nodding at the boy, made a motion with her finger over her upper lip.

The kid canted his head, puzzled, then understanding lit his dark eyes. Quickly, he brushed the cookie crumbs from his mouth.

Noel had to grin. "My name is Noel. Noel Paladín. And you are Val. Val . . .?"

"Val Paladín."

Noel's Adam's apple bobbed. "I beg your pardon?"

"Actually, sir, my name is Valentino Giuseppe Buonocore Aliberti Paladín."

"WE MIGHT AS WELL GIVE up any idea of getting any sleep," Noel said, lying on his back and staring up at the darkened ceiling.

There was nothing but silence from Heidi's side of the mattress.

His hand slid across the narrow expanse of sheets that separated them to palm hers. He knew she was hurting. "Heidi, what happened between me and Paola, that was before . . . before us."

"Well, now 'us' includes your eight-year-old son." Her whisper was raw.

Hell, could much more go wrong? He had to give it to the kid. He obviously had the Paladín grit. Hopping a Greyhound in Fort Worth bound all the way for San Patricio, then thumbing a ride with a Mexican migrant worker the rest of the way to The Barony.

He turned, dipped his head to kiss his tattooed name on her shoulder.

"We need to let his grandparents know," she murmured,

conceding. She had done so much conceding these last few months—cutting back her days at her San Antonio art gallery to three and operating out of The Barony. Difficult concessions when publicity and promotion and wining and dining were imperative to commercial success.

"A few more hours will be soon enough." Too soon. He was not ready to take all this on.

"After I tucked Val in, he went out like a light."

He only wished he could get some shuteye. "I'll call Mom at six. She'll have the Alibertis' phone number."

According to Val, his parents—Paola and her husband Luca—had been riding a motor scooter in Rome months before, when a car had clipped them and bumped them into oncoming traffic. The heir to a fortune, the poor little rich kid was now living with his only relatives, his maternal grandparents who obviously were struggling to take care of him.

Well, there apparently was another relative. His real father—Noel himself. Or so Val claimed.

Noel's mind couldn't even begin to juggle the logistics of what kind of international court battle might possibly be brewing. Nor did he know how to make all this right with Heidi. She was not even sure if she wanted children. She did not deserve to be loaded down with an eight-year-old without any forewarning.

He rolled to his side and cupped her face to turn it toward his. A sliver of early morning light filtered through the wooden shutters to expose her strained features, her shadowed eyes, and lower lip that her teeth were nibbling.

He knew what he was about to say could jeopardize their marriage. Her free spirit might not be ready to be hogtied by a child that was not her own. His throat felt like his heart was corking it.

"Darlin', I want to do what's best for Val."

Her teeth clamped even tighter on her bottom lip.

He sighed. "Maybe it's returning him to Italy to live with what's familiar to him. Surely there are some distant relatives there. Maybe it's returning him to live with his grandparents in Fort Worth. At least he knows them, and they come from Italy. I don't know what to do yet. But I have to ask myself what kind of father I'd be, walking out on my own child."

A mewl escaped her. "Or walking out on a child you and I might have. I know you. You could not stand looking at yourself. And I know that if I'm going to be the kind of wife you deserve, I can do no less."

A sigh of relief eddied from his pent up lungs. "I'd feared—I know that all this is crazy shit to be hap—"

"Noel, he's the mirror image of you when you were a kid. I think I fell in love with you then. How could I not open my heart to your doppelganger, *Mein Schatz?*"

He gathered her against his length. He had her—and with her came that addictive rush of transcendence in their coupling—and that was enough.

The Barony and its board meeting and his pipe dreams for the standards that the Paladín kingdom represented to him could go up in smoke, and he would be okay with it. He knew he could always find a way to make things work.

## WASHINGTON, D.C.
## NOVEMBER 1963

At the ungodly hour of three in the morning, Fiona was prowling with Steven through the files of Martin Biggs, head of the law firm that represented Garner's business interests—and he picked that ungodly time to skim his lips across her nape.

"You're not helping." Her head momentarily lulled back into the cradle of his chest and shoulder, while her protruding stomach nudged against the file cabinet. Her flashlight beam skittered across the page of the open file she had extracted.

She sighed. "You're incorrigible." She retrained the flashlight beam on the open folder.

From behind one hand, he cupped her breast, heavier now with her pregnancy. "Hmmm . . . I love your bountiful Madonna's body."

"Look! Look at this, Steven!"

Steven peered over her shoulder. "See right here," her finger jabbed at a page.

He peeked over her shoulder. "So? It's Biggs's response to a note from Garner's Committee for the Re- Election of the President."

"No, what's just below. It's a withdrawal from its slush fund—requested for Garner's miscellaneous expenditures incurred with the law firm."

He whistled. "I told you to follow the money, didn't I?"

"But that's not enough to indict Garner for some kind of criminal behavior. It's hardly grand larceny." Disappointment warred with a racing heart that at any moment they could get nailed.

"Time we skedaddle, my love. If the nightwatchman nails us—"

"I'll divert him, act as if I am going into labor, while you surprise him from behind."

"How in the name of all that's sacred do I let you get me into these peccadillos, Fiona Paladín Douglas?"

"Because I give enthusiastic, mind-blowing fellatio." Under his dedicated lovemaking, her confidence as a lover—and a wife—had skyrocketed.

Still, she was jeopardizing their futures, as well as that of their unborn child, by pursuing a vindication that had no direct bearing on her own life. Ridiculous . . . unless just doing what instinctively felt was right was worth all the risks.

She should close the file and get the hell out of that office. That would be the safe, sensible thing to do. She paused and shook her head. She had never been sensible. She flipped back a couple of pages. "Holy shit, Steven, look at this."

A note from Garner outlined Carnegie's personal security. What was Garner doing with the Secret Service policy manual?

She flipped back another page. It took her a moment to decipher that she was looking at the diagram of Carnegie's upcoming motorcade route through Dallas—except that someone had scratched out the final portion of the route and detoured the dotted line, indicating a new direction for the motorcade.

"What is that?" Steven asked, squinting at the diagram.

*"That,"* she muttered "is a coup d'etat." All these years of following breadcrumbs of information-leakage trails, with all their dead ends, may not have been so futile after all.

"Isn't Sam riding in that motorcade?"

"Yes—the day after tomorrow. We have to get a hold of him now."

"We may have a slight delay," Steven hissed, nodding at the office door's frosted pane, where a man with a gun was silhouetted.

## AUSTIN
## NOVEMBER 1963

AT HIS DRISKILL HOTEL CAMPAIGN headquarters, Sam stood on the ballroom dais once again, hand in hand with Gabby—and behind them, her parents and his mom. This time, the red, white, and blue bunting draped the walls and bandstand in honor of his special election to the Eighty-seventh Congress.

For weeks, he had been heavily preoccupied with the upcoming voting results—both the special election for the senatorial seat for which he was vying and, more importantly, the stockholders vote that would determine the future of The Barony legacy. And both were being held on the same date.

But the results of one were in. He had won the senatorial seat.

Here—in his home and heart of Texas—any dream, however fanciful, was possible.

In Sam's boyhood, Texas had seemed something of mythological proportions, like Mount Olympus or Camelot. And those deep feelings had not changed. The Barony still rated among legends spoken over campfires under Texas's expanse of star-spangled skies.

Other states might suffer under severe hardships of depressions or joblessness. But never Texas. Texicans shook off pestilence and plague like a horsetail swishing away pesky flies.

He had set his heart on following in the footsteps of his namesake Sam Houston by seeing, not only for Texas but for America, the realization of all its potential glory. Like Garner, Sam wanted to be a true public servant devoted to advancing the well-being of America's least advantaged so that all Texicans might flourish.

Sam Houston Paladín knew that he owed his own accomplishments not to any superb politician's skill he might possess but to both Garner for his backing and Gabby and his mother for those months of stumping across Texas's skyscraper cities and hayseed towns, proclaiming why they fiercely supported him.

"I believe in my husband, and you can too because of what my husband himself stands for," Gabby had told a rally last week. "Natural catastrophes, economic downturns, or government interference, my husband is determined to see Texicans through come what may with grit and dedication."

And his mother, who was weathering widowhood as well as could be expected, wrapped her campaigning last week at the Sons of the Republic of Texas meeting with, "You want Sam Houston Paladín at the helm because of his hard core of honesty and loyalty, along with his passion for all the glory and power that is the kingdom of our great state."

He may have won his bid for the vacated congressional seat, but he was still worried, as was the entire family, about the glory and power that was the kingdom of The Barony.

The stockholders meeting was also that same night. As he and his mother had tendered their proxies already, he had left instructions for Noel to call his hotel suite with the results, regardless of the time, leaving a message if he had to.

He leaned over and kissed Gabby's cheek, and the crowd broke out into cheers and applause. "Shall we dance?" he asked.

The band had launched into "This Land Is Your Land," Sam's campaign song. He slipped an arm around her waist, inhaling her subtle sandalwood fragrance. The revelers went wild. Amidst wolf whistles and coyote yips and the spine-rippling Texican battle cries, they danced there on the stage. Long ago, at the celebration of the passage of her father's Civil Rights bill, Sam had danced with her, and in his arms, she had been as stiff as steel. Now, she was pliant, her body flowing with his.

To make herself better heard, she stood on tiptoe and whispered in his ear, "We're also celebrating the next addition to the Paladín dynasty."

Stunned, he could only gape. Then, he felt his grin stretch to nearly both ears. "That makes all this—this celebration— seem paltry. Let's go up to our room and celebrate. Alone."

She laughed. "You randy ol' goat. It's only nine o'clock. I'll slip away now to see your mom to her room. Give the bash another hour of mixing and mingling. Then meet me in our room. You'll recognize me because I'll be wearing your campaign button—only your campaign button."

His imagination lit a fuse in his crotch. "You're on, sweetheart!"

At the end of an excruciatingly slow-passing hour, there was nothing he wanted more than to be alone with Gabby. She possessed the power to dispel the shadows in the distant recesses of his heart—and one of those shadows was his anxiety over the questionable outcome of The Barony stockholders meeting, most likely still in progress.

He got no farther than the bank of elevators when he remembered he was to meet Garner in the campaign headquarters suite one floor below to finalize the details of the flight to Dallas and the Presidential motorcade through its streets the next day.

"Gotcha in the fourth car back," Garner had told him earlier that evening, "riding with the mayor of Dallas. I'll be two cars behind Carnegie."

Which, Sam knew, would normally irritate Garner, who felt he was the better man. And the better man was always front and foremost. But surprisingly, Garner was taking it all in stride.

Perhaps Gabby had already shared the news she was pregnant with her father. That might have made being understudy on the nation's political stage easier for Garner, but that would piss off Sam, for sure. Sometimes he felt like her old man shared the bed with them, so anxious was she for her father's approval.

Worn out, Sam headed along the hallway toward the Cattle Baron suite Garner had reserved for the campaign headquarters. Using his key, Sam entered to find the living room, with its soaring ceiling and wet bar area, faintly lit. "Garner?"

"Back here, Sam," Garner shouted, his super-sized Texas twang filled with muffled laughter.

Sam headed back to the main bedroom . . . and stopped short at the open double doorway. Reclining against the backboard of the signature wrought iron king-size bed, amidst a tumble of sheets, was a buck-naked Garner. His arms were around the shoulders of two young women, a peroxide blonde and brazen redhead, who cozied on either side of him.

Garner grinned. "Got a little present for you in celebration of today's victory, Sam. Come give Rita here a hug. She's from Texarkana."

The redhead, who must have been "Rita," spread her arms wide, revealing pendulous breasts. "Welcome, handsome."

The blonde, who still wore a campaign party hat—and nothing else— giggled.

Sam felt like the crown of his head was going to blow like a volcano. "You can't be . . . be serious? You procured a whore for your own son-in-law?"

"*Whore!*" Rita screeched.

"Don't be a stick in the mud," Garner chided. "I know you love my little girl. Sex and love are like bananas and apples. One has nothing to do with the other."

Sam knew he would regret for the rest of his life the opportunity he was about to throw away. Self-interest, logic, and sensibility all pointed to continuing to ignore Garner's despicable behavior and curry favor with him. Sam's career was on the line.

But for him, it was a choice of that or throwing away his conscience. There was such a thing as principle, and without it, he was as lost as a gambler without Lady Luck.

"All these years, I have tolerated your philandering, because I th . . . thought there was still something of substance beneath your insecurities. Because you had a goo . . . good mentor in Sam Rayburn. Because Gabby loved you. But I was wrong, Garner. All you are is a manipulative slimebag."

Garner jackknifed upright. "That's *enough,* motherfucker. Your ingratitude is unbelievable. And I don't take that shit from anyone, let alone my son-in-law."

"No, it's not enough. I'm not finished. I want nothing more to do with you. Either in the political or the personal arena. If Gabby wants to see you, and I can't imagine why she would, she'll have to do it on your turf, you son- of-a-bitch."

Garner's smile was as thin as a razorblade. "I'll destroy you. I'll break you like a matchstick, son. And what you think of as your own turf will be mine by the time Knopf finishes with The Barony. And Gabby will wonder what she ever saw in you."

"You won't destroy me *or* The Barony."

But could Garner destroy Sam's relationship with Gabby?

## SAN ANTONIO
## NOVEMBER 1963

AT EIGHT O'CLOCK ON the fifteenth floor of the Chase Bank Building, the chairman of The Barony Ranch board of directors, Mel Knopf, smiled congenially and lightly rapped his gavel, calling to order the meeting of the stockholders.

Julian scanned the attendants, both seated at the impossibly long table and those standing. And, of course, there was the attorney and the corporate secretary who recorded the minutes, Knopf's flunkies.

According to parliamentary procedure, once the minutes were read, the roll call for votes on stockholders' proposals were to be handled in a largely scripted manner. Nevertheless, the meeting dragged on, running into overtime.

Why was Knopf stalling?

Julian's mental abacus clicked through the number of votes the Paladíns could count on. Damn, he wished Sam and Gabby and Aunt Mariana could be here. Sure, Julian had their proxies, but he'd feel a hell of a lot better with Sam at his side.

As it was, his father and his uncles—Preston, Darcy, and Byron—were here, along with Bridget, Noel and Heidi, Aunt Hannah and Jakob, Jack, Tim, and other familial representatives.

But where the hell was Fiona? She and Steven's Dulles flight was supposed to have arrived a couple of hours ago.

The vote count looked to be, by a goddamned narrow margin of one, in the Paladín's favor. All the proxy votes were in, with only Emma Wilder not even bothering to send in her proxy. Wheelchair-bound as she was, he had no worry about her making an appearance in time for roll call.

However, parliamentary procedure allowed Knopf to cast the deciding vote in case of a tie. If the unexpected should happen, like the last minute arrival of a stockholder— say, like Emma Wilder—to tie the vote, then only Fiona's vote could save The Barony.

Where was she? Had she maybe gone into labor and missed the flight?

Surely, the room's furnace was in overdrive. Julian's forefinger ringed the inside of his starched collar. His dress shirt was plastered to his back.

Bridget pressed her palm over his. He glanced at her, and

she smiled reassuringly. Lordy, how he loved that smile. Everything lay on the line this evening. Their future, their family's, The Barony's.

He leaned toward her and whispered, "Go to the outer office. Try to call Fiona from the receptionist's desk."

The hell of it was that even though the Paladíns may win this showdown, the Knopf faction would ambush the Paladín's again and again.

And he knew he'd blown it with old lady Wilder.

As if the thought of the cantankerous woman had summoned her spiteful spirit, the boardroom door swung wide and in she rolled, her wheelchair pushed by an elderly man with slanted eyes. She wore some kind of a black epoque velvet hat with a short veil that no doubt hid her gloating expression. Hells fires! So, *that* was why Knopf had been stalling.

Then the grinning bastard spoke. "And now comes the final item on our agenda—the dissolution of The Barony Enterprises, Inc. If you will look over the proposal that accompanied your packet, the board is open for discussion."

The door swung open again, admitting Bridget. Her expression grim, she circumvented the long desk to slide into the seat beside Julian. He inclined his head to hear her whispered, "No answer."

He took a swallow of his ice water and, fingers pyramided on the table, levered himself to his feet. He tossed his packet into the center of the table, polished enough to satisfy a Medici. "I have reviewed this pile of shit and am putting forth a protest vote against this proposed dissolution."

Knopf smirked. "We anticipated that, of course. The meeting is open for a yea-nay vote. Do I hear a second protest vote?"

"I second the motion," Jack said with a shotgun smile. *"Laissez les bons temps rouler."*

As always, Jack's nature was to draw the fabled line in the sand. Compromise was not part of his genetic makeup. It was not part of any of the Paladíns' gene pool. His features were as grim as Julian's spirit. They both knew that now, with the old harridan's vote, The Barony's fate was sealed.

And Fate wanted them to sweat because, alphabetically, her vote was the last to be cast. When her time came, her hooded eyes swept the length of the table and around the room, auguring each stockholder one by one. Each second was uncomfortable for a stockholder and prolonged torture for Julian.

His ancestor, Fiona Flanigan Paladín, was said to have believed family was everything. But then, she had come to Texas precisely for land. The Irish girl had believed land was life itself. And rancorous, unbiddable Emma Wilder, Obregon's issue, held The Barony's life in her pudgy old palm.

At last, her gaze settled on him. Without taking him out of her gunsight, she spoke to the room at large. "Not only am I voting against the dissolution of The Barony, Inc.—so you can just wrap that package of hogwash up in Christmas paper—but I am also casting a vote of no confidence in The Barony, Inc.'s present leader, Mr. Knopf, and proposing his removal from his office as CEO."

The room's gasps sounded like a collective asthma attack.

The corporate attorney found his voice, choking as it might be. "Objection. Your proposal was not entered onto the agenda and thus cannot be considered."

"Hogwash!" Emma Wilder said again. She looked over her shoulder at the old guy standing just behind her wheelchair. "Tell 'em, Judge."

The man bowed low, cleared his throat. "I am Justice Ren Yat Sun, of the Texas Supreme Court. A stockholder has the right to challenge a ruling of the chairman and items not on the agenda may be discussed with a two-thirds majority vote to amend the agenda."

Julian managed to shut his dropped jaw. He would not have thought it possible for Knopf's pasty face to blanche any whiter.

With obvious reluctance and a noisier intake of breath than usual, Knopf called a vote, which passed by an easy majority—and in a bizarre twist, put Emma Wilder's proposal to remove him on the agenda.

At that point, the old woman was granted the floor to speak. Elbows on the wheelchair's arms and plump hands clasped before her, she eagle-eyed the stockholders. "I'll make it short and sweet."

Her hooded old eyes arrowed around the room. "As a very wise young man recently told me, 'All I can give you is my opinion and advice. Knopf here isn't the kind of leader I would want to follow into battle.' And, that said, my advice is for you stockholders to replace him with that very wise young man—Julian Paladín."

Well, well, he'd always said his instincts were shot full of holes.

Now it was up to the stockholders—once again—to determine his destiny and that of The Barony.

## AUSTIN
## NOVEMBER 1963

A breast bared by the slipping satin sheet, Gabby stretched out an arm for the nightstand and fumbled in its lamplight for the clock. Sam should have been back fifteen minutes ago.

She knew too well how a constituent or legislator could buttonhole you, when after a long day all you wanted was to get off the cement floor and pry your swollen feet out of your stilettos.

For years, she had worked the conventions, rallies, and speaking engagements for her father and for his career. Living only to be the recipient of his wide megawatt grin that enchanted her little girl's heart, a grin directed solely for her.

Despite her determination as an adult to escape as far as possible from the controlling charm he asserted—running even to the earth's far ends through EIL and UNICEF—her love for her father, with all his vices and his virtues, had drawn her back. And she had somehow gone on to fall in love with another politician, one with the same spellbinding magic.

She swung her bare legs over the bed and reached for the black silk wrapper. She had slid only one arm through, when the hotel door's keyhole rattled, and Sam opened the door.

If she had thought there would be lust stamped on his features, she was wrong. Passion, maybe—but a passion flamed by fury. "Any word yet about the stockholders meeting?" he demanded, his words jabbing faster than a sewing machine needle.

Shaking her head, she shrugged her other arm into its wrapper sleeve and, quickly tying the belt, asked, "What's wrong, Sam? What's happened?"

Slouching into the plush chair by the suite's escritoire, his long legs splayed, he rubbed the bridge of his nose. "Do you think your EIL would let us sign up for a decade-long stint in Timbuktu?"

"Why?"

"Because I just told your old man to go to hell in a handbasket. More or less. And he told me he'd screw my political career, take possession of The Barony, and bring you back into his fold. More or less."

"So, you had an argument." She shrugged. "I'm all too aware of how hot- tempered my father is, but he always says fences can be mended."

Over his pinched fingers, Sam fixed her with a hard stare. "Gabby, as a reward to me for following the carrot he dangled, he offered me one of his whores tonight."

"You know how he's always joking."

He dropped his hand. Beneath his glare, his mustache,

trimmed at the corners of his lips with a slight downward curve, fairly bristled with his anger. "Damnit, Gabby, I just le . . . left her and another buxom beauty, both naked in the bed with your father in our headquarters suite."

Her stomach sank. "I know he has serious flaws, Sam. But those flaws . . . coming from his difficult childhood . . . well, they also bring incredible gifts with them. He truly cares about the deprived and the—"

"And the depraved. Goddamnit, I'm not in the mood for pla . . . platitudes, especially from his daughter. *My* wife." He levered his lanky body upright. "I'm rousing Mom and heading to the airport and The Barony. The family will be conclaving there after the stockholder's meeting, whatever the outcome."

"What about the motorcade in Dallas?"

"Fuck that. Right now, I need to consider my options. And, Gabby, you need to consider your loyalties."

She understood. There it was—the gauntlet thrown down between them. And she could not really blame him for feeling as he did. Her heart went out to him. The blow-up with her father and the showdown with the Board of Directors . . . it was a hell of a lot for one night.

She kept her mouth shut and dutifully packed while he called a cab to the airport, then left and went to wake his mother.

After all these years, Gabby had come to understand and appreciate Mariana. As senator, she had brilliantly walked the tight rope of diplomacy. Whatever Sam might later tell his mother about tonight, Gabby knew that her mother-in-law adhered to the maxim that silence at the proper season was wisdom.

Even as the hurriedly chartered Paladín flight winged back in the predawn to The Barony landing strip, Gabby's mind whirred with her father's wounding, self-serving behavior and her husband's uncompromising nature, demanding her heart and soul given over fully to him and The Barony.

Dear God, he had been no better than her father in using her for ulterior purposes. It had been Sam who put her in the intractable position of negotiating for a Paladín family member—and on their honeymoon—despite his avowal that the choice was hers.

How was she to balance her own values that wobbled between these two strong-willed men? Each whom she loved with all her being. Did Sam's way have to be all or nothing? Either, or? Why did Sam not realize that compromise was required both in politics and in love? A suffocated moan peeled from deep in her chest.

From the hanger, they took her Cadillac on to the *hacienda*, where Heidi, coffee cup in hand, met them in the tiled hallway. Her strawberry-blonde hair, unbraided, lay loosely over one shoulder of her white furry robe. "I thought you three were supposed to be in Dallas today?"

"Plans have changed," Sam said. "Can Diego get the rest of the luggage?"

Jack joined them in the corridor. "I got in on the tail end of the conversation. So, what happened, Sam?"

Gabby stood between Sam and her mother-in-law,

feeling trapped. Anticipating the ugly accounting of what had gone down between Sam and her father, her insides cringed. She should be inured after all these years of awful, and all too often accurate, allegations hurled at her father by political foes.

"Let's just say that Garner and I don't see eye to eye on certain issues, and as a result, my political aspirations will be hammered. And The Barony with it."

Jack glanced inquisitively in her direction, then clapped Sam on the shoulder, propelling the three of them further into the hallway. "Well, if there's one thing we Paladíns know, it's that families can squabble among themselves, but we always have one another's back."

She was hugely grateful the way Jack was quick to run interference. She was hanging onto her aplomb by a thread, while a headache was beating an insistent tattoo at the backs of her eyes.

Jakob and Hannah were emerging from a hallway bedroom, and Hannah hailed Mariana. "So, is my favorite female cousin coming out of retirement to oversee her son's political agendas?"

At once, Gabby tensed, her chest too tight, as she waited to see how Mariana would handle this. But her mother-in-law merely greeted Hannah with a hug and a warm smile. "I'm your *only* female cousin."

A barefoot Regina padded from around the corner, gave Gabby a peck on the cheek, and offered to get more coffee. Everyone trooped back to the den, where the rest of the Paladín clan was gathered.

In times before, mixing with the large, prominent family had come easily for her. They accepted her wholeheartedly. Being part of the Paladíns—joining in with their births and deaths, diplomas and marriages, losses and triumphs—had seemed natural to her. Now, she didn't know how to act. She felt estranged from them, shut out by Sam as she was.

Tim, Byron, Darcy, Pierce, and Preston were powwowing with Noel and Julian. On the TV screen flashed a photo of President Carnegie, waving as he descended from Air Force One at Dallas's Love Field the night before. She knew Sam should be there.

Nearby, the teenagers, Tejas and Jill, sprawled on the tiled floor in front of the television. Next to them, hunkered on his knees, was a dark-haired boy Gabby did not recognize.

Noel rose from where he sat on the stone hearth and crossed to give Sam a bear hug, then looped his arm around Gabby's shoulders. "Glad to see you both." He glanced at the boy. "Val, say hello to your uncle Sam and Aunt Gabby."

The boy sprang to his feet and proffered a small hand. "Hello, sir. Ma'am."

Both she and Sam's startled gazes switched from the cute kid to Noel. He grinned sheepishly. "A long story. I'll fill you two in later. Right now, more pressing issues. I tried to reach you at the Driskill late last night, cuz. If no one's already spilled the beans, we won against Knopf—he's been ousted, and Julian's our new CEO."

"Hey, Julian," Sam said, "you got a place for me? I may need a job." He made it sound like a joke, but she espied what no one seemed to notice, the tension flickering the veins in his temples like live wires.

Before long, the rest of the family would know of the fallout. She wanted to bolt—this was total madness, torn between the people she loved and each expecting her to desert to the other side.

Julian's mouth hiked a smile at one corner. "Anytime, man. But I got to warn you, restructuring, starting all over again from the bottom, won't be a cow patty toss."

"Once you grab a cup of java, Sam," Noel said, "let's all shoot the bull in my office. Besides, each of us need to sign a slew of documents from the meeting as soon as possible."

Julian came to his feet. "Ladies, we're not to be disturbed."

Bridget nudged her glasses on her nose with her middle finger, making sure her husband saw the shaft she shot him. Julian grinned and blew her a kiss.

"Anyone for mimosas?" Fabienne called from the den doorway.

Heidi headed for the kitchen. "Pop the cork, Fabienne. Ladies, follow me," Her headache beating against her skull like a kettle drum, Gabby managed a tight smile. "I'm going to change into something comfortable first if you don't mind."

She got no further than unpacking one of the suitcases that had been placed in the bedroom assigned to her and Sam, when Heidi appeared at the doorway.

"Gabby, I picked up a phone call in the kitchen, asking for a Mr. or Mrs. Sam Paladín. I hated to interrupt the guys, but it sounded sort of . . . important." Her brow wrinkled.

"Metropolitan Police Department. Do you want to take it? You can pick it up in our bedroom if you'd like."

At once, she worried that her parents may have been involved in an accident, but they were probably in Dallas by now, and the Metropolitan Police Department would most likely be Washington D.C.'s law enforcement. Shit, what was going on now?

"Hello?" she answered, minutes later from Heidi and Noel's spacious and dimly lit bedroom, the blue Princess phone's lit-up dial the primary source of light, other than the nightstand's alarm clock. "This is Mrs. Sam Paladín."

"One minute, please, and I'll connect you," an officious female voice said.

"Gabby, it's Fiona," came the harried female voice a moment later.

Gabby sank onto the edge of the huge bed. "Is something wrong, Fiona?"

"Hell, yes. Steven and I have been arrested. Look, I don't have much time. This is my one and only call allowed me. First, we need a lawyer to spring us. A good one, because the charge is serious. Burglary—meaning prison time. They've been holding us for over twenty-four hours now. Constitutionally illegal, but what the hell. Second, and most importantly . . . are you listening to me, Gabby."

"Yes, yes, go ahead."

"I think we may have found evidence of an assassination plot—targeting Carnegie. Today, in Dallas!"

"What?"

"Actually, the evidence goes back much farther. Thirty

years or more. A Benedict Arnold in our present day midst if we're right. Look, you're the last person I wanted to say this to, but the evidence may link your father with this assassination plot."

Her heart thumped hard against her rib cage. "You . . . you can't be serious. This is no joking matter, what you're sugg—"

"Gabby, whether we're right or not about your father, you've got to somehow stop this motorcade! Meanwhile, damnit, the authorities won't listen to us. All the evidence we found has been confis—"

The phone went dead.

Gabby stared at the receiver for a disbelieving moment, then replaced it in its cradle. Her head felt like it was going to explode. Was Fiona's accusation possible?

Yes, possible—anything was possible, damnit—but not probable. At least, not in Gabby's estimation. Rumors of assassination plots were always rife. Accusations by media and political opponents alike were volleyed like tennis balls. Except this one was more like a grenade.

Where was her father staying in Dallas? The Statler Hilton. The parade was due to start shortly. Her mind raced around like a mouse in a maze. What if the home phone was wire-tapped by the FBI or CIA?

In the bedroom's silence, the alarm clock ticked annoyingly loud, counting off precious seconds.

Could her father do something so heinous? But what if Fiona and Steven were wrong? Fiona had not sounded entirely sure. After all, she had placed the call under the highest duress. And given the raging hormones that came with pregnancy . . . .

She was afraid to look at the time. Her stomach was heaving . . . . What if she herself was wrong . . . what if . . . .

Her fingers drifted to the touchtone dial.

If she made the warning call—would it be to her father . . . or the authorities?

The old hinges of the *hacienda's* heavy bedroom door grated as if in protest, and harsh light slanted in, blinding her. The man's dark shape advanced toward her. She recognized that walk, with its animal grace. Her lungs squeezed shut, and her whisper was more a squeak. "Sam."

He stood over her, looking down. "I was looking for you. Heidi said you took a call. Are you all right?"

Bitter bile gagged her. "I . . . I have a killing headache."

"I'm sorry." His hands clamped on her shoulders, easing her back to recline on the bed. "Here, I'll get you a glass of water and aspirin from the bathroom's medicine cabinet."

She braced her forearm over her eyes, as if she could somehow hide from the awful choice awaiting outside her closed lids. From the bathroom came the sound of running water. Her breathing sped up. Oh, God, what if he had been listening?

He returned from the bathroom and settled beside her, the mattress giving with his weight. He slid a forearm beneath her neck, tilting her head to tuck two aspirin between her lips. His fingers lingered there, lightly tracing the bow of her upper lip, then the fullness of her lower one, before he tipped the glass of water to them.

As she swallowed, she stared up at him over the glass's rim. His scalding eyes, auraed by the faint light, were focused on her face with an intensity that seared her heart, yet her hands and feet felt frostbitten.

"Is something wrong?"

"No." Her hand trembled as she passed him back the glass, its water sloshing. She could not stand by and say nothing. She had to tell him about Fiona and Steven. She sat up so quickly, her head protested the pain. "Yes."

"You're shivering." Setting the glass on the nightstand, he gathered her against his side and began chaffing her arm. He was tender, solicitous, yet she sensed something unsettling underneath. "What is it?"

He was watching her with concern, his gaze both soft and fierce, and she could feel her face afire. "The call I took . . . it was from Fiona." How much to tell? "The line went dead before . . . before she could finish. But she and Steven have been arrested. For burglary, she said. She told me they needed a lawyer. A good one to spring them." She hiccoughed and could feel herself starting to hyperventilate.

"Shhh, Gabby." He ceased stroking her back and lowered his head, his mustache nuzzling her earlobe. "I can make a call," he whispered reassuringly. "Have a D.C. attorney on it within the hour. I'll take care of that now. You get some rest."

Her heart was racing. He went to move away from her, and she clung to him with desperation. A strangled sob tore from deep in her chest. How could she do this, become a whistleblower against her father? Her own *blood?*

Sam gazed down at her, his fingertip tenderly swiping a tear from her trembling lower lip. "What, my love? Whatever it is, I can make it right."

Not this, she wanted to scream. Not my heart being sliced in two.

She buried her face against his throat and whimpered. She knew she would rue this day, that her deed would haunt her every waking hour and, most certainly, invade the guilty refuge of her sleep.

But she could not dam up the words bursting through. "Sam, we've got to call the Dallas police." Her words were ragged gasps. "Fiona also said she and Steven uncovered a plot. Someone planning to assassinate Carnegie in Dallas today." She gulped, swallowing the redemptive poison of a daughter's possible betrayal. "And they think my father is behind it."

A sigh that was like a gust of wind ushered from him. She felt his knotted shoulder muscles go lax. "It's all right, Gabby."

She drew away to look up at him. "Did you understand what I just said?"

"The Dallas Police switchboard is jammed with calls." He shrugged. "But Uncle Pierce's plane is taxiing off for Dallas at this moment. This also may be his opportunity to finally settle his score with Aubrey's murderer."

Her mouth dropped open. "You knew. You knew all this time about Fiona's call."

"Yes."

Her mind flitted, sorting, arranging the pieces of the

complex puzzle that was Sam. Strangely, she felt relieved. She no longer had to shoulder the unbearable burden alone.

Tenderly, he kissed a single tear trickling down her cheek. His smile was a rainbow after a thunderstorm. "You meant what you told me when I asked you to marry me, didn't you? When you quoted that passage in the Book of Ruth . . . 'Your people shall be my people.'"

LATER THAT DAY, AT 12:40 p.m., a TV news bulletin interrupted the soap opera *As the World Turns*.

"Here is a bulletin report from CBS News. In Dallas, Texas, three shots were fired at President Carnegie's motorcade in downtown Dallas."

At once, the Paladíns homed in from various areas of the hacienda to listen to the electrifying flash.

The newsman, Walter Cronkite, cleared his throat, took off his black-rimmed glasses, and put them back on. "The first reports say President Carnegie has been seriously wounded by this shooting. More details to—"

Gabby shot to her feet with an outcry. Sam caught her as her knees gave way. "My God, my God!"

He glanced at his uncle Preston and raised a brow that asked the unspoken question.

Preston shook his head. "No. Nothing from Pierce yet."

Gabby's wail raised the hair on Sam's arms. "It's my fault. I waited too long!" He lowered her to the couch with him, pressing her damp face against his shirt to soothingly stroke her disheveled hair. "No, no . . . Uncle Preston had time to spare."

He looked up and caught his mother's stricken expression. She bit her lip, then murmured, "Unless he was . . . detained."

From the television came Walter Cronkite's dolorous voice, announcing the death of the President. In horror, Sam, Gabby, and the rest of the family watched a replay of the parade and then spectators flattening on the grassy knoll at the moment of the shooting. The motorcycle sirens wailing like banshees as they sped away, leading the President's Lincoln Continental limousine to the nearest hospital. On the streets, total strangers consoled each other. At the White House, aides wept openly in the corridors.

The next frame on the television was aboard Air Force One of Mrs. Carnegie's features stamped with majestic courage and Garner, looking sad but confident. "I remind Americans everywhere, there is still someone in charge."

As his swearing in began, the kitchen phone rang shrilly. Heidi rose to answer it. Sam had half expected this, a barrage of calls to start with him as son-in-law now to the new President of the United States.

But Heidi returned, her face ashen and her voice ragged. "It's the Department of Public Safety. Pierce's plane . . . and body . . . have been recovered in a cornfield outside Waco."

FROM ALL OVER that next day, reporters, correspond-dents, and photographers breached The Barony's fences. The public wanted news—rumors, gossip, trivia, it did not matter.

Backed by his mourning family and with Gabby at his side, Sam appeared on the veranda to give a statement.

Near the base of the veranda's stairs, a reporter, pen and pad in hand, shot her question in Sam's direction. "Senator, our deepest sympathies on the death of your uncle."

With a nod that was more a jerk of his head, Sam acknowledged the expressed condolence. Rage, shock, disbelief—they manifested at that moment in the wildly ticking muscle at the scarred corner of his lip, tugging down one end of his mustache.

"Would you mind," another reporter yelled out toward the back, "giving your Texas constituents your perspective of these chilling, senseless tragedies occurring one upon the other, here in your own home state?"

How could he get through the statement he had composed without stuttering? Bur with Gabby beside him, he knew he could get through today and the rest of his life. How had he ever doubted her love? He wrapped his arm around her shoulders and drew her close, securely, to his side. Crazy, how for the first time in their life together, he felt totally at peace. He loved her so fiercely—she was his home, as strong a fortress as The Barony.

"Americans have always picked up the pieces and moved past heartbreak," he said simply, then paused. And, by God, there was such a thing as justice—although his Paladín sensibilities would term it a "vendetta" he would be waging on behalf of the Paladíns.

Solemnly, his gaze swept the upturned faces below him, their absorbed expressions indicating they were awaiting some kind of direction from him, some compass to steer by on these troubled seas.

"We Texicans have loved and lost and rebuilt an empire like nothing the world has ever seen—our beloved Barony. And we will do it again, as will all Americans with our great country."

# AUTHOR'S NOTE

In researching the cold war/Civil Rights era, I found the following immensely enlightening and helpful: Robert Dallek's *Lyndon B. Johnson: Portrait of a President*; *Bulletins From Dallas: Reporting the JFK Assassination* by Bill Sanderson; Smithsonian Magazine's "LBJ Goes for Broke" by Robert J. Caro; and Joseph Califano's *The Triumph & Tragedy of Lyndon Johnson: The White House Years*.

# ABOUT THE AUTHOR

Parris Afton Bonds is the mother of five sons and the author of more than fifty published novels. She is the co-founder and first vice president of Romance Writers of America, as well as co-founder of Southwest Writers Workshop.

Declared by ABC's *Nightline* as one of three best-selling authors of romantic fiction, the award-winning Parris Afton Bonds has been featured in major newspapers and magazines, in addition to being published in more than half a dozen languages.

The Parris Award was established in her name by the

Southwest Writers Workshop to honor a published writer who has given outstandingly of time and talent to other writers. Prestigious recipients of the Parris Award include Tony Hillerman and the Pulitzer nominee Norman Zollinger.

She donates spare time to teaching creative writing to both grade school children and female inmates, whom she considers her captive audiences

Parris would love to send you a free e-book. Visit her website at www.ParrisAftonBonds.com today and claim your free book!